# SO BRIGHT A HOPE

## DAUGHTERS OF HIS KINGDOM BOOK 5

### AMBER LYNN PERRY

LIBERTY PUBLISHING

Copyright © 2018 by Amber Lynn Perry

ISBN-13: 978-1-945965-01-2

P.O. Box 4723

4801 W Van Giessen St

West Richland, WA 99352

Cover Design, Seedlings Design

Cover Photo, Danyell Diaz Photography

Published by Liberty Publishing

This novel is a work of fiction. Names, characters, places, incidents and dialogues are a product of the author's imagination or used fictitiously.

❀ Created with Vellum

*To all those who hope.*
*"Be of good cheer, and he shall strength your heart, all ye that hope in*
*the Lord."*
*Psalm 31:24*

# AUTHOR'S NOTE

During the American Revolution, becoming a prisoner of war was a serious and dangerous prospect. Many brave soldiers were taken, and many died in the horrendous conditions they were made to endure. Those who survived related heart-wrenching tales of abuse and neglect.

In Boston, during the siege, conditions were deplorable, and when Washington relieved the city with the taking of Dorchester Heights, he was shocked to find it in such a state of ruin. Much of the city had been destroyed—churches used as stables, fences and buildings torn down for firewood, food stores depleted.

As with my other stories, many facets included in this novel are true. Double agents did exist during the war, and Washington certainly could not have been victorious without them. Those spying for the Commander in Chief were required to exhibit great skill and tenacity, courage and secrecy. Anyone else was unfit for the job.

The contribution women made in the revolution can not be overstated. Seemingly small acts were indeed invaluable and we would not have the freedom we enjoy today without the unfaltering determination and unwavering hope of such remarkable women.

I pray you will come away from The Daughters of His Kingdom series with a greater understanding of and appreciation for the men and women who sacrificed so much. Let us strive to honor their memory and keep their stories alive.

Let us live truth—fearlessly.

# PROLOGUE

August 21, 1770
Boston, Massachusetts

Light from the street lamps snaked behind James Higley as he reached the end of the abandoned cobblestone street. Glancing behind, he halted and stopped his lungs, listening.

The very air breathed of treachery. All Boston was ill with it.

Though night's clouded arms had long since embraced the bustling city, a few stragglers still paced the streets. He remained motionless as the calls of night watchers and laughter of drunken sailors played tricks upon his ears. He allowed a guarded intake of salty air, then stilled again. Had he imagined the shuffle behind him? His back stiffened.

Footsteps. No mistake.

"Lieutenant Higley, I presume?"

James spun, his stomach in his throat. At the sight of the older gentleman before him, every tension drained. 'Twas Robert Campbell. Thank the Lord.

Standing straighter, he nodded. "Dr. Campbell."

The man's narrowed eyes reflected the pallid light of the road, and he dipped his chin in return. James waited for a reply, his pulse at a steady run. Crickets sang around them, a frog croaked. Water lapped at the wharf several yards away while James's heart beat loud in his head. Was the man waiting for him to speak? More, did he suspect?

James held back a dubious suspiration, fully aware of the picture his red coat afforded. The man was no fool. Though there were rumors that Robert Campbell's devotions lay opposite his outward displays, this moment would be the defining breath, the nail upon his coffin, unless James's suspicions were correct. He would not have requested a meeting, would not even have grappled with the idea of revealing what he prepared to, if he did not believe the wise physician treasured principles the same as he.

Robert studied him a moment longer, sincerity lifting the corners of his mouth. "How may I help you, Lieutenant?"

Though the late August breeze was warm, almost comforting, James's stomach churned. At least none seeing them would think anything amiss. James was a soldier, and Robert a well-known Tory. However, if they were heard…

James adjusted his stance, looking behind him. The glow of the street failed to reach the shadow where they stood, but would their clandestine meeting remain undiscovered? After filling his lungs, he began the declaration he'd rehearsed a hundred times over. "I have been a soldier for some time."

Robert's brow flinched. "Aye."

"I had always believed the king carried an interest in the betterment of the people of the colonies. For this purpose, I chose to follow my uncle and join the ranks of valiant men in arms."

"Noble of you." The man moved his feet, eyebrows lifted.

Noble. James ground the word beneath his boots.

As if beyond the sea, his mother's ghost called from beside her grave. *Traitor. Turncoat. Treasonist.* Then, from a fresher mound of

2

earth, another voice echoed through the streets of Boston. An innocent who might still be living, but for him.

James's throat constricted. He could hear the man's laugh, see his smile, almost feel the affectionate clap on his shoulder. A father could not have been so loved. Or so betrayed.

"Lieutenant?"

Robert's quiet petition dragged James away from the suffocating depths. He swallowed, praying God would forgive him, aid him in his act of atonement. Though in truth, 'twas so much more. 'Twas the beginning of everything new. Everything right.

Releasing a breath that carried his heart, James held the man with his gaze. "I have long enjoyed protecting and preserving those who pursue their...those who pursue happiness." How much could he say? How much should he say? Coming out with his purposes would mean endangering both of them if somehow the enemy lurked undetected. Leaving their safety in the hands of heaven, he revealed the rest. "In my current capacity, I enjoy that service...but..." *Lord, open his mind to my meaning.* "I should like to do more."

Robert stared, a hard look lining the space between his eyebrows. He pivoted his head, never moving his vision from James. "More?"

He nodded, fearing even the slightest sound would shatter the fragile ice that carried the weight of his future. "I understand...I understand that perhaps you might know of additional ways I may serve my country."

The doctor shook his head. "I am merely a physician and devoted Tory, Lieutenant. I know nothing more you can do than what you do already."

James stilled as the sky succumbed to an even deeper shade of black. He allowed his voice to reach for the cobblestone as he leaned forward, ready to run if the man cried foul. "You are not the only one who wishes for change—who wishes to make a difference, Son of Liberty."

All the world went silent. Even the insects that listened stopped their pleasant singing. What little breeze had blown, stilled.

Robert released his arms to his sides, and stepped nearer, until inches separated them. "You know not of what you speak."

So he wouldn't deny it? And yet, he wouldn't admit.

The muscles in James's face threatened to tick when he responded. "I do."

The clamber of boots along the street shut their mouths, and Robert tugged James farther into the dark as two drunk sailors passed at the opening of the road.

'Twas several long seconds before Robert spoke again, this time through a tight jaw. "Defectors are not treated kindly."

Defectors? James scowled. He matched his volume with the doctor's. "I do not mean to defect."

The man's expression shifted when at last understanding owned him. His eyebrows jumped slightly, his mouth firm as he allowed several inhales and exhales to stretch between them before he spoke. "What you suggest is impossible."

"Impossible?"

Robert shook his head. "'Twould be a death sentence. Your superiors would find out your involvement and such would be the end of you."

"They would not." Was the man meaning to dissuade him? "Even if such was a possibility, 'tis a risk I am willing to take. Do not you take such risks?" Again flashed in his mind, the man whose life had been lost, and his tenacity was redoubled. "Even if you believe me incapable, I will do it, with or without your assistance. I am unmoved."

"'Tis not that which concerns me." Robert's voice went deathly quiet. "What you desire to embark upon is nothing short of imperative." He paused, his hard gaze chipping away at James's very soul. "If you are not fully engaged, you may be the means of bringing down that precious thing we labor to sustain."

"I understand." How could he make him see his dedication? "I do not treat this lightly."

Robert's eyes narrowed further, his posture rigid. "Are you ready to make such a commitment?"

Hope buoyed, James squared his resolve. "This instant."

"Every man that undertakes this work must learn to trust no one, to keep every secret—to leave even those they love in the dark of what they do."

James looked past him to the center of Boston. He had no family. None that cared for him. His uncle, Thomas Gage, may be a general in the British army, but that meant little. The man hardly knew him. And as for a family of his own, 'twas something he little considered and little desired.

"What brought you to this?" Robert's sudden question moved his vision back to the man before him. "Why would a man in the service of the king choose to rally for the cause of freedom?"

Why?

The tears he'd witnessed two days past, the grief that was endured because of him—'twas that, aye. But much more.

The quiet wharf rallied behind him, and he breathed the salty air, filling his lungs with fresh strength. Declaring the truth he'd so long ignored but that now writhed with life inside his chest, would free him. "Liberty is the eternal gift. With it, we have everything. Without, naught at all."

"Aye." Robert peered off, the muscles of his face taut, somber. Slowly, he turned to him, a warmth in the twitch of his smile.

He reached for James, gripping his hand with the kind of power that is borne from an indivisible bond. A bond they now shared, and would until they attained what they, and so many others, sought.

"Welcome, Lieutenant, to liberty."

# CHAPTER 1

Sandwich, Massachusetts
February 5, 1776

Sugary snowflakes dusted the gray sunrise, its melancholy forcing Caroline Whitney to shiver under her cloak. She'd known this day would come.

"I hate to leave you." Papa's eyes drooped, his fingers tapping against the cocked hat he held in front of him. The small carriage behind him was motionless, a coffin with windows. "You're sure you will be alright?"

"You needn't worry over me." Smiling, Caroline nudged a basket toward him, forcing him to replace his hat and take the vittles she'd prepared. The scent of butter and cinnamon dusted the air between them. "This should keep you and Mama sustained until you reach an inn for the night."

His grin didn't reach his eyes, though gratitude did. "I don't know what I would do without—"

"I've included a book as well." She pointed at the basket, refusing to have him speak so. "'Tis Cato. Enoch's favorite. I am sure it will make the long hours more enjoyable. 'Tis always preferable to travel with a book."

Moving aside the cloth, Papa peered in the basket before peeking at her, this time a bit of his jolly nature returning. "Are you certain you can part with it? 'Tis your favorite, too."

Pretending none of the ache that swelled at the truth she refused to acknowledge, she grinned. "There are plenty of books to occupy me. I have just acquired both Plutarch and Voltaire, and I am eager to begin."

A laugh bubbled from Papa's chest to his face, dissolving, for a moment, the worries Caroline read in his posture. "How you can endure such books I shall never know."

"Oh, Papa." Her own tensions eased at his mirth. "Frivolous fiction does not fill me. In truth, I prefer writings with depth and veracity."

"I know." The lightness in his sound faded. He peered past her to the house, his mouth closing as if he refused utterance to any words lest they reveal too much of the grief behind the doors of his stoic exterior.

Righting her slumping posture, Caroline fluffed the sunken conversation. "I will have plenty to keep me occupied here. My chores, for one thing, and certainly I shall have company." Her gaze rolled to the carriage, and halted, unable to stay the dark nature of her tone. "We both know Mama needs this. 'Tis for the best."

And it was, truly. Though Caroline's heart still ached to journey with them. If only Papa might change his mind even now, and beg her to come along. But such hopes were futile. At five and twenty—naught more than an old maid—being left alone would not be seen as anything but what it was, a necessity. The home must be watched, if for no other reason than to ease the mind of the woman they had all but lost.

Papa glanced to the pale horizon, regrets heavy in his brow. "I will be gone only as long as it takes to see your mother safely to her sister's."

Caroline peered past his shoulder to where Mama sat in the coach, her back rigid and face forward. Gone was the color from her cheeks, gone the sparkle in her eye.

A lump formed in Caroline's throat, and she coughed it away. "Travel safely." To keep the emotions from consuming, she took the thick scarf from her neck and neared, wrapping it around his. "I fear the roads will be none too serviceable. Keep warm and know that all will be well here, I promise."

Father's jaw flexed, the lines of his face burdened with sorrow. "You must go to Ephraim's if you need anything. I have spoken with he and his wife, and they will be checking on you—"

"I am no longer a child, Papa." The laugh she offered eased the lines on his furrowed brow and she found strength to continue the act, to prove she felt none of the foreboding loneliness. She filled her words with strength, straightening her shoulders to prove her words. "Should I need anything, I have plenty to whom I may go. The soldiers are too occupied with Boston to be concerned with little Sandwich."

Papa rubbed his thumb against the handle of the basket before glancing behind him, his gaze no doubt focused on Mama. Facing Caroline, he lowered his voice. "'Tis this war that's done it to her. The loss of Enoch was too much. And...should anything happen to you—"

"It will not."

"She wishes you to come. You must know that."

Caroline lowered her chin, unable to speak until the lump in her throat had cleared. "I know."

"We are grateful you will stay on." He slipped the basket over his arm and took her hand in his, the warmth of his love spreading past the cold of his fingers. "For the house, the farm, aye, but too...Mama believes in her heart some word will come of him."

Caroline forced a smile at his words. Aye, the incurable hope she'd draped over all of them. 'Twas futile to make her see the truth of it. Enoch was never coming back. Caroline could see in Papa's eyes, he knew the truth. And yet, there was something in the way he blinked that said he yearned for the same.

Gripping tighter to his hand, Caroline took all his worries in through her touch, and did her best to soothe them. "We will do what we must. God will carry us as he always has."

And He would. So why was there still a hollow in her heart?

The flakes began to plump, resting on Papa's dark coat as he gazed at her. In their silence, a sermon preached between them, one that might have rallied her weary spirit, but merely offered it a different pew. There was no way to turn back time, to get back what had been taken. They had only to move forward, make the best of things without their "dearest boy" and to continue on with a shell of the woman who'd loved and raised them.

The horses shook their heads and the driver mumbled something to the restless animals. Papa's throat bobbed. "She will return to herself, Carrie. You will see."

Caroline braved another look, hoping Mama would peer out at her, smile and blow a kiss as she had always done when times were brighter, their hearts joyful—when they were free. But she did neither.

Taking a step back, Caroline rallied what strength she had remaining in the dregs of her spirit. "You best be going. Use what daylight you have, there are so few hours of it."

"You are right." Reluctant, as if the pain of leaving caused his limbs to slow, he neared and kissed her forehead before stepping back, tears in his eyes.

*Do not weep, Papa.*

To keep up the strength they both required, she put sunshine in her voice. "Anna Donaldson is expected this afternoon and we shall finish mending the shirts we've gathered for the militia."

He made his way to the coach, moving forward while looking back. "I am pleased you will not be alone during our absence."

9

"Nay, of course." She continued, knowing her jolly tone was what allowed him to move at all. "Most of all, I am eager for the time to read in solitude, I assure you."

At the door he paused. "I shall be home as soon as I can." He ducked inside and closed himself in the carriage, his mouth tight to hide the quivering of his chin. "Be safe, my dear."

Through the window, he nodded to her. The glistening of his eyes made the ache in Caroline's throat press harder. Mama neither looked, nor moved, and the effort it took to keep the stinging tears from falling was near impossible.

*Lord protect them. Give them peace.*

The driver yawed and the carriage jerked forward, snapping and crunching over the icy ground as it moved from the yard to the road. The flakes were thicker now, like lumps of cotton dumped from a heavenly bail.

She waved as the carriage grew smaller with its distance, until at last, was fully out of sight. Still she couldn't move for the memories that bound her knees and held her motionless in the cold. Enoch was gone, and now they. Not even a year had passed since her older brother had announced his plan to join the men in Boston and defend the freedoms that were rightfully theirs. Since then, their lives had never been the same.

Holding her arms beneath her cloak, she stood in the cold while the memories whirled around her, turning the wintery yard into spring, and her memories into reality.

"'Twas a clarion call," he'd said, a knapsack on his shoulder. The breeze toyed with his blonde hair, courage in his smile. "A man must stand for what he believes, or he will die in want of them."

She looked toward heaven, her bleak surroundings clutching her once more. *Or die because of them.*

Turning toward the house, Caroline fled the jaws of grief that nipped at her heels. She must look forward, to the future. Looking back only brought pain.

Shrugging off the snow-covered cloak, she heaved a sigh of wishes and wants, closing herself in the warmth of the house. At least now Mama might have a way to leave the sorrow behind. For a time. As for herself...

Caroline huffed away the self-pity, making her way to the kitchen to stir the porridge that had started to boil. *Oh, Enoch.* With effort, she eased her sadness into the chasm that had housed her heartache since that day last June when they learned of the battle—how Enoch had fought valiantly. How his body had never been found.

With a hard breath she closed that chapter of her memory, choosing instead to place her focus on her work around the house. Hours passed, and her chores were extinguished one by one, until at last, she found her place of respite in a chair beside the fire, a book in her hands.

A pounding on the door jerked her upright, and she looked to the clock on the mantel. Anna was not expected until later, but who else could it be?

Placing her book in the chair, she hurried to answer the continued pounding. "Welcome, Anna, I—"

Caroline stopped hard at the sight of the black-cloaked man on the stoop.

His cocked hat shadowed much of his face, but his angst was palpable. "Is this the residence of Mr. Jack Whitney?"

Still too stunned to speak, Caroline nodded.

He thrust a letter toward her, his raspy voice firm and commanding. "See that he gets this."

Taking it, she fought the fright that shocked her into numbness. "I...forgive me, my father has just—"

"'Tis imperative that he reads this at once."

After a brisk nod, the stranger ran back to his mount without another word, without even looking back.

Caroline charged out after him. "But he's not here, I—"

The man leapt onto the saddle and with a hard jerk of the

reins, pulled his mount around and kicked. Instantly, the horse charged, flinging up chunks of ice and dirt as it carried the rider into the thick veil of winter.

What in mercy's name could be so urgent? And why wouldn't he wait to learn Papa was not home, and wouldn't be for weeks—perhaps months?

She peered down at the little thing, and in two heartbeats, her neck went tight, her eyes blurry. That looked like Enoch's pen. *Nay.* She blinked away the mist in her vision. *Whatever is the matter with you?* Mama's dreams were infiltrating her own.

Wiping her fingers over her eyes, she scolded the weak part of her that always seemed to gain control when she was weary. Enoch wasn't the only person to form his W's and Y's in such a way.

She made for the house then stopped and lifted it again, this time allowing her eyes to linger.

Could it...possibly?

"Caroline!"

Spinning toward the sound, Caroline gasped. "Anna! What a pleasant surprise."

Anna waved from the opposite side of the road. "I know I am early, forgive me." Once beside her, Anna leaned in for a quick embrace, her red cloak dusted with white. "I might have waited, but I admit, I was eager to see you."

"I'm so pleased you're here. Hurry in out of the cold." Caroline ushered her into the welcome warmth of the house. "What a snowfall."

Anna swung off her cloak and hung it on the peg before resting a hand on the swell of her belly. "I suppose we shall have another foot or so by evening, would not you agree?"

"The way it is falling now I would not be surprised." Caroline's stomach pinched as her mind followed after her parents. "I hope it does not impede safe travel."

Anna moved into the kitchen, friendly compassion sloping her dainty brow. "Your parents left this morning." She looked out the window. "Do you think they will turn back?"

"Nay. They have been gone some hours already."

As Anna took a seat at the table Caroline visited the porridge pot once again, the note still in her hand. She watched the bubbling mixture, inhaled its spicy scent, and rubbed her finger and thumb against the paper, aching to open it.

"I have just heard there is a dance at Baldridge's this Saturday. Will you go?" Anna said.

Caroline peered over her shoulder from her crouched position and grinned humorously. "You know me better than that."

"Why will you not?" Anna placed her hands in her lap. "What of Leo? Perhaps he will be there?"

Leo thought naught of her, of that she was certain. Not that she cared. There was only ever one man she had believed might have desired her. Their parting almost three years past had left a gash in her so deep she'd vowed never to speak of it.

A laugh mended the sudden rift. "You are kind, Anna, truly. But I cannot think of going. Not now." She paused, her heart following after the carriage that carried Mama away. "Besides, I should much prefer to sit beside a warm fire with a book."

Anna leaned back in her chair, again running her hand over the growing babe in her middle. "What is it really, Carrie? What is it you are not saying?"

Still stirring, Caroline shrugged, both grateful and frightened at how her friend of so short a time could know her so well. "I am not...I am not like other ladies." There was no use in hiding what she felt. "I am too outspoken, for one thing—too apt to speak my mind on topics not suitable for such a gathering. For another, I am *old*." She rested a humorous tone in the last word, flinging another half-smile to her friend.

"Old? What a silly notion. You are in your prime."

Caroline laughed out right. "Well, I thank you for that. I much agree with you."

But the bachelors in town would disagree. To them she was past marrying age. She was candid, wild. Timothy had thought so. Had told her so. Had left her because of it.

*'Tis your riding, Carrie, 'tis unbecoming for a lady. To say nothing of your fascination with politics and taxes—those are conversations and topics for the men to engage in. You must change. I cannot love you as you are.*

Caroline shuddered and left the spoon in the pot, staring at the bubbling mixture. Perhaps Timothy had been right.

"What have you there?" Anna said, as if she understood Caroline's need to flee her own thoughts.

"Oh this…" Caroline rose and lifted the curio, turning it in her fingers. "Such a strange thing. A man was here not a moment before you arrived, dressed all in black and in a dreadful hurry."

Sitting at the table opposite her friend, Caroline studied the script, her pulse growing frantic as the ever-springing dream of her heart nudged her to open it. "'Tis addressed to Father. The man said 'twas urgent, and when I tried to explain—"

"You must open it." A look of humorless gravity owned the soft lines of Anna's face.

Caroline stalled, bouncing her vision from the note to Anna. "You think I must?"

Anna's black hair framed an expression rich in earnest. "Your father placed you in charge in his absence, and if there is an urgent matter then certainly someone must know of it."

The more Caroline held the folded parchment, the more it singed her fingertips. "You are right."

"Perhaps I should go." Anna pushed up from her chair. "I shall allow you privacy."

"Nay, please stay. I shall only be a moment."

Anna took her seat once again, a grin on her lips. "Take what time you need."

Shameful amounts of strength were required not to swipe it open. Unfolding it with care, she scrolled her vision across the words faster than her mind could relay the message. Her blood stalled in her veins.

*Dear Lord. It cannot be.*

Her limbs simultaneously weakened and jolted with strength. She lurched to her feet, her hand at her throat. "Nay."

Anna reached out. "Good heavens, Carrie, what is it?"

Caroline read again, disbelief blurring the words. 'Twas impossible. Lowering the letter, she put a hand on the chair and blinked to clear her eyes as her mind could not accept what the page preached to be true.

The shock jerked her lungs to take in quick sucks of air, and she pressed a hand to her mouth. "I do not believe it."

"Gracious, Carrie, you're frightening me." Anna leaned forward, reaching out. "What's happened?"

Hot springs of joy spilled from her eyes. Looking up, light filled every piece of her. "He lives."

# CHAPTER 2

*B*eneath his sturdy boots the snow crunched, and James Higley held his breath. Remaining motionless, he strained his hearing to cut through the deafening silence. No movement, no sound. Naught but the sting of winter's breeze to rustle the frigid air.

Still, his muscles tensed. Experience taught always to guard, always to suspect.

Daylight strained through barren trees, casting sickly shadows across the white-covered ground. Wearied from winter's long night, their shallow standing offered pitiful cover.

Glancing behind at the place he'd left his mount, James calculated his timing as the sun moved along the sky. He reached into his pocket and peered at the delicate face of his timepiece. Not thirty minutes until he was expected at headquarters.

The man whom he was to meet had better get here soon.

"Fox."

James turned at the whispered sound and answered in code. "Hound."

Breathing out as he hadn't done in days, James allowed a smile as full as last night's moon, his eyes hardly believing who it was that stood before him. "Why, if it isn't Henry Donaldson."

His friend of many years stepped forward, hand extended. "Captain Higley." They shook and Henry's face lifted, his eyes awash with joy when he chuckled. "Good to see you, old friend."

"I had not expected you to be the messenger. A pleasant surprise indeed." James tilted his head, unable to subdue his grin. He gestured to Henry's navy-blue regimentals. "The color becomes you." The tension in James's shoulders eased. "I am pleased to know we are once again fighting on the same side."

Henry's shoulders relaxed their rigid line. "I hope someday you will get to change your red coat for a blue one."

"Someday perhaps." James sobered. God willing, 'twould be sooner rather than later. But in truth, he knew his work was not yet done.

Henry allowed for a beat of silence, smiling. "I have many questions for you. But ones I suppose will have to wait for another time."

"Aye." James lowered his head. "As I have questions for you. You are married now, I understand."

"I am." Henry nodded. "Much has happened since last we met, and much to tell, indeed."

News of Henry Donaldson's defection from the British Army some months ago had spread through the regiment like fire. Though his action was defamed by most, James had inwardly rejoiced.

Henry tightened a grin over his mouth. "When this conflict ends we shall bare all our secrets. As for now..."

Aye. To business.

James surveyed the surrounding sentry of naked trees before speaking and lowered his voice. "You have news for me?"

"Aye. We've been commissioned to make camp some twenty miles south and watch for enemy movement. We had word a

17

transport might be coming up from New York. Do you know of any such thing?"

"Nay." The moving sunlight shifted the shadows and James's shoulders tightened. He looked at his pocket watch. He must hurry. "I shall find out and give you word."

"What of the two Patriots?" Henry's sudden question yanked James from his thoughts. "The ones we heard tell were helping you at the foundry. Are they still undiscovered? Did they make it out of the raid alive?"

The events of the past few weeks burst to life. Henry was not as acquainted with Hannah Young and Joseph Wythe as he was, but their courage was well known and admired. The determination of such people never ceased to impress, and worry. So many were willing to give so much, even to the end of their lives.

"They are well." James paused, sending a silent plea toward heaven they would continue to be so. "They were given to my watch, but I have let them go."

"You let them go?"

James stared out, pondering that night three days past when he'd done the very thing he knew could have him thrown from the army—or worse. "God willing, they will remain undetected."

"God willing *you* will remain undetected."

The message in Henry's words swirled around him like dust in a storm and dirtied his formerly unsullied confidence.

"A brave thing." Henry folded his arms, intimate knowing worn thick on his expression. He knew well the army, and those orchestrating it. He knew the depths of the danger. "What will Stockton say of this?"

"He will accept my story." James shifted his feet and held his friend's pointed gaze.

There was no other choice. Stockton *must* accept.

Suspicion crawled across Henry's brow. "So easily?"

James wiped a hand over the back of his neck, fighting away the prick of doubt that pressed deeper. "When I explain to the major that I was overtaken by Joseph and beaten down, I have to believe he will—"

Henry chuckled. "You do run a dangerous game, James Higley."

Answering his friend's lightness with his own, James produced a smile but felt none of the accompanying mirth that typically followed. Dangerous, aye. Deadly.

He filled his lungs before releasing weeks of tension in a single, rough breath. "Their lives and ours—in truth, the entire future of our country depends upon the lies we tell."

Henry unfolded his arms and moved his weight over his feet, his eyes studying. "You know not the good you do, I am certain."

Trailing back those five years, James's memory filed through his acts of service to the Patriot cause. He could only hope what he did was enough, both to make amends and to rally the cause he'd come to champion.

James cant his head. "I have but one request."

"Aye." Henry adjusted his stance. "Anything."

He paused before answering. "I require the imprint of your fist."

"What?" After a few beats Henry jerked back. "James, I cannot—"

"If I am to be believed I must look the part."

Lip between his teeth, Henry shook his head. "I'm sorry, I cannot without provocation cause pain to any person—"

"You must." James exhaled, knowing he would feel the same were a friend to ask such of him. "Believe me if there were any other way—"

The blow came quick and hard. Another one followed after, right across his jaw. Disoriented, James attempted to straighten when another punch to his gut threw him to the ground.

Eyes stinging and blurry, nose dripping blood, James groaned and pushed up on one hand. A light chuckle left his chest. "Remind me not to ask that of you again." He squinted to clear his vision as a smile formed past the pain. "Either you've gotten stronger, or I've forgotten the iron in your arm."

Henry crouched and extended his hand. "'Tis worse if you know it's coming." His gaze went to James's nose and he grimaced. "It looks the way you hoped, I believe."

"By the feel of it I'm certain it does."

He helped James to rise, and clapped him on the shoulder, a sudden solemnness possessing his face and tone. "I shall continue my petitions to Providence in your behalf. We rely on you. More than you know."

James nodded, his ears ringing both with pain and somber gravity. "Providence holds the future of all in this conflict." He inhaled as the initial pain began to subside. "And I believe, in the end, freedom will stand victorious."

The scent of a faraway fire drifted through the wintery air. He needn't look to his watch to know 'twas time.

"I pray next we meet 'tis under the flag of freedom." Henry's grasp lingered. "We have much for which to hope."

"Aye."

Unbidden, James reached for the timepiece in his pocket and smoothed his thumb over the inscription on the back of the object he most treasured, feeling the message more than thinking it.

A warm trail trickled down James's mouth. He dabbed it with his hand and chuckled. "Go, before I make you answer for your violence."

Henry replied, smiling. "God speed."

He watched as his friend retreated from sight.

Peering down, James studied the blood on his fingers, how it matched the color of the wool coat that covered him.

In moments he'd be called to explain his tardiness, and the reason for his bloodied face.

Would to God Henry's fist had done the job. For if it hadn't, 'twould be more than a bloodied nose he would suffer.

Caroline stared at the words, consumed by shock and unable to fully allow herself to believe she read what she did. Again she sat, her body heavy, the room misting away into mere shapes and colors. All that existed was the note in her hand and the letters that embraced her from the page.

The touch on her arm reminded Caroline she was not alone. "Carrie?"

She looked across the table and shook her head, wiping a tear. "Forgive me, I am…I am…" A laugh of joy sparked from her smile. "My brother, Enoch…" She looked at the paper. "'Tis from him. He writes to say he is alive."

Anna's face went slack. "But I thought he—"

"We all thought so."

The consuming jolt forced her to her feet as another measure of understanding cleared the fog of disbelief. Walking to the parlor, she continued reading, Anna following behind.

She read aloud where it began. *"Dear Father, These long months have been agony for me, knowing you believed me dead when I am, in truth, alive and in Boston."* Caroline stopped, her breath shallow. "I believe I am in shock."

Anna's kind gaze enclosed her in sympathetic comforts. "Is that all he says? There must be more."

"There is, aye." She'd been so consumed she'd nearly forgotten to continue. Caroline sucked in a shuddered breath then released it with forced calm. She placed a hand at her middle. *"Know that nothing else but your comfort and well-being have been on my mind every moment. As for myself, there are reasons I have not yet had time to write you…"*

She stopped, an icy thread snaking down the length of her spine. Flashing a look to Anna she swallowed and continued. *"I was indeed wounded in the battle, and believed dead for a time, until a soldier discovered me yet living, and I was taken prisoner with several others."*

All joy began a slow draining.

Anna stepped beside her, reading over her shoulder as she went on.

*"I have since been kept here, in this besieged place, its once pleasant streets resembling what one might deem the true paths of hell. I write not to make you mourn for me, but to tell you only that I have loved you all. Do not tell Mother and Carrie of this, I fear they will weep more at knowing..."*

Caroline's throat clogged and her knees threatened to buckle. Shuffling backward, she took the nearest seat. She lowered the note, her vision now too cloudy to allow any more. He was alive, yet a prisoner? Was he ill? Had he any hope of release?

Awash with the battering questions, she'd lost the strength to stand, to move—to think.

Anna knelt before her. "Shall I read it for you?"

Caroline met her gaze, and all at once, the friendship she'd known was heaven-made gifted all its benevolence to her hurting. Anna had grieved her own brother, sought him and mourned for him. Only to learn he was nothing as she believed him to be. Her path had been different, but her heart was the same. Praise God for such a person.

Able only to nod, Caroline felt the paper slip from her fingers.

Anna put her back to the fire, and read. *"I fear they will weep more at knowing my current condition, and should I die while in this prison, I would not wish for them to suffer at my death a second time."*

She paused, and Caroline supposed she looked at her, but her head was too heavy to lift, her mind hardly able to keep its footing.

*"We have little warmth, and even less food. I have suffered these many months with illness, as have all the others with whom I was taken. But we let not our tribulations dim the fire of our convictions."*

'Twas not Anna's voice now, but Enoch's that filled her ears, and her head lifted.

*"If we are called to suffer more, or to be carried across the sea, or if we die unknown and forgotten in the crevices of this woebegone city, know this—that I regret not what I have sacrificed and suffered, and would do it again even with the knowledge that such misery awaited. Freedom's value is immeasurable—and yet, 'tis so easily squandered."*

Caroline glanced up, a shimmer of something unnamable flickering in her chest. Of their own volition, her legs pressed her up. She needed to move. Pacing, she listened as her friend continued.

*"If you are able, if you believe at all in the goodness of Providence, pray for us. By the courage of a good friend, I am able to write to you and beg for your petitions on our behalf—as we plan to escape. If our actions or this letter is discovered we shall be—"*

Anna moved the first page aside—and halted. Flipping over the paper, she looked up, mouth tight and brow narrow.

Shall be what?

Caroline froze, her heart beating a rhythm that pained even more at the look on her friend's ashen face.

Shaking her head, Anna flipped both pages again before meeting her gaze. "There is…there is no other page."

"That cannot be."

Caroline strode forward and took the pages, confirming what her friend had said. Tendrils of dread weaved down her middle and coiled in her stomach.

Looking up, she met Anna's worry-bathed gaze. Neither spoke. Caroline's mind began a frantic search for conclusion. What had happened? Had it been lost? Had it been intercepted? She checked the paper for a seal. There was none.

*Oh, dear Lord.* Where was the last of it?

With a flick of her wrist she turned the paper to examine the date.

January 18, 1776.

Two and a half weeks ago. Why had it taken so long to reach them?

She ran to the door and flung it open. Charging into the snow, she scanned the yard and squinted through the blinding white. The rider was gone of course, but somehow she'd hoped...

Whirling back, she hurried inside. "I have to go."

"Where?" Anna closed the door Caroline had left open. "Caroline, you are in shock. You must allow yourself time to think."

"What is there to consider?" Caroline snatched her cloak from its hook by the door and swung it around her shoulders. Bolts of heat and cold fought for space in her bones. "My brother, whom we all believed dead, is alive—was alive at the writing of that letter—no, Anna, I cannot rest."

"Please, Caroline." Anna stepped in front of her and took hold of her shoulders. "I know the power of hoping to once again embrace one so beloved. But you cannot go in such a state. Come and speak with Eliza and Kitty about it. They will help you see more clearly—"

"How can I not pursue more knowledge when this portion of a promising opus is handed to me, as if from the very fingers of God?" Her muscles cramped, and she lowered her chin. "Anna, though I have not known you long, I feel you are one of the dearest friends of my life. Of course you mean well, but I must go. I must speak of this to my cousin, Hannah."

'Twas only then that Anna released her hold, a questioning look thinning her eyes. "That is all you wish to do?"

Caroline paused, picking apart the frayed ends of her own emotions, and lied past the truth. "Aye. Worry not that I shall do something rash."

Her mind trailed away and carried her gaze with it. Nay. There was much she wished to do. She wished to rush to that abysmal place and pluck her brother from the clutches of the enemy, cutting down any who attempted to stop her.

But how could she say such? How was even such a reckless

dream to be? She knew better than to attempt any such action. Still, her heart wailed to bring it to pass.

"I cannot bear this knowledge alone." She hurried to the kitchen and grabbed a sack from the cupboard, quickly filling it. "Father is now too far away to go after. And as Hannah knew Enoch, knew of his death, I wish to apprise her of this and ask what may be done, if anything."

Aye. When she spoke her purpose aloud it beamed with wisdom. 'Twas the right course. No rash action to hurry her into danger. God would show her the way, even if she knew not beforehand what she should do.

Standing in the kitchen, heavy sack in hand, she felt the weight of more than mere bread and cheese in her grasp. Crinkling the letter carefully into the inner pocket, she cinched it tight.

Her throat clogged so that her words were weak when she spoke. "I am grateful you were here. I could not have handled such news alone."

"I will not pretend I do not feel you should stay." Anna's face threatened to crumple, but she pulled a smile in place over the worry. "'Tis dangerous, but..." She flung forward and wrapped her arms around her, pulling Caroline into a sisterly embrace. "I would do no different than you." Pulling back, she took the wrap from her neck and put it around Caroline's. "Promise me only that you will not do anything rash."

Had she heard her earlier thoughts?

Caroline quirked her mouth and gave a breathy laugh as she strode to and out the door. "Such as what?"

Anna followed after. "I refuse to say lest I plant anything in your head."

Halting long enough to place a kiss on her friend's cheek, Caroline grinned as the cloud-like flakes rested themselves on her cloak. "I shall be back soon and will tell you all."

Warm with emotions that collided in her chest, Caroline

turned and hurried to the barn. Her brother's letter replayed again and again from the safety of its place in her sack.

Swinging open the barn door, Caroline halted as a firestorm of all she'd harbored wailed upon her, and she closed her eyes. With a hard breath, she opened them. Enoch was alive—or had been two weeks past. God willing, he was still. If he was not, God alone would have strength to drag her from the one thing she must do. Enoch's battle might in fact be over.

Hers however, had only just begun.

# CHAPTER 3

"*I* should have you court-martialed." Major Ezra Stockton paced in front of James, his barreled chest accentuated by his crossed arms. The small room they occupied smelled of sweat and rage. "I am disgusted with you."

James stood erect, face forward, his head throbbing. The trickle of blood from his nose he'd wiped away before being summoned, threatened to trail to his mouth a second time. Stockton had never questioned him before. Would to God he didn't now.

Stopping, Stockton released his arms and pointed a taut arm toward the door. "I gave you strict orders to watch over those two and now you wish me to believe you failed because of mere weakness?"

The blood began its impending decent from his nose. James raised his chin, preparing to speak, but Stockton's boom filled the officer's quarters.

"How dare you let those two Patriot spies get free under your watch." He neared, the crimson color of his face glowing red-hot. "Your blunder is a blotch on my command, and I refuse to be so defamed by one in my regiment."

James offered a quick nod. The man they'd hung had taken the blame for the two he had set free, and Stockton seemed at the time to believe them innocent. James should have known something would change the man's mind.

Stockton released a growl that rumbled through the room. "If you wish to retain your rank and serve in my regiment then I demand exactness in the performance of your duty."

"Aye, sir."

"You promised me these three days they were being watched over and had I not pressing business I would have checked on them myself." He ground his teeth, examining the wounds on James's face. "You think me a fool."

"Nay, sir."

"You think I would actually believe such a story?" He jammed a finger against James's chest. "I must now explain this to Pitman who had expected this very evening to question them."

Thick curses exploded through the air. Stockton was known for his temper, but such had always been endured by others. Now, it seemed, 'twas James who would feel his wrath.

A trail of sweat beaded down his neck as the reality of his actions flooded his lungs. Five years he'd worked against them under their very watch, and thus far, they'd been blissfully ignorant. But this...this ruse he'd devised kept his head only just above water in a wind-swept sea. It would take but a single wave to press him under.

Images of the past whispered through his soul—of the death he'd witnessed and the vow he'd made to no longer give his life to the king, but to freedom—and twisted at parts still raw and grieving. He must not be moved from his post, must not be demoted. There were more reasons for his secretive work in this cause than his passion for liberty alone. That had come gradually. 'Twas the horror he witnessed that night, the black-heartedness of the army, that proved the last straw, turning him.

Crossing to the desk only feet from where James stood in the middle of the room, Stockton slumped in the chair and wiped a hand down his face. "*Quod factom est.*"

James fought the urge to raise a brow. Had the man said what James thought he did? What little Latin he knew, the message Stockton had spoken was more a quiet question than a condemnation.

Braving a look to his superior, James pretended ignorance. "Sir?"

Stockton leaned back fully, extending one arm to the table. He kept his head bent and eyes diverted. "Pitman calls me weak. Says that I am as reluctant as Howe in this conflict." He raised his head and spoke to the window. "Reluctant, perhaps, but not remiss." At this his vision hurled against James and struck him through. "Why I am compelled to trust in you, Captain Higley, I cannot say and it goes against my better judgment. After this most recent blunder I have every reason to suspect you have motives other than the success of this army. You have time and again called me to question your abilities, yet…" He wagged his head, sighing. "Yet there is something of myself I see in you. Your determination, your respect for authority, your intelligence. Which is why I am granting you a—"

A knock at the door halted his speech and a groan emerged from Stockton. "Come in."

Creaking, the door opened and an errand boy entered. "Major Pitman is here to see you, sir."

The long slow inhale was followed by a slight raise of one eyebrow. "Tell him to wait."

The boy bowed and excused himself.

Stockton glared at the door as he started speaking. "I believe we are expected to move in a few day's time. Which means we will not be returning to the foundry."

They were not? This he hadn't heard.

With a heave, Stockton pushed to his feet and circled the desk. "If you were not otherwise so reliable I would strip you of your rank and dispose of you. But as it is, I am in need of captains who can take orders and fulfill them." He came within inches, his voice nearly inaudible. "I am giving you one last chance. Do you understand?"

James kept his vision forward. "I do, sir."

"Good." Stockton allowed more space between them. "I have an assignment for you—"

The knock came again and this time the boy entered without an invitation. His face was flushed and his features hard. Poor boy. Pitman's wrath left scars to rival Stockton's.

"Major Pitman needs to see you now, sir—"

"Tell him to wait!"

The boy retreated and Stockton's glare snatched James at the throat. "Meet me at the foundry at sundown. 'Tis empty and, as I have something I wish to speak to you about, it will be the best spot to converse." He whirled and waved a finger. "You are dismissed."

"Aye, sir."

Pivoting on his heel, James exited and made his way through the foyer, past the muted cajoles and sneers of those in the parlor. Once in the barn and beside his mare Ginny, he allowed himself to finally and fully breathe. Releasing the caustic fumes he'd held in for too long, he wiped a hand down his face. *That was too close.*

Moving his hand away, he noticed the blood on his fingers and reached for the cloth in his pocket, cleaning it away.

He replaced the cloth and rubbed his head. Was he doing enough? 'Twas a risk—everything he did put him closer to discovery. So why did it seem as if his efforts did more harm than good?

"I hear you were nearly court-martialed. Shame. I should have liked to witness that."

Not moving, James leveled his shoulders, disgust pluming at the sound of a voice he'd grown to loathe.

"What are you doing here, Greene?" Ducking to give Ginny

another measure of grain, he fought the urge to whirl back and ease his rage with a fist to flesh.

Matthew Greene neared, resting a hand on Ginny's rump. His eyebrows lifted when James turned to face him. He tsked and shook his head. "Lost a fight, did you?"

James scowled. "I thought Pitman had a mission for you. Why don't you go about it?" Keeping civil took amounts of strength he no longer possessed. "I have my own business to attend."

"Like allowing Patriot spies to go free?"

*Don't engage him.*

James's bones threatened to crack. "Get out of my way."

He prepared to leave when a hand on his arm yanked him back.

"Stockton may be blind to your motives, but I am not." Greene's fomenting hatred was his weakness, though he considered it a strength. "'Tis your uncle's station that provides you with protection from discipline."

James jerked his arm from Greene's weak grasp. Lengthening his spine, he narrowed the space between them and peered down at the man who had been his nemesis since their first crossing from London.

"If you were not so concerned with your own advancement you might see there is other work more worthy of your feeble attentions, Lieutenant."

James made his way to the yard, when the cold of his enemy's vitriol splattered over his back.

"Then you have not heard? I am no longer a lieutenant." He paused. "I am a captain now. You and I are equals."

Twitches of rage threatened to swing his fists. "You and I will never be equal."

Greene continued, a sickening smile on his face. "I have been given carte blanche to apprehend the man who is subverting our progress in this war. Pitman believes in me. Far more than Stockton believes in you it would seem."

Riddled with the scent of self-absorbed delight, Greene's expression forced James to ground his teeth or risk spewing his mirrored dislike. Would that the man might someday get what was owed him. But that was for God to judge and for James to endure.

Craning to peer behind him, James spied a huddled group, his vision landing on one who might relieve him of the plague of Greene. For a time at least.

Adjusting his feet to give a more relaxed stance, James rested his hand on the sword at his side. "Abrams is neglecting his post again."

Greene's brow folded instantly as his eyes swept to the indignant private.

"He still refuses to say where he was the night of the raid." James shook his head, inwardly chuckling at how easily Greene could be baited. His glare was already on the man.

Greene raised his chin, suspicion dangling from his tone. "How do you know this?"

"You are sadly under-informed, *Captain* Greene." James shook his head and slapped Greene on the shoulder. "A sorry state for one so trusted." He made his way to the line of tents that formed their small camp.

James moved forward, but Greene spoke from where he stood. "You would help me, James Higley, by sharing such information?"

Stopping, James peered over his shoulder. "I would never help you."

"Nay. You would never help anyone but yourself."

James prepared to enter his tent, but paused as Greene's bitter words scarred a path down his skin. "'Twould seem the legend behind your scar is more truth than fiction, hmm?"

Hot exhales melted the ice that formed on the pole of his tent in front of him. *Say nothing.* Yet the urge was strong, and James fought the battle with a clenched jaw.

Before he could lash out and do damage to the man's exterior that only a surgeon could repair, he flung open the canvas door and ducked inside.

The cream-colored walls surrounded him, but 'twas the memories that closed in, suffocating in their oppression.

"Go, nurse your wounds, Higley. It appears you need it."

As the sound of Greene's footfall faded, James held a hand up to his ear and traced his finger along the jagged place the tip of his ear had been—the remembrance he carried of that night, and would always carry.

A reminder that he must continue at all costs to fight the very people who believed him trustworthy.

At all costs, he must go on.

# CHAPTER 4

Stomping across the ice-crusted ground, Matthew Greene sneered, grumbling in bitter silence.

Who was James Higley to think he was so honored? Greene kicked a rock, his cold hands in his pockets. Everyone knew James was only in the army because his uncle put him there. His rank bought and paid for like the rest of his life. Never had to work for what he wanted, never had to make his way in the world.

As for Greene, he'd fought his way to captain. *And Father had said I would never make it past private.*

That eve so many years ago throbbed hard through his memory. Father's slurred speech, his wobbled stance and blood-shot eyes were the only way Greene had ever known him. Greene's jaw hardened, remembering how he'd told Father he was leaving, that he wanted more from his life. Father had just laughed and slumped in his chair by the fire.

"You think you're better? Nothing can change who you are. You're a Greene—a worthless sot like the rest of us. The bottle is your future. No Greene will ever amount to anything."

*I shall prove you wrong.*

Making his way through the lines of tents, the small camp seemed suddenly…smaller. Pitman—Major Aldor Pitman—of all men, was the only one who saw his potential. How was it that his superior, a man with little knowledge of his strength or abilities could see what Major Stockton had never seen? Greene had strength and perseverance. It was because of him alone, because of his determination and will, that the raid on the Patriots had happened at all.

"Captain Greene."

Greene halted and turned on his heel to see Major Pitman striding toward him, his attendant Private Rawlings at his side.

"Good day, to you, sir."

Pitman motioned to the man at his side. "Prepare my horse. I shall be ready to ride within a quarter hour."

The attendant bowed and marched away to do as commanded.

Pitman flicked his wrist at Greene, and Greene followed.

"I've just had a meeting with Stockton." His neck twitched as if he were still filtering through the contents of their exchange and found it vexing. "We've encountered a change of plans." He marched up the steps of the house next to headquarters and strode in, the few soldiers littering the entryway scattered to positions of attention when he passed on his way to the study.

Greene followed close behind, an uncomfortable foreboding settling in the middle of his gut.

Pitman entered the small but elegant room. Removing his hat, Pitman motioned for Greene to shut the door, and much to Greene's chagrin, ignored the particulars he'd hinted at moments before. "Tell me you have gleaned some helpful information in the few days I've been gone." His jaw twitched. "The news I've just had from Stockton makes me long to see justice met where it is due."

Clearing his throat, Greene nodded and said the thing he should say, not the thing he wished. "Aye, sir. I have acquired information that has promised excellent leads."

"Leads?" A vein in Pitman's forehead bulged. "I didn't advance you with this assignment for you to find leads."

Greene pulled back. "I have had only three days—"

"Plenty of time to give me names, Greene. I want names." Pounding his fist on the table he emphasized his words.

Sweat formed on the back of Greene's neck. "I have questioned Higley."

"Good. I never trusted the man." Pitman's color normalized.

At least Pitman too sensed in Higley what he did. The man was secretive, devious and weak. Worse, he was clean. Few suspected him and despite their efforts, no evidence could be found to prove what Greene surmised to be true. The man was not what he seemed.

Keeping his posture rigid, Greene kept confidence in the folds of his brow despite the doubt that crept over him like a fog. Pitman wouldn't be pleased with the crumbs he offered to one famished for meat. "He told me Abrams was missing that evening."

Pitman raised his brows. "That is all? That is your lead?"

Greene's neck grew hot. "I...he said..."

"I am sure he forgot to mention that he too was missing that very evening and no one seems to know his whereabouts for the space of several hours."

Rage thickened in his chest, lodging there in a heap. No surprise James hadn't mentioned it.

"Whoever this informant is, Greene, I need him." Curls of anger journeyed across Pitman's long face. "He is threatening the very life of this army. He's close. I can feel it."

Greene's brow twitched. "Aye, sir."

Pitman stared through black eyes before moving around his desk and sitting. "There will be a reward for you on the other side of this if you are successful."

A reward?

Pitman paused before continuing, "Another forthcoming

advancement may be yours, Captain, *if* you bring him in to me alive." He looked up. "He is nothing to me dead. There will be time enough to end him."

Another advancement? Greene's chest swelled with more than breath. "I understand, sir."

"However," Pitman said, thick brows folding. "If you are unsuccessful, you will find yourself at the bottom where you began."

The bottom. *You will never make it past private. No Greene will ever make it out of the slums.* Greene swallowed and shook his head as a question tumbled through his mind and out his mouth. "How much time will I be given?"

Scribbling something on a page, Pitman looked down as he spoke. "I need to have him by week's end. We are being dispatched to Boston." He stood and handed the paper to Greene. "There are several soldiers unaccounted for and I believe they may be hiding out between here and the foundry we no longer occupy. Find them and bring them in. It may well be among these stragglers that you discover the man you're looking for."

"I shall leave immediately, sir—"

"Before you go." Pitman sighed and kept his quill dancing. "Find Abrams and question him." At this he stopped and looked up. "Trust no one. Suspect all."

Greene stood straighter, arms firm at his sides. "Aye, sir."

Pitman rested his attention again on his writing. "You are dismissed."

Greene bowed. Striding from the room, his pride bloomed more as the reality of his future cascaded over him. If only Stockton could see him now—could see his glory and how success looked on him. The promise of a detachment, more missions, more work for the king. *Ha!* Stockton had thrown him from the regiment like rubbish. Pitman at least saw his greatness. These rewards were too long in coming.

He snarled, moving toward camp, calculating the next move he must make. Where was Abrams, anyway?

Rolling back one shoulder, Greene looked behind him while his brain did the same, unable to leave his nemesis in pleasant solitude. James was as trustworthy as a snake and just as dangerous. Pitman was a smart man. Why would he take James's word as veracity? And why—why hadn't he insisted on investigating James further? They both knew he'd let those Patriots go. Was Greene the only one so dedicated?

The thought rankled, but he strode past their pickets. James would be questioned, he'd be sure of that. For now, 'twas Abrams he needed.

Removing his hands from his pockets, Greene splayed and curled his fingers to encourage the blood to find them. The camp was small, the row of canvas tents only fifteen long. And there, at the end of the row, was a fire surrounded by a handful of crouching soldiers, their arms outstretched over the flames.

Their conversation hushed even before Greene was fully beside them. A dozen suspicious eyes narrowed in his direction.

He straightened his back and flicked his finger toward Abrams who sat at the far side of the fire.

"Come with me."

Sighing, Abrams rose slowly. "Whatever you need, don't make it long. This is the first real warmth I've enjoyed in days." His face cut into a lecherous grin. "Though I do keep plenty warm at night."

He whooped and the others laughed.

Not amused, Greene stood rigid until Abrams came beside him. Gesturing the direction he'd just come, Greene started to walk and Abrams followed beside him.

"I need to speak to you about the night of the raid."

Abrams kept walking, an irritated undercurrent in his tone. "What about?"

"Where were you?"

The man continued his forward attention. "I don't see how it matters. 'Twas three days ago."

Greene stopped in front of his tent and opened the door, ushering his companion inside. Abrams ducked in and Greene followed, letting the door slap closed behind him.

"It matters because there is a traitor among us."

Without permission, Abrams took the only chair in the small space and slouched. "What makes you so interested in finding him? Pitman's made you his little monkey and suddenly you'll do whatever he says, is that it?"

He'd forgotten how irritating this man could be. "I hear you were not at your post that night." He held back, waiting for a reaction, but there was none. "Do you deny it?"

"Why should I?" Shifting in his chair, he huffed. "What does this bloody army offer us? No warmth. No food. They promised glory but have given us only grief." A bitter laugh shuffled through his chest. "Aye. The night of the raid while the rest of you were scrambling, I was finding pleasure in the arms of a woman. Court-martial me if you must. 'Twould be better than suffering any more in this hell hole."

Greene pressed out a gravelly breath and pivoted. The words were careless, threatening perhaps, but were they treasonous? He ground his teeth. Was this man even capable of such crimes? Intelligence was a necessity for such actions, was it not? Abrams seemed less endowed than some. Then again…Greene pondered. Every man had his weakness—a spot that, if grazed, would make him fall to his knees. Greene had been in the army long enough. Surely he'd heard something of Abrams.

Like the flick of a match, he found it.

Relaxing his posture, Greene tilted his head and one brow. "You have a son, do you not?"

Abrams face slackened, and his jaw flexed. "How do you know—"

"Your dalliances have caught up with you. Should Pitman discover such a thing I suspect he would—"

"I know nothing." 'Twas after a hard length of silence, Abrams answered. "I admit I was gone but that is all. Had I any additional information I would tell."

Greene neared. "How do I know you speak the truth?"

"I have nothing else to say because there is nothing else." Abrams sat higher in his seat and straightened his gaze on Greene. "I give you my word that I am not the man you seek."

That was already clear, but at least he'd made the man recognize his earnestness. "You are lucky, Abrams. For the man, when he is caught, will be faced with a firing squad, if he is not first faced with being drawn and quartered."

Abrams leaned forward and wiped a hand over his mouth as if the horrid realization had begun a descent through his mind.

Of a sudden, the careless confidence returned and a grin toyed with one side of his mouth.

He inhaled and allowed for a satisfied sigh before speaking. "I wonder if perhaps my dereliction might prove to be your salvation."

Unlikely. Greene tilted his head. "How is that?"

Abrams sat back again as if the chair were large and plush. "I recall after leaving a certain establishment that morning..." He paused, his lips sliding upward. "I saw a soldier on horseback speaking with two others at the edge of town. They were sharing a mount—a man and a woman."

The tiniest spark popped in Greene's chest. "And?" There had better be more. For if this story revealed a name, he believed that name would be synonymous with traitor.

"There is nothing more to tell." Abrams stood and walked to the door of the tent.

Greene rushed after him. "Did you see the soldier's face?"

Abrams slowed, irritation puckering his mouth. "Nay."

Grabbing his arm, Greene jerked him around. "Did you see anything else? The markings of his horse? The epaulettes on his uniform? Anything?"

Shaking his head Abrams tugged his arm free and strode from the tent. "Patriots are liars, Greene, and liars are tough to catch."

# CHAPTER 5

$\mathcal{T}$he sun bent low in the horizon when Caroline rode into the yard of Eaton Hill, the frosted air clinging to her bones.

She slowed her mount and surveyed the quiet yard, assailed by memories of times more blest. Of springtime picnics when she and Hannah chased butterflies as children, of summer nights spent stargazing. There had been joy here, love. Now nothing could be seen but shadows and ice-covered ground, nothing felt but foreboding.

The uncle she'd loved had been killed here only weeks ago—and by a soldier's hand. The very land seemed to mourn his loss.

Caroline urged her mount further on, her lips pursing. No movement, not even any horses in the open barn. A worry niggled in her middle and she sat straighter. They would never keep the barn open.

Dismounting, she patted her horse, more to reassure herself than her four-legged companion. "I shan't be long, Shadrach." After leading him to the barn where he could rest and find refuge from the cold, she made her way to the lightless house. She'd expected to see a burst of activity on reaching Eaton Hill, certain at least Joseph would be in the foundry, but not even a hint of life could be seen in the place that was usually bustling with noise. No sound of hammers beating, no smoke even from the chimney.

A cold pit formed in her stomach.

Stepping to the door, she knocked. The expected tap of Hannah's footfall never came. She knocked again—this time harder—and stepped back, rubbing her gloved hands together to fight off the cold. That small hope she'd carried, that perhaps Hannah was in her bedchamber and dressing or occupied in the kitchen, died when still there was nothing.

She knocked again before putting her face to the wood. "Hannah? Hannah, 'tis I, Caroline."

Naught but mocking silence answered.

Where was she? Caroline tapped her hand against her skirt, glancing behind. Where was Joseph? Something had happened. Her memory leapt to the night Hannah had explained her work as a Patriot spy, and the danger that lurked in the places where safety should have been. The need to act consumed Caroline.

She reached for the handle of the door, and it gave. Pushing it open, she stepped in. The scent of stale logs in the fireplace, and the temperature inside nearly as bitter as out, made her muscles spark.

"Hello? Is anyone here?" Shaking her head, she ignored the warning that blared in her ears. "Hannah? Joseph?" All was well, surely. They were merely away, or had been called to some place, or were perhaps on an errand in town.

Or they were discovered. Taken.

Her hands shook as the horrid possibility took a more formidable place in her chest. "Hannah?"

Caroline hurried to the kitchen and halted. The table was littered with forgotten food and dishes. A chair was toppled, the fireplace cold.

*Oh, Dearest Lord.*

She spun, her voice echoing through the lonely house. "Hannah! Joseph!"

Clutching her skirts, she raced upstairs, certain her fears would be eased when she entered Hannah's bedchamber. At the doorway, Caroline's stomach churned harder. The bed was unmade—the quilt missing and the drawer to her dressing table open.

Putting a hand to her head, she groaned, her knees turning weak. Hannah was gone—something had happened. Nothing could be more certain. She began a slow descent, praying in her heart for strength. They had already suffered so much, and now her dearest cousin, the one with whom she'd shared all her secrets, the one who knew her better than she knew herself, was gone. Captured, perhaps even now on her way to stand trial for the courage and bravery so few others were willing to prove.

Along those miles she'd ridden here, those quiet moments on the road, she'd told herself she should not think ill of their enemies, but should pray for them as Christ admonished. Caroline's limbs shook. How could she? Those men thought they could take what they pleased, that they could demand, dictate and demean.

It was too much to be borne.

She strode to the parlor, giving in to one last hope. If Hannah had left, on her own and not in duress, she would surely have taken the family Bible. Opening the small cupboard beside the fireplace, her heart skidded to a halt. There it sat, untouched and unopened, like a doleful mute, unable to share what it knew—what had happened.

Caroline straightened, her arms slack at her sides. A cold sweat covered her skin. What had happened? How could this be? How could—

A sound from outside turned her head to the window, and her pulse jumped. Two riders, both in red, entered the yard.

Panic swept through her, sucking all strength from her limbs.

What were they doing here? Would they come inside? As if they heard her thoughts, they answered with a dismount, both hitching their horses to the post outside.

*Dear Lord, help me.*

Her blood chilled and she ran to the kitchen, but the door was blocked by a toppled chair. Her throat threatened to close as the men's voices came muffled through the walls, growing louder with every frantic breath.

As if aided by heaven, she turned and salvation opened before her. The closet. 'Twas just her height and...

The voices were clear now and without a second thought she hurled herself into the closet and pulled the door closed—but it stopped within an inch of latching. Her bones threatened to crack as she tugged and tapped. It would close no further.

The front door swung open and the two men burst in.

Caroline welded her back to the closet wall behind her. *Lord, protect me.*

"—left his place entirely." The first soldier paused and glanced across the space. "We can be sure no one is here."

The second one entered and shut the door. "I understand, sir."

Taking his hat from his head, the older of the two moved to the center of the parlor, a sharp word cutting through his teeth. "At times I feel I am the only one truly seeing the precarious nature of our position." He looked to the younger one, his mouth splayed in frustration. "Another round of privateering boats has just intercepted one of our largest ships off New York."

"I had heard." The other one crossed his arms. "They are a nuisance but can easily be brought down."

A mouse squeaked and scurried across Caroline's shoe. Her entire frame went rigid. She kept her eyes fixed on them, and by the grace of heaven, their conversation went on unhindered.

"They are more than a nuisance, they are a hindrance." The older one pointed toward the door with his hat. "If they are not put down we will find ourselves in the midst of a conflict that will

45

take years and countless lives to end." Dropping his arm to his side, he shook his head. "A frigate is scheduled to arrive in Boston, the Nancy, in two week's time. I can only hope we have enough men to keep her from being taken."

"She is so vital, sir?"

"Critical. Her cargo is our lifeblood. Muskets, ammunition, food and other necessities she carries will strengthen our weakening men in Boston and keep our real condition a secret from Washington. We can no longer sustain this siege or I fear we will be forced to concede defeat before we have even begun."

Crossing the length of the room, the lean one, arms across his chest, peered down. "Do you think we will not take Dorchester?"

A growl rumbled through the room. "I have spoken of such many times." He put his hands behind his back. "And I believe change is in our future."

The younger soldier stood straight, his shoulders broad and accent rich. "He means to act?"

He shook his head. "General Anderson has just arrived from London, and I have reason to believe he might be the person to exact the progress we need to snuff out this vexatious rebellion once and for all."

"I have heard promising things of him, but I am not acquainted with him, sir. Are you?"

"I am not, but your uncle is and has spoken well of him."

Still pacing, the older one pulled a letter from his pocket and handed it to the other. "I am tired of wasting time. These skirmishes do nothing but fuel a fire already at dangerous strengths. Which is why I have devised a plan."

Opening the letter, the second soldier shifted his weight over his feet as the older man continued. "If I can convince Anderson that my design to defeat the rebels will be successful—which I am certain it will—then we may have a chance of convincing the others, which will in turn convince Howe, and we may at last be done with this bloody civil war."

After a quiet exhale, the soldier refolded the paper and returned it. "What is it you wish me to do, sir?"

At last releasing his hands from their position at his back, the man took the nearest chair. "I am sending you to Boston ahead of me."

"Ahead of you?"

"Anderson may be brilliant but his ego needs stroking. If we wish to entice him to our side we must flatter him. And in truth, I cannot think of anyone more qualified than you."

For a moment the younger soldier didn't move, but his head twisted sideways, and continued to twist—in her direction.

Her pulse thundered through her head so hard she feared they could hear its percussion. Had she been seen?

Just then he turned away and put his back to her. A wave of cold relief washed over her muscles.

"I do not see how someone of my station could help in such a capacity."

The older man stood. "I expect you to use your powers of persuasion—God knows you've been granted a greater portion than most—so that when I arrive several days after, he will be all too eager to listen to my proposal to take Dorchester Heights and support me when I present it to Howe."

Nodding, the captain pivoted her direction, his vision lingering dangerously close to her hiding spot.

He stepped forward and turned away again. "I will not fail you."

The major strode toward the door. "Tell no one of this. You are to leave immediately and wait for my arrival by week's end."

"Aye, sir."

He placed his hand on the door, and looked back. "Your work is imperative. We must end this conflict once and for all. Every day we waste means more death for both sides. God knows we cannot sustain this much longer."

Pulling the door open, he gave one last nod, and strode out, the other following.

The sound of the door latching into place echoed through the quiet house like a hammer to a coffin.

Blood still pumped wild through her veins, her bones brittle. How long until they rode away? She must stay until they were gone, but how long would that be and could she be certain 'twas safe?

Minutes passed, every blink an eternity.

Putting her face close to the open inch of space, she squinted, hoping to see the hands of the clock on the far wall of the parlor, but 'twas too far.

Her muscles twitched, the urge to bolt to safety almost suffocating.

Pressing the door open slowly, the hinges screamed like demons and she cringed. No sound, no movement through the window. Aye. She must go. Now.

As if consumed by something from another world, she bolted. Racing to the door and across the yard to the barn.

Once inside, she hurried to Shadrach and gripped the pommel of the saddle when a voice from behind turned her hot blood to ice.

"Good afternoon."

## CHATPER 6

$\mathcal{T}$he woman didn't move. Her arms were still at the saddle when she turned toward him. Eyes wide, cheeks drained of color, she looked as if she'd seen the devil himself.

He'd known someone had been there, listening. And had known they would appear. Perhaps not so quickly or so soon, but he'd known it.

The only thing he hadn't known was this person was a woman.

God be thanked Stockton hadn't questioned and continued on when James said he wished to stay behind a few moments longer to check the foundry for forgotten munitions.

James stepped from the shadows and motioned to her mount. "Is this your horse?"

She jerked back. "Get away from me."

Raising his hands, he stopped his advancement. "I mean you no harm."

He offered a smile, hoping his sincerity would remove the blatant fear in her colorless face. Dropping her hold of the saddle, she straightened and went still as a marble block. Her mouth formed a firm line while strands of light-blonde hair strayed from their pins beneath her cap.

Pricked by a thousand woes, James let his mind sort through them double-time. This woman had overheard every word spoken between him and Stockton. She knew enough to be dangerous.

What he must determine now, was *how* dangerous.

Idle conversation might gift him the time he needed to think. He softened his posture. "If I may be so bold...tell me, what are you doing here all alone?"

"I..." Her voice was a fragile thread, but the courage she held in her shoulders sang hymns of a character woven in strength. She raised her chin. "This is my cousin's foundry. What are *you* doing here?"

He quirked his head, calculating. She was Hannah's cousin, then. The resemblance was clear—both in complexion, and bravery. But what could he say to her? The truth? If only...

James gestured toward the house. "Your cousin has graciously allowed us the use of the foundry for the advancement of the British army, but we are no longer in need of it, as you see."

Pink tones rose from her neck into her cheeks as she answered through her teeth. "Is that so?"

Something in her eyes, in the way her chest moved swiftly up and down made him speak before thinking. "You should have made yourself known."

Her dainty eyebrows rose. "Whatever do you mean?"

So she would play at such games, would she? "If you are anything like the person you claim is your cousin—"

"She *is* my cousin."

"Then I suggest you use the better part of wisdom and tell me exactly what you were doing in that closet."

"I was..." What hint of color painted her cheeks slipped away when she lifted her chin. "Are you accusing me of something?"

"Should I be?"

She tucked a blonde strand behind her ear, forced calm in her taut voice. "Allow me to go on my way, and I am sure we can both be certain we will never mention this incident to anyone."

The slight twitch in her neck and the quickening of her breath told she lied. Brave of her. Foolish.

He took a step forward. "You spied on a private conversation between two officers. Such an act could prove you guilty of treason."

She shuffled back. "What?"

His conscience clubbed him in the gut. *Idiot.* He could have chosen better words. But risking discovery in any respect could be the end of him. Of all of them.

Then, like a flash in the pan, the truth burned his eyes. If she revealed what she'd heard, as well intentioned as her act may be, his work could be undermined. It must be shared with the right sources, in the proper way. What he'd learned from Stockton about the Nancy, about his plan to take Dorchester, was information vital to the Patriot's and any alteration could bring damage beyond repair.

His mind raced. Being called to Boston was a Godsend. Such proximity to Washington would allow for swifter transfer of intelligence. And with him in the den of officers where information was thicker than fog...

*Lord, what am I to do with her?*

In a burst, she whirled and reached for her mount.

Lunging, he grabbed her, but she fought, kicking and clawing. "Let me go!"

She thrashed, forcing him to hold stronger. Gripping her at the shoulders, he swung her to the wall and held her there as much with his eyes as with his strength. "That I cannot do."

"Please." Her trembling increased and tears formed in her eyes. "I beg of you, let me go. I will not tell what I know."

The unmistakable rhythm of horse and rider echoed through the yard and every sinew pulsed with warning.

Still holding to her, James forced his stare to open her trust. "Stay. Here."

Perhaps she believed him, perhaps she was inert with fear. Either way, it mattered not. Only that she obeyed. If any other soldier discovered her, whatever blissful future she had designed for herself would be slayed.

He strode to the yard, then halted hard when the man who sat tall on his mount twisted on his saddle to greet him.

"Ah, if it isn't Captain Higley." Greene looked around, a mocking jovial expression over his face. "What brings you here—alone?"

"I could ask the same of you."

"I am in search of camp stragglers—loners and possible defectors." His grin widened as he looked to the house, then the foundry. "I thought we'd left this place after the raid."

"We did." After years of practicing necessary deceit, lies came to him quick and full. "Stockton asked me to be sure the stores were empty before we made for Boston."

"Stockton is moving out as well then, is he? Not surprising." Greene again peered about the yard. "You have seen no others?"

Muscles taut, senses firing, James prayed the woman would do as instructed and stay where he'd left her.

"You'll find only myself here. Though a few others are returning from Sandwich this evening, I believe." James forced a relaxed pace as he moved toward Ginny, hoping Greene wouldn't dismount, but he did. "I am just on my way."

"I have to admit, I admire your perseverance, Higley."

James fought the urge to deform Greene's smug grin. "Do you really?"

"Aye, indeed I find myself amazed at your ability to continue on when you are the mock of the regiment—perhaps the entire army. What with your uncle a disgrace and your rank entirely because of him."

"I am the laughing stock of the army, am I?" James pretended misunderstanding. "I thought that honor went to you, Greene."

"At least you haven't lost your humor." Greene chuckled and stalked near him. "You see, I have been doing a bit of discovering and it seems that Abrams was indeed gone that night. But...he saw someone. A soldier, that is, speaking with a man and a woman the morning of the raid." He paused. "Strange is it not?"

Darkness crept over James's back, but he shrugged off its threat, refusing to answer.

Greene thrust a finger at his chest. "They have been gone days, not hours like you wish us to believe."

"You would take the word of a man who was derelict in his duty and no doubt full of drink?"

Greene struck forward, facing James nose-to-nose. "The evidence against you is piled high."

James leveled his spine, pulling him a full inch above his opponent. "Prepare your arguments against me and let me answer for myself."

"Perhaps you've forgotten what it is to fight for king and crown, for it seems you fight only for—"

A splash of color from the barn and thumping of hooves hit James's senses like musket fire. He whirled with a prayer. *Lord, no.* The woman rode from the barn like hell burned at her heels.

Instantly his shoulders cramped. He should have known she would attempt an escape.

"Who goes there?" Greene yelled and whirled for his horse. "Halt!"

Racing to Ginny, James mounted and yanked her around, kicking her to instant speed.

The woman's horse was swift, her skill in the saddle clear as she rode, her body low and arms tucked as she moved with the rhythm of her mount.

"Stop!" Greene shouted as he rode up from behind. "Stop in the name of the king!"

Racing up beside the woman, James reached for the reins of her horse. She attempted to hit him away, but her strength was nothing to his, and in seconds, he'd stopped her.

Greene rode up beside them, jumping from his horse. "Get down."

The woman flung a frantic look to James before obeying. She said nothing when Greene took her at the arm, his eyes a whirlwind of fury.

"Who are you? What were you doing at the foundry?"

Leaving Ginny, James hurried to them. "Greene, leave her be."

Greene's face contorted. "Coming to the aid of another spy, are you?"

"I am not a spy." The woman's tone was harsh, yet quivered.

Greene released her with a shove. "You have one chance to convince me."

James came between them before she could answer. "Why distrust her at all? She was merely—"

"Merely what?" Greene's face curled in disgust. "Here you are again, coming to the aid of the enemy."

"You are too quick to judge."

Blue veins bulged from his neck. "You would have me let her go?"

"You know nothing about her."

"And you do?"

James could feel fear exploding from the woman behind him. Aye, he knew something of her. He knew her courage and that she cared about her cousin. He knew that deep in the dark centers of her pale blue eyes, there was sorrow. And pain.

Greene tilted his head to see her. "Only the guilty run."

"She is not on trial."

"Fine." Greene stepped back, his chest rising. "I will make you a deal. You bring her in for questioning—*questioning*—not a trial, and I will suspended my decision to name you as the informant once and for all."

James's throat constricted. *Devil.*

"I need only for you to prove to me your devotion to the king with this one last act." Greene's eyes narrowed. "A simple task."

The sun's descent on the distant horizon was imminent, the surrounding twilight a premonition to more than the mere end of day. "I do not answer to you, Greene."

Greene moved back a step and put his hand on his sword. "Nay, but we are equals now, in the sight of the law, and if you wish to retain your position, you best come with me."

"Bringing an innocent woman to answer for innocent actions is—"

"Then you refuse to do it?"

From every pore came the kind of hate he'd witnessed from others but never felt. Greene had taken James in the very thing he was incapable of doing. Subjecting this woman to the wrath of Pitman, or Stockton, was unfathomable. She'd admitted to James straight out her relation to Hannah Young, a nail to her coffin if ever she revealed such to them.

He clenched his jaw. "I will not do it."

Greene snarled. "Then I will."

"Nay!"

Both men's attention went to the woman whose face was crimson, her mouth firm and nostrils flared. Stepping aside, she moved from the safety of James's stance. "I will go nowhere with either of you."

Looking at her where she stood behind him, James studied her jutted chin and the raw strength that led her to dangerous ground.

"You are all the same." She flashed a look to James before gouging Greene with the daggers in her eyes. "You believe you can make demands and take whatever you wish when you wish it."

Greene stepped toward her, his stare growing lecherous. He reached for her cheek and prepared to stroke it. "I like your spirit."

*Smack.*

Greene's head snapped sideways. He grabbed his face, glaring, then lunged. "How dare you—"

James came between them again, grabbing a fistful of Greene's shirt. "She is nothing to you. Forget her."

"Striking an officer?" Steam plumed from his nose. "She should be punished for more than that."

"Like you punished my cousin?" Leaning into her words, the woman's foolish bravery came alive in her cheeks. "You take my uncle's foundry then you—"

"Your cousin?" Greene's narrowed eyes circled in question. "Who is your cousin?"

James's stomach coiled and he wished he could snatch her words from the air, and stomp them into oblivion. She had no understanding of what she'd unwittingly divulged.

Who was this woman who carried so much fire?

"My cousin is Hannah Young." She squared her shoulders. "You have done something with her and I want to know what."

Greene's expression plumed with snide pleasure. "I am certain you would like to know." The tone of his voice fell to their feet. "One spy must protect another."

"I am not a spy!"

Greene's rage foamed and surged like a turbulent sea. "Tell that to the court!"

He reached for her again, and again James extended his arm in front of her. "Take her and you will be taking in an innocent woman. Even Pitman will not take kindly to that."

"Who are you to care about what I do?" Greene all but foamed at the mouth. "Who are you to care about one Patriot—man or woman?"

"I care about what is right."

"This *is* right, Higley." The shape of her hand showed red on his face, his eyes aglow with fire. "She is coming with me."

# CHAPTER 7

*A*ll the courage she'd felt before, all the coursing heat of conviction she'd used to strengthen her words, went suddenly dry, chapping her veins in its absence.

He would take her? Accuse her of being a traitor, and then what?

*Dear Lord, what have I done?*

"She will go nowhere with you." The tallest one stood between her and the devil, his broad shoulders straight and firm.

"Get out of my way."

Greene plowed forward, but the man from the barn gripped him, holding him back. "I cannot do that."

"You would impede the progress of the king? Out of my way!"

"Your fight is with me, Greene. Not with her." His English accent punctuated his intention.

Greene's nostrils flared, his fingers twitching. "How right you are."

Fist flying, the man's face contorted. Whooshing down, his arm circled, hitting only air as the other dodged and plowed his own fist into the man's gut.

Reeling, Greene stumbled backward.

Caroline's heart threatened to pound from her chest as she looked to the man who remained between her and her captor. Who was he and why would he do such a thing?

A lifetime of thoughts charged through her mind. She looked from the two, to the horse, to the road. Should she take a chance and run?

"You've already dug your own grave." Greene straightened, grimacing. "You have no pitiful story to keep you from punishment now."

Plowing forward the man roared.

The thud of fist against flesh cracked through the trees. She cupped a hand to her mouth, gasping, as the man's body went limp. Greene fell to the ground, a trickle of blood streaming from his mouth.

Biceps flexed and chest pumping, the soldier from the barn stared down before slowly turning toward her.

His jaw flexed. "You are brave, woman. And foolish."

"I have done nothing." She shook her head and stepped backward. "You must believe me."

Relaxing his stance, he turned from the man on the ground and came toward her. Caroline's skin shrunk over her muscles as she took another step back. "Stay away from me."

"You have done more damage than you can know."

"Damage?"

He came nearer and every fear she'd born from childhood, real or imagined, combined to take shape in the form before her. A Redcoat. A soldier. The enemy.

She shuffled backward, and he kept coming.

Where was that courage? Where was that immortal strength she'd felt only moments before? The sting of the slap still pricked her hand. Could she do it again? The man continued toward her, and the urge to protect herself crashed and faded like a wave on the sea. This man was taller, his shoulders more broad, his expression a threatening wilderness.

Striking him could mean the end of her.

"Please, I beg of you." She continued her backward movement until she bumped against the saddle of the horse behind her. Her voice quivered. "Let me go. I give you my word I won't say what I know."

The angles of his face flinched, and some unnamed emotion flashed behind his eyes before resolve gained hold and reigned there.

"Forgive me, woman." He took her at the elbow. "But you are coming with me."

Greene gasped awake, his head throbbing. A horse nudged him with its nose before moving away as if it had done its work in waking him.

Blinking hard, he stifled a groan and pressed himself to his feet. The rock in his middle and pounding in his head pulsed against an already bleeding rage.

Greene stared down the path where hooves had made dents in the snow. Higley had taken her. *Only the guilty run.* He balked, blinking to clear his blurry vision. Letting those two spies free was one thing. Helping this flagrant rebel woman to escape capture now was beyond reproach.

And who was that woman? How dare she strike him? How dare she meet his gaze as if she were his equal?

Greene snarled, staring into the dark wood, his breath pluming in the biting air. Nay. She'd seen herself as more than—better than.

The sting of her slap inched downward, past his heart and into his soul. Her cousin was Hannah Young. He should have known. Insolent patriotism ran in their blood, it would seem.

Here again the beloved James came to the rescue. At the thought, a razor of truth skidded over his smooth pride. Here again, James had thwarted him.

The more the memories repeated, the more a noxious hate broke free from its cocoon and unfolded its power in his chest. More was at stake than Higley's life. More even than the woman's. 'Twas his own. *No Greene will ever amount to anything.*

Greene's jaw ached. He rubbed his mouth and stomped toward his mount. All those years, tormented, but now—now he would prove he was something. Prove it not only to Pitman, but to the man who no doubt was as drunk now as he was the day Greene had sailed for England with that insufferable traitor.

Only the guilty run.

Greene shrugged away his acknowledgement of any pain.

If James wished to run, so be it. Every predator must give their chase before victory.

Every Patriot must feel their zeal before the noose.

Beside him some paces, a horse rustled and Greene looked to it. The animal peered at him with its large, knowing eyes, as if to deride him—blame him for what had happened to his rider.

"She's never coming back for you."

He strode forward, mind combing through what little knowledge he had of Patriot spies and their ways of transporting messages. They used all means. He tugged a bag from its tie against the saddle and reached in. Not the most promising place, as they were typically more secretive, but he dumped it anyway, watching the foodstuffs plunk against the ground.

Nothing. As he'd suspected.

He clutched the bag, preparing to toss it away when the crackling sound of parchment rustled through his ears.

Taking the bag again he opened it wide, his heart pumping. There, inside was a small pocket—and in the pocket, something folded.

Tugging the paper from its hiding place, he let the bag fall, and turned the paper in his fingers.

"Well, well, well." He sneered at the horse that stared him down. "What have we here?"

# CHAPTER 8

*C*onstant prayer was all her mind could produce. Thought of escape, rescue—'twas all a dream. Impossible. No one knew where she was, thus none would know where to look when night fell and she still had not returned. Caroline stiffened, trying to ignore how close her body was to the man whose horse she shared. A horrid realization cascaded over her already cold skin. None would suspect her missing. None would even know she'd been taken. Anna was likely confident Caroline was safe and happy, relating the news and woes of her heart to Hannah.

Her heart stuttered as the shadows deepened. She blinked to clear her thoughts and redirected her mind lest reality steal any strength she had remaining. *Do not think of Hannah now. God will carry her. Think of escape. Of getting free.*

She squinted up to the sky, then to the horizon, attempting to surmise their whereabouts amongst the sea of snow-covered trees. They traveled north, northwest perhaps, on an unmarked trail with no towns or landmarks to give any indication of where they headed.

Boston?

The thought made her grip on the saddle weaken. Would she

be held in prison? Hanged? She wriggled her tired rump on the small bit of saddle she occupied, and her breath slowed. She had done nothing, yet would be found guilty nonetheless.

With naught to occupy her mind but the past and impending future, her thoughts took flight. Hours earlier this man had taken her, but spoke nothing since. She looked down at his arm around her waist. This man who held her was all too eager to find his superiors and present his prize, it would seem, as they'd stopped but once and he appeared none too eager to halt their journey any time soon.

She wriggled in the saddle once more, and he tightened his hold. Whoever this Redcoat was, he seemed statue-like from his silence and the way his large frame was firm and broad. Since the moment he'd found his place on the horse behind her, he'd held her there. Not possessive or angry. Never once attempting anything untoward. More, he seemed protective. Almost...kind.

The very thought struck her like a sip of sour milk. Redcoats were none of those things. Any nature of his that seemed at all gallant was a guise. Caroline turned her head, peering into the endless wood. Nay. They all were devils. 'Twas Providence protecting her from him, no doubt, until she could once again be free.

Shifting her position, she attempted to bring feeling back to her leg, and the pain of it caused a petite grunt to slip from her throat.

*Keep quiet, Carrie.*

If they were to stop she feared what he might do. The thought raked hard through her fragile security and she drew in a deep breath, praying again. And again, she censured herself. What a fool she was. If she'd only waited longer, not tried to flee Eaton Hill so soon, perhaps she wouldn't have been caught at all.

Just then the solider tugged on the reins and the horse came to a slow stop.

Caroline went rigid.

Without a word he slipped from the horse and looked up to her, reaching out his hands. "Come. Stretch your legs, we've had a long ride."

Instinctively, she moved toward him then stopped when brilliance illuminated her mind like a bolt from heaven. She swooped the reins into her hands and leaned forward. With a kick and a yell, she prepared for the animal to spring forward and carry her to safety.

The horse didn't move.

Panic swept in. She tried again, this time kicking harder. "Yaw!"

As if she were nothing more than the saddle itself, the animal adjusted its feet, ignoring every tug and touch she gave it.

In vain Caroline tried one last time, but all her frame was now benumbed as horror washed through her blood like a frigid sea.

From the side of her vision, she could see the soldier step back, arms crossed. He said nothing. She was trapped, and he knew it.

To her shock, he remained there, looking at her with an illegible expression—an expression that made her all the more wary.

"Are you finished?" Arms still crossed, his thick biceps strained the seams of his jacket.

She looked forward, then back at him, scowling, proving to him, as well as to herself that she could not be made afraid. "Where are you taking me?"

An eyebrow twitched. "Tell me why you were in the closet."

Such command in his voice made her startle and she tried to blink away the sensation. "I told you I would not tell what I heard."

"A dangerous lie." The smile that flashed over one side of his mouth betrayed his amusement and the realization smacked hard. He found her a simpleton. A weak, useless female that would tremble at his every word.

In a quick jerk she swung down from the horse, but her numb

leg buckled and she tumbled back. Just as quickly, he reached for her, his strong arms holding under hers to break her fall.

He helped her to straighten, keeping one arm about her shoulders, but she pushed him away, balancing on one foot as feeling pricked its way back into her veins. Courtesy begged her to thank him, but such formalities were reserved for gentlemen.

She spun to face him, her limb gaining strength with every second. She stared, feeling the weight of his returned gaze. 'Twas as if he could see through her, all the way to her weakest parts. To her fear, even though she pretended devoid of it.

Of a sudden, as if his mysterious powers took hold of her she began to blurt the truth. "I am Caroline Whitney, cousin of Hannah Young, and I came to the house this morning in search of her. Upon finding her missing I prepared to leave when you arrived and…" She stopped for a breath and watched his eyes. Something flickered in them and suspicion clutched her chest. "Tell me where she is."

"You suppose I know of this woman." He tilted his head, mouth firm. Bits of light streaked across his dark hair, revealing hints of auburn. "I cannot give you the answer you seek."

He neither confirmed nor denied it, which made her believe he did. She took a step forward. "I know soldiers were quartered at Eaton Hill, and to find the house in disarray and she nowhere in sight—and to know you and your superior were familiar with Eaton Hill…" Arms at her sides, she mimicked his domineering stance. "Tell me where she is."

He shook his head. "I cannot tell you, for I do not know."

His gaze struck, true as the sun's brightness. She turned her head away. 'Twould be simple for him to say such, even if he knew they'd been taken.

"I can tell you this." The depth of his voice forced her eyes to his. "Any person, male or female who engages in spying for the enemy is not dealt with kindly."

"I have already said it, but shall say it again. I am *not* a spy."

He looked forward, jaw shifting, before his gaze grabbed her again. "The truth matters naught when you are suspected. All enemies to the crown must stand trial."

"I..." The protest died on her lips. He *was* taking her to Boston.

Her knees lost their strength, then in a storm of brave panic, regained it ten-fold. Turning, she bolted, not thinking, not caring. Knowing only that she must get free of him.

She made it two steps before he grabbed her arm, the strength of his fingers reaching all the way to her bones. Yet, there was no pain at his grasp, no malice in his touch. Somehow, that scared her all the more.

"Miss Whitney." Beside him, she could feel his warmth, could hear him breathing in the cold, quiet wood. "You have no choice but to come with me."

Caroline looked over her shoulder, the unshed tears burning her eyes. "Why?"

The hold on her arm loosened, and that look returned, the one that seemed to reach out and down through her spirit, as if he wished to tell her something, but couldn't. His timbre turned rough, almost a whisper. "You must trust me."

There, in his deep green eyes, a secret rustled, and something took flight within her. Something small and swift that carried away a twig from the dam of her resistance. Did she trust him? More, could she? What other choice had she but to go with him? Surely the Lord would offer a way for her to be free of him, for her need was more than a personal one. Enoch needed help— needed escape.

A scowl threatened, and she allowed it as she returned his unfaltering stare. "Can a woman trust the word of a soldier? I think not."

His chest raised and lowered as a hard sigh left his mouth. He glanced down at her skirts, then her feet and back up. "Are you well enough to begin again? We have many miles to cover, and already 'tis too dark."

Caroline looked to the horse. He still had not said where they were going. Every instinct fired, protesting in a volley of fierce anxiety.

Pivoting to face him, she raised her chin. "Will you not tell me your name, sir? I would like to know how to address my captor."

Amusement colored his eyes a brighter green, when all too swiftly their darkness returned.

He nodded before splaying his large hands around her waist. As if she weighed no more than the clothes on her back, he lifted her onto the saddle and found his place behind her, his arm settling in the same spot it had been before.

He would not tell her his name? She'd heard it spoken, but with all the commotion, she couldn't bring it to mind. "You will not reveal yourself to me then?"

She turned back and jolted from his nearness and the softness of his breath on her cheek.

"I am Captain James Higley, Miss Whitney. And do not worry. I shall not imprison you long."

Greene dismounted, legs buzzing with the need to make chase, the note singeing a hole in the pocket of his coat.

As he strode into the small camp behind the house that served as Pitman's regimental headquarters, he hid an inner grin. Pride swelled his chest as he took a long breath of smoke-scented air. 'Twas a congenial companion, pride, and its surges of energy, the very thing that kept him from dwelling on the continual throb in his jaw. The sooner he found men to help him, the better. His chance had arrived—had been handed to him almost as if the very arm of God extended down—and he would not squander a second.

Cutting across the snowy ground, he made for a small group of hunched soldiers, authority in his voice. "Reece."

The boy plucked up at the sound of his name and turned from his place beside the cook fire. "Aye, sir?"

Greene halted and lowered his volume, knowing the other curious privates craved a slice of the conversation. "Where is Pryer?"

Reece shook his head. "I do not know, sir."

"What do you mean?" They were in the same company, saw each other every day, how could he not know? "We ate together this morning. I don't see how he's suddenly disappeared."

Reece's genial nature continued to shine in his youthful face. "I haven't seen him since then either, Captain."

Filling his chest, Greene softened the blunt end of his frustration with a steady breath. "Where is Abrams then? Don't tell me he too has gone missing."

Motioning over Greene's shoulder, Reece relaxed his stance as if grateful he could help in some way. "Abrams is in the livery, sir. I've just been there."

Greene twisted to look behind him. Abrams's willingness to help was a given, even though Greene knew little of his actual nature. Abrams was rancorous at best, ruthless to a fault. From their conversation earlier, it seemed he was all too willing to toss Higley to the lions. He needn't men of brains, but brawn.

He tapped a finger against his leg. If only Pryer would return from wherever he was. The man was dedicated and driven by motives that mirrored his own, and their history of friendship would ease the stress of their duty. Despite his weakness for women, Pryer was as dependable as the sunrise.

With Abrams and Pryer—if he appeared—he had two men… what about a third? He paused, feeling the presence of the youthful soldier behind him. Reece was young, unseasoned and betimes too jolly for soldiering. However…Greene granted himself a quick glance at the boy before turning away again. He was quick to follow orders, asked no questions.

Releasing a harried breath, Greene turned about and placed a hand on the boy's shoulder. Walking several paces away from the others whose ears seemed pinned upon the air, Greene carried his volume at a whisper. "I have been given an assignment."

The boy's eyebrows went up. "Sir?"

"'Tis an assignment I cannot fulfill alone." Greene removed his hold, but kept his voice low. "I believe I have discovered our informant and must follow after him."

"Of course, Captain." Eyes round, the boy stood tall, attentive. "I am ready now, if you wish, sir."

"Good. We leave within minutes." He pointed back toward the small fire. "Gather your things and prepare your mount."

Reece nodded and turned to follow orders. Greene called after him. "You said Abrams was in the—"

"You're looking for me?"

Greene spun at the curt sound, not surprised to see Abrams's pinched expression.

Facing him, Greene met the man's pointed stare with his own. "I am."

Tilting his head forward, Abrams offered pretended courtesy as he polished his unsheathed bayonet. "What now?"

Perhaps the inclination to invite him was devil-sent. Greene allowed himself a moment to reflect as Abrams stared him down. Greene tapped his fingers against his leg. It would take more than fulfillment of duty to find the traitorous pair and bring them in. It would take hate. Hate for the rebels, for their inglorious cause. Hate for those who forced them on this inglorious mission. More, 'twould take hate for the man who betrayed them all with his traitorous heart.

Abrams carried enough of that for the entire army.

He caught Abrams's gaze and squeezed with dominance. "Where is Pryer?"

Abrams shook his head, and peered at his polished weapon, pretending he hadn't felt the power in Greene's stare. He shot his chin back up, a faux smile on his lips. "He's not here."

A flash of ripe irritation soured his tongue, but Greene kept his response cool. "Where *is* he?"

Abrams shrugged. "Gone. Won't be back for days, I venture."

"Days?" Greene let fly a curse. "How is it I have no knowledge of this?"

Abrams turned his attention to the bayonet in his hand, a vacant expression punctuated with a grunt as he looked back up. "Pitman sent him on a mission or some such nonsense. Left not long after you." The next bit was under his breath. "What the devil are we doing just sitting here? The sooner we destroy every blasted Patriot, the sooner we can leave this God-forsaken place and get back to our miserable lives."

"You are bored, I understand that. Boredom for any soldier is akin to misery." Humility had its advantages, and Greene knew when to use it. "But our common dislike of a certain officer might persuade you to work beyond the camp." He paused, patient as Abrams's eyes narrowed. "I need your help."

Abrams scowled in disbelief, his quiet enough for Greene to continue.

"It seems our friend, Captain Higley, has gone somewhat rogue."

Only an eyebrow twitched. "Is that so."

The man's curiosity was a promising sign. "It seems he has again shown his weakness for the Patriots by taking from my capture a Patriot spy." He paused, straightening his back. "I've been commanded to bring in any suspect and he is the grandest of all. But I cannot do it alone."

Greene took a step back, waiting for the response he knew was forthcoming. 'Twas then Reece joined them, shrugging his knapsack over his shoulder like a schoolboy ready for adventure.

He grinned. "Ready."

"You're not bringing him along?" Abrams slipped the bayonet into its place at his side, stabbing Reece with a look as deadly as the blade he'd polished.

"Aye." The truth slipped out of Greene's mouth, followed by a curse. "I'd hoped to have Pryer."

"He's been sent on a scouting party." Reece shifted his bag on his shoulder. "Just heard some of the men talking."

"Scouting party?" Greene swiped a scowl in Abrams's direction. Would it have been so painful for him to divulge it?

Abrams offered a miniscule smile, a capstone to his former indifference. He had known, and clearly had no intention of telling. Greene's chest plumed with toxic malice. The man might not live past morning if he continued this way.

Greene turned to Reece, forcing a rough exhale. "What else did you learn?"

"Just this morning Pitman put him in charge of taking a group of men in search of the Patriot camp we know exists, it would seem, but have not yet been able to find."

Greene wiped a hand over his rough jaw, wincing when the sore spot reprimanded his touch. "When will he return?"

Reece bobbed a shoulder. "Doubtful he'll be back even by week's end."

Week's end? Blast. Greene had to start now if he wished to follow the scent of his prey.

Myriad thoughts formed in the back of Greene's mind. How could he do this with only two men—and two so opposite? He craned his head to look behind him at the pitiful handful of soldiers that hovered over the shallow flames, attentive to the conversation but pretending not to be. Greene pressed out a hard sigh. It wasn't as if he had a charming array of compatriots to choose from.

He'd have to move forward and make the best of it.

Raising his eyes to Abrams, he cut past the barbs of the man's stare to stab with his own. "We will go without him."

"Just the…three of us?"

"Aye."

Greene strode between them, letting them follow on the command of his wake as he passed. "Ready your mounts, boys. We've a traitor to find."

# CHAPTER 9

*T*he cold turned bitter just before the sun slid past the unseen horizon. Darkness had its hand upon his shoulder, and its grip tightened. Hours they'd ridden, and hours more lay ahead of them. James readjusted his hold on the woman who shared his saddle, and contemplated the decision he'd made the moment he'd known there was no other choice but to take her. The safest place for her was as far away from him as possible. He knew not where Henry Donaldson and the others camped, but it couldn't be far. Once she was safely within their protection he could finish his journey to Boston and think of another reason why he'd set this "spy" free. No doubt Greene would defame him. But he'd deflected such attacks in the past. 'Twould be no different than before.

James's back ached and his belly cramped from hunger. Not that the need for food commanded him, but nourishment would offer the strength to continue. A quiet sigh from his female companion brought to mind the other truth concerning him. If he suffered the pangs of a day without eating, she surely fared worse. 'Twas hard not to notice how slight she was with her body against his for so long. She was not painfully thin, but she had no reserves either.

He gazed past her sloping shoulder and scouted the landscape for the house he knew was there, for the light in Mr. Albert's window—the signal he was home, and waiting to help. Always eager to give aid, the old friend had made him promise to stop whenever needed. Now, after so many polite promises, he would follow through.

James craned his neck, peering as far left and right as he could, but saw nothing. Blast. Where was the light? No light meant no signal, which could mean danger.

Exhaling his thoughts, he pulled back on his reins and Ginny stopped. If he traveled alone he would continue on through the night without reservation, but the woman would need rest. They'd broken their ride only twice, and if not for the water left in his pouch plus the few bites of hard bread, he felt sure she might have fainted, though she would never have revealed her need. In fact, she had said nothing since their second stop when her fiery spirit and sharp accusations had turned her fair complexion a striking pink.

He flung the recollection away. Her quiet was more than welcome, despite the fact that their combined silence made the tedious journey all the more draining, even for him.

A flicker caught the far corner of his vision. He looked left, and there he saw it. The cabin. But no light. His spirit sank. 'Twas the moon's faint glow that caught against a window.

The woman slumped against his arm as sleep dragged her down.

"Miss Whitney?"

She jolted and sat up, looking back to him as far as her neck would allow, but said nothing.

He answered her unspoken question. "We shall stop here."

Her body stiffened, tempting an explanation that he quickly

dismissed. Any attempt at chivalry only seemed to upset her. Better to leave her thoughts where they were.

Guiding Ginny toward the small cabin, James studied the darkened yard, the unlit house.

James tapped his horse onward to the front of the house and pulled her to a stop. Squinting, he studied the vacant windows to make out any shadow, any movement, but there were none. Not even a sound from the barn. The itch to continue toward the secret Patriot camp made his leg muscles twitch. If he continued through the night he could easily reach it by morning.

A rustle in the naked branches made the hairs on his neck stand on end. The one truth he'd felt at his heels since the moment he'd left his adversary unconscious on the ice, crawled toward him from the trees. Greene would be after them, if he wasn't already. Nothing was more certain.

The man would want blood—and a mere trickle would not suffice.

He prepared to turn back to the road when the woman rubbed her head, and reason beckoned him. Nay. He must stop. Even a few hours of sleep would revive her. Traveling on with a woman so wearied would make the journey more treacherous, not less. 'Twas a risk he must take.

He slipped off the horse and instead of slumping toward his outstretched arms as he expected, the woman held herself up, blinking hard against the exhaustion that dominated her.

She peered at the house, then to him. "Where are we?"

"Halfway." Best to keep facts at a minimum, even if he himself couldn't vouch for their veracity. For her safety as well as his.

"Halfway to where?" The conversation seemed to energize her. In a graceful motion, she swung her leg over the horse and hopped to the ground like a seasoned rider. Spinning, she faced him, an unspoken command in the tilt of her head.

An emotion popped in him, one he couldn't name and frankly

didn't wish to. He might have supposed a woman in such circumstances to be flighty, inconsolable and desperate. She was not. In fact, despite the fear he could read so well in her eyes, she pretended to feel none of it. A rare trait. An admirable one.

"We shall spend the night here." He paused, calculating her inaudible response. "'Tis...the home of a friend."

Though darkness lent little illumination, he didn't need it to know a shade of color drained from her cheeks. Over time, he hoped, she would come to see he was not that sort of man.

He raised his palm and lowered his voice. "Stay here until I return."

"You still have not told me where you are taking me." Her pert mouth pinched as her chin shot up. "I demand that you tell me."

Stunned at her quiet force, he eased a vacant expression over his face to hide the amusement that flickered within. He'd forgotten how appealing a woman with a will of her own could be. With a subtle shake of his head, he doused her burst of rivalry with that of reality.

He started toward the house. "The less you know, the better."

"Am I to be tried?" The words burst from her, sharp, yet weak.

He halted and looked over his shoulder, allowing her question to settle into the cracks of his understanding. A parcel of truth sprung from his mouth before he could stop it. "The man who nearly took you, Captain Matthew Greene, believes you to be a spy—"

"But I am not—"

"Either way." James neared her. "He believes it, thanks to his discovery of you. If you had stayed in the barn as I instructed none of this would ever have happened."

Eyes round as the moon and just as wide, she balked. "You believe this to be my fault then."

*Is it anyone else's?* He resisted the temptation. "Because you attempted to flee, you are in danger of being imprisoned and tried as a traitor, Miss Whitney. As for myself, I have a job to do. I cannot trust you to stay silent, and I cannot trust you stay safe, therefore, against my own desires, I must keep you with me until my job is finished."

Through the darkness, he could see her dainty brow pitch, but her gaze never left his. A few strands of hair swayed around her neck where they'd loosened from their pins while a procession of emotions circled in turns over her face—anger, resentment, grief.

She inhaled and looked away, holding her arms around her. Would that be her reply? If it were, there was more said in her silence than any words could convey. By now she'd learned to obey him. Perhaps fear him. Which of the two, he couldn't tell. Either way, 'twas for the best. Any more foolish attempts to flee could prove disastrous.

He made for the door, considering another ill. He'd not had time to send Henry Donaldson a message and let him know of his coming. Only a handful of men knew of his work with the Patriots. If he were found and taken by unknowing rebels...

The thought cramped across his shoulders. He prayed they would bring him in, instead of kill him.

At the door, he cupped his hands around his eyes and peered into the nearest window. Dark as pitch. He gripped the latch of the door, praying it would give. It took only a gentle nudge and the well-worn wood lifted, unhitching and swinging open into the black room.

Every sense spun into action. His heart raced. Blood filled his muscles, ready to fight. A mouse scurried in the far corner and his arms flexed. The scent of a recently abandoned fire met his nose. Did someone wait for him? He remained quiet, unmoving, until utter silence allowed him to hear only the gentle thump of his pulse and Ginny's breathing from the yard. His fingers twitched, ready to reach for the pistol at his side should the enemy lunge from the shadows. Mr. Albert's trade rarely took him away from home. Perhaps he merely visited family. Or was there another, more nefarious reason for his absence? Pray to God it wasn't the latter.

A single step brought him in. At his side a small table rested, and on it, the stub of a candle in a crude tin holder. Once lit, the soft glow reached only a few feet into the room where the kitchen table rested. He lifted the wan light and stepped in further, swinging around to be sure the space held no secrets. His pulse slowed. There was no one, just the furnishings of a simple country cabin. A bed, a hearth and cabinet full of the provisions he—and the woman—would need.

"Whose home is this?"

James whirled around. "I told you to stay until I came for you."

The candle's light reached for her, but hadn't the strength to illuminate more than a faint form. "I…" She wrapped her arms around herself and walked in further. "My legs are aching to sit."

Of course. He should have thought of such.

James motioned toward the bed and stepped aside. "You may sleep here."

"And you will sleep in the barn." She whipped around to stare him down.

"The barn?"

"You cannot expect us to spend the night in the same room."

His patience had thinned to dangerous levels. "If you would wish me not to protect you, Miss Whitney, then I will certainly."

The tightness around her mouth eased as humility seemed to grasp her. "You think Greene will—"

"I know he will."

She flung a gnarled look toward the bed, then plunked down in a chair beside the window. "This will suit me well enough."

"As you wish." Irritation strummed over his politeness and he stepped back. "I will see to my horse."

He set the candle on the table and strode out, wondering if it might serve him better to leave her here. That mouth of hers was a reckoning force.

Leading Ginny to the barn, he circled over the dismembered parts of what should have been a mission sent straight from God. Stockton had given him the opportunity he'd been wanting—needing. But now with this woman…he dropped a pail in frustration and Ginny looked up as if to scold him for the out-burst. He sighed his apology and after the saddle was removed, her coat properly brushed, he stroked her nose before she nudged him aside and bent for her supper.

With a shake of his head, James started for the house again, wearied to the bone, but not interested in sleep.

Once inside, he shut the door, latching and locking it before he turned back around. The sight freed a frustrated breath from his mouth.

And she'd said she preferred a chair.

"Miss Whitney?"

There on the bed, her head on the pillow and legs still on the floor, her torso rose up and down so calm it appeared some magician had placed a spell upon her.

Taking a few steps forward, he proceeded with caution. "Miss Whitney?"

Beside the bed, he paused, assessing her position. She couldn't sleep like that all night. If her legs were uncomfortable before, surely this would make them worse. He reached down to lift them onto the bed, then stopped. Nay. The movement could wake her and she would never believe his tale of innocence.

The need to step away called like the drum of war, but something compelled him and in a swift motion he bent and lifted her legs onto the bed and stepped back, holding his breath. Not even a finger moved. Only her chest lifted up and down, the softest sound of breath leaving her nose.

James exhaled a harbored breath and tugged the blanket over her then stepped back, allowing himself time to study the woman who believed herself his captive. How old was she? Three and twenty perhaps? Younger? She looked vibrant, healthy. Beautiful.

James crushed the untimely thought and forced formality.

Where was she from? Did she have a family? Was she married?

James whirled around, furious at himself for allowing his mind to wonder so. But the thought remained. If he had had a wife and she had been taken, he would be apoplectic with rage. James strode to the table and reached for a loaf in the center basket. Tearing off a piece he counseled the wayward parts of himself. The woman was a stranger, a person he knew nothing about and 'twas best he kept it that way. As soon as he met with the Patriot company he could leave her with them and be on his way to Boston.

He sniffed the loaf and replaced it, suddenly void of appetite.

His fingers found their way to his pocket, and he pulled out his timepiece. Holding it in one hand, he caressed the delicate carvings with his thumb, a lump forming in his throat. The face of the man who'd gifted the precious timekeeper took form before him, that smile, that knowing in his eyes, embraced all the grief in his soul. James blinked, his chest constricting.

Only the commander of heaven and earth could protect him now. He had done everything possible to fulfill his covenant, and now all his hopes and prayers rested in the hands of the Almighty.

He leaned back in the chair and turned the watch, reading the inscription on the back, feeling that cold, familiar melancholy. He snapped his fingers round it and tucked it back to the safety of its hiding place.

Against his will, he looked to the bed where she lay, fighting the strange notion to discover more about her. She looked so much like Hannah Young that her confession they were cousins rang factual. Both had light hair, both silken complexions and eyes as clear as a mountain spring. Only this woman's eyes were blue...and her hair such a striking shade of blonde he almost wished to reach out and see if it felt as soft as it looked.

Growling, James raked his fingers over his head, slaying that thought and moving to the next one.

Whoever she was, her family would not rest until she was returned. All the more reason to get her to the Patriots as soon as he could. There he could discuss what was to be done—could be sure Greene would not discover her. Or him.

There, he could discard this unwanted distraction and narrow his attentions on what needed most to be done.

# CHAPTER 10

*C*aroline held her breath. He was beside her, she could feel it.

Despite the heavy hand of weariness that pressed against her eyes, Caroline schooled her face to show ease, her breath to slow, her eyes to remain closed. Let the man think she slept. She could not place herself at such risk in the presence of a stranger—a soldier—by being so vulnerable.

The instant he'd left for the barn, she'd given in to the beckoning of the bed, almost certain he would not return until morning. But it seemed his intention to stay with her was intrepid.

Of a sudden a touch on her legs froze her and she nearly broke her act by crying out when her legs were lifted to the bed. But just as quickly the touch was gone and a blanket was rested over her legs.

His soft footfall echoed against the floor as he stepped back, and for a moment, he waited there, before quietly moving to the center of the room.

Her mind struggled to comprehend such an act of kindness—and from one that should have taken her, used her. Was that not what such a man might do?

Caroline struggled to calm the confusion rising in her chest. Was it just a ploy? Some scheme to trick her into trusting him? She squinted her already closed eyes. Yet he seemed sincere. Honest. How she could sense it, she didn't know, but the duality of her emotions was enough to tear her in two.

Her whole body ached. Physical weakness did terrible things. Or so she told herself. Why else would she feel herself succumbing to fear and doubt? Where was sleep when she craved it—the blissful night to come rescue her from reality?

She covered her face with her hand and struggled against the moisture in her eyes that threatened to wet her pillow. Nay. She would not cry. Doing so might alleviate a measure of pain, but would also alert the soldier who sat at the table not ten feet from her.

*Oh, Enoch.* They were both prisoners now. This morning there had been hope. Hope that she would see him again, perhaps even aid in his rescue, had Hannah and Joseph been at Eaton Hill, but now…what had she but shattered promises of a future that might never be? Hannah was gone, perhaps imprisoned, or worse…'Twas too much.

*Lord, help me. Grant me peace—wisdom, Lord. I need it.*

Like an embrace from heaven, the burden against her chest lightened and the lump in her throat receded to a small pebble. Wiping at her eyes, she reminded herself of truths she'd nearly allowed to slip free. Now was not a time to succumb to doubt. Was she weak or strong? This was the time for her to decide.

She blinked and the moisture wicked from her eyes. She was strong, aye. Whether true or no, she would believe herself so. Thoughts of Enoch, thoughts of Hannah and Father—they would keep her pressing on. There was nothing else but to be valiant in the face of tribulation. If Enoch could suffer so terribly for so long, could she not endure a bit of hardship?

If only there was some way to escape.

Peeking through the slits of her fingers, Caroline took a thorough study of the soldier who'd taken her. Who was this man who claimed she must trust him—for her safety? Was he not her enemy? He'd as well as kidnapped her and prepared to take her she knew not where. And yet...were he so evil would he not have used her ill? Berated and spoken as the other soldier had? Her memory tipped backward to the moment in the wood when he'd stopped her horse and stayed between her and the other menacing foe. He'd...protected. Truly. But why?

Allowing her mind to calculate, her heart to discern, she peeked through her fingers at him, praying he believed her still asleep.

Sitting forward, elbows on the table, he held a timepiece in his fingers, a thoughtful, mourning expression over his sculpted face. Slowly, he turned it over in his hands, and his brow grew somber.

Breathing out heavy, he sat back and replaced it in his pocket, instantly looking up. His gaze full upon her, and he stilled.

Caroline's breath halted in her lungs.

"I thought you were sleeping."

She swallowed and moved her hand away from her eyes. How had he known she'd been spying on him?

"I was." Pushing up from the pillow, she sat aright, her spirit as weary as her body—but both were captives of her mind, and sleep was not to be had no matter how she craved it.

He straightened in his chair. "I didn't mean to wake you."

His congenial nature clashed with the image she fixed in her mind. Redcoats were all the same. He was no different. So why did he act as if he were?

The pale light of the candle that flickered in the center of the table allowed the most pitiful of light, but 'twas enough, illuminating in perfect shadows the lines and angles of his face.

Caroline blinked away her girlishness with a formal acknowledgement of the obvious. He may perhaps be the most handsome man she'd ever seen, but that gave her no permission to stare—or to think any longer on the fact. *Silly. An embarrassment should anyone else know you thought such a thing.*

She straightened her back as she sat on the edge of the bed, her weary legs longing to stretch, and focused her wayward attention on the three books that were stacked beside the candle. At any other time she would have rushed to them, rife with curiosity and the need to open their pages. Perhaps she should. Perhaps the action might rid her of a portion of the fear and awkwardness that seemed so eager to thicken her spirit with anxiety.

"You like books, do you?"

She startled and looked up to see her captor pointing to where her eyes had been.

"You may read them, if you like," he said. "Since you are unable to sleep."

Had her attentions been so obvious? It rankled her that he'd noticed. More, that in his kind, gentle way, he showed true interest.

"Thank you, no." She hadn't seen what books they were and pretended disinterest, though in truth curiosity itched in her fingers.

Pensive, he stared at the books himself. "I have most recently read Cato."

"Cato?" Immediate interest flicked to life, though she forced pretended apathy. "And how did you find it?"

"Most remarkable, indeed." He looked down at his hands, then up again—at her. "In truth, I believe it might be the most provocative work I have enjoyed in some time." Peering out, his brow drew together as he began to quote the section of the play that was written on her heart with iron pen. "How beautiful is death, when earn'd by virtue. Who would not be that youth? What pity is it that we can die but once to serve our country?"

His voice was clear, strong, as if he meant the words more than stated them. What soldier in the king's army would read such a play, let alone find the message in its symbolic lines? A fountain spring started in Caroline's chest and she balked in the quiet halls of her spirit. Who *was* this man?

It took only seconds for the awkwardness to return as her absent reply moaned in the silence. Moving in his seat, no doubt realizing she refused to say more, he opened his mouth to speak when her stomach made a ghastly rumbling noise that echoed through the small room.

She wrapped a hand over her middle, her cheeks heating at the embarrassing sound. She hadn't eaten since morning and her body refused to let her forget it.

A flicker of amusement played with one side of his mouth. "Help yourself." He gestured with his head toward the wooden bowl on the table, bread-stuffs filling it to the brim.

She pursed her lips and looked away. Was he indeed so generous? He could not be. "I have no interest in food."

"Well…" his voice was rich, genuine, and the things it did to her muddled understanding made her squirm in her stays. "I shall bring some for morning when we leave. Get some sleep if you can. We must leave at dawn."

Standing, she faced him from her place by the bed. "How can I possibly sleep when I have been taken from my family and—"

"I am sorry for that." His deep accent rumbled through the room, cutting her voice silent. He rose to his feet and moved to the window. "I am sorry for what your family has had to suffer. This war brings its woes upon all, I'm afraid."

*My family?* He spoke as if he knew them. Why would a soldier make such a confession? And one so drenched in sincerity? Caroline didn't move, letting the words settle around her like dust from a beaten rug.

He turned at the waist, motioning to the bed. "You should rest at least."

Stunned motionless, Caroline stared, her brow cramping in question.

Shrugging, he turned back to the window. "Do what you will. As for me, I shall be keeping watch."

"All night?" He must be joking. "You will not sleep?"

He said nothing. Only stayed at the window, unmoving, his attention fixed. Caroline's stays suddenly cinched tighter. Was he really so concerned—for her? Nay.

Her stomach growled again and her eyes trailed to the bowl of bread. She'd never been so famished.

Perhaps a bite…

She walked to the table, stepping over the pride that wished her back. If she were to keep the strength she needed to find some way to escape him—make a way to safety—she must have something in her belly.

Reaching forward, she halted when he turned, his eyebrows up.

"I thought you were not interested in food." There was mirth in his voice that mirrored the glimmer of candle light in his eyes.

Bother. She dropped her fingers to the edge of the table, feeling a fresh shame bleed up her neck. Must he say anything?

He chuckled. "I am only joking."

Braving a glance, she slid her vision toward him. His smile was wider than she'd seen it, a few white teeth peeking through his lips. Her heart fluttered and she looked away when he spoke. "Eat your fill. You will sleep better."

'Twas as if he'd heard her thoughts. Caroline stayed herself, denying the pang but the scent of something edible made her salivate and she reached for the morsel. 'Twas soft and plush, pure heaven in her mouth.

"The man who owns this home will consider it a blessing to have housed us."

She scowled. "You know the owner of this home?"

Again he looked back, yet said nothing. A slight raise of his brow indicated his irascible emotions, but Caroline brushed them away, pretending his strong gaze did nothing to her middle.

Though it did. It created fear. Nay...she paused. Not fear. More, respect. Mystery.

"You may take the rest with you come morning." He spoke toward the window. "We will ride at dawn."

Before she could drown in the turbulent seas, she hurled herself against the steadying force that held her upright.

"I refuse to go any further until you tell me where you are taking me." There, she'd spoken it. Though she refused to hope it would produce an answer.

His head lowered ever so slight. "You'll know when we get there."

"Am I some prize to you?"

At that he turned around. "Prize?"

Caroline's fears climbed upon one another in a mad dash to her mouth. "I have told you time and again, I am no Patriot spy, though in truth I would not hesitate to be." That last bit she nearly regretted, but chose to raise her chin and hold his gaze despite the tremor in her hands. "I cannot see how any gentleman could capture a woman and carry her miles from home without the courtesy of telling her where she's being taken—especially if that place is to her death."

Her voice quivered, and 'twas only then she realized the true depth of her fear. Though a sorry state of being, she had to admit she felt it. She could be killed...

"I have told you, Miss Whitney, I do not take you for my own pleasure." By degrees his expression turned soft. First his eyes, then the muscles in his face. Sighing, he put his back to the window. "All I can tell you is that where I take you...you will find refuge. I promise."

Such an answer shouldn't satisfy. 'Twas cryptic, secretive. Caroline held to the familiar worry and swung to the next rung of frustration that waited to carry her. "How can I know you do not lie to me? How do I know that anything you tell me is true?" She stepped forward. "How do I even know James Higley is your real name?"

"You have only my word, I suppose." Compassion met resistance, battling hard in his gaze. His voice swooped low. "But I tell you this, placing your trust in me is the surest way to safety. Resisting me, the surest way to trouble."

Everything in her wailed in protest. Nay. He lied. They all did. Every soldier followed only the rules of the flesh—orders of appetite as well as the orders of their superiors. She should despise him. His fellow soldiers had killed her uncle, done nearly the same to her beloved brother and might have done that very thing to Hannah. She should despise him and she did, but not enough. Not nearly enough.

And that made her fear most of all.

Rocking in the leaking boat once again, she moved back to the bed as the soporific effect of those few bites began to take hold.

Then, like the crash of a felled tree, the weariness assailed her and she lay back, hoping to dream nothing of her plight, nothing of the morrow, and certainly nothing of the mysterious man in red.

# CHAPTER 11

*A* longer night he'd never known. Every sound from the unfamiliar house jolted his senses. His head ached. A remnant from the blow his friend had given him, he told himself, and not from the way his mind had labored all night to keep his eyes away from the sleeping sylph.

Sunlight peeped, hinting at a cloudless sunrise that would bathe the sky in pink. Beautiful, surely, but without clouds, the temperatures would be bone-chilling. He looked behind him, careful to avoid the bed when he studied the small room for a cupboard or trunk in which might be hidden a few blankets.

He gnawed his cheek. Mr. Albert would be heartsick if James didn't take what was needed, there was no question. Still, it felt a slight to do so when the man had so little himself.

Weakness overcame him and he allowed his eyes to shift toward the woman at the moment she turned in the bed and rested on her back. Thick strands of light-gold hair curled along the pillow, framing her head like sunbeams.

He shook his head and turned to the window, examining the horizon. He needed the blankets, should he find them. She would need the warmth, and when he could, he'd return them. The small cloak she wore would not be enough to keep off the claws of this depth of cold.

The sun gifted more brightness to the sky, and James looked to the bed, then to the door. Perhaps he should let her sleep a few minutes more. He needed to ready Ginny as it was, and with nothing to gather but bread and blankets...aye. He could leave and return without her knowing he'd even left.

Careful not to make a sound, James hurried to the barn, his skin pinching at the bitter February air. When he entered, Ginny lifted her head and spied him as if to say she knew what he'd been thinking.

A pair of blue eyes, pink cheeks and courage enough to fill a chasm owned his mind, though he pretended otherwise.

"You think you're so smart?" He rubbed her nose then prepared her saddle, giving her one last handful of food. "She'll soon be gone and all the better."

He paused, recalling the slap she'd given Greene. Such bravery he'd hardly seen in the men he served with. And to find it in a woman...

James shook his head, leaving Ginny in the tepid warmth of the barn, and made his way toward the yard. 'Twas dangerous territory to tread upon. He must leave this open ground or risk the very battle he'd long promised himself he'd never be strong enough to win.

Mid-way to the house, he stopped hard. "Miss Whitney?"

There, at the side of the house, she jerked to a halt, guilty as a child caught snitching.

He strode toward her, "Where are you going?"

She placed a hand on her chest and breathed out. Shaking her head, she looked away. "Nowhere. I...thought..." The way her lips pursed and her posture rested, James fought a self-directed censure.

Hers was not a look of someone attempting to flee, but of one attempting to find. She'd thought he'd left her—and had gone in search of him.

Stepping forward, he offered the kind of smile he hoped she would accept as genuine, naught else. "I was readying Ginny."

"Oh." She swallowed and returned his smile with her own. "Of course."

She shuffled backward and hurried to the house when the sound of an approaching rider snipped his forthcoming response. Was it Mr. Albert returning? He'd hated to use the man's house without the chance to thank—

James halted, his muscles numbing and cramping in the same instant.

'Twas not one rider, but several. And a hint of their red-colored coats through the trees made his pulse thunder through his veins.

Just as he'd feared. They'd been followed. And found.

If only they'd left before sunrise.

James hurried forward and took Caroline at the arm.

She yanked against his hold. "What are you doing?"

He pressed her toward the house and shut the door as the riders rounded the corner to the yard.

Gripping her at the shoulders, James prayed his gaze could grip her sensibilities. "We've been found."

Her face went white. "What?"

"Whatever happens, do exactly as I say."

Unmoving, she stared at him. If he read her right, and surely he did, her thoughts were as he'd hoped. She'd learned from their first encounter that following his instructions was more likely to lead to safety than chasing after her own ambitions.

She shook her head. "Perhaps 'tis the owner of the house, come home at last."

The child-like hope in her voice opened a window to her spirit he had yet to see, and it softened him.

"Nay. 'Tis not the owner." That would have been a mercy.

He released her and hurried to the window. His pulse tripled, and his chest went hard. What were soldiers doing here? It must be Greene. Yet, on second glance, 'twas clear none were him from their size and coloring.

Perhaps he'd sent out a search party.

There was little James could do against four men. He had only one shot in his pistol and the dagger he kept at his belt. Though his combat skills were unmatched, if their muskets were aimed, he would have little chance.

If only he—

James's mind skidded to a halt when the first man dismounted and started for the house. What was Mark Pryer doing here? James pulled away from the window and looked at the woman whose eyes were round and pale with fear.

He'd have to think of an excuse as to why he was at this house, with a woman.

A knock sounded on the door. "Open in the name of the king."

Caroline's face lost every sheen of color and her expression went slack. A silent scream leapt from her eyes and he rushed forward ready to whisper a consoling word when an idea struck.

He pulled at his neckcloth, speaking over his shoulder. "Uh... one moment." Then he turned back and unbuttoned the first buttons of his waistcoat, untucked a portion of his shirt and reached for her but she knocked his hands away.

"Are you mad?" She whispered through her teeth.

Pryer called from the other side of the wood. "I shall give you to the count of ten before I break open this door."

She glanced at him, this time with more pleading than ire, and he reached for her again, palms raised. "You must follow my lead. Do you understand?"

Pryer's voice hit against the door. "One. Two. Three"

James flung a look to the door, then to her, speaking fast. "Remove your cloak and take down your hair."

"What?"

She shook her head and refused, forcing him to do more than he'd wished. He untied the ribbon that held her cloak at her neck.

"Four."

Her mouth dropped open and she knocked his hands away, sliding back. "How dare you—"

"Five."

James clamped a hand over her mouth and whispered in her ear. "You must trust me, Miss Whitney."

"Six."

He removed his hand from her mouth, still keeping his tone at the smallest of sounds. "I shall do my best to persuade him, but I cannot do this alone." He stuck his fingers into her hair and removed two pins at once, releasing a cascade of silken locks.

"Seven." The voice behind the door grew louder.

She scowled, but didn't resist, and he took her refusal to speak as compliance.

"Eight…"

At that James spun on his heel and whirled to the door, swinging it open when Pryer spoke nine.

"What is it?" James growled, employing every performance skill he'd learned to master. "Pryer. What are you doing here?"

He stilled his breath, waiting for an answer from the man James knew held little regard for him. In truth, Pryer hated him nearly as much as Greene. But there was one weakness this man carried that Greene did not. And now was the time to exploit it.

Stepping to relax his stance, Pryer quirked a brow. "I could ask the same of you?"

James glanced behind him, allowing Pryer full view of Caroline before closing the door. He kept his voice low.

"I've been put on assignment. And this home is on the way to my destination."

Pryer's eyes narrowed, his attention clearly teetering at the sight of her. "What destination? You travel alone?"

"I was to meet with a few others in Framingham by sunrise

this morning, but...I fear I shall be late." He looked behind him to the door before facing Pryer with a small shrug. "A man must allow himself what pleasure he can."

A smile started across Pryer's face. "Aye, he must."

James chuckled in jest at the comment, though the action of it was so foreign he could only pray to God his act would be believed. "You are surprised?"

"Nay, of course not. I had simply not known you to chase after women." He crossed his arms, then looked back to the three others who waited silently on their mounts. "You found one to your liking, hmm?" Leaning forward, he whispered though partially open lips. "There are so many maids in these country towns, yet so few well enough versed in the ways of men and women." He leaned forward yet again. "Tell me, how well does she—"

"You didn't reveal to me your own business." James relaxed his stance, fighting the urge to put his fist through the man's jaw for suggesting such filth. "What brings you about this road so early? Pitman has shown his trust in you then, it would seem."

Making polite conversation might distract him.

Pryer's attention was still at the house, but he answered with half interest. "We suspect a Patriot outpost is camped within the area, and I've been tasked at seeking out all residents in hopes of attaining information they are sure to have." He focused at last on James, and his chest puffed out. "Using that information, I have been charged to discover them, disband them and bring them in."

The last was a lie meant to impress, and James played his part, nodding in approval. He could never bring down an entire Patriot outpost with only three other men.

James glanced back at the door, pretending to be more concerned with returning inside, while his mind raced across a wide-open field. He would have to hurry to Henry's camp—warn them to disband before they could be discovered. Despite the fact

Pryer could not defeat them, they could hurry to Pitman and gather more men.

"I hope you find those blasted rebels." He shifted his own stance and inclined his head, making a show of his eagerness to return inside. "If you'll excuse me."

He nodded his farewell and turned to the house, but Pryer's voice stopped him. "And what's your assignment, Captain? I hear Greene has now been tasked with uncovering the informant. I might have thought such would have been given to you."

Hand at the door's latch, James peered over his shoulder and offered a light tilt of the head. "Greene is best for the job." Or so his arrogance makes him. "As for me, I fear Stockton has not authorized me to disclose the details of my work. But I am sure you will learn of it soon enough."

"You're still that man's pawn, are you?"

Releasing his hold on the door, James turned back to study his opponent. A sheen of suspicion shadowed the man's face. James offered a hard look. "I cannot choose from whom I take orders."

"Nay, but you can choose to whom you are loyal."

James froze, eyes narrowing. All ease had left Pryer's tone, the statement carrying a deadly charge. James turned to the door, refusing to respond to such degradation.

Pryer grabbed him at the arm, sneering disdain seeping through his teeth. "Everyone knows you let those two Patriots go free."

Word traveled fast. James jerked free from his hold and turned back. "Think what you will, but I did nothing." The lie slipped easily from his tongue.

Pryer's words were black. "This informant might not be so difficult to find if only one would open either eyes."

"What are you saying?"

"Are you truly so blind?" Pryer sneered. "Pitman should have commissioned me with the task of bringing the traitor in." He stepped forward, eyes inky with hate. "I would know exactly who to lead to the noose."

James's blood went cold, but he'd practiced not to feel it and offered a disinterested grin. "And who is that?"

A mocking laugh heaved from Pryer's mouth. "You really are a fool, Higley." He moved back a pace and glanced again to the others waiting for him. "Had anyone else your position they would have seen by now that their superior is leaking secrets to Washington."

Stockton?

A cold breath splashed into James's lungs. He held his breath, allowing the winter air to sit in his chest as he calculated. How many others believed this? Had Pitman ordered Greene to follow him for that reason? He blinked the thought away. Greene's pride would never have allowed him to keep such a thing behind his teeth. If he knew, he would have spoken it. Nay, this thought must be Pryer's alone.

James continued his act, and growled through his teeth. "What are you saying?"

Anger twitched over Pryer's mouth. "Every command of his you accept is a direct act against the king."

"You accuse me of treason?"

Pryer shook his head in disgust. "Stockton ordered you to let those Patriots go, then accuses you of the action? Were I you, I would think twice about accepting a command from him again."

So that is what he thought?

James turned to the door and pushed it open. "You are mad, Pryer."

"And your judgment is weak." He took another step backward, then motioned to the house with an upward cast of his chin. "How can you be certain this woman isn't using you for more than pleasure?" Bitter rage held James's teeth together as Pryer's face beamed with a smile straight from Satan. "Of course, even if she is, I might like a turn with her. It's been too long since I've—"

"Stop." James lowered his chin, his voice a blade. "This one is mine."

His mouth twitched. "Possessive, hmm?"

Fists curled, James strained to keep his arms at his sides. "Of her, I am."

"A new side of Higley, I see. You almost make me impressed." Walking backward, Pryer put a hand on the sword at his side. "I'll be sure to find you when both our missions are complete so we may take up this most interesting subject once again."

At last he moved back and prepared to mount. James's muscles were hot and throbbed with battle-ready blood. Removing his stare before these four men retreated would place him and the woman in too vulnerable a position. But Pryer sat on his saddle, unmoving, answering James's glare with his own, when the thought cut across his throat.

He doesn't believe me.

Pryer had known James long enough to understand that chasing after women, using them in such a way was not in his nature. The man suspected. He waited for proof.

James sauntered into the cabin, hiding the spike of anxiety with easy movements, before shutting and latching the door behind him.

Caroline stood just where he'd left her, hugging her arms around her chest. Ashen and shaking, she looked ready to collapse.

Wishing not to frighten her more, he extended his hand to her, whispering. "You must not believe everything you hear."

Her throat bobbed, followed by the barest thread of voice. "What am I to believe?"

He moved toward her, knowing he must give more of a show, for surely Pryer peered in at them, salacious voyeur that he was.

She backed away as he neared until the table stopped her movement. She raised a hand to strike him, but he caught it before her action could be detected by prying eyes.

"I will not harm you, I give you my word. I would never." James stared down at her, all of him wanting only to comfort her, make her believe he would not do the thing she feared he would. He quieted his voice another rung, and raised his hands to her face, praying she felt both urgency and sincerity at his touch. "But he might, if he doesn't believe you to return my pretended affections in kind."

Her eyes searched his and she whispered in return. "What... what do you mean?"

Releasing his hold on her wrist, he cupped her face, closing the remaining inches between them. "We are watched." She stiffened, her eyes sweeping to the window in fear, but he circled his thumb against her skin to calm her. "If we are to go free, you must allow me to show you what it is to be wanted."

# CHAPTER 12

*C*aroline's frame went simultaneously weak and rigid. He would truly ask this of her?

As his warm, rough hands held her face, then wound into her hair, her mind caught upon the word *ask*. 'Twas not forced or commanded, his actions toward her. Even in such a moment, he treated her as a thing of worth. She blinked, treading the deep waters. His gentleness meant little. Was this not what she'd expected from him all along?

He lowered his face to hers, his eyes searching, hesitating, pleading.

With his breath on her cheek, she flung a look to the window. There, as he said, from his mount the soldier watched through the pane, shoulders level and posture rigid. She released a small gasp when James's nose nuzzled into her ear, his lips dusting her skin. They must prove something—what she did not know, but he'd asked her not to question. And somehow, something within persuaded her to comply.

Lowering his hands from her face, James took hers and placed them on his chest. A spray of tingles dashed over her skin, feathering down to the center of her. *Good grace.* What was happening?

She tried to breathe. This wasn't right. He was the enemy—more, a stranger. A man who'd taken her from her home, her family. A man who prepared to do she knew not what.

So why of a sudden did she feel...to trust him?

"Do not be afraid." Never had she heard his voice so smooth, his accent so deep. His hands were at her face. "He will see us close and believe you to be mine." His lips caressed her ear as he whispered. "I will not force anything upon you. I promise."

Every sensation charged with life. She closed her eyes and found herself growing ever more stiff, and yet, ever more limp in his arms.

The tiny hairs on her skin stood on end when his breath tickled the hair around her ear. Slowly, she closed her eyes as all in the room began to darken. The fire crackled loud, the scent of cold and wood and something completely male consumed every thought. The heat of his body ignited her own, and she felt certain her knees would lose their strength. Even before, when she fancied herself in love, she'd never been held like this. She fought against the pull, but still it begged for study. He must know well his way with women for his touch to be so possessive and yet, so perfectly gentle.

He smoothed one hand into her hair and the other to her back, his voice a rich, soothing pool. "Look at me."

Nay.

Even with the inner refusal to guide her, she obeyed, and at once, she froze. All feeling, all resolve, all thought fled in place of the stranger that held her. Breathing turned shallow, vision blurred. Was he a stranger? Indeed 'twas true. So how was it that some unreachable part of her seemed to run to him, as if she'd known him, in fact had yearned for him, all these years.

His gaze swept over her face, eyes hooded in so real a way it seemed 'twas not some act, but truth of feeling that led him to hold her like a man in love.

Slow, dream-like, he closed his eyes, descended, and pressed his lips to hers. Caroline gasped, tense and refusing to breathe. As if he knew her tension and wished to ease it, he pulled back until his warm mouth hovered above hers, lip dusting against lip, breath marrying. 'Twas less a kiss now than before, yet the heat in her blood flooded harder. The cabin faded, the light and sound once so strong were now merely phantoms. All that existed was she and the man who held her.

In a swift motion he descended in full, his mouth covering hers, hands at her back, cradling her against his solid frame. Somehow both of her own hands were at his back and she gripped for fear her legs would lose their strength. Pleasant heat blazed through her middle as his mouth continued to explore hers.

Then, as quick as it began he pushed away and made for the window. "They've gone."

Caroline rested her weight on the edge of the table. Desperate to calm the uncontrolled speed of her pulse, she breathed in short shallow breaths and covered her mouth with her hand. She could still feel his fingers in her hair, his soft lips molding against hers. What had happened?

He spun back to her, tucking in his shirt and righting his neck-cloth as if their kiss had not completely undone him as it had her. He motioned to her hair. "Pin yourself right, we must leave. Immediately."

With that he charged out, leaving the door open behind him.

At last the room came into being once more. The cold swept up her skirts, reality slapping her awake.

Such a kiss. Timothy had never held her like that.

Whirling to the table she took the pins in her fingers and fumbled to straighten her hair. This stranger should not have pressed her so close, that was for certain. How could he hold her one moment then march away the next? The more she considered it, the more her face turned hot as embarrassment crept up her neck. It had all been an act—as of course it was meant to be—a ruse to deflect the enemy and it appeared their theater had worked. So why had it felt like more?

She shoved the last pin in place and stared forward with a huff. What an actor he was. To hold and caress her in so intimate a way when clearly their nearness had done nothing to him. He had some talent indeed.

Caroline peered out the open door and swept a hair from her face. Their forced closeness had done nothing to her either, except make her realize how much she truly wished to be free of him. The cad. 'Twas not to be borne.

A stripe of resentment unrolled down her spine, gifting her the strength to straighten. Who was he to capture her, force such attentions, and in the end, leave her in some foreign place?

His disposal of her could not come soon enough. By tonight she would be free of him.

She closed her eyes. Though never would she be free of the memory of his kiss.

James charged across the yard, his entire body aflame. The cold morning air whirled around him and he welcomed its chill. Shaking his head, he splayed his fingers, trying in vain to flee the trance her kiss had placed on him. Never had he imagined a pretended moment would leave him so...so what? What *was* this sudden malady?

At the barn he flung open the door with such a jerk it smacked against the outer wall. Was he weak? Nay. Nay, 'twas something different. Something deeper within him struggled. An unreachable, intangible place.

A quick inhale returned her to him in memory, the feel of her silken skin against his fingertips, the way her untried mouth succumbed to him. *Her hair.* Those corn silk colored locks were smoother even than he'd imagined.

Grumbling, he marched toward Ginny. He would not have supposed she had never kissed a man. If she had, it hadn't been done right. Again that heat assailed him, and he slowed. The sensation of her delicate hands against his waistcoat continued to singe through to his skin. That sweet sound she'd made...

He growled inwardly, cursing Pryer. 'Twas all that man's doing. James had seen the lascivious hunger in his eyes. If not for him—if not for the need to prove the woman could not be used— he'd never have been forced to do what he'd done.

The shock on her face rolled through his mind.

She feared him before...what must she think of him now? God willing she would not feel even more so. Closing his eyes, he rested a hand on Ginny's neck. He hadn't intended to hold her so close, to kiss her so deeply. How long *had* they kissed? It seemed only seconds, but surely 'twas more. Pryer had long since gone, perhaps had left the moment after James held her to him. But the feel of her had spread through his veins like a tonic, darkening the world around him until all that existed was the woman in his arms.

Panic swept up his back and he pulled his shoulders straight. He'd been warned of this. Warned that attachments of any kind would weaken the mind. Such a risk could never be taken. After his foolish attachment to Kitty Campbell, hadn't he learned?

A storm of regrets assailed him. What advantage might Pryer have taken in that moment? Of course, if James had known such a kiss would have stolen his sensibilities, he'd not have done it. He'd only pulled away when the heat between them had all but...

James shook his head to free his mind of the seductive memory.

Evening could not come soon enough. Once this woman was in the safety of the Patriot camp, he could move forward. Forget her. He knew nothing about her. How was he certain she wasn't spoken for—married?

He took Ginny by the reins and led her toward the house. Her large dark eyes blinked as if she read his thoughts and he clenched his teeth. Nay, he could do it. He could forget the fire in her spirit, the spark that ignited his skin at her touch. He must.

His mission was the cause. And there was no place—would never be a place in that—for a woman.

# CHAPTER 13

"*D*o you even know where we're going?"

Abrams's complaint dredged up a host of curses, but Greene held them behind his teeth, contemplating the many ways he could dispose of his murmuring companion. "Keep your mouth shut, Abrams, or I'll shut it for you."

"Ha!" Abrams, who rode beside him on one side while Reece rode on the other, leaned forward to look over at Reece. "He doesn't know."

"I know exactly where we're going."

All he went on was instinct, and his instincts had never failed him before. 'Twas what had risen him to captain. How many fellow soldiers were still stuck at private? Abrams was a clear example.

He endured another round of mocking from the scum-of-a-man, resisting the urge to explain. They wouldn't understand or accept any explanation. Gloating and satisfaction could come when they found them. And they would. The scent of victory was near.

The soft thud of an approaching rider met Greene's ears the moment Reece announced it.

"Sir, someone's—"

"I know."

Greene tugged his horse to a halt and the others followed suit. Whoever it was that approached would meet a blockade. 'Twas best to be the one with the advantage, not the other way around.

The louder the sounds became, the more his pulse thundered. There was not one rider, but three, possibly more. The snow's dampening effect muffled what he might have heard in summer, but he heard enough.

"Ready your weapons."

Greene brandished his pistol, and the click of metal on either side told his companions followed his lead.

If 'twas a band of Patriots, they would be ready for them.

Close enough now for them to hear voices, Greene strained his attention paper thin, but still he couldn't see them. Or make out their conversation.

"Here they come, boys."

Tension radiated between them like heat from a bonfire.

As the riders rounded the corner, Greene readied his aim then quickly lowered it, blinking in shock.

"Pryer?"

"Greene." Pryer pulled his horse to a stop. "This is a surprise indeed." The three men behind Pryer halted in a straight line. "What are you doing here?"

"That's what I'd like to know of you." Replacing his weapon, Greene examined Pryer's men. He'd seen them before but didn't know their names.

Twisting in his saddle, Pryer gestured to his small group. "We've been tasked with ousting a Patriot camp. There's been talk of one nearby, but so far we've yet to discover it."

"Pitman put you to this?" If he hadn't, Greene might have authority to call him to his service.

"Aye."

Curse.

"What about you? I venture you are doing more than picking daisies." Pryer's playful remark might have produced a grin were Greene's mood not so sour.

Holding tight to the reins, Greene summed up his mountainous frustrations into a single sentence. "Under Pitman's direction, I am on the hunt for the man—and woman—who narrowly escaped my capture."

"James Higley bested him and now he wants revenge," Abrams said.

Greene swung about, glaring. Abrams would get a fist in his face.

Smiling wickedly, his companion shrugged, reveling—it seemed—in the way it made Greene's hate rise. If the man wanted to fight...

"James Higley?" Pryer's expression slackened. "And a woman you say?"

Must he air all his failures? "Aye."

Pryer shot a glance to his companions before nailing a hard look to Greene. "When did this happen?"

"Yesterday."

"I cannot believe it." A curse leaked from Pryer's lips. "I have just seen him."

"You can't be serious." Disbelief made love to want, turning Greene's entire frame motionless. "Do not jest with me."

"I do not jest." Pryer's hard eyes and clenched jaw gave testament to his veracity. "Not hours ago I encountered James at the home of a known Patriot—with a woman."

"I knew it!" His horse's ears swung backward when he yelled. "Tell me where he went and I will follow him." He swung about, motioning to Abrams then Reece. "You will keep your eyes open. 'Tis likely they—"

"Don't waste your time, Greene." Pryer leaned forward, his hands resting on his saddle. "There are greater prizes than a sycophant captain not worth his weight."

"What?" Greene inhaled to soothe the stabbing irritation. "Nay, I will *not* stop, Pryer. James is not simply a groveling minion. He is the informant."

Pryer twisted his head. "Are you certain of this?"

"Very."

There was no proof but he needn't any. James's refusal to bring the woman in was a blatant indication of his lenient heart. After explaining what he knew, what had happened, Greene rested back in his saddle, grateful he at last could tell his tale of woe. Nothing could be clearer. James Higley was a traitor if ever there was one.

Pryer turned his head. "I will give you that he's a vagrant, and his actions questionable, but I wouldn't place the guilt upon him."

He'd always liked Pryer, but in this moment, any friendliness was replaced with mere civility. "You don't know him like I do."

"Think harder, Greene." Pryer leaned forward. "Stockton has been orchestrating him. Who else was responsible for the escape of the Patriot spies if not him? He was living with them for weeks and used them as couriers for his information while James was doing nothing more than following orders."

"Stockton is a fool." The mere feel of the name on his tongue made Greene's sinews stretch. "But you will not convince me otherwise about James. His station was bought. He has time and again proven he cares nothing for the king." He let his pronged reprimand fall before finishing. "Where have they gone? What direction?"

"I cannot say, but my guess was north. I only followed this path because of an intercepted message that suggested a camp this direction."

"Don't believe everything you get from courier hands, Pryer." Missives with intentional misinformation were everywhere. "Nothing is this way, I guarantee you that." A thought pressed up through the soil of his mind. "James prefers leaving a clean trail..."

Pryer's eyebrows lifted. "And?"

"He wouldn't leave this woman alone or let her flee without

protection. His foolish attachment to chivalry makes him incapable of that. Nay...he would wish her free, wish her safe. He would take her to the only place he knows."

Pryer tilted his head. "And where would that be?"

"Like any good gentleman, he would return her to her people. He would bring her to camp."

Realization dawned over Pryer's face like the sun on a hillside, then darkened again. "But how can you be certain?"

"There is no way to be completely certain." He was not averse to speaking truth in such times. "But my instincts tell me, if we find the Patriot camp, we will find James."

Greene offered a pause, allowing his friend a moment before he asked the question. "Care to join us?"

Pryer's eyebrows were cinched when he looked up.

He needn't speak his concern aloud, his thoughts were easily read in his face and Greene answered. "You will receive credit for your part, and I for mine. I don't care to take your victory from you." He added the next for effect only. "We are too good of friends to allow anything else."

Pryer smiled politely, bowing his head. "In that case, we go a-hunting."

~

"Can we stop a moment?"

Caroline's voice didn't sound her own. 'Twas fragile and hollow, but as she'd not spoken a word since the moment of their unintended kiss, she was grateful her voice could produce anything, for the sake of her cramping legs.

All the morning hours she'd sat rigid against the man who held her, losing the battle of her mind. Ignoring him as she wished was impossible. Feeling his chest rise and fall behind her, hearing his quiet breath, toyed with her memory, singing to life all those secret pleasures.

The horse stopped before James replied. "'Tis a good spot to rest."

He slipped from the horse and raised his arms to assist her. She hesitated, but complied. 'Twas her weariness, naught else that drew her to accept his offer. Or so she told herself.

Once she was settled on the ground, he pulled away, as if touching her had singed him.

"You are free to stretch your legs, move about as you need but do not venture beyond the road." He twisted to look behind at the thick grove of trees before returning his attention to Ginny. "We must be on the trail again within a quarter hour."

Caroline replied with a swift nod he didn't see. She stepped away, a sigh leaving her lips. 'Twas a blessing he had become so austere. She needn't additional complexities to make her journey to this unknown destination any more unbearable.

She rubbed her fingers against her eyes. A quarter hour of straight legs and ground beneath her feet would be heaven. Several paces ahead was a large tree, its trunk bending outward, beckoning her to rest her weary back.

The small grunt that escaped when she leaned against it startled even herself. A breeze swirled, and she shivered. How had she missed such a chill? She squinted upward, noting a dour February sky. 'Twould snow no doubt.

There, back against the tree, hands clasped around her, she allowed herself a glimpse of him where he stood some paces away. Nay, more than a glimpse. She allowed herself to study him as the myriad questions, myriad sorrows aligned in her spirit, waiting for their turn in thought. This soldier who had taken her...did he know the devils who captured Enoch?

Enoch!

She gasped and pushed to her feet. The letter? She'd left it! How could she not have thought of it until this moment? Everything had happened so fast...

Dizzy, she reached for the tree beside her. She'd hoped her

beloved Shadrach would leave and find his way home, but…what if he had not? What if the other soldier had found her note and planned to—

She swallowed and shook her head. Nay. He wouldn't…would he? Enoch was already a prisoner. There was nothing else they would do to him. Was there?

The possibility sank in her stomach as one grief rolled toward another, stopping at the feet of her rescuer. Sitting against the tree, she spied him. The other soldier had accused him of setting two Patriots free. Had he truly done it? If so…why?

Were not all Redcoats as hell-bound as Satan himself? Perhaps this man planned to take her there with him.

Then, like the helm of a ship, all the small moments of his gentlemanly goodness, his kind and gentle ways, turned her thoughts from the fall of water that crashed beneath her heart. This man was not like them. Not like the ones who took and demanded and killed. Was he?

Caroline's skin pricked as another wintery chill winged past. Such a vile matter, this war. She could hardly make one thing white and another black. Was there not some middle-ness to all of this?

She sniffed and dotted her eyes. She must be strong. This man might be less the devil than she supposed him, but still he was a stranger. Still, the enemy.

Surely, He who knows all had listened to her prayers and would use this ill to a greater good. Caroline rubbed her hands over her arms beneath her cloak as she flung another look to James. *James.* How long had she been thinking of him as such?

She huffed and pushed from the tree to walk several paces into the wood, easing the discomfort from her legs. A prayer formed in her heart, all the raw parts of her confusion linking arms and singing.

*Lord, I thank thee for keeping me safe—and I pray thee, continue. Help me find a way to escape him. Help me find a way to help Enoch.*

"Miss Whitney?"

The call of her name shot through the wood and she spun with a jerk.

"What are you doing?" James's gaze impaled her as he charged forward. "I told you to stay on the road."

He stopped before her, an even measure of harshness and worry in his stare. Caroline's middle went flighty under the scrutiny of his stubbled face. Unable to meet his gaze, she motioned to the trees. "I was only—"

"You know not the dangers these woods conceal." He whirled and strode toward his mount, speaking without facing her. "We must leave immediately."

"Leave?" Her legs had barely begun to regain their natural feeling. With a quiet scoff she followed after him. "I refuse to be hauled from place to place like...like some sack of grain."

Pausing, he peered over his shoulder, an eyebrow lifted and a smile twitching. He found her humorous, did he? How he dared find anything in this situation *humorous* was beyond her. He treated her as an imposing brother would treat a sister, not as a gentleman would a lady.

He finished his march to Ginny and tightened the girth of the saddle. 'Twas then she noticed the pistol tucked in a pouch in its side. Her pulse flickered and her eyes jumped back and forth between the man and the weapon. Should she?

Her mouth went dry, her palms cold. She didn't wish to kill, only to escape.

The more she considered, the more her limbs chilled and her neck tightened. Could she? God only knew what ill end awaited her if she attempted another escape. Even at the thought, another crept in, making its home in her chest.

This man, Redcoat though he may be, was not what he seemed. Rather, not what she had supposed him to be. Perhaps trusting him, giving up her safety into the hands of a stranger would be—

"Do not think it."

His sudden words clutched her throat and she was forced to clear it before pretending innocence. "Think what?" She forced a laugh that did little to conceal her guilt. "What do you accuse me of?"

The look he tossed over his shoulder was a sermon.

Caroline straightened her arms at her sides and raised her chin, accepting the challenge. "I was already admonished not to attempt to flee and I gave you my word." Lying's offensive palate tempted her to grimace, so she held her mouth tighter. "You think I would go against orders, Captain?"

Looking away, James chuckled light in his chest, allowing Caroline a full glimpse of the frightful scar on his ear. She fought back a gasp. Gracious heaven. How had he come by such a thing? 'Twas healed, but jagged and red, as if it had been there for some time.

Before she had time to ponder its gruesome history, he turned back to her, no hint of any former merriment in his eyes. "You should school your cheeks not to redden when you lie, Miss Whitney." He faced his mount again, reaching into the pack. "Your husband must find your impertinence wearying."

Caroline pulled back, mouth open. "I..." She shook her head and shifted her feet. "I am...I am not married."

He pivoted round again, extending that familiar half-eaten loaf toward her. "Is that so?"

Her cheeks which, according to him, were red before, now burned hot as fire. She looked away. Had he asked her three years past, she would have told him marriage was imminent. Timothy had loved her, or so he'd claimed. So she'd believed, before the truth of his thin attachment was revealed. Their parting left dry, abandoned rows in the fields of her soul. Unyielding. Fruitless. At five and twenty she held little that would attract a man. Her mother's worry-induced petitions wagged before her like a pointed finger. *Act the lady, Carrie. Wear this hat, dress this way. Stop your riding. No man wishes a woman who speaks her mind. You will frighten them all away.*

And it seemed she had.

She could feel his eyes on her, and pretended it didn't offer a kind of painful delight. What would it be like to have someone care for her—truly care? Caroline huffed and brushed an errant hair from her forehead. This Redcoat was not the sort of man in whom she would take interest were he the last soul on earth.

The sooner she escaped him, the better. Better for The Cause, better for Enoch. Better for her heart.

# CHAPTER 14

*J*ames studied the woman whose porcelain complexion blared with color as she stared into nothing. But her cheeks were not now red from falsehood, rather embarrassment.

*I am not married.*

The words splintered through him, and 'twas only his practiced skill that allowed him to conceal the shock.

From the moment of their kiss, curiosity had plagued him to near blistering obsessiveness. Her answer to the statement he'd hardly practiced before speaking, left his mind utterly blank. He was grateful he'd not kissed a married woman, but…how could that be? 'Twas difficult to believe a man had not yet made her his. Her wit was alluring. Her indomitable spirit enchanting, to say nothing of her beauty.

Something had grasped her, some memory, as she stared away, and he used the moment to memorize the gentle slope of her nose, the soft line of her jaw. He'd never seen hair the color of sunshine.

She looked back to him as if she'd felt his stare and wished to scold him with her narrowed eyes. The look had the opposite effect of what she intended as she tucked a silken strand behind her ear. He could almost feel her fingers against his skin, and the sensation reached through him, stitching a hidden smile in his heart. Such fire and innocence. A rare combination in a woman.

"We best be going." The anxiety he'd held pricked over him as it had when he found her walking through the trees. They were watched, or so he suspected from the few snaps and rustles that made their way from the wood. This was no place to linger.

When she didn't immediately begin to mount he took her at the elbow. "There is no time to waste, we need to—" A sound from the trees cracked in his ears and he spun, his hand already at his pistol. Someone *was* there.

Her face shot up and she whirled, her back against Ginny. "What is it?"

James scanned the forest, frantic to determine the location from which the sound had come. Quiet owned the wintery air, begging his pulse to calm, but he refused. He knew better than to be fooled by temporary silence.

A flash of movement caught his side vision and he stepped forward, guarding the woman with his body.

He could hear her breath coming in short, quick huffs.

"What is it?" She repeated, this time whispering, one hand on his arm.

Every sinew, every muscle throbbed. Thank the Lord she didn't require his assistance to ride. If indeed they were ambushed, he could command Ginny to carry the woman away. That is, if he could fight down the men who surrounded them.

How many were there? Again, he scanned the wood, but saw nothing. Had Greene brought his men this far in so little time?

He felt her hand on his back as she spoke soft, her voice ready to snap. "Is someone there?"

James nodded slow, preparing instructions in his mind before speaking them. "Prepare to ride when I signal."

She gripped his arm and pulled him to look at her. "Alone?"

The fear he witnessed in her eyes dimmed the temporary anger at losing his sight on where the enemy waited. Holding her at the arms, he poured reassurance into his stare. "If I am to protect you, I must—"

He heard the approaching footsteps before he heard the man's words.

"Unhand her."

James's jaw cramped. 'Twas just as he'd feared. Patriots.

A rough hand jerked him around as a pistol's cold barrel was shoved against the side of his head. "Look here, boys. Seems we found ourselves a soldier."

Caroline stepped back, stunned into muteness. She looked to James, dread crushing her bones at the sight of the gun at his temple.

Three more men emerged from the trees like spirits born of her fears, their muskets aimed at the man she'd begun to trust. The urge to lunge for the pistol in the saddle pooled hot in her limbs. But what could she do, one woman against so many? Even an accurate shot would not save them, but seal their fates.

"Are you alright, miss?" The man gripping James craned his neck to her, a ring of concern in his eyes.

She hinged her mouth open, still nothing emerged but a grunt of confusion.

His gaze narrowed. "Has he hurt you?"

Caroline's mouth went stale as the events of the past day consumed. Even if she told the truth of James, would they believe her? That he was not the kind of soldier they thought him to be?

That mattered naught to them, and it ought not to matter to her. For he *was* a Redcoat.

The man yanked against James's coat. "We heard there was a

runaway soldier that might be of use to us if we could capture him —and it appears we have." He looked to Caroline. "I am only sorry we couldn't rescue you sooner."

"I..." Her chest pumped, stealing her voice. Dearest Lord, what should she say? Why could she not speak? "I...he took me..." The rest clogged in her throat. She longed to say more. To say he'd not harmed her. To say he'd been kind.

"You're safe now." The man then pierced James with a stare while a sneer hooked through his face. "You, soldier, are coming with us."

Caroline's legs lost strength as her mind cleared, at last accepting the miracle of her rescue. She was saved. God had heard her prayers. She reached out to hold onto Ginny's saddle as her knees threatened to buckle. The world dissolved into haze, a mix of colors, muddled voices and shapes. Tears pooled in her eyes. *Thank you, Lord Almighty.*

"Rogers, see to the woman. Caleb, bring the rope."

The words splashed against her, clearing her vision as one of the men led her away. They would tie him? She looked over her shoulder, shock and relief and worry all joining hands to encircle her.

Like a lamb to the slaughter, James submitted, allowing the tallest Patriot to bind his hands behind him, naught a word on his lips despite their taunts and jeers. He looked up, and she caught the gaze he sent her. Her heart leapt to her throat. Too much to say in a single look. Too much left wanting, too much to question. As if of their own strength, her legs slowed, willing her to go to him, help him, stay with him.

Stay?

Such a thought was traitorous. She would never see him again. And so it must be.

So why did this heavenly rescue feel more like a pain rather than a salve to her heart?

"Come with me, miss." The gentleman at her side led her onward. "We'll take you to the outpost, then find out how to get you back home."

She offered a shallow nod of gratitude. Not that she felt so little, only that a torrent of confusion drenched her mind and slowed her action.

The Patriot helped her onto his mount at the edge of the trees as the other three continued their objurgating mockery.

The tallest one stood back, watching and saying nothing as the shorter two searched James's pockets.

"No notes, sir." The black-haired one peered to his superior, then back to James, and reached into his inner pocket. His movements stopped short and his head rose, a smile on his face as he pulled the pocket watch from its resting place. "What is this?"

James's stoic expression hardened, his nostrils flaring. "That is mine."

The man chuckled, tossing the shiny timekeeper to the leader. "Pure gold, I reckon."

James wished to speak, Caroline could see it in the cut of his ticking jaw. 'Twas then his deep, threatening voice shook the ground. "Give that to me."

"You have no property, soldier." The leader of the small group neared, standing nose to nose with him. "All you have now belongs to my commander." He lifted the watch and shifted it back and forth, examining it with disinterested care. "You won't need this where you're going."

James lunged, but the men at his sides held him back.

Caroline's blood stalled in her veins. What did they mean? She swung her gaze back to James, whose stare was on the trinket as if his heart had been torn from his chest.

The tall one chuckled. "Come men, let's deliver our prize."

Limbs shaking, the words sprang from Caroline's mouth before she could stop them. "What will you do to him?"

As the two lead him to the road, a gun ever pointed at his back, the leader turned to her, satisfaction lighting his brown gaze. "That, my lady, is for Captain Donaldson to decide."

# CHAPTER 15

Caroline sat on the hard cot inside the tent, a blanket draping her shoulders, a stone in her heart. The steaming cup in her hands should have warmed her, the scent of strong coffee should have calmed, but they did neither. Having arrived at the Patriot outpost not a quarter hour past, she'd been whisked away to the solitude of this small, forlorn bit of canvas on sticks. Her chest pinched. How long was she to wait? Where was the leader of this Patriot band she was promised would come?

What had happened to James?

She stood, placed the cup on the over-turned box that served as a table and walked the few steps to the tent door. The urge to charge out buzzed through her legs, but she stayed them. *Patience, Carrie.* Still, the clawing need to know more left its marks within her. Though she'd tried to glean what information she could from the men who'd rescued her, they said little.

A cloud of voices drifted past the tent and she moved a step closer to the canvas, straining her ears to hear any of what they said. A single word slipped through. Lobsterback.

Caroline gripped the blanket tighter. Closing her eyes, she lifted her soul to the One whose omniscience could carry her through this veil of confusion and chaos. The enemy deserved nothing but what they themselves cast to others. To people like Hannah who sacrificed. To her brother who languished in prison. To her uncle who lay dead. So why should she care what future awaited this man she hardly knew?

"Miss Whitney?"

The door to the tent swung open and she jumped back, a hand at her chest. "Forgive me. I did not hear you coming."

"'Tis I who should apologize, I should have announced myself."

Whoever owned such a stunning pair of eyes, Caroline knew not, but their blue color matched his regimental coat, as the kindness in his face matched the knowing command in his stance.

He grinned, removing his cocked hat. "Miss Whitney, allow me to introduce myself. I am Captain Henry Donaldson."

"Henry!" A smile burst from her heart to her lips—the kind born of a familiarity they shared, but only she knew—and made the cold ease a mite from her limbs. "You are Anna's husband."

The grin he had offered before doubled as intensive wondering owned his wide expression. "How do you know—"

"I am from Sandwich. Your wife is a dear friend of mine." Her soul cried in joy for her friend. "She will be so pleased to know you are well."

A hundred emotions took their turn in his gaze. "How is she?"

"She misses you dreadfully, which I am pleased to say is her only malady." Such love in one's eyes Caroline had never witnessed. She pooled her words with richness in hopes of easing the obvious pain he felt at missing her. "Never have I seen a woman so healthy who carried a child, I can assure you of that."

The muscles of his face ticked with emotion and he cleared his throat. "I am so pleased to hear it." The tight smile he offered was a polite benediction to a conversation clearly too dear to his heart to speak of without the birth of tears.

He motioned toward her. "I came as quickly as I could." His

voice lowered. "I am glad my men came upon you. You are not hurt?"

"Nay, I am well."

"A miracle then." He motioned for her to sit, and she obliged while Henry took the chair beside the box.

"Have you seen..." She knit her fingers and placed them in her lap, aching to keep the rising anxiety from his vision. "Have you seen him yet?"

"Nay." Henry's studying gaze tore away the facade. Her attempt to fool him with her calm was futile. He reached out and placed his hand on hers. "Do not worry, you are safe now."

Sitting back, he exhaled, all politeness and sincerity bundled in soft sternness. "I know it may be painful to retell, but I feel that understanding what happened will help me best know how to move forward."

Caroline drew a long breath. Clutched by memory, her gaze drifted away, but with effort she regained it. "I had received word from my brother that—"

"Henry, I heard you called for me."

The man who burst in stopped mid-step, jaw open, eyes wide. "Miss Whitney."

Caroline's shock matched his, and she rose to her feet. "Dr. Smith."

Her old friend neared, hand outstretched. "What brings you here?" His joy was genuine but faded as the ever-ready physician reigned in his actions. Looking her up and down as if to be sure she didn't suffer some hidden ill, he released his hold and stepped away. "Do not tell me you were the one who was found with the soldier."

"I am."

Nathaniel's eyes darkened. "We encountered your cousin much like this not long ago."

"I know." Everything she'd kept within flooded her heart, that former boulder being edged away with every pump of blood.

"Hannah told me of her work as a spy in confidence, and from that moment I have worried over her."

Henry rose, his knowing look reading through her words. "Tell us all that happened."

Caroline inhaled, her chest crushing from the memories. "I went looking for my cousin when I learned that my brother is being held as a prisoner in Boston."

Nathaniel jutted his head, brow heavy with hope. "He is not dead?"

"Nay." The kindness of a friend, and one who also had known of Enoch's assumed passing, made the retelling only pulse, not pain. "He wrote to us, telling us his plan to escape, but I hadn't details, as the last of the letter was missing."

She waited, and the men's silence petitioned for more. "I hurried in search of my cousin, knowing I must share the burden and seek wisdom of what to do as my parents have left for New York and there is no knowing when they will return."

"You wished to help him."

"I admit I did. Though I cannot say how I believed such a thing possible."

Henry crossed his arms, his jaw flexing. He threw a look to Nathaniel. "If there is one prisoner, there are others."

"Aye," Caroline answered, "he spoke of others in his letter." Her throat thickened, images of fathers, husbands and brothers suffering in quiet agony with none to ease their pain. "The letter was posted over two weeks ago and arrived only yesterday. I fear...I fear perhaps it is too late, but I cannot rest until..." She let the rest fade into silence.

Caroline hugged the blanket tighter. 'Twas a foolish hope, but it kindled life in her bosom she hadn't felt since learning of his death. Perhaps this was God's way of—

"You are brave, Caroline." Nathaniel's gentle words brought her gaze up and away from the cyclone of unquenchable thoughts.

He extended his hand. "Would you allow me to read it? The letter I mean. I wish only to know—"

"I do not have it." She dotted her gaze back and forth between the men as she retold her harrowing tale. How she'd raced to her cousins, and hidden in the closet. How she'd been found in the barn then chased at her attempt to escape. Her shoulders drooped and what strength in her gaze gave way, and she stared at the floor, her brow cramping. If not for James, if not for his bravery in her behalf...Her memory relaxed into the past. The way he'd placed himself in front of her adversary. The way he'd kept his vision on her while the Patriot's had carried her away, as if he wished to be at her side, protecting her. Her chest tightened.

What would these Patriots do to him when they questioned him? Had they already? Had he spoken?

Holding her vision against Henry's intent expression, Caroline revealed the ugly truth. "Your wife beckoned me not to go. It is because of my actions that the letter has been taken and perhaps my brother will now truly be lost."

Not until that moment had she considered the consequences of her actions. Her skin pricked at the memories, shame and despair rising like Erebos to consume her. Why hadn't she put the letter in her pocket? What had she been thinking? Why had she even relinquished the bag at all? Her eyes burned. Now, because of her, Enoch might truly die—either from illness or by the hand of their mutual enemy.

Henry placed a hand on her shoulder. "Your brother is in the hands of God. Worry not over him, 'tis not your fault." When she found strength to look up, she saw compassion beaming through light blue eyes. "Do you remember anything from their conversation? Any names?"

"I...I don't know if I recall." Anxiety had stolen her coolness. Why could she not remember? Her stomach rose to her throat. "The first man, I do not remember his name, Greene, perhaps? But the man who took me, his name is James Higley."

Nathaniel jerked backward. Henry's face went slack.

"Did you say Higley?" Nathaniel said.

Caroline stalled. "I did." Her throat parched. His name stirred them, but their cryptic reactions made it impossible to tell what they felt at hearing it.

Henry's angled jaw flicked, his mind working as he stared at his friend. "Did you know?"

Nathaniel shook his head, mouth firm, then turned to Caroline. "Stay here and warm yourself. We'll return as soon as we've... taken care of him."

Those last four words burrowed into her chest as the men bowed and rushed out the door. Take care of him? What did that mean? Would they torture him? Kill him?

Caroline shuffled backward, slowly lowering to the cot.

*Forgive me, Lord.* She closed her eyes and dropped her head to her hands.

She'd only ever wished to help. To perhaps find a way to rescue her beloved Enoch—at least aid somehow. In the end, she'd only brought trouble.

Despite her intentions, she could do naught but regret that she had done anything at all.

In the center of a large tent, James sat on the ground where the dutiful Patriots had tied him to the pole that held up the heavy canvas. The rope at his wrists was rough, tight. He curled and stretched his fingers to entice a thread of blood to his buzzing fingers.

He scowled. Where was Henry? He should have been here long ago. Again he wriggled his arms and hands, trying to find relief to the growing numbness. The action gave his mind a subject to meditate upon. Something other than *her*. But the memories accosted him despite the effort, holding him tighter than the rope at his wrists. Staring at the wall of the dirty tent, his mind found the place it wished to rest, and he allowed it to linger. The way her face had lost color when the men appeared, the roundness of her eyes when she'd been led away from him—how her voice had cracked when she'd asked where they would take him. 'Twas nearly as if...

James shook his head and growled as he let his breath free. Where on earth was Henry? He moved his wrists again. There was little time for him to sit here when Greene was at his heels. Washington needed to know of the supply ship and the movement of the troops. More, he needed to get to Anderson and begin his mission to befriend the man ahead of Stockton's arrival to Boston. Every moment he spent in the presence of military leaders was vital. Every intelligence he could glean was like manna to a soul starving for victory.

"Managed to get yourself caught, did you?"

Henry burst in the room, his expression stern with shock and rich with friendship.

James leaned his back against the pole, reserving a smile. "A pleasure to see you, too, Captain."

The joy that streaked across his former compatriot's face matched the emotion in James's chest. "Pined my absence, hmm?" Henry tugged a knife from his side and knelt beside him, grinning. "Your nose is bruised. Someone hit you did they?"

James craned his neck to look behind, hidden mirth in his words. "I was accosted by a Patriot rebel not long ago."

"Is that so?" A quick slice and James was free of the rope. Henry rose, extended a hand, and helped James to rise as he slipped the knife back into its sheath. "The man must have a fist of iron."

"He does." Chuckling, James clasped arms with his friend, a spread of warm brotherhood streaming through his blood. With a strong pull, Henry tugged James into a brotherly embrace.

He stepped away and smacked James on the back. "You are

fortunate not to have a hole in your chest. Those men might have shot you had not Miss Whitney been with you."

"How is she?" The words came out too quick. James forced disinterest in his stance and tone as he massaged his wrists. "She is still...here? Or have you sent her home?"

"She is still here."

Something foreign winged through James's chest, and though he could interpret the coded signal it sent to his heart, he ignored it. He would never see her again, and he was relieved.

"So, this is our prisoner."

Both men turned as Nathaniel entered through the tent door.

James went still, gauging the man's study of him. Last they'd spoken, their interaction had been strained. But that was months ago. No doubt the man remembered it as well as he—the time James had come seeking Kitty Campbell's hand in marriage, not knowing how her heart was already twined with the doctor's. Time had shown James 'twas not love he'd felt for the woman, but admiration, respect. That he'd even considered an attachment when he knew full well the dangers, caused shame to bleed in his stomach.

Never again.

Nathaniel neared them both, and as if to prove he carried no ill will, the vibrant smile and hard slap on the shoulder he offered James was as real as if they'd been life-long friends. "'Tis good to see you."

"Thank you, Doctor."

Stepping away, Nathaniel raised a brow, a side-ways smile tipping his face. "I might have guessed I'd find you bleeding, if not dead."

Henry laughed quietly. "I was just telling him that very thing."

James rubbed his wrists again. "I am nothing if not lucky."

"Luck has nothing to do with it." Henry's tone turned serious. "Providence carries you, James. You do His work in this cause."

In truth, God *was* in this war, and more than ever they relied on His grace to guide them.

"What news?" Nathaniel's gaze swung between him and Henry. "Miss Whitney tells us you are on some mission for the enemy?"

She'd spoken of him?

He bobbed his head, forcing away the question he wished to ask. "I've been tasked with traveling to Boston to befriend an officer ahead of Major Stockton's arrival to the city. The mission could not be better timed."

"You are headed north, then?" Henry asked.

"Aye." James paused, pacing to the table where a pitcher rested. He motioned to it in question. "May I?"

"Of course," Henry answered.

Nodding his thanks, James poured himself a drink, not realizing how parched he was until the liquid coated his throat. He set the empty glass on the table. "With Washington so near it will be easier to share information. Distance creates difficulty that is often insurmountable. Not only that, I've attained intelligence about a supply ship with goods privateers must intercept."

"When will you finish your journey?"

"As soon as possible. And so must you."

Henry's scowl was instant. "What do you know?"

"I encountered another soldier on my journey here who is looking for a Patriot outpost such as this." He poured himself another drink. "I suggest you disband and make ready to move farther north immediately."

"Immediately?" Nathaniel's question rumbled. "Two of our own spies have yet to come back from their journey east and are expected to return before morning. Can we not wait until then?"

"'Tis a risk." James gnawed his cheek. "Leave no later than morning and I suspect you shall be well, so long—God willing—as I was not followed." Battling the recurring image of the brave woman he'd helped, James took another drink. "I might have been able to move forward on my own mission without interruption, but for..."

Her name was nearly on his lips but he denied it, knowing the familiarity of its use would only make him think of her more.

"I should like to hear your tale of it." Nathaniel leaned against the pole in the center of the room, arms crossed and eyebrows up. "Miss Whitney says she was taken by you for overhearing. Something about her hiding in a closet? What exactly did she hear?"

James leaned back against the table, palms holding the table's edge. "She claims she went to the house looking for her cousin. When Major Stockton and I arrived to discuss his wishes in secret, she hid in the closet in hopes of remaining unseen." He sighed, recalling the worst of it. "I would have let her go had not Greene spied her attempting to make an escape. The man is a hound, poisoned with the scent of ever-elusive success in his snout. He wishes me dead."

"Does Stockton know Caroline is with you? Does he know what she heard?" The depth of Nathaniel's question carried the burden of history with it. Stockton had nearly hanged the doctor's wife for her believed interference with the army's intelligence.

James breathed out, crossing his arms as he pondered. "Greene might possibly have told him, but 'tis doubtful. He wishes to uncover proof of my worthlessness and pin the name of traitor upon me, so I feel he will keep this to himself and Pitman."

"Pitman?" Henry scowled. "Is his regiment still at Plymouth."

"It was when I left, aye." James pushed up from his leaning position. "Both he and Stockton were none too pleased to discover Hannah and Joseph had escaped under my watch."

Nathaniel released a sigh that was far more than breath, 'twas a prayer. "Thank the Lord." He moved toward James. "Now that they have found safety, what shall we do with Miss Whitney? You no longer believe her to be in danger, do you?"

James maneuvered back to the table, and pulling one map from underneath another, smoothed his hand over it. "If I know anything of Greene, I know his will is a fortress. He will never rescind from what he wants until it is his." Recalling how she'd slapped him, James fought a smile, then a frown. "He claims Miss Whitney is a spy and said if I was to bring her in, he would not accuse me of treachery. Otherwise, he would name me as the informant."

Neither man offered a response, but they needn't for the depth of his words to be read in their solemn eyes and firm jaws.

James sighed. "I had to take her." He looked up. "But here I must leave her and hope that once again my tale will be believed though I fear perhaps, if I cannot befriend this new major as Stockton intends, then I will lose my post...and therewith my contribution to the cause."

Speaking aloud his fears made them tangible, growing arms and threatening to choke. An image, ever present in his mind, brought to life the face of the man he'd betrayed, and the vow he'd rather die than deny. James had given his life to a cause that mattered, to an army that fought for something eternal.

He reached for his timepiece, but felt only wool and linen where the treasure should be. His muscles flinched. Blasted Patriot. Why take a trinket that meant nothing to them?

James growled. "I have worked for nothing but this cause for five years, and now it seems my work will come to naught."

"Not unless you take her with you," Nathaniel said.

Peering past a heavy brow, James quirked his mouth. "Take her?"

Henry flung a look to Nathaniel then stepped forward, his mouth parted and eyes bright, picking up where his friend had stopped. "If you take her with you, as your prisoner—" He stopped and he raised a finger. "Take her as a token of some sort, proof of what you and Stockton have learned during your time here. Proof that the Patriots will take all measures to secure their wills. You can, with her as your envoy, prove that the poison of rebellion has infiltrated even the minds of the fairer sex, and that your work must be completed or the Empire is at risk of losing everything."

James blinked, allowing the shocking suggestion to sluice over him, filling his mind with light. How had he not considered this?

Yet...

He shook his head. "If I bring her as bait—as you suggest—how can I be sure she will be safe? I cannot place her in greater danger—"

"Captain Donaldson, sir?" A man appeared at the tent door, and James bristled. 'Twas the man who had taken him. Though he'd done naught but his duty, James's fought the urge to charge forward and demand the timepiece. But he couldn't risk a brawl.

Henry turned toward the door and paused. James could see his friend's mind working. "Doctor Smith, will you see to his business? I am not done interrogating our prisoner."

Nathaniel bowed, tossing a volume of script to James through his eyes. "Of course."

A whip of movement, and he was gone.

Once alone, Henry neared James, his voice a hollow thread. "You must keep your mission secret, and Miss Whitney must be kept safe, this I understand." His chest lifted and lowered when he peered to the tent door and back. "I can think of none more skilled to see her to safety than Ethan Barrik."

"Who?"

He gestured to the door. "The man who found you."

"Him?"

Henry paused, no doubt sensing James's growing apprehension. "I count myself a faithful judge of character, James, and I believe him worthy of our trust in this case."

Henry's cant head and tilted smile warmed only the surface of James's growing supposition.

Rubbing a hand over his mouth, James glanced to the door, imagining he could see her several tents down, her pale gold hair and pink cheeks—her shoulders straight and chin high. She was proud. In the best sense. A trait he would be loath to see dimmed by the fiery darts of their common enemy.

He grit his teeth before turning to his friend. "Are you certain the man is trustworthy?" Greene was a stray bullet with a course for one's head. If this Barrik fellow did not take care, he would cause both himself and Caroline to hang.

Henry's hand came down hard on James's shoulder. "Have I ever led you wrong?"

James looked away. If he believed anyone, 'twas Henry. The man had never been anything but forthright, so...so why did his skin crawl at the thought of Caroline in anyone else's care? He knew 'twas selfish to think himself the only one with skill enough to keep her safe. Yet his muscles ached to be the one to do it.

His thoughts must have scrolled in his eyes, for Henry answered as if he'd read them. "She could be in no better hands than his, I am certain."

"Of course." The reply was forced, but there was nothing for it. What else could he say?

"You can make your escape at dawn."

James lifted his brow. "Dawn?"

Henry's expression was a mix of companionship and caution. "If you wish to leave now—"

"Nay, staying through the night will allow more talk and planning between us here. Washington will want a report if I am able to reach him without another interruption." He smoothed his thumb over the stubble beneath his chin, when without warning the thoughts in his head shot from his lips. "When will Barrik take her back?"

If Henry detected the slight catch in James's voice, he didn't show it.

"I shall speak with him now." Henry walked to the door, then stopped and peered over his shoulder. "Until this evening."

He left without another glance, and James's muscles altered between tense and calm. It could have been any small band that caught him, but for God's good grace it hadn't. Would that the rest of his journey might go as smooth.

Would that Caroline might find peace and safety.

If Henry trusted Barrik to such a degree than he should as well.

He should trust all of it to God. And he did.

Yet, he couldn't shake the premonition that the darkest of his days were still to come.

# CHAPTER 16

*G*reene slipped from his saddle, keeping his feet silent against the snow. The others did the same.

He scanned the hushed wood until his vision discovered the tree-circled tents that peeked out at them from the wintery light. His soul coiled with delight. Just as he'd suspected. The Patriots could not have left a more perfect path to follow. It had taken time, but such always did and it paid to be patient. God was on his side, there was no doubt of that.

James would be found. And the woman. Their futures were set. Nothing so simple.

He motioned with a tilt of his head and Pryer came beside him. His low voice mirrored the question in his crumpled expression. "We will not wait until dark?"

"I can take no chances." Greene turned to see Abrams at his left. "If James is here, I want him. Now."

"And what of the woman? Is she free for the taking?"

There was more to Abrams's question, and Greene curled his fists to keep from pummeling the man into submission.

"You will go with Pryer to apprehend James." A caustic memory brought a sting to Greene's face. "The woman is mine."

Pryer's men filled the holes in their small line. Muskets were drawn, loaded and at their shoulders. Only seven of them, but the Patriot band was small enough. Twenty or so, it seemed. His small band looked at him as if he were omniscient, and the sensation was tantalizing. What a pleasant taste was power.

No Greene would ever amount to anything? An inward grin made his chest rise. *If you could see me now, Father.*

Nodding to Pryer, he grazed his vision over the others. "You remember your instructions." Turning, he peered to Abrams and Reece who took their respective positions, one reluctantly, the other with boyish determination.

Looking to the young soldier who stood beside him, Greene took his command and polished it. "Reece, you will stay here."

The boy's face warped. "Sir?"

He'd considered bringing him, but Reece was too clean. Greene needed men who weren't afraid to bloody their hands.

"Guard the horses until we return."

Stepping backward, Reece nodded, his mouth a thin line. "Aye, sir."

Striding to the front of the small pack, Greene kept one hand on his sword, his pistol in the other. While his men made chaos and found their traitor, he would find the woman. Alone.

They moved forward, following his crouched position in a long line on his left and right.

A movement from the camp caught his eye and he stopped, the rest following suit. There, at the center, in front of a small tent, stood his feminine adversary. God himself could not have granted him a more benevolent gift.

She *was* here. Just as he'd suspected. How they'd come upon her, he didn't know, but didn't question. The Patriots were badgers in their tenacity, and to take her meant they must have taken Higley as well. That is, if they had been together. But why would they not have been? Greene studied the small camp as his mind whirled. Unless Higley had already been killed in the taking of her, he would be here as well.

His mouth twitched. How good this felt, being moments away from victory. Moments from bringing one, possibly two, radicals into captivity.

This moment was proof that he, Matthew Greene, was everything his father had never been.

Calculating, he reorganized his already laid plans.

A flick of his wrist brought Pryer beside him. "Like we discussed, create a distraction and locate Higley. I will go for the girl."

Pryer's expression hardened with delight. "On your command."

Greene looked behind, a harsh whisper scraping through his throat as he lifted his musket. Never had his smile felt so real. "Make ready, boys."

From one side of the small tent to the other, Caroline paced. She stretched her fingers and peered at the door too many times to count. Henry and Nathaniel had left an hour past—or more—and had yet to return.

Anxiety buzzed and sparked through her limbs. Perhaps she should have said more of James, then they would not have thought him so much the enemy. She stalled, rubbing the fabric of her skirt between her fingers. The one time she'd peeked out the door, she'd seen nothing of them. Did they only speak with him? She could only hope that they—

"Pardon me, miss."

Caroline raised her head with a jolt, smiling only after she recognized who it was that entered the tent with hat in hand. 'Twas the man from the wood.

"Good day, sir."

She curtsied before side stepping to allow him further entrance. His tall frame brought his head so near the top, he bowed it to keep from touching the canvas ceiling.

His presence boomed through the small space and Caroline fought the urge to squirm. Even in silence he was as commanding as when he'd come upon them hours ago. And yet, there was something else about him, a calm, captivating strength behind the marble.

She opted for a show of friendliness, despite their lack of introduction. "I do not believe I know your name, sir."

As if he were unused to communicating with the fairer sex, the man moved his fingers along his hat, a whisper of friendliness behind his whiskered face. He cleared his throat. "I am Ethan Barrik, miss." His voice was deep. "And you are Miss Whitney. Captain Donaldson has just spoken with me about your situation."

Had he? How much had he shared? Her ears heated. She'd hoped all she'd spoken to Henry had been in confidence. But perhaps stories like hers were not ones that could be kept silent.

"I am sorry for what you've endured," he said. "The Redcoats believe they can do what they like, when they like. We are here to teach them all the reasons they cannot." His eyes blazed, as if he meant to singe the very words into the seats of parliament.

Caroline dipped her head, able only to speak a quiet, "Thank you."

He stepped forward, keeping his pointed response polite but strained with intent. "I have been instructed to take you home to Sandwich in the morning."

Her head shot up. "Indeed?"

"We would leave this evening, but..." He shook his head. "Captain Donaldson believes after your ordeal, a bit of rest will do you good before we head out again."

There was a secret behind his words, something he knew, but wouldn't reveal, and from the way he looked at her, he saw the same in her own face. She moved away, fighting the miserable strain of thoughts that refused to abate.

No matter what her heart cared to feel, 'twas her mind she must obey. James Higley was a stranger and a Redcoat, true. Yet when all that was stripped away, all the fright, all the horrors of war, he was a gentleman more than a soldier. And as such she would choose to remember him.

"Well..." Ethan cleared his throat again. "I shall see to the horses then."

He bobbed his head and made for the door when Caroline's vision landed on a heaviness in his coat pocket and she reached out.

"Wait."

Stopping with a jerk, he turned back. "Aye, Miss?"

"I..." Caroline swallowed, allowing herself a few seconds to think of what exactly she wanted to say. "I wonder, do you still have the timekeeper you took from, from..." *My captor? The soldier?* What should she name him?

The man's eyes widened and he faced her, reaching into his pocket. He retrieved it and held it out to her. "Forgive me. I should have known he would have taken such a thing from you."

Caroline's jaw opened, but no sound emerged. Did he think... "Oh, nay, I didn't mean—"

He took her hand, turning it slowly before placing the cold, heavy object in her palm. She looked up and held her breath. His eyes were dark, but welcoming. He closed her fingers around it, and stepped back. "It is home now. As soon you will be."

Without another look, he turned about and cut through the tent door, out of sight.

Caroline peered down. Opening her hand, she studied the gold trinket, remembering how James had cradled it as if 'twas more than a simple timekeeper—as if it held his heart.

Smoothing her fingers along the back, she felt the soft imprint of an inscription and turned it over. There, pleading to be read, the words inscribed on the smooth gold backing cried up to her.

*To have all, you need only have hope.*

*L. Armitage.*

Suspending her motionless, the delicate words sang through her heart, its prayerful refrain a melody only her spirit could hear.

Caroline looked up, a thought so wild consuming her she almost couldn't breathe. Could she? *Should* she?

Shaking her head, she dropped her hands to her sides. 'Twas foolish of her to even think of bringing it to James herself. But such would allow her to see him one last time. She stalled. He might be bound and gagged. Could she bear the sight?

Growling, she shook her shoulders. *Foolish, Carrie.* Nay. 'Twas more than foolish—'twas dangerous. A woman visiting a prisoner? She'd have to be mad to even consider it.

Yet...

Without allowing a second thought, she clutched the watch and strode through the door of the tent into the bleak winter. The small camp was alive with activity. About ten men or so. Some hovered bullet molds over flames, some with mugs to their lips. Muskets on every shoulder.

She clutched the watch in her fist. Did she dare it? She must. But where was he? Perhaps he'd already been taken away.

"Miss Whitney?"

Caroline spun with a gasp, feeling like a child caught in mischief. "Captain Donaldson."

He bowed politely. "What are you doing away from your tent? Are you unwell?"

"Nay, I am well, I thank you. I simply..." Did she think she could keep her secret from the man? Best have out with it, or surely her red cheeks would give her guilt away.

She exhaled and allowed her shoulders to drop. "I confess, you will not be pleased with what I am about to say."

"Has something happened?"

His genuine concern endeared him to her all the more. Anna had married the best of men. "Nay, I..." She lifted her hand, revealing the treasure it held. "This belongs to Captain Higley. I would hate for him to be separated from it. 'Tis such a lovely thing, and I had thought that perhaps I should—"

An explosion in the far wood slashed through her words and a ball whizzed past her ear, piercing the wall of the tent behind her.

Her heart leapt to her throat as Henry whirled, arms flying.

"Take your positions!"

Frozen, Caroline stared. A line of red advanced through the trees, weapons aimed.

Soldiers.

They'd come for her.

~

The report of a musket drilled through James's chest and he raced to the door of the tent. Slapping it open, his shoulders cramped.

They'd come for him.

He scanned the chaos, the need to find Caroline as vital as breathing. Then, as if guided by heaven, he found her standing motionless in front of a tent on the other side of the camp—the perfect target.

"Caroline! Run!"

He rushed forward, but the din of the attack drowned out the call of his voice. He growled and rushed back inside, praying Henry had left a weapon. He found nothing, and there was no time to go in search of one.

Rushing out again, he measured the line of soldiers. Not many, but enough to kill several and take even more. 'Twas the raid all over again.

He kept his sight on Caroline and charged toward her when a Patriot yanked him at the arm with a roar.

"You'll not be freed so easily." The man shouted, pointing to another militiaman. "Help me!"

James's muscles went hard with blood and he plowed his fist against the man's gut. Two others approached and he crouched, ready to fight. He allowed only a second for his vision to find her, as Ethan Barrik raced forward and hurried her away.

The blow to his side and another to his jaw sent him stumbling. They came again, but he straightened as rage ripped up his back. He didn't wish to pain them, but he would.

A punch to one face, then the next left each man flat out and reeling. Racing forward, James was forced to stop when the point of a sword met his chest.

"Surprise."

James snarled, his fists curled. "Pryer, let me go. We are on the same side."

"Are we?" He pressed the tip of his weapon into James's waistcoat. "Stockton has you trained well."

Another soldier appeared at Pryer's back, his glare as cutting as his brandished blade.

Pryer motioned with his head and the soldier moved toward James, taking his hands and wrenching them behind his back. "Greene tells me you have a price on your head."

"Where is he?" James's pulse thrashed so hard it strained his veins. The soldier prepared to tie him and he jerked, freeing one arm. "Where is Greene!"

Rarely had he felt fear. But he did now. And not for himself— for the woman he'd risked so much to save. He scanned the camp, his pulse thundering when he could no longer see her.

Pryer chuckled as if he hadn't heard him. "It seems you came upon this camp before we did. And 'tis a pleasant thing for us. They have made our catching of you that much—"

A shot rang out from behind James, and the soldier at his side went down in a heap as Henry rushed forward, smoking pistol in hand. Pryer's eyes widened and he raised his own weapon but Nathaniel swung up behind him, holding a knife to his neck.

He threw James a fierce look and yelled. "Go!"

Without a second thought James leapt forward, but a grasp on his arm stalled him.

"Wait." 'Twas Henry, a ready pistol in his grasp. He shoved it toward him. "God speed."

Whipping the weapon from his friend's hand, James charged to the place Caroline had been taken, knowing he would take time to thank Henry in the future. God willing.

Holding tight to the pistol, he fled, leaping benches and dodging fires as the men fought and yelled around him.

Putting fire in his feet, he barreled past the tent where Caroline had been and raced into the wood, praying he would not be too late.

Caroline's limbs were stiff, heavy, as the tenor in camp evolved from shock to organized rage.

Men raced and yelled, others crouched, shooting into the white cloud that approached.

"Miss Whitney!"

She turned as Ethan Barrik ran toward her. Grasping her arm, he pulled her beside him, shielding her with his body.

"Come with me."

More balls whistled over their heads and he pulled on her arm to hurry her.

"This way."

Heart at her throat, Caroline struggled to breathe. Her blood pumped wild until her arms and legs moved as detachments of her, thrusting her forward without her command. She must get to safety.

Holding tight, Barrik led her to a horse hidden some yards from camp.

Reaching for her, he prepared to lift Caroline to the saddle when a voice cut through her skin.

"Let her be."

Caroline looked to Barrik whose glare was on the man behind her. She dare not turn around.

Should she attempt to mount and ride to safety?

Barrik threw her a silent command to stay and despite all that screamed she do anything but, she remained motionless.

Moving in front of her as James had done before, Barrik's deep voice raked across the ice-covered ground as he raised his own weapon.

"On your way, Lobster. Or you will feel the cold lead of my gun."

Greene tilted his head back and the laugh he let free threw barbs into her back. "You wish to frighten me? 'Tis the woman you should be wary of. She cannot be trusted."

How dare he speak as if he knew her? He knew nothing! Slowly, she turned and every vein, every sinew cramped to stone. His weapon was drawn, and aimed not at the man in front of her. But at the knot of her cloak.

When her gaze locked with his, a smile moved over his lips. "Did you think you could get away so easily?"

Her frame quivered, and she curled her fists. This was the kind of soldier she knew—the kind of Redcoat she loathed.

"You will not have me." The words came out as if spoken by some foreign mouth. Her voice didn't even sound her own. 'Twas clearer, stronger. The fear she felt was tamped down by this bright flash of courage. "Nor will anything you do stop the progression of our cause."

Greene didn't move. "Such proud words will get you nowhere." His vision swung to Barrik. "If I have to go through you

I will." He flicked the gun sideways. "Step away and I will grant you your life."

"My life is not yours to take or leave," Barrik growled.

Nostrils twitching, Greene looked ready to spew fire. His glare stayed on the man while he spoke to her. "Come with me, woman. Give up the fight and perhaps your sentence will be lessened."

Barrik clicked the hammer of his gun and raised his arm to aim at Greene's chest. "She will go nowhere with you."

Greene tilted his head. "Foolish."

Two guns exploded simultaneously, but only one man fell.

Caroline screamed as Barrik writhed on his back, his hands clutching his chest. "Nay!" She dropped to her knees beside him as Greene charged forward. "You devil!"

He skidded to a halt and kicked Barrik in the head before he grabbed her at the hair, pulling her to her feet. "You have made me a fool once, but not again." He yanked and she cried out. He gripped harder, his gravelly voice cutting her ears. "Stop fighting me!"

"I will never stop fighting you." Clambering, Caroline tried in vain to claw her way free, but his grasp was iron.

With a yell he hurled her forward and she stumbled, landing on her hands and knees.

In seconds he was behind her, pulling her up by her cloak. He whirled her around, one vice-like grip on her arm, the other at her jaw. "What happened to your gallant rescuer?" His breath burned her nose. "Did they kill him? Hmm? Or will that pleasure be mine?"

Upper lip twitching, Caroline spit in his face.

The back of his fist came swift and hard to her jaw. A shock of pain unlike anything she'd known bolted through her face and head. Her eyes watered.

Greene neared, his exhale hot as he whispered beside her ear. "Do not worry. You and I shall have a bit of fun before I parade you through Boston like the traitor you are. Your cousin might have gotten away, but you, minx, shall not."

"Let her go, Greene"

Caroline whirled. "James!" He'd come for her.

Greene spun her around, his arm at her neck. "I should have known you would not be far behind."

James didn't move, his shoulders indomitable and glare sharp enough to cut flesh. "Enough. Let your quarrel be with me."

# CHAPTER 17

*T*he arm around Caroline's neck choked her, the rough wool of his coat pressing hard against her throat.

Barrik lay on the ground, writhing from the hole in his shoulder and the blow to his head that bled down his face.

Greene's available arm was extended, his breath hot on her ear as he spewed his hate to James. "I told you I would come for you."

"I never doubted." James paced forward with slow, methodical steps.

Caroline pleaded through her eyes, grappling for help from the one who'd helped her before. But his gaze never once fell to her.

"You truly believe this woman is worth so much trouble?" James's eyebrow twitched.

Greene's grip tightened and Caroline gagged for breath, tugging at his arm. *Air, Lord.* The world turned fuzzy and her limbs began to lose strength.

"You seem to believe she is." Greene wrenched her sideways and put his arm even more forward. "She herself is proof you are not what you say you are. You are the informant."

"Perhaps I am." His eyes flicked to Caroline. "Perhaps she is a spy." He walked closer, than stopped. "Are you willing to stake your future on it? Standing behind a hollow wall will give you little shelter."

Greene's grip tightened then suddenly released and Caroline fell to her knees gasping for air. Hands on the cold ground, the wood swirled around her as she sucked in huge breaths.

James went past, not once looking down. His eyes were on Greene. "Your conflict is with me. Not this woman."

"My conflict is with every Patriot!"

She struggled to her feet, coughing from the constriction of Greene's unyielding hold.

Stopping some feet away from Greene, James stood. Legs apart, shoulders straight and broad, his voice bellowed through the trees, louder even than the tumult that continued from camp.

"I tell you, Greene, you are wasting your time."

"You refused to bring her did you not? What other evidence is needed?" Greene's face turned crimson. "I have worked my way to captain. Toiled and pained to receive this honor. Everything you have was given to you. Your place in this army was bought. Where is the honor in that?"

Caroline's blood streamed through her as did cold confusion. What should she do? Wait? Speak?

The two men parried with their words and deathly gazes.

She peered at James who stood in front of her, again between her and Greene. In his hand a pistol. Was it loaded? There was no way to tell, and yet...

Owned by something primeval, she lunged and yanked the pistol from his hand and aimed it at Greene. "Get out. Now."

Greene's expression flattened before a mocking laugh echoed across the cold air. "Shoot me and your fate will be sealed."

The pistol grew heavy in her grasp as doubt clawed over her. What had she done? She could feel James's gaze but ignored the pull to look.

"I do not wish to shoot you." Her voice wobbled. "I wish only to be set free."

"That is impossible." Greene's vision never left her, and despite her efforts, it destroyed her pretended courage like a wave to a wall of sand. "I said I would find you, and find you I have. There is nothing you can do to keep me from my duty."

He took a step forward and she a step back. Her arm quivered. "Come no nearer!"

"Your fear betrays you." He continued toward her. "You will not shoot me."

"I refuse to be taken when I have done no wrong." Caroline allowed herself a quick look to James. His mouth was tight, ripples of anger moving the muscles in his jaw as he stared at their mutual enemy.

"You bloody Patriots!" Greene's tone boomed like cannon fire, his face red and sweating as he yelled and pointed to the camp. "You've brought this on yourself. This is your eternal future if you continue to go against the king."

In a burst, he lunged and Caroline's finger twitched against the trigger.

A flash of light and explosion from the gun moved slow, dream like. Greene's head whipped aside and a stream of blood sailed from his neck. He grabbed at the wound and fell backward.

Shock clutched her throat at what she'd accidentally done. *Dear Lord, help me.*

~

James lunged for her as she dropped the pistol. Her open mouth and round, fear-filled eyes screamed a truth he already knew. She hadn't meant to shoot.

Caroline went still, trance-like. James grabbed her at the arm and pulled. "We must get you away from here."

Stuttering, she moved with James but her gaze was still on her victim. "I...I didn't mean to—"

"Caroline!" He tugged her on, hoping the action would free her from the fear. "We must leave!"

Her frame quivered. "Is he dead?"

From the way Greene clutched his neck and groaned upon the ground, 'twas clear he was hurt, but not mortally.

"You've not killed him." James tugged her away, praying she could find presence of mind to move as swift as needed. "We must leave. Immediately."

Looking to James, her panic clutched him like a crying child. "Where will you take me now?"

Her hand in his, he kept her beside him, speaking the truth he hadn't prepared. "I don't know."

"Higley!"

James skidded to a stop, his hold still on Caroline. Henry Donaldson barreled toward them, then slowed and raised his hands. His wide stare jumped between them, landing squarely on Higley, a secret missive in his eyes, and his voice. "What are you doing, Higley?"

Higley pulled Caroline closer to him, fearing somehow her knees would give way. Knowing also, he must continue to act for her sake, and for anyone else who might be watching. "She is coming with me."

In the second it took him to speak the words, the truth of what he must do consumed him. There was no other choice now.

"What?" Caroline turned to him, the strength in her grasp a hundredfold. "Nay! Please!" She jerked forward, arm outstretched to Henry. "Do not let him take me!"

The plea cut him to the core, his chest pooling with sympathy. No doubt she was afraid. If only he could take her hands, explain his reasons, promise she would be well. But there was no time. Attempting to make clear all that must happen while she was so consumed with fear was a futile attempt.

"Go swiftly," Henry said. Every communication could be read in Henry's eyes, the pull of his mouth, the lowering of his hands. In his expression, a hopeful benediction rested, and he took a step back.

Caroline read it as well as James, he could tell, from the way she jumped and writhed to flee him. "Wait! Henry, no!" Her voice crashed through the air like sharp spears of ice.

Henry's throat bobbed and without another look, he turned and ran back to the melee of the camp, shouting for the doctor. "Nathaniel, come quickly! We've more wounded."

"Nay!" Caroline cried and wrenched at James's fingers. Her knees weakened and she grappled for him as she struggled for strength. "Why? Why are you doing this?"

He held her at the shoulders. "Caroline." He shook her gently. "Caroline, listen to me—"

"I shot him. I...I didn't mean to. I was trying to get away."

"Which is why you must come with me. Now."

"With you?" Her words came out in fractured bits, her volume rising. "Where? To Boston? To trial? Nay! I cannot—"

He shook her again and his motion rattled her jarred composure into stillness. There was no time to waste, though Nathaniel and Henry had the attack well in hand, standing here with Greene who was likely to regain consciousness any second was akin to standing in their graves.

"You trusted me before." He held her with his stare until the resistance in her stance subdued a degree and he repeated what he'd said before, this time more measured. "You trusted me before. You must trust me again."

Her eyes glistened and she swallowed. "I'm afraid."

He caressed her with his eyes as he couldn't do with his hands. "You needn't be. Not with me."

She blinked a few tears free. "Where then are you taking me?"

James eased his grip on her arms.

"I have no other choice, Miss Whitney. I am taking you to Boston."

~

Muddled voices droned in and out as Greene lay on the ground, his neck pulsing and head throbbing.

The warm liquid spilled from his neck, and he slapped a hand to the wound. Gasping, he sat up with a jerk as the world around him cascaded back to full light and color.

Curse that woman. Curse every bloody Patriot!

"Stay where you are."

Three men burst from the camp, themselves spattered with blood, most likely not their own.

They neared, two with weapons outstretched and aimed, the other with strips of cloth.

"Tie this one up first, Willem, while Dr. Smith sees to Barrik."

Greene's face cramped as recognition socked him in the gut. "So, you're the infamous Henry Donaldson, are you?"

Donaldson's face coiled into faux civility. "And who are you, Redcoat?"

Greene had encountered him a few times, though they'd never spoken. But his cowardly run from grace was not unlike Higley's and that was all he need know of him. 'Twas right those two should keep an unholy alliance. Both were worthless. Both traitors.

The younger soldier rounded, yanking his hands behind him. The instant his hold was taken from his neck the flow poured from the gash, as did the pain.

Helping Barrik to sit, the third man spoke something, patted him on the leg then rushed to Greene. Crouching beside Greene, the doctor kept his attention at his wound, his brow folding anger between his eyes.

"Captain Donaldson asked you a question." He whipped a

bandage from his pocket and pressed it to the gash on his neck. "What is your name?"

They couldn't demand anything of him. Greene swallowed a grown. The humiliation pained worse than the wound, but he covered that reality with ire-painted words. "I am a captain. You are a man demoted." Greene spoke to Donaldson, chuckling despite the searing tear in his flesh. "Your rebel army is worthless —nothing more than a shoddy mix of country boys throwing pebbles at a giant."

Donaldson's chest raised and lowered. "You won't tell me who you are? So be it. We will learn soon enough." He looked to the doctor. "Are the others safe?"

He nodded and stood. "The ones that lived."

Greene's jaw hardened, and his chest pumped up and down as the merciless reality impaled him. He had to accept it. They'd failed. James had fled—and with the woman who'd shot him.

Hate and rage married in his blood, becoming one and burning a trail of passion through his veins. How dare she? How dare James? If the need to find them before was paramount, now 'twas the only reason he breathed.

"Get him up."

Donaldson motioned with his weapon and the Patriot behind him tugged upward on his arms, forcing Greene to stand.

The doctor strode to Barrik, letting the man lean on him as he helped him to camp.

Donaldson kept the weapon aimed at him, coward that he was. "Put this nameless captain in the tent with the other prisoners and tie his legs."

The Patriot at his back shoved him forward and Greene stumbled, but never wavered his deadly glare at the traitor in front of him.

"You will regret this day."

He glared. "I believe that honor is yours."

With another nudge the Patriot moved him onward. *No Greene will ever amount to anything.*

Greene's mouth twitched as he marched through the small camp, the powder-darkened faces of the soldiers watching him as he went.

Every self-made man had impediments. No one's story was told without tribulation. So it was with him. This was merely a setback. Nothing more.

With a kick, the man forced Greene through the tent door and onto the ground. His knees caught his fall before his face could, and the exertion forced more blood through the gash on his bandaged neck.

He scanned the group as the man whipped him round and tied his feet at the ankles.

Reece sat in the far corner, slumped and frowning like a whipped puppy. If the boy had had any sense he would have taken a horse and fled. Now, they would have no rescue. The second he looked up Greene would cut him through. Idiot. He should never have brought him.

Abrams too had been taken and tied. Blast!

Why had he thought he needed help? He would have been better off alone.

The soldier pushed up and stood back, his expression knotted with hellish satisfaction. "Welcome to the Continental Army, boys."

# CHAPTER 18

*N*ight draped its frigid cloak across the cloud covered sky as James tugged Ginny to a stop. Little moonlight could be seen through the covering of clouds and trees. A fitting benediction for the kind of day it had been. Cold, dark. Frightful.

James's jaw ached from clenching. Here they were again. Exhausted from riding and fatigued from lack of food. But tonight there would be no cabin, nothing to fill their bellies, and no bed to sleep in.

He dismounted and helped Caroline to the ground before taking two bedrolls and tucking them under his arm.

Surveying the spot he'd chosen for them to make camp, he reserved a murmur. Not perfect, but would suffice. Thank goodness they would make Boston by tomorrow. It might take all day, but at least they needn't spend another night without shelter.

He peered up at the sky, praying God would withhold the snow that hung heavy above them, before marching to a spot beside a large tree. After brushing away the snow with his boot, he unrolled one woolen blanket and rested it on the ground. *Blast.* Reality socked him in the gut. These blankets wouldn't be enough.

To keep her warm through the night, he would need to keep her close.

He leaned his head back, squinting. The trees would provide proper cover should God ignore his prayers. With a sigh, he spoke over his shoulder. "We shall stay the night here."

As expected, she didn't move.

"Come." He motioned her forward, but still she refused to acknowledge him. "We shall need our strength for tomorrow's journey."

Her mouth pinched harder and she twisted away.

Stubborn woman.

He marched forward, stopping some inches in front of her, hoping his closeness would force her to relinquish her pride. It didn't.

The grumble that left him relieved none of the frustrations that roared like a frenzied army.

"You think I wish to have you along?"

That brought her head around.

He held her gaze. "You think it was my intent to bring you to Boston?"

"Wasn't it?"

What little light hovered around them revealed streaks of tears over her cheeks. Blast. He hadn't heard her crying. She'd been so silent.

He tempered is tone, but the fire still burned. "I did what I had to for your safety—"

"My safety?" She straightened her arms and jutted her head. "Am I not in more danger with a Redcoat then I would be with a camp of Patriots?"

Was she really so ignorant? "That camp was ambushed. I—"

He cut back his words and let his arms fall against his legs. Argument was futile. She was tired, cold, hungry and frightened. Knowing how such ailments worked woe upon trained soldiers, trying to make her see reason under such duress was pointless.

He pulled in a long breath of cold air and held it before pushing out all his frustration with it. "You need rest."

"I need rest?" She quirked her head. "You think I need rest?"

The storm in her eyes was about to batter him. James squared and prepared to be doused.

"I shall tell you what I need." Her dainty nostrils flared. "I need my mother to be herself again. I need to know my cousin is safe." Cracked and thick, her volume rose. "I need my uncle to not have died at the hand of a soldier. I need my brother to be alive!" She gasped as sobs carried the rest of her words. "It is men like you who have taken so much from us. Our lives were simple. We wanted nothing but to live in peace and freedom. But you wish to strip us bare!"

The tears flowed again. She shoved him, and he allowed it, listening.

"Now I am taken and with no recourse. Did you not think of what you have done? I've been left behind by my family, by the future that I'd wanted and now I have only the knowledge that I'm to be taken and tried when I am innocent."

She shoved him again, this time harder. "I am no spy, Captain Higley! But let me tell you this." She spoke through her teeth. "Were I, I would not hesitate to do everything in my power to undermine what you do!"

He remained silent, allowing her fractured revelation to shatter around them. A beautiful, tender truth that showed the soul of her that he found so remarkable. "I do not doubt you."

Quivering, her delicate features crumpled. "I didn't mean to shoot him. I only wanted to get away."

His throat thickened at the sight of her pain. A pain that seemed to reach out and hold him.

James swallowed, praying his voice would stay even. "I know." If only he could hold her...

He forced his arms to stay at his sides or else he would pull her to him.

Falling victim to the despair she held within, she dropped her face into her hands and sobbed.

Never had he known what to do with a woman's tears. The sight and sound of them tore at him, and the urge became impossible to resist. He neared and folded his arms around her, resting his cheek on her hair. The sensation was instant, powerful. *Heaven.* Not that he relished her tears, only her closeness, and the hope that his embrace could soothe her grief. Her sobs went on and she held to him, her fingers gripping the back of his coat while her soul slipped through and gripped his. There, in the insignificant wood, in the cold and dark of night, a side of his mountainous resistance sloughed away.

*Dangerous, James. Don't do it.*

But how could he not? One moment of intimacy was not a commitment. Holding her while she cried was not forgetting his vow. He knew such a thing was impossible—love, a family. A spy did not have such a life.

He closed his eyes, and moved his hand over her silken hair, inhaling the sweet scent of her skin. How good it felt to be needed. Not by some intangible thing, but by someone living. By her.

Her tears continued, and he allowed it. Weeping inwardly at what she and her family had suffered, but selfishly savoring the way she clung to him, the way she seemed to find in him the balm for her agony. He must savor it. For surely 'twould not last.

"James?"

She spoke through her tears as they began to calm, and the sound of his name on her severed voice made his own thicken.

He answered with his mouth against her hair. "Aye?"

The reply he craved, whatever it might have been, never came. He held his breath, hoping by his patience he might learn some secret part of her, but she remained silent, as if whatever she'd planned to say she'd chosen to keep hidden.

Perhaps 'twas he that should speak. Perhaps he should...

In a hurried motion she pulled away and lowered her face, dabbing her eyes.

The yearning to reach out and touch her, hold her against him again and soothe away the remainder of her tears made his muscles ache.

Caroline sniffed. "Forgive me." She raised her head and offered a tight smile before looking away again. "I know you are not to blame. And though you are the enemy, I find myself...puzzled over you."

Puzzled?

She turned to him. Confusion and yearning shimmering in the dark centers of her eyes. "I cannot believe you are what you say you are."

*If only you knew.*

A pain started in his center, a dagger of secrets both thin and sharp that stabbed straight through. What would she do if he revealed himself—told her he'd saved her uncle, set her cousin free?

What would she do if she knew he loved liberty as much as she?

The questions rained hard, more like jagged hail stones than mere drops. A woman as strong as she would be grateful at such a revelation. Perhaps...

Then, like a harsh rescue by some unseen being, he was assaulted by the raw edges of reality. Nay. He couldn't speak of it. Not ever. He'd promised himself, and the man he'd betrayed, that nothing would separate him from his duty. Most especially, not a woman.

Brushed by a wintery breeze, James rolled up any weakening part of him and tucked it securely away.

He stepped back, creating a much needed distance. "I may be the enemy. But that doesn't follow you cannot trust."

She dabbed at her eyes and sniffed, her gaze averted. Her mind worked. He could see it through the way her full lips pulled tight and her eyes studied some faraway place.

Then, she faced him. "Tell me this." Her neck corded and she breathed through her nose. "Why have you brought me? I know there is some reason."

Guilt left its slimy trail over his raw conscience. *To use you.* Nay. "To keep you safe."

"Why have you such an interest in my well being?"

"Why?" His volume began to rise with his unbidden frustrations he'd once thought he'd been rid of. *Because I'm beginning to care for you.* "Because I refuse to have you suffer by him."

Her face crumpled. "Do you believe me innocent?"

Hope drilled through her gaze and he couldn't help the answer. "I do."

Her shoulder's instantly dropped. "Then why bring me?"

"You wish to know why?" The truth blurted from his lips, a protective redoubt that would keep the rest of him safe from the barrage he feared might overtake him. "I am taking you to Major Anderson as a token. Proof that the colonials have poisoned even the minds of their women and will use them against the crown as quickly as they will their men."

Her face blanched and her mouth dropped open. "But...you told me you—"

"You are innocent, I know." He pulled back, spitting out the bitterness. "Bringing you in will prove that I am not what Greene claims I am and will soften the major toward me."

Caroline jerked. "You will use me?"

How miserable that sounded. He didn't wish to use her. The urge to tell her his mission, his work for Washington and his promise to get her free thickened his tongue and nearly spilled out in a whisper so low not even the snow would hear.

"I have a use for you, aye, but not what you think. You will have a way free. Believe me."

God would provide the way. He always did.

She stared at him then walked past. He followed her with his eyes, not missing how her frame trembled. Was it the cold, or his presence, that caused her to quake? Perhaps it was his revelation.

Sitting down beside the tree, she tucked her knees up and peered forward as if she were numb both inside and out. Painful silence danced between them, when suddenly she spoke.

"I cannot say what it is, Mr. Higley." Her tone was thick, fearless. "But something within begs me do the very thing I know I should not." She looked up. "You have twice now saved me from a man I know wishes me ill. And though I am inclined to run from you, I shall trust you—I shall go along with your scheme." Her tone sobered. "On one condition."

Condition? "And what is that?"

"That you help me save my brother."

⁓

Caroline sat motionless, clinging to her knees, dumbfounded at what she'd said. The words had sprung from her mouth without her consent, and she could only pray God had placed them there and that the Redcoat she'd come to trust would agree.

James didn't move, his broad shoulders straight and posture firm. The muscles in his jaw flexed as if he chewed over the prospect. She'd grown accustomed to that look, to the way he thought over things. He was not like other men she'd known who spoke without thinking nor acted without considering the consequences. Where James had wisdom and patience, Timothy had—

Caroline looked away, the thought stealing both her strength and her purpose. Why would she think of him now—after all these years? Allowing any thought of that man, of what he'd done and said, was a drain to her precious energy.

*I can't love you the way you are.*

She squinted and turned her head more, straining to squeeze the past from its hiding place, like dirty water from a rag. The only reason she thought of Timothy at all was because of James.

'Twas his gentleness, his sincerity, his strength of character—his mere proximity that forced her mind to places she didn't wish it to go.

"What do you mean 'save' your brother?"

James's quiet response tugged Caroline from the enclosing thoughts. She faced him, grateful the real purpose of her heart had been placed on the altar between them.

She licked her lips, fighting the shivers that rolled up and down her spine. It must be the chill. 'Twas a frigid night, and now they would be forced to sleep without shelter. Lord, help them. Her gaze drifted from his face to his chest and the memory of its firmness beneath her cheek as she'd wept threatened to dissolve the pillar that kept her resistance from collapsing.

His waistcoat and jacket were rumpled from where she'd gripped and spilled her emotions over him. He hadn't resisted, hadn't pushed her away. The way he'd held her, stroked her hair. The way he'd whispered against her ear...Her gaze fell to the ground. No one could truly be that genuine, that kind. Not really. Not forever.

"Caroline?"

She perked up, the melodious sound of her name in his masculine baritone sent pleasurable twirls through her center. *Do not think of him, Carrie. He will use you and you him. You have a purpose. Focus on it.*

"What has happened to your brother?"

James's quiet question coaxed her away from the sweet torture to which she'd succumbed and she pulled her posture against the tree, trying not to show how much she shivered.

"My brother is being held prisoner somewhere in Boston, and I wish to get him out."

James's eyes narrowed as he walked near her. "How long has he been there?"

"Since Bunker Hill."

She gauged his response, but he gave none. Though the British had won, they had suffered unthinkable losses. For the first time, as she studied him, waiting for the flinch of his brow or the tilt of his head, Caroline found herself devoured by the need to know more of him. Had he been at that battle? Had he lost a brother of his own? Perhaps he was new to the colonies—a recent arrival on one of the many ships the king sent almost daily? Who was James Higley *really*?

He continued closer, his boots crunching over the snow. "You wish him released from prison, then?"

"Released, or aided in escape." She shrugged, praying he saw strength over fear. "I care not how it is done only that it be accomplished."

Why must he come nearer? James stopped inches from her, looking down. "And you believe I can help you?"

She swallowed, her neck straining as she looked up at him from his towering position. "I do."

Slowly he crouched, resting his arms on his knees. "You say you are inclined to trust me."

Caroline's mouth refused any utterance. She nodded.

His eyes shifted, and he studied some far off place behind her. "'Tis my turn now to ask—why?"

Her pulse thudded and she gripped to what warm strength she had remaining. "I...I already told you, I don't know why. Need I a reason?"

A single eyebrow quirked and he tilted his head. "Most would feel compelled to trust for some reason, aye."

He pushed up and strode toward his mount. He tugged from the side of his saddle another rolled blanket and searched through a pack.

Caroline watched him, a weakness somewhere deep taking hold. If only he would hold her again, take away her fears—and keep her warm. "If you wish an answer, I suppose I can...think of one." Raising her chin, she tried to finish without revealing her chill in jostled words. "You are unlike the others."

He pivoted from his spot, still looking in his pack. "What others?"

"Greene, of course, and...and others." Perhaps it was the cold that loosened the lock on the past and set the ghosts free. Perhaps she believed she would never see him when their work was over and revealing her hurt to him was a safe way to unhook its claws. Perhaps she was simply a fool. Either way, it sprang free. "I knew someone, once, and...he was nothing like you. That is all."

Arms laden, James stepped toward her again, another blanket and other items in his grasp. Without asking permission, he knelt before her and draped the heavy wool around her. Not once meeting her eyes, he wrapped a scarf around her neck and tugged it up around her ears.

She should stop him. Tell him such an act was too familiar, too intimate. But her lips were frozen shut.

"There, you should be warmer now." He sat back on his heels, then moved his gaze, lacing it to hers.

Her breath hitched, and this time, not from cold. Caroline stared, shivering, and yet despite the frigid air, a real warmth started in her center. 'Twas his eyes that did it, the secrets and securities that nested in them. She could hardly see from the way the clouds and branches denied almost all light from the moon, but it seemed...it seemed that betimes the green of his eyes shielded demons. Yet, other times, as now, it revealed more than it shadowed. For somehow, the James Higley she craved to know shared a piece of his secret with her. Aye. Despite its clever wrapping, he shared it nonetheless.

In a blink the magic was gone, the warmth all but vanished.

He looked away and cleared his throat before holding her with another stare, this time, one more somber. "We have no shelter and I fear we may not make it through the night if we do not share each other's—"

"I understand." The answer leapt from her mouth, her response made more emphatic by the way her body shook.

"You understand?" His eyebrows flew upwards.

"You want us to share our warmth, Mr. Higley." A small, disparaging laugh breathed through her nose. "I am too cold to care about society's view of propriety at this moment. We do what we must."

A smile trickled over his face, followed by worry. Without an answer, he took the blanket from her hold and readjusted it before sitting beside her at the base of the tree. With the blanket over each of them, he moved his arm around her, tugging her against him.

Instinctively, Caroline swiveled toward him, too tired and too weak from cold and the shock of the day's danger to protest her own actions. A dream such as this she could never have imagined for herself. The quiet sound of his breath, his firm body and his strong arm around her made all her foolish dreams burst to life and dance in vibrant colors.

She might never again be held so close. Might never again spend the night in the arms of such a man. If her mother's words were prophecy then she'd lost her future when Timothy left. *Why must you speak your mind so, Carrie? You've turned him away.* Caroline closed her eyes. *If you only knew, Mother. If you only knew.*

Closing her eyes, Caroline conceded to the exhaustion and rested her head against James's broad shoulder. The chill took possession of her mouth and her mind, for she spoke, but it seemed more a dream than reality. Her teeth chattered lightly. "You are nothing like him."

"Greene?" James moved his head slightly, answering only after a few long breaths against her hair. "I should hope I am not."

"Nay." She didn't speak of Greene. *You are nothing like Timothy.*

Sleep swept in and out like waves on a beach, lapping at her strength and tugging her under. Her words droned on in spite of what little resistance she offered, her voice sounding less and less like her own.

She moved her head against him one last time, until at last

sleep pulled hard and held her. Still, her mouth found strength to move. "He pretended he cared, but...he lied. Then he left. But you won't..." A phantom filled her dreams and she shivered harder, holding to the one person she felt her soul knew, even if her mind did not. "You won't."

~

Any thought of sleep, any previous need, retreated into the blackness.

James's eyes were open, but he could see little as he stared forward, consumed by the words she'd spoken before falling asleep against him seconds ago.

Who had lied? Who had left? Not her brother surely. The thick, dreaminess in her voice had carried just enough grief, just enough regret, to reveal what he was certain she hadn't intended.

But still there were questions. Had she known this man long? Had she loved him?

She hugged James tighter in her sleep, and his pulse beat stronger before he mocked the weaker parts of himself. They each had secrets. Each carried a past. And there it should lie. Curiosity was a killer and he had best remember to leave secrets buried deep.

His scar ached in the cold, and he stifled a mocking laugh. 'Twas a fitting reminder of his purpose. A fitting reminder that this one night, in the dark and cold, might be his only time to hold a woman so close, to hear her quiet breath, and rest his head against her hair.

Regret cut over him like knives. Caroline Whitney was not just any woman. She was unique, beautiful and courageous. There were so many reasons to build a wall around his heart. Whoever had hurt her may have lived a lie, but he needn't know them to know that his lies were bigger, more dangerous, and more painful should she know them.

If God hadn't warned him before, He surely did now.

A rock formed in his gut. James had a duty to perform. He would be her protector, her guide, her help until his mission—and hers—was complete. But that was all. He could never be more. God help him.

# CHAPTER 19

$\mathcal{T}$he soft shuffling of a horse's hoof tempted Caroline's eyes to open. Heavy with the fog of sleep, it took a full three breaths before she remembered where she was, why she was there—and who she was with.

James's strong arm rested around her, his head back against the tree. The first hint of morning peeked at her through the covering of clouds, leaving marvelous, pale shadows across his face.

The urge to study him longer was a need she nearly obeyed. The horse made another sound and she turned her attention to it. She peered forward, allowing her mind to race to the places it wished to graze, however noxious the grasses. Yesterday's encounter in camp, the accidental shot at Greene lived like poison in her veins.

A shiver rippled up her spine, and not from physical cold. Greene had hated her before. What would he do now? Had he even lived? Perhaps she'd killed him. With exhaustion no longer holding her captive, her mind broke free, pondering the bitter dregs she'd refused to ingest hours earlier. The thought of taking a life—any life—stole the light out of her chest. She prayed to God he still lived. Though if he did, not only would the man accuse her of an act she hadn't committed, he would wish her dead for attempting to kill him. There was no doubt of that.

As reality cascaded over her, an avalanche of shock and fear, James released a deep breath and a sudden calm smoothed over her. Here, in the arms of a stranger, she'd found the only person she could trust. *James.*

Some faraway melody sang of a wavering dream, but 'twas too muddled to recall in full. Had she really said something of her past to him—revealed the wounded parts of her? Surely not.

Caroline's heart twirled in her chest the more she considered all she'd learned of him in two days. A question swelled through her chest. Why would he take her to Boston, only to promise to let her free?

She scowled toward the sunrise. Why would she allow it? Why would she go with him and not run from him while she could?

The cold clawed deeper and she tugged her cloak closer around her, but the action did nothing to change the way she felt. Not without, or within. James's nearness had stopped her shivering as he'd said. If only her heart would stop its flutters.

There was too much mystery about him to let herself fall prey to childish infatuation. His red coat aside, he was still a stranger. A roguish, handsome one.

*Please, Carrie. You shame yourself.*

James adjusted against the tree, his arm still around her, and she harbored a silent groan. How long until they were on their way again? Being beside him like this, forced by the nature of the silence and their situation to ponder the better qualities of him, was almost a greater torture than considering the formidable situations that led her here.

A sniffle tickled her nose and she reached for a handkerchief in her pocket when her fingers dusted over the timepiece hidden safely in the folds of her dress.

Carefully, she removed it, smoothing her cold fingers over the even colder metal. Whatever secrets this man carried were his alone. Somehow, she felt she knew him, felt she might go beyond mere trusting. But all that must be forgotten.

Theirs were lives destined for different paths.

She turned it over, the inscription shining through the air and into her spirit.

*To have all, you need only have hope.*

Caroline slammed her eyes shut and released a hard breath. If only 'twas truly that simple. She could not hope herself free. She could not hope Enoch alive—for indeed she might discover him dead after all.

She sniffed again and ran her fingers over the delicate words. What the days ahead carried, she couldn't know, and needn't. 'Twas enough to know that God would lead them. It would have to be.

Careful to keep every movement slow and silent, Caroline prayed for stealth as she slipped the watch in the outer pocket of James's coat, and with it, the hope of a future she would never have.

James feigned sleep as Caroline's dainty hand moved his coat pocket. Something dropped inside and he remained motionless as she stilled. Her gaze coated him, he could feel it, but didn't dare move. Moments passed until she shifted free of his arm and stood. He watched from slitted eyes as she stretched her shoulders back and moved her neck, no doubt stiff from hours in such a position. Walking toward Ginny, she petted the horse's nose before walking some paces into the wood. An urge to follow her shocked through his muscles, but he forced an instant calm. He would have seen deception in her eyes. She didn't plan to run.

In case she spied him from her place of solitude, he moved with practiced covertness and felt for the object she'd gifted him.

The instant his fingers touched the smooth, round object, his heart leapt to the heavens.

The timepiece.

How had she taken it? When? There hadn't been time to check the pockets of the wounded soldier before he'd taken her to safety. He'd believed it lost forever. But now…

He leaned his head against the trunk and looked up, aching in places long since devoid of feeling. Throat thick and eyes stinging, he peered toward the thin sunrise. How good she was. He must thank her. But there would not be time now as they must away, and mentioning things of the heart would only lower the defenses he must have at the ready.

Morning approached. Thank the Lord. And with it, the annunciation that his greatest work was upon him. The sooner they got on their way, the sooner he could ride toward his larger goal.

Only God could show him how to fulfill Stockton's wishes, and those of Washington. Only God could show him how to keep this woman safe, and how to set her free.

Free from capture. Free from his heart.

# CHAPTER 20

*H*ands tied at his back, Greene stared forward from his position on the ground in the center of the prisoner's tent. After so many hours of being alone in the dank, forgotten corner of the camp, Greene had supposed they'd been left to die until five minutes past sunset, when the doctor had come in.

"Your gash is deep." Crouching beside Greene, the doctor reached around for his bag, a lantern beside him. "You'll need it stitched."

Greene jerked back, paining his already throbbing neck. "You will do nothing to me."

The man's expression slid precariously over civility. He shrugged a single shoulder and pushed up on his knee. "If you choose to risk infection, that is your choice." Once his full height, he looked down, this time, a sheen of pathetic compassion in his eyes.

Compassion? As if Greene needed compassion. Who did he think he was? Some benevolent savior come to rescue him? He sneered. The pretended caring of the Patriots scrubbed salt into every raw wound. *If not for that woman...if not for James...*

Stepping toward the door, the doctor rubbed his hands with a cloth. "I'll check again in the morning."

Greene cocked his head. "I'll be gone by morning." He grinned with every ounce of hate he could press into the edges of his mouth.

"Will you now?" The doctor put the cloth in the bag before snatching the lantern and moving toward the door of the tent.

The doctor said nothing as the rust of disdain colored his complexion a hearty red, no longer any hint of pity. Good. Anger made them equal combatants.

"How are they?"

Donaldson pulled open the tent door and looked in, surveying their bounty of prisoners.

"Well done, soldier. You've caught us." Greene tilted his head, ignoring the pain the action caused. "What will you do with us now?"

The man refused to acknowledge Greene as he spoke to his companion. "Barrik is stable."

"Good." The doctor grabbed his bag and made for the door. "One other Lobster has died, but the rest will survive until we learn what Washington wishes done with them."

The words, like shovels, dug a pit in Greene's middle. Three had died altogether. All of them Pryer's men. He swung his gaze to the man whose head was bowed, lips tight and colorless. Pryer deserved no pity. Only the strongest survived. Every soldier knew the risks. Every leader accepted them.

Donaldson strode in, his hard gaze surveying Greene, then the others.

Greene followed his stare to Reece and Abrams who slumped in the far corner. Abrams nursed his animosity—'twas clear from the twitch of his mouth. Reece stared blankly at the floor, fear tracing his face and posture.

Wriggling to ease the pain in his arms, Greene looked up. "Though we've never met, I feel as if I know you."

Donaldson's gaze swung to him, unamused. The expression plucked delight from Greene's chest. "You are infamous. A traitor to the crown—the man who ran to the Patriots like a child runs to their mother."

Red seeped into Donaldson's eyes. His fists curled and he might have spoken, but the doctor touched his arm.

"Come."

Donaldson didn't move.

Greene side-glanced Pryer whose own interest in the altercation had brought life to his expression.

Best make the most of this.

Greene lifted his stare, shielding himself with disdain. "You were acquainted with James Higley were you not?"

He waited, then continued when no response was had.

"It seems he too has gone the way of the wicked and given his soul to the devil." His mouth twitched upward. "He's a traitor. Just like you."

"And yet 'tis you here, Greene, wounded and bound." Donaldson's unshaven jaw flicked and he rolled his shoulders. "I see it isn't working out for one of us."

Greene allowed a harsh smile and quick laugh. "For now." A grin sprouted over his lips. "I will find your friend and give him the justice you were too cowardly to face."

"You are going nowhere." A coiled snake hissed in Donaldson's expression, ready to strike.

The doctor tugged at him again. "Let's go, Henry."

Greene's fomenting pleasure radiated from his skin. "The devil was a traitor to God and the likes of you and Higley are no different here among men."

"Talk all you will of traitors and devils." Donaldson wrenched free of the doctor's grasp and leaned forward. "When this conflict is over we shall see who is the victor and who ends up in hell."

Donaldson scanned the group as if calculating some unvoiced

plot against them, then turned on his heel and slapped the tent door open, the doctor following close behind.

When their steps fell silent, Pryer spoke. "You will escape, will you? How?"

Greene wriggled his foot from his boot. There, tied to his ankle was a dagger the size of a pen.

What a dimwit Donaldson was.

Scooting around, Greene reached his foot toward Pryer.

Reece blanched. "What are you doing?"

'Twas as if the boy preferred this mire to soldiering. Greene didn't acknowledge the question.

"Take the knife out and give it to me."

Pryer scooted round and tugged the dagger free then, with his head wrenched back to see where he cut, sliced the blade back and forth over the thick rope that tied Greene's wrists.

The moment the last fragment broke free Greene plucked the dagger from Pryer's hand and moved to the one at his knees.

Pryer leaned forward. "Cut my hands free. Your knees can wait."

Winds of anticipated freedom blew through Greene's limbs and he cut more wildly at the rope.

"Cut me free!" Pryer spoke through his teeth, his words scraping over the air like a stone over grain.

With a snap the rope broke and Greene hopped to his feet, slipping his boot back into place.

"Sorry, boys. This is up to me now."

Pryer's face turned crimson. "How dare you—"

Greene lunged, the tiny weapon at the man's throat. "Any man who exposes me will never speak again."

He looked to the others. Every face was a maze of hate. What did they expect? They'd failed him. And he would be a fool before he let that happen again.

Let them hate. When he found Higley and exposed him, when

he was moved to major and commanding his own regiment, what would they say of him them?

Hurrying to the door, Greene peered out. Surely God prepared his swift escape. Only one man stood guard. A small one at that.

Lunging, Greene cut the blade across his throat, killing him before he could make a sound.

Dropping the body to the ground, he raced toward the wood and fled.

~

God be thanked the day's journey had gone as it did. No snow, no wind. Smooth travel, if there was such a thing. What he'd thought would take a full day had taken half the time. Another mercy of God, no doubt.

James pulled Ginny to a stop in front of the large home that served as officer's quarters on Boston's Beacon Hill. Only his rank and knowledge of some of the soldiers had gotten him across the neck as easily as it had. They'd said nothing of Caroline, perhaps suspecting her to be his woman.

His woman.

He looked down where his arm hooked around her small waist and fled the battle he'd been fighting since they'd left that morning.

She would help him forward his mission. And he would help her. That was all.

With a gruff sigh he dismounted then helped her to do the same.

Adjusting her cloak, she peered around. "So this is Boston, is it?"

"You have never seen it?"

She shook her head. "I have never been past Plymouth."

"Well...'tis hardly as grand as some make of it." He wanted to wink but didn't. 'Twould be too familiar. She would hear the jest in his voice just the same.

Sighing, Caroline's delicate brows pinched. "I suppose I shall not see the rest of it, if I am to be used as bait."

Bait?

"I never said anything about—"

"'Tis well, James." She turned her face to him. "I have resigned myself to it."

James trailed his gaze through hers, wading through the depth of their calming blue when a thought, foreign and lured with spurious temptations, dragged him into dangerous waters. What if he took her—right now—and ran. Away from the war, away from the blood and carnage that surrounded them. Would she go with him?

Would she want a life with someone like him? Could he keep his secrets from her forever?

She didn't look at him, but stared at the house some steps away where two soldiers flanked the doors as if awaiting some foreign dignitary.

Turning, she gazed behind to the town below, where the tall white steeple of the North Church stood out among the sea of homes and shops girding it.

Her throat bobbed and 'twas as if he could hear her thoughts before she spoke them. "How long will this venture be?"

The same question plagued him. "I cannot say."

"Will I be kept in a cell? A dungeon?"

He didn't know and didn't wish to answer. Prayers flew to heaven in her behalf. Were Anderson any kind of gentleman, he would keep her in the house—a prisoner of her room.

"It matters not." Arms at her sides, she looked to him and nodded. "It matters only what we do tonight."

"Tonight?"

She spun to face him. "We begin the search for my brother."

Many parts of her intrigued him. Her determination certainly one of them. "We can begin only as soon as we are able. I fear tonight—"

"Nay? Well, if you do not, then I shall."

"'Tis not that simple—"

"Is it not?" Her arms moved round as she spoke. "My beloved brother, whom we believed dead these many months, is within these city walls, and you wish me to wait?"

Determination was one thing. Rash impudence was another. "Acting without first thinking, without preparation and planning, will prove disastrous." He held her stare. "You must follow my lead, Caroline."

She pulled back, her cheeks red and lips pursed. "I believe since I am your prisoner, I must be Miss Whitney to you."

He snapped his teeth. Using her first name was somehow like breathing, it happened without thought. But she was right, and the distance that followed such formal familiarity would keep them both safer.

"You are right, indeed. *Miss Whitney.*"

She stepped back, as if she wished to place a wall between them. "Let us get on with it then, shall we?"

The separation pulled and James felt a pinch of something he pretended didn't pain him.

He nodded. "Follow me."

James tied Ginny to the hitching post, all the while pouring every morsel of his faith into God's goodness. Without Providence to shield and guide them, both would be brought to an early grave.

He motioned her to him, and 'twas then, he noted the tremor in her knitted fingers. She'd not trembled the full ride here. Was she so nervous?

He berated himself. And why shouldn't she be? Why shouldn't he? He could only hope the major was as benevolent as his avowed reputation. If not, he would have to see to her escape and that of her brother more quickly than he thought.

Starting the long walk up the wide steps, James memorized the placement of the doors, the windows, the width of the house and its distance from the road. He would need these specific locations in his memory for the time he let her free.

Made of brick and two stories high, it boasted large windows in front and two massive chimneys on the sides. It seemed the kind of place one read of in books, not something that should grace the modest hills of the Massachusetts seaside.

He heard her sigh and swung her a sideways glance. "Do not be afraid."

She stared forward, voice fragile. "A futile request."

James swallowed, berating himself. "Speak only when spoken to."

Suddenly she stopped. "Will you be with me?"

The fear she tried to mask lived in her eyes.

*I would not leave your side.*

"I hope to be." How vapid that sounded, how hollow. He sent another prayer toward heaven. There were more reasons to worry over her safety. Men like Pryer and Greene were rampant in the army. If any of them dared touch her...

*Protect her, Lord. Protect us both.*

They continued the last length of walk until the two soldiers eyed him at the door.

The one on the right spoke, and his voice played tunes inside James's memory. "Higley?"

James studied the long boyish face of the soldier he hadn't seen in years. "Edmond?"

Tall and thin as ever, Edmond Blakely grinned wide and extended his hand. "What a pleasure it is to see you, sir. I thought you'd been stationed in New York."

"I was indeed, but have since been stationed here." James peered to the other soldier, who, though silent, was saying enough with his eyes as he stared Caroline up and down.

The mongrel. He'd known she would attract attention. But

how to keep it at a minimum was more a trial than he'd realized, and they'd been here naught but sixty seconds.

He inhaled, turning his attention to Edmond. "I'm here to see Major Anderson."

Edmond nodded, smiling. "Of course." He opened the door and motioned forward. "This way."

James bowed his thanks. "And you may introduce me as *Captain* Higley."

Once inside, Edmond turned, his eyes wide. "You've been promoted, have you? I am not surprised. I too have been promoted, but to lieutenant. Anderson seems to appreciate my dedication. Since you and I were last together, I returned to England with part of my company, and I have been in his service since that time." Stopping, he looked to Caroline. "James, where are your manners? Will you not introduce me to your lovely companion?"

James growled inwardly then pretended all the rough civility he'd practiced. "She is not my companion. She is the reason I must see the major."

"Aw. Well then..." Edmond's geniality wilted, but only slightly, before he started toward the expansive hall.

In the large entry, a high ceiling and chandelier announced whoever owned this home had immense wealth and consequence. That is, before the army took it upon themselves to make it their own.

Edmond turned and raised his hand. "Wait here."

The soldier stepped toward a closed door, the echo of his boots bouncing off the dark walls.

James forced himself to play his part, to keep his act always inscrutable, though the pain of not looking back, of not taking Caroline's hand to stroke away the worries, made his fingers twitch.

Blessedly, Edmond reappeared seconds later. "He shall see you."

In a moment." He looked to Caroline and gestured to a chair beneath a large mirror. "You may wait here."

Caroline's dainty neck bobbed and she sat, placing her hands at her knees. Edmond took James at the arm, leading him toward the partially closed door. His voice was a mere whisper. "It has been years, James." A sudden sobriety owned him, his brow drawn and tone thick. "How are you?"

So much implied in three simple words.

His friend's genuine caring rubbed off one of the memories' hard edges but the rest remained. "I am well."

"I must admit I worried over you, knowing how you felt about…"

Edmond cleared his throat and lowered his arm. James's scar burned, but he pretended not to feel it. He knew what his friend would say and wished to deflect it before it hit the air.

"Lieutenant then, hmm? Congratulations, old friend. How long have you—"

"I still think of it. Don't you? What happened with Loden?" Leaning forward, Edmond lowered his tone another step, clearly intent on unearthing the recollection James was loathe to relive. "He was a good man, despite what he did. I still cannot believe him—a Tory—capable of crimes against the king. But it seems—"

"'Tis in the past." *Blast.* The man spared no time getting to details. "I have moved on."

"'Twas nothing short of a tragedy." Edmond continued and James steeled himself against the forthcoming barrage. "You are not the only one to be shocked by it, you know. We all were aghast at the news—his hanging the worst of it, of course. But he was guilty, I suppose. There was naught else to be done."

The more he spoke, the more James went rigid, his bones filling with iron and holding him motionless. A door opened beneath him and he fell hard into the rotting past he'd tried so hard to forget. The foul stench made his eyes burn as the memories clung to him.

Then, as had happened so many times before, everything began to change. The hall became a humid night, the ceiling a starry sky. And Loden before him, bruised and chained, reached out with tears on his cheeks.

*"I am innocent, James. You must tell them."*

*"You know I wish to, but how can I tell what I do not know. All evidence points to you."*

*Loden clung to James's sleeves, his face red with pleading. "Believe me!"*

*Quivering, James held back tears. "If only I could."*

"You don't still blame yourself?"

Edmond's quiet voice blinked James back to the present. Such a question. He stared into the corner, his head almost too heavy to lift. The answer hadn't changed.

He looked back to Caroline who sat rigid in her chair. Here was a chance to prove himself. To show he was not the man he'd been before. If God would let him, he would make it right. Until the day he died.

Facing his companion, James pressed a hard smile to his mouth as he stepped out of the pit where he'd fallen. Surely the man wouldn't belabor it any longer. "Are you pleased to be back in Bost—"

"Your ear looks ghastly. Never healed proper did it."

Enough. "Is Anderson ready for me?" If not, James would tie this man's mouth shut. "I am happy to wait elsewhere."

As if surprised at the sudden question, Edmond shook his head. "Nay, he is ready now."

Thank the Lord.

James bowed and moved down the hall, passing a smile to his friend and speaking a secret prayer that he might not be forced to endure another such conversation.

At the end of the grand hall, a large door rested a few inches open.

"Major Anderson, sir?"

James pressed the door slightly when a thick voice peeled through the small opening.

"Come in."

He took in a long breath before striding through the doorway. "Good day, sir."

At his desk and engrossed in whatever was on the paper before him, Major Anderson spoke with his head down. "You are lucky I have so much trust in my lieurenant or I would not have granted you such a hasty audience." He sighed, still looking at his work. "What do you want?"

"I am Captain James Higley, sir. Major Stockton sent me to see you."

At this his eyes flicked up though the rest of him remained motionless. He waited, the large clock at the wall ticking loudly. "Did you say Higley?"

"Aye, sir."

The man removed a pair of spectacles and squinted as if his mind tried to correct a blur. "Are you any relation to Thomas Gage?"

*Would it entice you more or less toward me?*

James nodded, knowing he couldn't deny such even if he wished to. "I am indeed, sir. He is my uncle."

"Ha!" Placing his glasses on the paper, the man stood and rounded the desk, arms out. "How delighted I am to see you."

James froze at the man's surprising warmth then quickly regained himself and mirrored his geniality. "And you, sir." Bowing, he allowed a real smile on his face despite the cold shock that coated him. Had he met the man before but didn't recall it?

Anderson extended his hand and James took it.

The major squeezed his grip and patted James on the arm. "To what do I owe the pleasure?"

He would get straight to business then. Good.

Righting his posture over his ride-weary legs, James nodded. "Major Stockton has—"

"You know, I adore your uncle. I really do. 'Tis a shame so many deride him. But don't worry that you shall hear such talk from me." Major Anderson stepped back, inspecting James with a wistful grin as if his memory carried him to a different place. "Very fine man, indeed. And his wife—so lovely."

James smiled, stuttering. "Thank you, sir. I...I do agree."

Major Anderson clapped him on the back and led him toward the desk, gesturing to a chair. "It has been far too long since I have seen him. How is he?"

Seeing as how James hardly knew the man himself he struggled for the proper response.

"Since his return to London, sir, I cannot say, but I like to believe he is well."

Pondering, the man nodded. "Aye, let us both believe that is true." Anderson flipped back the tail of his coat and took the seat opposite James at the desk. "Tell me then. What can I do for you?"

"Major Stockton has sent me as an envoy sir—as a welcome, really—to the city. We are most pleased you have arrived, as it seems we are in need of good leadership."

Anderson's eyebrows went up. "Howe is your general in command is he not? Does he not provide good leadership?"

"Indeed, sir. Of course." Every word was a lead weight. Placed wrongfully, they would drown him. "We are simply grateful to have additional help against the provincials, sir. They are gaining strength."

"'Tis their hubris that provides them Greek-like toughness. But it shall be short-lived."

A more perfect interlude he could never have orchestrated. "I have brought you...a gift of sorts."

"A gift?"

James rose, laughing politely through his nose. "A token more like. Proof that our work here in the colonies, our effort to eradicate their rebellion, is vital."

He motioned to the door and Anderson quirked his head. "Lieutenant?"

Slowly, the door swung revealing Edmond first, then Caroline.

There at the end of the hall she stood, her hands clasped in front of her, her chin level and eyes as clear as springtime.

Edmond motioned to her and she neared, walking down the hall as if James had called her to the gallows.

James's spirit flew to her, took her by the hand and whispered words of comfort. If only she could feel them. By the tightness of her mouth, she did not.

Anderson's expression jumped over several emotions before descending on curious delight.

"Well, well, well. What have we here?"

# CHAPTER 21

*C*aroline held her breath as Major Anderson swept his fingers through the air, beckoning her forward. "Come, I shall not bite you. Look at her, she appears like a deer in a wood, ready to flee from danger."

Caroline did as commanded, going as far as the center of the room before she stopped.

Anderson came round to her, inspecting her with pursed mouth and squinted eyes. He looked to James, chuckling. "She appears to have slept in the dirt. Have you brought me a street urchin?"

Straightening, she rubbed her finger against her thumb to ease a modicum of tension. Certainly she looked a mess. She'd thought of it several times, but Anderson's comment made reality stare her in the face. Having not washed or changed since before leaving home, and the thought of how her hair must be...She groaned inwardly, a wave of embarrassment rolling through her.

Unbidden, her eyes raised to James and every former thought fled. His eyes were soft, his intent unmistakable, despite what he professed. "Major Anderson, I have brought you a Patriot spy."

The man jerked back, surprise more than shock in his words. "A spy? You jest."

"I do not, sir." James smiled like a Roman with his bounty, but she could see past his act. "I apprehended her in Plymouth."

"You don't say." He put a hand to his mouth. "The Patriots are making women do their work for them, is that it?"

"I work for no man, but for The Cause." Caroline shrank back at her sudden gumption, an instant rush of regret flooding her limbs. *Why can you never stay silent?*

Both James and Anderson stilled, their eyes round.

"She speaks!" Anderson looked to James then Caroline, his easy tone dipping for a harsher one, but it leveled at curious civility. "I am inclined to think you do not know what you do, my child. Those who work against the crown are not treated lightly. Why not stay at home and sew stockings like the others?"

Caroline's neck and ears heated as she met him eye to eye, the need to speak her mind an impossible appetite to cure. "If I were to give my time to anything of lesser importance than one's liberty, sir, I should think myself unworthy."

"Unworthy?" Anderson crossed his arms, studying her as if she were some foreign curiosity before turning to James. "Do all these Patriots speak such a way?"

"Remarkable, is it not?"

James chuckled before scolding her through a granite stare. Couldn't he read her regret? She didn't wish to cause trouble. But how could she not speak the truth?

Anderson took another step back, looking her up and down without the slightest hint of shame. "Tell me, what is your name?"

Caroline swallowed, wetting her throat. They hadn't considered if she should use her real name or a faux one. Too late for that now. "I am Caroline Whitney, sir."

Arms still crossed, he tilted his head and stared for so long the silence began to suffocate. His chest lifted and lowered before he changed his stance and rested his arms at his sides. "Are you sorry for what you have done?"

Caroline balked inwardly but kept an even exterior. "Sorry?"

"Aye." Anderson spoke slower, as if to emphasize his words. "Do you wish to renounce your actions and commit to a life of service to King George?" He stepped back and shook his head like a father about to scold his child. "I cannot conceive of someone as young and—forgive me—as lovely as you, wishing to throw their life away for something that has no value?"

"No value?" Caroline thrust her head forward. "Sir, you cannot truly believe that—"

She turned her head and instantly her gaze collided with James. His expression was a reprimand, his posture a warning. Her stomach went hard and cold in the same moment. *Stay the course, Carrie. Be yourself, but be wise.*

Stepping back, she lowered her chin. "Forgive me, sir."

"I will not argue with you, child." Anderson became ever more the admonishing parent, while beneath his benevolent exterior, a monster crouched. "Will you or will you not denounce your actions and give yourself another chance at a peaceful life?"

The urge to speak her heart, to let fly all her treasured beliefs, all her reasons for what she believed nearly exploded from her skin. But she kept it back by the grace of God alone.

Caroline straightened her arms at her sides, praying some heavenly help would give her strength to speak while staying calm, civil. "My peace, Major Anderson, comes not from a life of ease and serenity, but from living my conviction, no matter the consequences."

She allowed the words to settle on the air as a rich reticence fell around them. She could not have said anything more true. Thank the Lord for giving her the ability to speak what lived in her heart.

"Most fascinating." Anderson's mouth bowed down, his hand over his chin. He looked to James, then to Edmond, who stood just outside the door. "Lieutenant Blakely? Have my wife's trunks arrived yet?"

"This morning, sir."

"Good." He released an audible breath as if he hadn't known what to say until that moment. "Have my men bring them up to the guest quarters. And you will tell Olga she's to attend to this woman with whatever I command."

"Aye, sir." The soldier bowed his head in acknowledgement.

Caroline threw a frantic look to James but he could offer naught more than a miniscule tilt of his head. What did the man mean by speaking of guest quarters? Was she to stay here?

"I find myself quite taken with this coquettish Patriot spy, Higley." Anderson's mouth tilted at one end.

James straightened. "Sir?"

He made his way toward his desk. "I wish Miss Whitney to stay a while."

"Here?"

At his chair, he stopped, a look of disappointed shock on his face. "Why ever not? I believe we could glean some insight into the mind of a colonial rebel from having her among us. And in truth, some dank, cold prison is no place for such a lovely lady." He winked at Caroline before flipping his coat tails back and sitting. "I should like my fellow officers and soldiers to learn from you before I decide what is to become of your future."

James blinked, pure shock in his eyes. "You are most generous, sir."

Anderson sat, sorting through his papers as he spoke. "My wife has sent her maid along with her old gowns before her, as she is still on her way from London. She is not expected for another week, and I take it upon myself to offer Olga and the gowns to you for the time being." He looked up briefly then nodded. "You appear to be about the same size."

Caroline's frame flared hot, then cold, as a thousand questions fanned through her. She cleared her throat, remembering her manners. "Thank you, sir."

"Dinner is at eight." Without another glance, he brushed them away. "You are dismissed."

The lieutenant neared, arm extended. Goodness dwelt in his eyes and the ample slope of his smile.

Bowing her head, Caroline followed him out, praying James would do the same. There was so much to say, though 'twas unlikely she would be allowed to say it, or anything at all for that matter. A mere look would have to satisfy.

Following the smiling stranger into the hall, she left a trail of prayers behind her.

She and Enoch were both prisoners now, but not for long. James had given her his word. And whether 'twas wise or not, she had made the decision to take it.

～

James bowed then marched to follow her out when Anderson called him back.

"Captain Higley?"

Wrangling a curse, he pivoted back, all politeness, while his insides twisted with the need to be at her side. He needed to soothe her harbored fears, pledge again his promise to protect.

He nodded. "Aye, sir."

The thickness of the man's stare poured over him like tar. "Have you quarters yet?"

"Nay, sir."

"Good." Anderson pressed his attentions on his paper. "I should like you to stay here as well. Seeing that you are Stockton's envoy, it follows you should be housed here until he arrives."

James dipped his head, fighting the delighted disbelief that coated his posture. "I should like that, sir." A clear answer to an unspoken prayer. *Thank you, Lord.*

"I hear so many different tales of you." Anderson rested his palm against his desk and sat back, a sheen of commanding superiority owning his frame as he studied James from a distance. "I should like to know what is true once and for all."

"Aw, well." Chuckling, James chose levity in place of gravity. "I should tell you, Major, *everything* you hear of me is true."

The very tips of the major's mouth twitched up, and his eyes squinted ever so slight. "I like that."

With a swift bow and cordial grin, James hurried into the hall, praying Edmond had waited for him. But they were gone.

Panic struck dissonant chords. She couldn't have disappeared so soon. The thought that perhaps some secret deception had been played on him dried the blood in his muscles.

Spinning about he scanned the expansive entry and the stairway that led to the chambers above, when he saw a brush of color disappear around the corner above the stairs. In a rush, his blood began to flow again. Thank the Lord. She'd already been shown to her room.

Good. James righted his posture. He needn't see her. This distance was much preferred to closeness. He neither needed nor wanted the distraction she gave. Washington required a man with full purpose of heart, not one made weak by vicissitudes of the heart.

Marching toward the door, he set his mind on finding the livery for Ginny and penning a cyphered message to Henry. There was enough to keep him occupied until dinner. More than enough.

# CHAPTER 22

*L*eft alone since the afternoon's introduction, the dinner she was to attend was long in coming. Even with her exhaustion and hours aplenty to rest in her bedchamber prison cell, she could not find respite in sleep. With her mind continually on Enoch and the knowledge she was so close—that soon they would find him and free him—was too much to consider and prepare to fall prey to slumber. Even if she had the enjoyment of a relaxed mind in such a circumstance, she would not have had the means to employ it, as nary a single book was to be found in her prison. The thought produced a sigh. A room was not a room without a book.

No matter how she pined for her brother, or a way to ease her tensions, there was much that stood between her and her goal. For now, there was dinner.

The bath the maid had assisted her with was as blissful as heaven. With clean hair that smelled of a spring garden, and skin that tingled after the delight of scrubbing, she felt presentable for the evening. Though she wasn't intending to impress anyone, certainly. James was about business and so was she. This dinner was a necessity. Dressed as if she were attending some foreign ball, she would play her part. For the greater good.

Caroline stood in front of the tall looking glass, begging her lungs to breathe. Never had her stays been pulled so tight. She attempted another inhale, but a shallow gasp was all her lungs could allow.

She reached out to the chair beside her and pressed a hand to her stomach. How would she be able to make it through the evening without fainting, let alone eat?

'Twas all for Enoch. That she must keep before her. That alone would carry her through. And tonight they would find him. They must. There was no time to waste. She could, and would do whatever it took. *Dear brother, I am coming for you.*

Lifting her eyes again to the mirror, she stalled, allowing her mind to ponder on what she'd yet to truly admire. Such a gown. She twisted this way and that, examining the back of the soft green gown and marveling at the way it plumed when she moved. Lovely. Its delicate moss color, its floral pattern and pink bows that lined the center of the stomacher were nothing short of breathtaking. A piece of art, truly. The softest of lace and most delicate ribbon fringed the neckline and sleeves. The Anderson's were of wealth, no doubt. Caroline smiled to herself. Perhaps she could endure the discomfort for an evening. She'd never seen her waist so impossibly tiny. Is this how all the ladies in London dressed? Paris?

Chosen for her by Anderson's wife's maid, Caroline looked down to the stomacher. Perhaps the woman had had no choice but to tug the stays ridiculously tight. The pins holding the gown together seemed ready to spring from their hold.

How small *was* this officer's wife?

Caroline smoothed her hands down the bodice and promised herself tiny sips of air would be sufficient. Dinner could not last long, could it?

She reached up and tugged at a thick curl that rested against the cream of her shoulder.

A trail of foolish thoughts paraded through her mind. What would James think of her? She swallowed. Did he think of her at all? She assumed he would be at dinner, but what if he was not? What if he'd forgotten her—left her here? Nay, of course not.

She dusted her fingertips over her lips. Often in the looks he gave, those times when he thought she couldn't see through him, there was something in his eyes, a softness that she craved to know the meaning of. In truth, she craved to be the reason.

Straightening, she inhaled to flee the captive imaginings, and her breasts swelled high. Caroline blushed and pulled at the lace. Must it be cut so low? She'd never worn such a gown. As if consumed, her mind filled once more with James. He had likely seen ladies dressed this fine a hundred times or more. 'Twould be nothing to him. *She* was nothing to him. She didn't wish for his attention no matter what her frail, girl-like heart might choose to entertain.

*Knock. Knock. Knock.*

"Miss?"

'Twas Olga.

Caroline twisted toward the door. "Come in."

The squatty woman entered and waddled forward, her round cheeks ruddy, and her gray-streaked hair pulled back in a bun.

Not once looking Caroline in the eye, she neared and turned her at the waist, examining the gown.

"Good." She brushed her hands toward the door. "They wait for you."

Caroline's legs went wooden. They did? She didn't know what to expect let alone where to go. She leveled her posture. *You are no weakling, Carrie.*

She grinned at the sour woman before hurrying out, praying dinner would end before she fainted. From now on she would tie her stays herself.

Below stairs at last, she stopped in the large hall that opened into the entry, listening for sounds from the dining room to invite her in.

The hush of voices turned her about and she stared down a dimly lit hall, her fingers trembling despite the chorus she repeated to herself. This would not last. Soon she would find Enoch and return to Sandwich and this whole thing would be nothing but a memory.

Continuing down the hall, she prayed for more air when from a dark corner a hand reached out and tugged her into the shadows.

Fear squeaked from her throat as the man spun her around and pressed her back against a wall.

Caroline gasped. "What are—"

"Shh."

A finger pressed against her lips and every fear smoothed at the touch. She needn't see nor hear to know whose firm hand held her.

"James," she whispered. Her muscles slumped as relief took the place of panic. "What are you doing? Are you not coming to dinner?"

His reply was hushed, his face inches from hers. "I've been waiting for you."

As her eyes adjusted to the weak light that filtered in from the hall, her heart fluttered. Clean-shaven and in a new red uniform, James appeared more the hero from some fictional tale. Shiny buckles and buttons winked with the pale light, but not as much as his eyes. Nay, he couldn't be real. No one was so perfectly masculine, and at the same moment, so tender. But his fresh scent and the way his soft breath met with hers in the quiet dark testified he was real. Completely, wonderfully real.

Caroline fumbled to recall what he'd said so she could answer him, but his closeness vitiated her thoughts, and her tongue.

Thankfully 'twas he that filled the silence. "I feared, since you were whisked away so quickly, you would think I had abandoned you."

He did? Her knees weakened and she pressed her palms against the wall behind her. The fact he worried over her did mystical things to her middle. She swallowed and offered a playful grin. "I hadn't thought at all about you."

His smile flashed white, and she could feel his gaze roam over her.

James released his hold, his voice near silent. "I wanted to find you before you came to dinner."

She whispered not only for secrecy, but to hide the tremor his closeness spawned. "Oh?"

"I wanted to thank you."

"Thank me?"

He was silent before replying, his accent a pool of warm honey as it kissed her ears. "You returned my pocket watch. I am indebted to you."

"I..." Her skin flashed with heat and her mouth went dry. "It didn't seem right such a thing should be taken from you. 'Tis clear...'tis clear it holds meaning to you and I—"

"It does." He embraced her with his words. "And I will forever be thankful."

Her pulse ran mad and she waited before answering, in hopes her reply wouldn't reveal more of her feelings than she wished. "You are..." She exhaled slow. "You are most welcome."

That he should feel such a depth of gratitude made her swell with pleasure. The more she learned of his heart, the less she noticed the dye of his uniform. He was not merely a soldier. He was a man. A good one. One she might actually...

She shifted her feet to readjust her thinking. "Was that...was that all you wished to tell me?"

"There is one more thing." James nodded toward the hall. "We have a guest."

Her stomach pinched. "A guest?"

His answer was long in coming. "Major Pitman arrived not long after us."

"Should I know him?"

"Nay, but I do. And now he knows of you."

Caroline's already pinched lungs tightened all the more. "He does?"

"Do not worry." Caution rimmed the richness of his voice. The trembling of her fingers started again, and instantly his warm hands covered hers, as if he had seen her fears through the dark and wished to comfort. "I have tempered both him and Anderson. Besides, they are helpless in the face of feminine beauty. You will be safe so long as you do nothing rash."

She locked her knees to keep from toppling. Her fingers trembled more, and his grip tightened. "I don't know what to do, or what I should say."

James's smile, like a gift, coated her in warmth. "Be naught but yourself." His whisper caressed. "Say what you feel, with grace and conviction, as you did before." He leaned forward, his lips near her ear. "They will be smitten."

How to speak? Her words came out broken. "For my brother's sake, I pray I do well."

The beat of her heart echoed between them. Surely he could hear it.

If her legs had strength she would flee to the safety of the hall, but they refused any action. They knew where she wished to be, and would keep her there.

James pulled back, releasing his hold on her, that familiar wry smile to his lips. "'Twas dangerous of you to wear such a gown."

"Dangerous?" With effort, she found strength for her voice. "Well, we are at war, are we not?"

He tipped his head toward hers. "With such beauty and strength, I daresay you will have the power to win them to our side."

Caroline pulled back and studied his eyes as they roamed her. "Our side?"

James straightened, a sudden mask in his expression. The magic between them still sparked, only dimmer. "They will be lenient when they discover your Patriot friends have set you free."

She tugged her hands from his, grateful he'd moved away. "That is your plan then? To make it look as if I have been rescued? And what of Enoch? When shall we go in search of him? I am ready tonight."

James didn't move, didn't speak. He stared at her in the small space, as if a universe lived within him, and he wished to share it, but hadn't the power.

"As am I. But we must wait, Caroline."

The cadence of her name from his lips made her own voice quiver. "Please, James."

"I gave you my word, and I will not rescind." His hungry eyes seemed to yearn to pull her to him. "We will find him, but we must be wise. If we move forward too quickly it will bring only more suspicion upon us and we cannot risk—" Of a sudden he went rigid and she nearly spoke but his upraised hand silenced her.

Someone approached.

Holding her at the waist he swung her back, shielding her from view with his tall, broad frame. He looked down at her, begging her silence with his own. Caroline held her breath as two men carrying large trays of food walked past, their faces forward.

Every carved muscle of his face tensed, all but the ones that ringed his eyes. Slowly, he lowered his hands from her waist, his timbre a caress. "Come. They are waiting for you."

# CHAPTER 23

From across the table, James spied Caroline. Her pink cheeks and tight mouth were easily read, if only by him. She refused to meet his gaze and his masculine pride rallied. Neither of them could deny it, the torturous beauty of the tension between them. She felt it. He knew she had, the same as he. And 'twas the reason she averted her gaze. Though 'twas just as well. Her tilted head offered a far better view of her delicate features. He told himself not to look, to instead focus on the savory scent of the soup, the conversation, but like a feather carried in a blustery wind, he was helpless, a captive to the pull of his heated pulse. What was it about her? How had she, in so little time, disarmed him?

It should cause him to rally his defenses. It should shake him to the core. The fact that it did neither, was a frightening truth that made him writhe in his jacket.

She prepared to take a sip of her soup when her gaze flicked upward and collided with his. His heart flared, though 'twas only his admiration for her, nothing more, he promised himself. Courage shone through her eyes, while the soft smiles she used to mend her fears bade parts of him to explore places he knew he shouldn't venture.

She needed him, did she not? He was, of course, the reason she was here.

The urge to brush the toe of his boot against her ankle, to offer her a bit of strength, became almost too much to ignore. He looked to the clock, then to the servants bringing in the next course of the meal. Dinner had just begun and yet it seemed to have lasted half his lifetime.

"You arrived in town today, did you?" Anderson peered at Pitman across the length of the table.

The long-faced major nodded, finishing his bite. "'Twas a simple journey from Plymouth." He reached for his glass, offering Caroline a transitory glance. "I am pleased with the change. There is a greater need here than the country towns."

"Captain Higley has done well, wouldn't you say, Major?" Anderson spoke with food inside his cheek. "Bringing us this lovely spy as proof our work here is vital. I daresay I am quite impressed."

Impressed. A lie. The man was a fuse, and any comment could light him, leading to the kind of explosion that would kill them all. James brought a spoonful to his mouth, not gracing the comment with any hint of expression.

Pitman replaced the half-filled goblet, speaking as if Caroline were not sitting feet from him. "And what information have you gleaned from this person? I take it you have made her talk."

Anderson shook his head, dabbing at his mouth with a napkin. "That is why I have asked her here. I wish all of us to be recipients of this woman's fiery spirit." He turned to her. "Tell us Miss Whitney, what do the Patriots now, hmm? What is their initiative?"

Caroline's mouth opened and when nothing emerged but a small squeak she smiled, her cheeks flaming red. Her eyes flew to James and she rested her utensil, placing her hands in her lap.

"Major, I..." She cleared her throat. "I don't know what you wish me to say."

Anderson leaned back. "Tell us what they are planning, where the troops are strongest, where Washington is keeping his stores, you know. I doubt such would be hard for a spy to share, come now."

Her face blanched and she blinked, her mind clearly working, but not quick enough.

James's back cramped, angered at how the man would put her in such a position. "I had ample opportunities myself to glean information from the time I discovered her, sir, which I assure you I made use of. I fear she knows nothing." James doused her with calm through a gaze he hoped she could feel as well as see.

"Nothing?" Pitman, who had yet to acknowledge her, swiveled, his glare scraping over her as if he could attain what he craved simply by looking. "I find that hard to believe."

"I fear it is true, sir." Caroline straightened, facing her opponent with all the strength and grace James knew she possessed, and he could do naught but be awed. "Captain Higley discovered me attempting to gather information that I could share with Washington but I was apprehended before I could glean anything of consequence. As for the reverse, I have nothing I can share, other than my conviction that liberty is paramount and we aim to achieve it."

Anderson leaned toward Pitman across the table. "Do you not find her fascinating?" Sitting back, he shook his head with a wistful chuckle. "For myself I am quite intrigued with how her mind operates."

Pitman, his long face devoid of emotion, prepared his fork. "I can see that."

"And I daresay, 'tis a good thing I am taken with you, little one," Anderson said, "as I have been given charge of the prisoners of this dilapidated town and I should most sincerely hate to see you forced to have to join them in their cell."

James gripped his fork, praying to heaven she would keep her calm. By God's grace she did, though he could read the whitening of her cheeks and prayed the message was not apprehended by any but him. She thought of her brother.

Caroline prepared another bite, her exterior and voice strangely calm. "I am indebted to you, sir."

Anderson grinned at the compliment. "Pitman, your officers are fond of a good party, are they not?"

"I am sure they are." Pitman blinked, as if he would silence the man with his reticence.

Undeterred, Anderson turned to James. "No doubt you would wish an evening to stand by your prize, wouldn't you? And see how everyone is taken with her beauty and brashness."

Brash? She was hardly that.

James sat back when a servant appeared, taking away his bowl and offering him a plate of seared rabbit in a sauce that smelled of onion and herb. He nodded his thanks before acknowledging the comment. "If you would wish it, sir, I am sure it would be enjoyed by many."

Anderson's brows flicked up. "But not by you?"

"On the contrary." James quickly filled his mouth, saving himself from any further answer while his mind sped into the future in search of a speedy conclusion to their charade. The thought of a household full of men and officers made his skin crawl. Especially knowing Anderson wished to make Caroline the center of attention. Danger was written all over the suggestion. The longer they stayed, the more precarious for her—and for him.

Anderson took his knife and cut the meat on his plate. "Well, either way, I should like to host something gay in honor of my arrival." He peered to Pitman. "Sir, you are welcome, but I can see you are not the kind to enjoy reveling."

At this, Pitman's mouth twitched. "You know me well, it would seem."

"You are not all that difficult to unravel." Anderson used his knife to slide meat onto his fork. "So long as you send your officers, I shall find a way to supply a few ladies. You need not attend if you prefer."

"I should be most happy to accept your invitation." Pitman raised his chin, almost hailing a smile. "If for no other reason than to perhaps find out more of this *spy*."

James's blood went cold. There was something sinister in the man, something dark. He'd known it existed, but had yet to see past the coldness that always crusted him.

"Excellent." Anderson grinned more like a boy than a man. "'Tis settled then, I—"

"Excuse me, sir." A soldier at the doorway, uniform dirty and hat askew, bowed before entering. "I must speak with you."

The young man whom James had seen before, but didn't know, waited for Anderson to motion him forward. He bent, speaking into Anderson's ear.

Anderson nodded. "How many?"

The soldier straightened. "Three, sir."

Sitting back, Anderson sighed, looking to Pitman before he answered, his gaze hard and words quiet. "A hundred stripes each, keep them in chains. I shall see them in the morning."

"Aye, sir."

Bowing, the disheveled soldier marched from the room, his sword and buckles clinking as he left.

After releasing another harsh breath, Anderson took up his utensils once again. "Those prisoners are a menace. I must find something to do with them."

James's stomach cramped and the juicy morsel in his mouth lost its savor. He raised his eyes to Caroline, and struggled to swallow his bite. Her breathing went shallow, her lips pale.

"Having trouble, are you?" Pitman raised the fork to his lips as he directed his attention to Anderson.

"I loathe to admit such, but so it is. I wanted them as near to me as possible, but the chapel we've converted into a prison is a useless place. There are too many windows..." He rested a beat, his facial muscles tightening. "'Tis the third time in as many weeks that our prisoners have attempted escape."

Caroline dropped her fork to her plate, complexion sickly. James nearly jumped from his seat to her aid, but the belt of their secrecy detained him.

"Are you alright, my dear?" Anderson spied her, inquisitive. "You look positively pale."

She took her fork again. "Forgive me. I am well."

James's muscles ticked with the need to extract her, take her to safety. To a place they could talk—a place she would be safe. He cursed himself. Why had he brought her? Perhaps he should have left her with Donaldson after all.

"I have tried various methods to keep them humble, but to no avail." Anderson shuffled the food around his plate. "I feel this time that a good suffering might do better than another hanging, for it seems they've grown accustomed to death." He spoke of horrors with no hint of remorse as he took another bite of meat.

Pitman leaned back, shifting in his chair. "They must be shown force." The man knew nothing of compassion. "I am glad to hear you are willing to do what must be done."

"Indeed." Anderson relaxed away from the table as if half his meal had satisfied him. "They are brainless and impertinent. Three were hanged last week and yet they continue to escape. 'Tis time for harsher measures to be enacted."

Caroline's face grew ever more devoid of color and her hands fell to her lap. Eyes round, she threw a look to James that made every protective instinct jump to readiness.

James clenched his teeth and strained to keep his back from cramping. The news seemed to clutch her throat, refusing air to her lungs.

Anderson sat up again, jockeying the food around on his plate more than eating it. "Tell me, Miss Whitney, what kind of dangerous fire is it that burns within you Patriots, hmm? What is it that possesses you—that makes you do things you would otherwise not when your life is on the line?" He didn't wait for a reply before looking round the table, smiling. "I hope to gain that secret from you before long."

Caroline blinked, her skin ashen. "I…" Her head bowed and she touched her forehead, swaying. "Forgive me, I—"

James bolted from his chair and rounded the table before Anderson could rise.

Caroline fell against him, her eyes half closed. "James…"

Anderson neared, his expression pinched. "She's fainted. Take her to her room."

Scooping her in his arms, James did as commanded, though he would have done so with or without permission.

Hurrying from the room, he made for the stairs and scaled them two by two. The door was cracked open and he rushed in, laying her on the bed, but she tried to push up.

"Caroline, you need to rest—"

"Please." She pressed his hand away, her voice thin as she sat up straight, a hand at her stomach. "I can't breathe."

He mustn't have heard right. "You can't breathe?"

Caroline shook her head, a hand at her chest. "Help me."

Panic swept him. She was in earnest.

"What can I do?" James knelt in front of her, his wild pulse tapping out his fears.

She strained for air. "My stays."

A momentary shock tugged his head forward. Her what? He shot a look to the door. Should not the maid-servant do such a thing?

When her breath hitched again he crashed through the sheet of resistance. There was no time to fetch the woman. His fingers flew over the pins of her dress.

"Do you think he's dead?" Caroline's words were pinched, a mix of strained breathing and suppressed tears. "Do you think he was hanged?"

He could feel her eyes on him as he worked, but he focused on the task, not answering. What could he say? The odds were not in her brother's favor.

He removed the last few pins and her stomacher fell away. Blast. He sneered away a curse. The ties were in the back.

"James..." Her eyes blinked slowly, and her head fell toward his shoulder, her body heavy.

Nay. He needed to move faster!

Holding her against him he tugged at her sleeve, but the gown was like a glove.

He spoke more to calm himself than her. "I must remove your gown so I can—"

"What are you doing?" The maid burst in, her face a gargoyle. "Get out of here!"

He didn't move. The urge to scold burned through his chest and he released the valve. "You've tied her stays too tight. She can't breathe."

The woman ignored him. Coming forward she pressed him back and took the spot James had been in. With ease of experience, she slipped Caroline's arms out of the dress. Her fingers flew over the laces at the back of her stays, until they were wide and open.

Caroline's shallow breath eased into long, steady inhales and exhales. James's shoulders drooped as relief spilled over him. He mimicked her long draws of air, not realizing panic had withheld air from his own lungs.

Her head came up, and their gazes met, sealing something inside of him like wax upon parchment. Seconds turned to hours as he fell helpless into the cool blue depths of her eyes. She seemed to thank him, to wish him nearer. The compulsion to obey was agony to resist.

"Go!" The pudgy woman motioned wildly to the door. "Get out."

James shuffled backward only when he was sure Caroline had

enough strength to sit upright on the side of the bed. His frustration at the maid refused to abate. How could he be sure she would not tie them up again? Why did women have to wear such ridiculous contraptions in the first place?

Moving toward the door, James left on the wake of his ire, which helped him ignore the fact he had left something of himself at Caroline's side. Something of his heart he would need back before she left—before he let her go for good.

He stepped into the hall and latched the door.

"How is she?"

James whirled to see Anderson standing in the center of the dimly lit hall, arms at his sides, head cocked and brow heavy.

"She is well, I believe."

The man responded with a shadowed expression that whispered of suspicion. The air thinned.

"I'm glad to hear it," Anderson said. "For I should like her to attend the party tomorrow evening."

James grinned, keeping his voice low. "All due respect, sir. Are you sure that is most wise? Seeing as she is your prisoner, I—"

"She is indeed my prisoner, but she is unlike any prisoner I have ever known. She is most lovely. Her mind is keen, and her tongue sharp. I am certain the other officers will find her most intriguing."

*I am sure they will.*

"You are right indeed, sir." James's skin pricked with self-inflicted rage. This was all his fault. "I wonder, however, if 'twould not be better if she—"

"Your bringing her here could not have been more providential. She may not know anything of worth, but she will give us an insight into the mind of a Patriot. Thus we can use their own thinking and tactics against them. Don't you see?"

Aye. He saw it. Clearly.

All James could offer was a mandatory smile and quiet hum. He curled a fist, pressing away the angst that built through his chest and down his arms. Would that James could get both her and her brother free by then, but the likelihood was hopelessly doubtful. That is, if her brother had not already been killed.

"I shall request Olga to have her dressed and down by six o'clock tomorrow, for I have a feeling she will not be joining us for the remainder of dinner." Anderson turned for the stairs.

At least the man could see reason enough to allow Caroline that.

"Lieutenant Blakely will be guarding her door," Anderson said. "During the day, she must remain above stairs."

"All day, sir?" The traitorous words were out before he could slay them.

Anderson stopped and pivoted back, his neck craned. "She *is* my prisoner. Would you have her stay in town with the others?"

James's legs went rigid. Had he lost all his senses? "Nay, sir."

His volume snaked around James's neck and began to squeeze. "You had better watch yourself, Higley." He neared, shadows from the candelabra rippling up his face. "Loving the enemy will only bring you pain."

Love? He breathed a laugh. "Sir, I don't—"

"I am no stranger to that look in your eye."

Heat crawled up James's neck. Thank the Lord for the darkness of the hall. "I'm sure I don't know what you mean."

"Of course you do not. Love makes a fool of both men and women." He closed the space and bent forward, his inflection a dark cavern. "Be careful what you do, boy. Give your heart to the enemy, and you will become one."

Ambling backward, he turned at the stairs, leaving James to dangle in the noose of his meaning.

Running a hand over his neck, James tried to free himself from the stranglehold. What had he done? A whipping would not be a just enough punishment. He knew better. He knew full well the dangers. Allowing any feeling for this woman was not only dangerous for him—for his future, and for the work he'd devoted his life and heart—'twas dangerous for her. Already he'd led her into a web from which untangling might prove near impossible.

He had a mission, as did she.

His greater purpose—his greatest want—must keep him from unearthing the one thing that could prove most dangerous of all.

# CHAPTER 24

$\mathcal{L}$ying on her back, Caroline stared upward into the blackness. Dressed in a less constricting gown and lightly pulled stays, she looked up from her position on the bed, tracing Anderson's words again and again in her mind. *Three men hanged.* Blinking, she inhaled, relishing the blissful sensation of lungs that could fill while she fought back threatening tears. Nay, he could not be dead. She must hope. Enoch was alive—she knew it. She would find him. She must.

The inviting coverlet and pillows beckoned her to rest, to ease the fears that bound her. But her mind resisted. She squinted, her memories spotty. What cut through the misty recollections with most clarity were things she wished would fade. *James.* A delightful warmth spread through her chest. He'd lifted her as if she weighed nothing, touched so gently—and the worry in his rich baritone. That warmth began to spread through her limbs and tingle in her middle. He seemed to care for her. But why? They hardly knew each other. She imagined the spark between them, surely. Handsome features, bravery and strength—both of body and character—were things of fairy tales.

But the way he had looked at her in the darkened closet. The way his fingers felt upon her cheek.

She growled at herself. Slapping her hands on the bed, she sat up. The events of the past days were too much for her, clearly. She was losing her head. Such girlish imaginings were beneath her.

Standing, she made her way to the clock on the mantle and sighed. Midnight. And not a wink of sleep within her. How could she sleep with the knowledge that her brother was in the city, that he was so close.

Again she closed her eyes, this time, praying. God knew the end from the beginning. He would not have led her here if Enoch was gone. Caroline flung her eyes open as a thought beamed through her mind. Had James gone without her? Under cover of darkness was the best time for secrecy, or so she suspected. So why not? She pulled her lip between her teeth. The idea was not entirely ridiculous. Anderson had mentioned a chapel, had he not? That it was near to Beacon House and had many windows. Her pulse jumped and she tiptoed to the window. Pulling back the heavy curtain, she peeked out. There was little to see past the glass, but a few lanterns glowing in the far streets of the city. 'Twould not be difficult for her to find such a place. Especially since she knew where to go.

Aye. She could do this.

Caroline craned her head to the clock once more, her mind afire. Dare she? The more she considered it, the more her chest began to burn. She must. How could she wait? There was no time to lose, especially if prisoners were willing to risk death in attempting to escape. James might have been gone hours, he might not be gone at all. Neither mattered.

Her limbs jolted and she pumped her fists, whirling. How could she not attempt it? God had brought her this far. She was not about to let a night go by without doing something. Enoch could at this moment be in need, waiting for someone to help him.

She hurried to the trunk by the bed and shuffled through it until she discovered a thick petticoat to put on over her existing one. The layers would add warmth, for no doubt 'twould be bitter. Skirt in place, hands gloved, she swiped her cloak from the chair and tied it around her neck.

Careful not to alert those below, she moved on silent feet toward the door. The metal hinges of the door screeched and she cringed, waiting for the sound of footfalls in the hall or a voice to call out. Silence answered.

Exhaling her relief, she pulled the door wider and peeked her head out. Down one side of the hall was no one. Thank the Lord. He had heard her prayers. She turned her head to peer the other way and stared into the red of a soldier's jacket.

"Going out?"

Her throat parched and she raised her head, inwardly castigating her stupidity. Her guard. How could she have forgotten about him?

"I...I was...I only..." She sucked in and said the first thing that sprang to her lips. "I need to use the necessary."

The embarrassing excuse laughed her to scorn. Her skin scalded and a sheen of sweat formed on her brow. *Really, Carrie?*

The man, whom she remembered from the time of their arrival, thinned his eyes. "Now?"

Caroline's stomach pressed up into her throat, but she forced courage into her spine and kept her gaze level with his. "Aye, now."

"Have you no pot?" He pointed a rigid finger back to her room, while the light of the hall revealed a tenderness in the lines of his face, as if she amused him.

Her throat grew thick. "I do, I do...but I—"

"There is a storm brewing, or didn't you know?" He nodded his head toward the wall and crossed his arms. "No one is going out tonight."

Her hopes deflated. With a storm out she would most certainly be lost and however could she be of help to Enoch then? And if she were caught? 'Twas a foolish venture.

Then again, what was a little snow when one's brother awaited rescue? Should she not do whatever she could? He would have done the same for her. She need only—

"Oh, don't pout." The guard shook his head, eyes scrunched and mouth tight as if he couldn't decide whether to smile or scowl. "Follow me."

"Follow you?"

He secured his hat. "'Tis none of my business if you freeze to death."

Caroline blinked. "You're in earnest?"

"Wait another moment and I might change my mind."

She nodded in gratitude and followed him to the stairs.

God would provide a way, storm or no. She was no stranger to cold. *Thank you, Lord!*

Through a small hall to a back door, she followed the enigmatic soldier, already shivering from anticipation. This night she might at last see the brother she'd thought she'd lost forever. How she would find him, return, and explain it to James she hadn't any thought. Then, reality struck her like ice down her back. In truth, if she found Enoch, she might not return at all.

Her guard opened the door and the brisk scent of cold met her before his words. "'Tis just there. See it? Only a few yards distant. I'll let you out, but know I am watching. And should you attempt any escape—"

"I shan't, of course." She smiled to him coyly. "You cannot believe I should like to stay out any longer than I must, do you?"

Her hands and feet drained of blood while her insides pooled with it. Nodding to him, she ventured out. The soldier followed, staying by the outside of the door as she marched onward. Once at the small shelter, she stopped and turned to look at her guard who, as promised, watched her. Her pulse raced as she swung open the door, and she smiled in shock. In truth Providence was with her. The opening faced opposite the house. He would see her enter, but if she moved carefully, he wouldn't see her exit.

For a moment she paused, reconsidering her hasty decision. The cold flakes hit against her hair and cheeks. Wishing to do a good deed, and possessing the ability to perform it, were two different things. At least she knew in what direction to venture.

*You can do this, Carrie. For Enoch.*

She peeked around the corner, holding her breath. There her guard stood, arms crossed against the hounding flakes, head turned away. Now was her chance.

Gripping her skirts, she slid backward and raced into the night.

$\sim$

"James."

James stirred, certain he'd imagined the sound of his name. 'Twas the first real night of sleep he'd had in far too long and his body hungered for it.

"James. Wake up."

This time a firm hand shook him and he bolted awake. He squinted until the form before him took shape.

"Edmond?"

Running a hand over his eyes, James tried to clear the fog from his head and the frustration that he'd been roused from the first warm bed he'd enjoyed in months.

Edmond's expression was unreadable in the dark, but his tone, though quiet, raked him. "She's gone."

All weariness vanished and he swung his legs over the bed. "Who?" He knew the answer, but hope begged him ask nonetheless.

Edmond looked to the window, his words stretched thin. "The girl."

Instinctively James grabbed for his breeches and boots. "What do you mean she's gone?"

James dressed as Edmond moved to the door, distress visible in his rigid stance. "She begged the use of the necessary and I kept watch from the door of the house, but after a good quarter hour of her not returning, I went in search of her."

A macabre display of scenarios painted James's thoughts as he sprung to his feet. "You let her out?"

Impossible.

Edmond looked pale. "I...I didn't think—"

"Clearly you did not." James rubbed his fingers over his eyes. "And you didn't find her in the yard?"

"Nay." He pointed. "The snow is falling hard, but it seemed her tracks led toward town."

James growled, cursing Anderson for not having put him in charge of her watch. The major had no doubt decided against it, believing James's intentions to be compromised. Edmond was a good soldier, but his kind heart led him to act with dangerous leniency. Any other would not have given in to whatever persuasion Caroline had used to get her way.

What had she been thinking? Was she truly trying to escape? Or was she searching for Enoch?

The latter question pulsed of truth.

She was going to the chapel—the place Anderson had said housed his prisoners.

Snatching a scarf and hat from the bedside table, he shoved past Edmond. "I'll go after her."

His friend followed. "I'm coming with you."

"Nay." He pressed him back. "You must stay."

The soldier shook his head. "If Anderson discovers I've let her go he'll dismiss me and I couldn't stand the shame."

Should Anderson discover it, Edmond's punishment would be more than a mere dismissal.

James pressed out a harsh breath and spoke through his teeth. "Stay at your post. I will go after her. Alone."

He didn't wait for an answer before striding to the back door.

The cold sneered at him even before he entered it, and when he did, the chill and worry pounded him.

*Caroline, why would you do this?*

James growled as he raced to the barn and saddled Ginny, that question tapping nails through his conscience. The answer was easily had. He'd told her he would do his part to search for her brother, and he would. She wished it to happen immediately, but didn't understand there had yet been time. Sneaking around in the middle of the night in such foul weather was heaps more than foolhardy.

The woman needed a tongue-lashing. And she would get one once he brought her back.

He mounted and kicked Ginny forward. The night was dark and the snow thick. 'Twas all but impossible to see anything through the fuzzy blackness. Sucking in long draws of cold air, James moved along the only road that led to town. The urge to call to her scratched at his throat, but he clamped his teeth. Yelling was futile in such a snowfall, not to mention the danger it would cause in drawing more attention to himself as well as to her, if in fact he was able to be heard past the din of the storm.

A movement to his left turned his head, and his hope.

There, along the street walked a cloaked figure. But for this person, the streets were empty, everyone else too sensible to make their way about in the middle of so thick a fall of snow.

He tapped Ginny onward. The closer he got, the more his heart pounded his ribs. It must be her. The shape and height matched her perfectly, and that plucky stride was unmistakable. With every pump of his pulse the anger at her rashness, the foolishness of such a thing, yanked the remaining composure from his already deceased patience.

As he neared, she stopped and whirled around, hands at the hood of her cloak. Eyes wide, she gasped and jumped back.

He pulled Ginny to a stop and launched to the ground, taking her hard at the arm. "What were you thinking?"

"J...James?" Her mouth opened as if any word she might say were lodged somewhere within her. Her eyes said enough.

A gust came and he raised his voice to be heard above it. "I knew you could be impetuous, but this is unthinkable."

She shook her head. "Nay, you don't understand, I—"

"Do you know what might have happened?"

"Nothing has happened."

Caroline's threadbare tone niggled at his conscience, but he ignored the pull and focused on her belligerence.

"Not yet. You could have died in this cold. You could have been followed, captured. The consequences are endless!"

She shook her head, quick and shallow. "I had to look for him."

"Had to?" He exhaled toward heaven and released his hold. "Not in the middle of the night. Not in a storm."

"Should a fall of snow keep me from trying?" She pulled back, a flash of emotion in her shadowed face as she spoke.

Was that a crack in her voice? He pretended not to hear, keeping his distance despite how the urge to comfort kneaded his back. "You should have trusted me." Frustration soothed his confused anxieties. "I told you I would help you search for him and I will. But timing is critical."

"Aye, it is." The flakes stuck to her dark hood as she scowled, her dainty brows pressing hard. "You heard what Anderson said. Three were hanged already—"

"Aye, the very reason 'tis foolish for you to venture out."

"Foolish? My brother may be dead!"

James bent forward, a finger pointed at her chest. "As may you be if you do not do what I say!"

Caroline shrunk back, pressing her lips together. A slash of regret cut over him. He should not have raised his voice. But she had to see this was no game.

"Come." He reached for her and she moved away. He stared her down, wrangling his wild anger into forced civility. "'Tis too cold, too dark and too dangerous. There will be no finding him tonight."

She raised her brows and her chin. "If the darkness and weather are too much for you, Captain, you may return, but I will not until I have—"

"Enough."

He stared her down. Why the sudden urge to kiss her into silence drowned out every other thought he couldn't say, but he despised it. He took her by the arms, too consumed with the throbbing of his heart to give way to reason.

"We are leaving, Caroline. Now."

She tugged against his hold. "Let me go!"

"Stop!" Shaking gently, he spoke through clenched teeth. "Listen to me." The defiance melted from her face, while the tension in her frame heightened. "There is naught that can be done. Not now."

"When?" She shook like an animal afraid of capture.

The cold whipped him, castigating his already bleeding frustration. "Soon." The anguish in her eyes called to the feelings he knew he must neglect, and he straightened his back to flee them. "We need more time before we can win what is necessary for our cause."

"Our cause?" Caroline yanked free of his hold. "Again you say it as if we are on the same side of this conflict, James, but we are not."

Frustration nurtured anger, cramping his shoulders. "I will not have you—"

"All you have done is force my hand. I want only to find my brother and be free of you."

Grabbing her at the waist he lifted her onto the saddle and swung up behind her.

"Worry not, Caroline Whitney. You will soon have your wish."

He tapped Ginny to move and battled like a solitary warrior against an army of thousands. She frustrated and allured him. The sooner she was away from him the better. He needed a clear head, which she destroyed with her own intoxicating strength and beauty of soul. With every step of his horse, every intake of breath, his heart beat faster, wishing and wanting things he shouldn't.

They had better find Enoch. And fast. For both of their sakes.

# CHAPTER 25

$\mathcal{H}$ ot tears trailed down Caroline's frozen cheeks as James urged Ginny up the hill to Beacon House.

The truth offered a bitter palate. James was right. She had been rash, but was she so very wrong to have made such an attempt?

She sniffed, and he stiffened. Pride was a paltry bandage for her wounds, but she wrapped it over her anyway. Let him know she cried. Why shouldn't she? He had been harsh—nay, rude. She'd gone along with his scheme, had nearly given into his charms.

A blaze of feminine rage warmed her to the core.

Did he think himself a prize? Perhaps he expected all women to fall prey to his gentlemanly ways as she had nearly done, to forget what he'd promised and give in to whatever he wished.

James tugged his mount to a stop at the back of the house and swung off, then prepared to assist, but Caroline dismounted without his aid. Stomping to the same door she'd escaped from, she refused the gaze she knew he gave her.

At the stoop, she pivoted, then jolted, surprised at his nearness.

"You are lucky," he said, "that I found you when I did." The husky nature of his timbre didn't toy with her at all...

She tilted her head. "You had best watch me closely, Captain. Or you might find I am indeed more clever than you give me credit."

"I do not doubt you."

Caroline squirmed. Why was he suddenly so polite?

Under the eaves, the snow no longer dusted them. His angled features were drawn, taut, his dark hat and hair dusted with snow. Bowing forward, his face came far too near. "Another venture like this, however, and I fear you will find yourself truly in danger."

Ha! Did he think to frighten her? Was her life not already in the balance? "The next time I go in search of my brother, I shall find him, and it will be no thanks to you."

She turned, but he grabbed her, pulling her flush against him. His mouth was on hers and though she pushed against him, his hands were at her back, a strong, unyielding hold. Tender, then brusque, his lips folded over hers, and she succumbed, returning his passion with hers. How had this happened? She didn't know, nor did she care. He released a quiet moan and she echoed him, a streak of heat pouring down her center.

Everything faded. The snow, the dark, the cold—'twas all a dream. The only reality, the feel of his hands on her face, his warm, wet lips against hers. His breath came quick and hard, the same as hers. Feeling her way up his chest, she caught herself from falling. Their first kiss, though forced upon by circumstance, had been all but a dream in its perfection. But this...this was a kind of pleasure that poured through her like fire, its burning bringing her to life.

His hands cupped her face, then knit into her hair before one hand slipped down to her back, pressing her ever harder against him, as if he wished to mold her frame to his. The way his mouth folded against hers, the way he whispered her name as he kissed her...this was how a man loved a woman.

Slowly, he pulled away, his warm exhales still kissing her wet lips.

She couldn't move, couldn't slow the mad pace of her heart. Every muscle pulsed with want, the embers of their passion springing life to the far corners of her soul.

She looked away, but he tipped her face up to his once more. "Take care, Caroline." His voice rumbled, a gentle warning. "Anderson is not as innocent as he appears."

Caroline opened her mouth to reply, but no sound emerged. Clearing her throat, she tried again. "I am not afraid of him."

"You should be." He brushed his thumbs against her cheeks. "He wishes your attendance at a gathering tomorrow evening, and I can tell you, his motives are anything but benign."

"What do you mean?"

His eyes roamed her face, his timbre a caress. "You are to be the center of the festivities and the height of conversation among a bevy of British officers who will come to gawk at the beautiful Patriot spy."

Beautiful? Did he really think so?

There were more pressing considerations, but now, still held in his arms, she could hardly fit two thoughts together.

Blinking, Caroline forced herself to pull away further. "Then?" *Stay focused, Carrie.* "After that shall we search for him?"

James's eyes still trailed her mouth, kissing her again with his gaze. "I will find out what I can tomorrow." He too stepped away, but the heat between them lingered. "I give you my word, the moment we can act, we will."

Caroline reached for the door, desperate for distance, while fighting a need to spend the wee hours talking to him, laughing, discovering the man behind the mask.

She rushed in, whispering over her shoulder. "I will be ready."

James followed her in and closed the door behind him. She didn't look back, thank heaven, as she tiptoed up the stairs and out of sight. His pulse still thundered, and all the places on his chest and neck and face where her hands had been tingled.

Dark and quiet—that's what he needed. He needed to shed this consuming emotion. He rubbed a hand over his mouth, but the feeling of her impossibly soft lips lived on his. Closing his eyes, he entered his room and sat on the cot. He needed sleep. He needed to get her out of his head.

He'd given in despite the warnings. He had told himself no. To ignore it, to move on, to forget her. An impossible task.

A breeze whistled past his window and he looked up, tempted to march back out and stand in the cold. A handful of snow on his skin wouldn't cure him, but it might help. Gads. He'd never endured so much heat. And despite how he shouldn't, he wanted to do nothing else but live that way forever.

# CHAPTER 26

The stinging scent of smoke hung heavy in the wintry morning mist. Despite the devastation the siege left in its wake, the streets were alive. Merchants marched up and down, women with laden baskets and scarf-covered heads barked commands at racing children. A dog barked. James smiled. How good it felt to be back again. If only the people here didn't look at him with distrust knit in their brows. Someday, he hoped, he could live as one of them. As a Patriot.

He marched down the street, a note in his inner pocket. He'd yet had time to deposit any intelligence to Washington, and since duty to Caroline called him down town, 'twas the perfect time.

Duty to Caroline.

He shook his head. No duty called him stronger than the one to which his soul directed. The Glorious Cause, the dedication he'd given after the tragedy of this place—of Loden's betrayal. He was changed now. He was as much a Patriot as Hancock and Henry, Adams and Revere. And yet, there was more that weighed on his heart, and ever would. He must continue to give the utter most farthing. To make right his wrong. Loden's memory deserved nothing less.

Nodding to a gentleman on the street, James slowed then turned a sharp corner and pressed his back against the brick. He hadn't been followed. He'd been sure of it. But caution was as natural as breathing and he peeked out, verifying the fact before he went to work.

Tugging free a loose brick, James pulled the folded paper from his pocket and secreted the vital missive behind the red square before securing it in place.

James stepped back, saying a prayer over the little piece. Someone would come, he knew, before tonight, and God willing the crumbs of intelligence he had would be worth something. It may not be much now, but he would get more. Much more. If Anderson continued to trust him, and if Stockton kept him here, there would be no better place than this to garner information.

The snow-muffled clomp of a horse's hooves approached and he slunk back, grateful when the rider appeared more occupied with the snowy road than the alley. Pulse flicking hard in his neck, James waited, listening. Emerging at the right moment was critical. Were he seen by anyone, most particularly a soldier, 'twould prove disastrous—especially for Caroline.

His gaze drifted out when the memory of last night's kiss scolded him once more.

The heat still singed, but the inner parts of him, the wiser man that lived at times outside of the boy, whipped him into humility. What had he been thinking? Did he really believe such an action didn't carry consequences?

He was a fool to put her at such a risk—to put his mission in jeopardy.

Certain of the emptiness of the adjoining street, he made his way out of the alley, considering the other vital reason he'd ventured into the city's streets. Finding Enoch would not be impossible. And when he did, she would be gone from him in days —perhaps sooner—which was why giving into such primal appetites was nothing less than...

He sighed and rolled back his shoulder. Nay. She was more than that to him. More than some urge to satisfy. That's what scared him most.

"Higley."

Kicking up slush, James halted. "Edmond, what are you doing out?" The next question blurted. "Who's guarding Car—the prisoner?"

Edmond pressed his hands into his pockets and gave an exaggerated shiver. "Beemish took my rotation for a few hours. I'm about business in town, thank the Lord. I couldn't take another minute indoors. But gads, 'tis miserable out here. Can't wait to get back." He chuckled and motioned with his head at James. "What are you doing?"

Perfect interlude.

On his way down from Beacon Hill James had surveyed the nearest chapel—the only one large enough to house prisoners, but it had proved empty. So had two other chapels, several homes and a large inn. The few soldiers he had casually spoken with were as dense as they were drunk and offered none of the information he craved.

Edmond, he hoped, would provide the answer.

"I'm about nothing really. Just enjoying a bit of air." James started walking again and Edmond followed. "Anderson says he's in charge of prisoners, hmm? Big job."

"Eh." Edmond grinned at two ladies who passed, following them with his head as they moved down the road. "There are but few remaining. However, they are miserable to contain."

"So I heard." Acting the passive conversationalist, James nodded to a townsman as he spoke. "Last night Anderson said they were being held in a chapel. You must be relieved they are not at Beacon House."

"Thank the Lord." He smirked. "Your lady friend is difficult enough to keep an eye on."

James quirked a brow. "Whose problem is that?"

"I know, I know." Edmond blushed and shook his head.

Quiet for a moment, James breathed slow before asking the ever burning question in a casual tone. "So where are they?"

"The prisoners? They have been moved. This morning in fact."

This morning?

James bit his cheek and kept every wild frustration behind a sober exterior. "A large undertaking I imagine. Surprised we were not asked to assist."

If only God would have given him such a blessing. The intelligence he could have attained would have been priceless.

"It was quite secretive I understand," Edmond said.

Nodding, James stopped at the corner, waiting for a large horse and carriage to pass. "So where are they now?"

Another pair of ladies walked by, smiling and giggling as they crossed the street. Edmond grinned, doffing his hat as they went past. "Good day, ladies—"

"Edmond." James tugged his friend around. "Tell me."

Edmond raised his brows, clueless to what might be upsetting him. "Tell you what?"

"Where are the prisoners being held?"

Edmond started across the street and James stayed beside him. "Undisclosed."

"What do you mean? No one knows?"

"None but the majors. Too many attempts at escape, so they've chosen to keep the location a secret." Edmond stopped and twisted to face him. "And why are you suddenly so curious? Worried your pretty little prize will be moved and you'll not have a way to find her for another dalliance, is that it?"

Not that the worry plagued him into panic, but the thought had crossed his mind.

James peered up the hill to Beacon House, his mind on a million things at once. What if she were moved? What if her brother was dead? How would he get her to safety?

"Don't worry." Edmond tapped him on the shoulder before continuing up the shallow hill. "If I know Anderson, and I am certain I do, he is too enamored with her to put her in such a place. Besides." A smile slid over his lips. "When there is something to be gained, you can be assured Anderson will make the most of it."

James remained still for a moment, watching his friend trudge up the snowy hill.

Aye.

'Twas the very reason he planned to get her out. As soon as he could.

But first, he must get through the day by keeping busy. He must get through the night without giving in to the one person that weakened him the most.

~

Morning had dawned, but with none of its usual pomp, and now that evening was upon him, Greene cursed the woe-begotten day of travel. Gray clouds emptied their chill, and the misery that went with it. Accursed New England winters.

Greene rode up to the officers' quarters in Boston, his rump aching from a full day in the saddle. At last he'd arrived, though he almost believed he'd freeze before he reached the besieged town.

He dismounted and peered about him. Though night, the windows of the houses and shops were lit, as was the street. The snow had not ceased falling, yet however dolorous the storm, the weather was nothing to the nature of the town itself. He'd known Boston before the siege, and it resembled little of its former glory. Dilapidated buildings, fences torn down, trees leveled. The common was littered with rows of tents, and along the streets, soldiers trudged, their hollow eyes and pale skin a testament to their suffering. He breathed out hard, shaking his head. This is what the Patriots wished, was it? Their countrymen benumbed and starving? A curse mumbled over his lips. *They* were the devils. But of course pride would never afford them a vision of the truth.

Greene shook his head and strode through the door of the modest brick building he'd been informed housed the officers. 'Twas a den of activity.

A soldier buzzed passed and Greene tugged at his arm. "I am looking for Major Pitman."

A scoff and a shake of the head was the only reply the stranger offered before striding away, as if the interruption was a grave impediment.

Greene smiled mockingly then moved in deeper, scanning the crowd for a familiar face. At last he found one.

"Ben!"

Flipping around, the man's gaze found him instantly and he excused himself from his conversation before striding down the hall, hand extended. "Matthew Greene." His grip was firm, friendly. "What brings you here? I thought you'd been transferred."

Word traveled fast, but in a leaky transport. "I was, aye, but not far. I'm in Pitman's regiment now."

Ben nodded. "What can I do for you?"

"I'm looking for Pitman. Is he here? 'Tis urgent."

Squinting, Ben twisted to look around. "I have not seen him since this morning. Jameson, have you seen Pitman?"

From the doorway at the side room, another soldier looked up, papers in hand. He motioned to another man. "Ask Gerald?"

Greene scoffed behind a smile. Would they ask every man in the army? The war might be over by the time they found him.

"Gerald?"

A balding fellow with narrow eyes neared, his brow raised. "Aye, sir?"

"This is Lieutenant—"

"Captain," Greene corrected.

Ben dipped his chin, impressed, then continued. "*Captain* Greene is searching for Major Pitman on urgent business. Have you seen him?"

"Nay, sir," the man said. "But I did hear that several of the officers were invited to a party at Beacon House in honor of Major Anderson's arrival. I believe he was one of them." He swung a brief look at Greene. "I suspect the gathering will go on for some time. If 'tis urgent, you might seek him there."

Greene stayed motionless in the tide of questions that hugged his ankles. Should he seek him? Confessing he'd been so close and failed again might be the last nail to his coffin. The waters rose higher and he looked around, hands on his hips. If he didn't reveal what he knew, of the Patriot camp, and the other men still held captive, he would risk more than demotion.

Sighing, he let his arms rest at his sides and bowed. "Thank you, gentlemen."

He prepared to leave when Ben pointed. "Your bandage appears to need changing."

Greene reached up and felt the cloth at his neck, the memories he tried to ignore flashing through his mind like the woman that shot him. His pulse thudded as the thoughts of cold and curses and blood swirled around him. Lowering his hand, he looked at the splotches of red on his fingertips and warred for the perfect malediction.

"What happened to your neck?"

The innocent question from the small man beside him flourished his already overgrown hedgerow of hate. "I was shot. By a female Patriot spy."

Both Ben and Gerald's mouths popped open.

Ben quickly regained his composure, but the shock still lived in his voice. "A woman?"

"Aye, a woman."

The thought rankled.

Greene pivoted on his heel and marched to the door while Ben called after him.

"Did she get away? Did you apprehend her?"

At the door, Greene halted, his hand on the cold metal handle. Looking over his shoulder, Greene gifted his friend a harsh grin. "She did, and I will."

# CHAPTER 27

*S*tanding at the foot of the bed, Caroline looked to Olga who stuck the last pin into her gown, and smiled. "Thank you for all your help. I couldn't dress alone—not in this gown, I am certain of that."

Olga peeked up, her round face revealing a shallow dimple in one cheek. It seemed the sour woman had softened some, for she hadn't laced the stays so dangerously tight, nor had she brushed Caroline's hair so mercilessly. She may not speak much, but the attempt at a smile was a step toward civility.

Olga motioned her to turn, nodding approval as Caroline adjusted the lace at her neckline and replaced the two thick ringlets over her shoulder.

One pin still between her teeth, Olga grunted with a scowl and Caroline stopped her movement. With her thick fingers, she slipped one last pin in the lace beside the stomacher.

Caroline dare not look in the mirror. If she did, she feared what she might see. For certainly 'twould not be the strong Caroline she wished to be, but the weak one—the one who pretended courage, but felt none. She was no better than a child, playing in her mother's gowns, imagining what it would be like to be grown and—

She stopped the rest of the thought, ashamed of the place it would take her. She would play the part Captain Higley required of her, if only to keep true desires in obscurity. She would find her brother and release him with or without *his* help.

After their kiss last evening, she'd been possessed by it and the fact shamed her. There was plenty to concern her, and the mere kiss of a man was what she cared about most? Disgraceful.

Olga raised a finger and left the room, indicating that Caroline should wait while she went to see if the party was ready for her.

She wiggled her feet in her shoes and brushed her hands along the width of the dress. Such a magnificent silk. Though similar to the last gown in shape, the construction of this sky colored gown was more delicate and refined, tucking perfectly around the shape beneath it. With elegant white, lacy sleeves and a petticoat to match, she felt more a queen than a convict.

As her gaze slid to the dressing table, she paused, a peculiar warmth spreading through her center. Two books sat beside the brush, gifts from James, or so Edmond had said that morning after breakfast.

"Captain Higley understands you like books." Edmond had handed them to her with an amused smile. "He hopes you will find these enjoyable."

That warmth continued to spread to her chest and up to her cheeks. Lifting the books, she couldn't help the smile that slid up her lips. Machiavelli's The Prince—and Cato. Her heart fluttered and she pressed a hand to her chest as she pondered once more its significance. How had he known she loved the book so? He must have read it in her eyes the time he'd spoken the lines she loved. How was it he always seemed to see into the depths of her? More, why did she not care? Why did she welcome it?

She dropped her hand to her side as more questions plagued, the seconds before her arrival below stairs ticking louder.

What would she say to him when she saw him? What would he say to her? Would they—

Olga hurried in, motioning behind her and there in the hall stood Edmond, his uniform cleaned and pressed, his posture proud but gentle. Caroline strode forward then stalled when his eyes fell softly upon her.

"Good evening, Lieutenant Blakely." Her voice faltered. Would he speak of last night? She'd not seen him since and feared perhaps he might harbor resentment.

He shook his head and cleared his throat before unabashedly trailing his eyes from her head to her feet. "Good evening, Miss Whitney."

Caroline's cheeks flushed. She must be passable then. Perhaps James might think...

*Don't be a fool, Carrie.*

She smiled at him and curtsied, grateful he'd not spoken of what she feared and prayed he wouldn't. Straightening, she motioned toward the stairs. "Shall we?"

Edmond bowed in kind, and offered his crooked arm. "Allow me."

Caroline nodded to him before tossing Olga a grin of thanks. As she moved down the stairs, her heart started a strange quivering. *Ignore it.* 'Twas nothing. Anyone would feel such a way, knowing she would be the sole lamb in a den of wolves.

Her palms went clammy, and she held more tightly to the fan in her gloved hand. In the hall, she could hear the hum of voices, and she sighed to relieve the angst that built in her lungs.

"Don't be afraid."

Caroline looked up to see Edmond spying her. "You look so lovely I doubt anyone will think anything of your politics." His mouth quirked. "So long as you don't make an attempt to escape."

She dipped her chin. There was the admission she'd known he would speak. Lifting her face to his, she allowed the hint of a smile. "For you, I shall make such a promise. But only for tonight."

He beamed, answering with a wide smile and soft chuckle that made him appear suddenly more handsome than she'd noticed before.

In seconds, the wash of gold light from the large sitting room bathed them as Edmond halted at the doorway.

All conversation ceased and everybody turned toward the door. Her skin seared and of a sudden she forgot how to move. Dotted with at least fifteen or more officers and a good handful of women, the room was as regal as any she'd seen. A fireplace as tall as she, bookshelves touching the ceiling, upholstered couches and high-backed chairs situated precisely around the room. She swallowed to remind herself 'twas not a dream. Along the back wall was a long table on which rested a vibrant display of desserts and foodstuffs.

Anderson strode forward, arm extended, his nature as warm as the crackling fire in the fireplace. And just as deadly.

"Ah, my dear. There you are." He made his way to her, taking her by the arm. "Gentlemen, ladies." The din of the room hushed. "This is the lovely Patriot I was telling you about, Miss Caroline Whitney. What a delight it is to have such a curious rebel in our midst, is it not?"

Every eye was upon her, and the mere knowledge made beads of sweat form on her back. He led her into the room, as Caroline's bones dried and threatened to crack. How did the room suddenly become so hot?

Two men came toward her from one direction, two more from another.

They bowed, taking turns introducing themselves. One of them, Colonel Cumbers, particularly tall and handsome, stepped in front of the others and offered his arm, his bass voice as smooth as honey.

"Miss Whitney, such a pleasure indeed. Wilson, fetch her some wine, will you?"

The Wilson fellow bowed and spun to do as commanded while the others followed her as if dragged by an unseen power.

Caroline's blood singed her skin and she flipped open her fan, grateful Olga had thought to include the trinket with the gown.

"I have heard so much of you, Miss Whitney. I must say I am pleased at last to meet you." Colonel Cumber's tone was caring, sincere.

Caroline looked up, startled at the way his gaze seemed to memorize her. She prepared to reply when her mind caught on something at the back of the room, and tugged her vision aside like a child begging for attention.

When her eyes found their mark, her breathing stopped. There, in the corner, skirted by three women, was the man she promised she would think nothing of. The ladies, all beauties, used their ample bosoms, minuscule waists, creamy skin and wide smiles like bait. James spoke with them and chuckled, a glass in his hand, completely unaware of her.

Her stomach dropped to her knees and her skin chilled. Would he not look at her? Had he even known she'd come in?

"Tell me, Miss Whitney." Colonel Cumbers nodded his thanks to Wilson who neared with a goblet of Madeira. "Major Anderson has informed us that you were taken in the act of attempting to gather information for Washington." He stopped, his half smile no doubt an attempt to beguile. "Such a brave act."

Caroline lifted the vessel to her lips. "Brave? I would not think of myself as so." The smile she tempted over her lips made Colonel Cumbers drop his vision to her mouth. She'd never had call to be flirtatious, though it seemed natural enough. And why not? If James could kiss her one minute then forget her so easily, she could do the same. She took a sip, flinging a coy look to each man that circled her.

She raised her chin and inhaled, relishing the spark in the men's eyes when she tilted her head just so.

"'Tis true then?" Wilson leaned against the side of a large chair. "You really did it?"

"Indeed." She kept her voice low, cool. "And how can you be sure that I am not, even now, doing that very thing?"

A mix of chuckles and murmurs jostled through the group, eyebrows and smiles lifting. Flinging a quick look to James, a stripe of jealousy burned her. Would he not even look at her?

"I must admit I would never have imagined a colonial woman to have such spirit, nor such beauty." Colonel Cumbers's gaze trailed over her once more, stopping at her neckline before slowly trailing back up.

Caroline took another sip to wash away the discomfiting sensation.

"Do you truly believe your cause to be just?" a soldier at her left asked.

She turned to him, pretending a coquettish nature that was, in the moment, frighteningly easy to exhibit. "The cause of liberty is the cause of mankind, is it not? And those of us who wish to see future generations live with such a fortune, must be willing to invest."

"What kind of investment is required?" The insistent fellow whose name she didn't know, evened his weight over his feet. "Surely you don't believe 'tis something worth risking your life over?"

A high-pitched laugh and inaudible comment from the corner behind them made Caroline's stomach churn. Her ire perked even more. James must be having a jolly time entertaining his admirers. Well. So could she.

She took another sip before answering, despite the fact she neither cared for the wine nor wished anything in her stomach. "I do. If I did not, I would not be here."

"But you do have liberty, Miss Whitney, already." This time, 'twas the errand boy, Wilson, who spoke. "What makes you wish to break off from the very country that gave you all that you have?"

"What *do* I have, young soldier?"

He jerked back slightly, a questioning cant to his head.

She painted a half-smile over her lips and let her gaze dot over each man that surrounded her, willing James to look her way and see how much attention was poured over her. "I think it impossible that you should misunderstand our discontent." Caroline straightened her posture, and held her glass at her stomacher. "If we are taxed, and forced upon, and ignored and reproved on every turn, would you not say that is the very opposite of liberty?"

One soldier, silent from the beginning, now spoke, and his tone stank of resentment. "You would see the entirety of the colonies break away. You would see men die—and an entire country torn apart—simply for the selfishness of the few?"

Her insides trembled at the dagger in his glare, and she forced herself to ignore away her fears. There was nothing he could do to her, was there? "There may be some who disapprove, but—"

"Your numbers are embarrassingly few, Miss Whitney." His shaven face was littered with scars, but 'twas the hate in his eyes that made him hard to look upon. "'Twill only be a matter of time before your cause is a mere line in the annals of history. And looking back, you will have the blood of thousands on your hands."

The blade of his glare winked in the light of a rage he didn't care to hide.

She swallowed, trying to find a way to smile when surrounded by those who liked only what they saw on the outside, but who hated what she was within. Resentment against the one who was responsible for this pitted in her middle. James had brought her to this and he was heedless of her plight. She should have known better than to give in to him, to let him hold her and kiss her as he'd done.

"Come now, Miller. You speak too harshly to the lady," Cumbers said.

Thank heaven for at least one who would stand up for her. He offered her a kind smile before turning to the combative soldier. "She alone is not responsible for the unrest."

"Nay, but she is one of the many. An ant cannot tear apart a beast on its own, but thousands of them…" He tsked and shook his head. "They must be squashed. Every one."

Squashed? Did he really mean to—

"That is enough, Miller." The colonel's reprimand slashed the air, and it seemed the entire room went silent. "I believe you need some air, sir."

Aiming all that remained of his hatred upon her, the man bowed, then turned and marched for the far corner, two other soldiers flanking him on either side.

"How goes it, gentlemen? Isn't our Patriot prisoner a most curious creature?"

Anderson filled the empty space in the circle, goblet in hand. "I daresay I am inclined to keep her here for the duration of the war." He gave such a look, it almost appeared as if he winked at her.

"Ah, I vote to keep her here, Major." Colonel Cumbers's meaning came out heavy. "I am sure we can find plenty to keep her occupied."

Caroline squirmed in her stays. Did he mean what she thought he did?

"Gentlemen, allow me a moment to speak candidly with Miss Whitney. You shall have your time with her, I promise you that."

The three remaining men bowed, eyed each other then left, leaving Caroline to grapple in waves too high to swim from. Would that she could snatch a book from the rows of shelves against the wall and find solace in words and pages.

*Lord, give me strength.*

She could play the part. Whether she was weak or strong

SO BRIGHT A HOPE

mattered not, only that she fulfilled. And that she kept her mind away from the one whose heavenly accent dusted above the din.

James didn't need her. Fine. She didn't need him either.

~

"Captain Higley, I am so pleased you've come."

James bowed politely, pretending to listen to the woman who returned his genial expression with too much amour. His mind was occupied elsewhere.

The moment Caroline had entered the room, every mouth had gone silent and every eye turned. Why not? She was the bounty— a Patriot spy, alive and in their midst. Not only that, she was lovely. His pulse tripled at the thought and he tried to forget the vision of her by smiling at the women surrounding him, but despite their own obvious beauty, their charms left him vacant, wishing for another glimpse of the woman whose spark and spirit were the real qualities he craved.

He lifted his chest, forcing himself not to look in the direction of the conversation he could hear from across the room. He would know her voice among a thousand. Again he inhaled long and slow, hoping 'twould dispel the brief glimpse he'd had of her beauty when she'd entered, but doing so only etched it deeper. And from the battalion of soldiers surrounding her, they wished to adore her, study her like a work of favored art.

If any of them dared touch her, or made any kind of advance...

"I'd feared perhaps I wouldn't see you again after your last visit. But you did promise to return and here you are." The blonde woman giggled, and James fought the urge to roll his eyes. Instead he grinned, which only made the woman blush as if he'd meant to flatter her.

Another woman, tall and thin, leaned forward, no doubt hoping to catch his eye to her ample bosom. He ignored the obvious attempt.

"You have moved up in rank, sir," she said. "I am most impressed indeed."

"Thank you, miss."

A third woman, as tall as the second and equally brash, leaned toward him, her voice sultry. "Is it true you were the one to bring in the woman spy?" The red-head turned, taking another look at Caroline. "I heard tell she was a beauty, but from the look of her she appears a miserably skinny, freckled thing. Nothing remarkable at all."

She was not miserably skinny and hadn't a freckle on her. He took a sip, ruminating over the myriad ways he would like to draw comparisons.

"I heard tell she slept with three different majors with the intent to gather information."

The girls gasped and giggled while James's blood boiled. Whoever started those rumors would have their throat extracted.

"What is she like?" The tall one's eyes were wide, craving gossip.

He lowered his glass. "Stay away from her, ladies. That is all that I can safely tell you."

Their mouths flopped open and several put their hands over their bosoms.

"And to think she is here, in this very room," the tallest said, once again taking the reins of the conversation. "We might be at risk simply being here."

The blonde one tilted her head with a scoff. "Oh, you are so dramatic, Winnie."

"Well…" Her cheeks pinked. "He said she was dangerous."

The redhead batted her eyes. "We needn't worry when Higley is near, ladies. That I can assure you."

James swallowed his drink to stifle a groan. *Lord, a battlefield, I beg you. 'Twould be heaven compared to this.*

"You were not long ago in New York, is that right, Captain?"

He opened his mouth to reply when Caroline's smooth tone

moved toward him like a ribbon, tying around him and holding him motionless. If only he could hear what she said—what they said to her.

The three women exchanged words and more giggles, and he succumbed to the need to see her.

Lifting his glass to his lips once again, he allowed himself only a fleeting glance and slayed the boyish hope that perhaps she would feel his stare and be forced by the same need as he to turn to him.

'Twas as he imagined. She stood regal, gracious, a glass in her hand and surrounded by at least five soldiers, all drawn to her like a moth to flame. He clenched his teeth and lit the fuse to his pride.

"Ladies, how lovely you look this evening."

Edmond neared, and James grinned. Never one to ooze with charm, Edmond nevertheless seemed oblivious to the fact. James found his boyish naiveté an endearing trait and would have smacked his friend's back with gratitude for saving him, would not the gesture have been too obvious.

"Edmond." He raised his glass and nodded while the ladies waved their fans and painted trite smiles over their disappointment that he'd interrupted.

Bowing, Edmond grinned. "Would you be so kind as to allow us weary soldiers a moment of conversation alone?"

"Why certainly," the blonde said, bowing intentionally low. "Captain Higley will know where to find us."

Batting fans and producing smiles with promises behind them, the ladies dispersed in a huddled group.

James tugged at his neckcloth and wiped his hand down his chest, grateful the noose had been cut.

"You saved me."

Edmond laughed quietly. "I could see you were in a bit of distress."

"Was it that obvious?"

"Only because I know you."

Caroline's voice tapped James on the shoulder and he turned, noting one soldier's red face and her pale one. Blackguard. He'd said something to her.

The need to bolt to her defense filled his limbs. Just then the man spun away and Anderson filled the hole in the group. A worse replacement.

Perhaps he should—

"Thank you. For your help."

James turned to him. "Help?"

"For not berating me after...after my blunder last night." Edmond's gaze drifted down. "I should have said so earlier today, but I guess my shame held my tongue."

James clapped him on the arm. "It turned out well."

Smile tight and posture relaxing, Edmond's eyes drifted to where James's continued to go. "She is lovely, isn't she?"

James bobbed a shoulder, hiding his true appreciation of her beauty with a half-smile. "Indeed."

"Quite a wit, too." Facing him, Edmond's expression drooped. "Where did you find her? I should like to learn your side of the tale. I have heard some vibrant accounts of her and I am aching to know if they are true."

"They aren't." James's neck and shoulders tensed. "Gossip is fueled by hate and jealousy."

Edmond chuckled. "Protective are you?" He eyed her, then looked back to James, failing at his attempt to stifle a grin. "Don't worry, I haven't any designs on her. Though I can't say the same about the others."

James tightened his jaw and inhaled to brush away the billowing worries.

Again, James looked her direction. The sight made him cringe. Anderson stood far too close to her.

His jacket grew increasingly uncomfortable. "Warm in here, isn't it?"

"She looks a bit like Miss Gray, don't you think?" Edmond

looked behind him to the blonde that had been beside them only seconds ago.

Was that her name? James hadn't known. He chuckled, shaking his head. "She looks nothing like her."

"She does. I'm surprised you don't see it."

For as much as he liked Edmond, the man was getting on his last nerve.

"I do not see it." He leveled his shoulders. "All that is similar is the shade of their hair, and even than Caroline's is paler, more like corn silk than honey."

Edmond's eyebrows rose slowly as he tilted his head. "Strangely specific." He made a face and lowered his volume. "And since when did you start calling her that?"

Blast.

The tips of James's ears burst with heat, his scar aching. He grew careless. How could he let slip that bit of familiarity?

Edmond patted him on the shoulder. "I am pleased to see this side of you, James. Your joy has been too long in coming. The fact you are a soldier needn't muzzle a life of love and family." He released his hold and leaned forward, whispering. "But why did you have to fall in love with the enemy?"

The mention of the words pulled James at the throat. Love?

Why must everyone come to such a word? Why not attraction? There was no harm in that word. Even affection. Why not that? But love?

Nay.

He rolled back a single shoulder. She would never feel anything for him—he was the enemy. Even if she'd kissed him as she had, even if their hearts seemed somehow bound together by an unseen, unmistakable power.

Whatever he felt for her, it was not love. Of that he was certain.

# CHAPTER 28

*C*aroline stared out at the happy party goers, pretending her skin didn't tighten at Anderson's closeness. Best to keep conversation flowing or her nerves would win over her courage. "You are new to the colonies then, Major?"

"Nay, I have been to the colonies many times before, but never to New England." He twisted to face her. "Your kind are mysterious indeed."

Tilting her head, she pretended ignorance. "My kind, sir?"

"Aye, you Patriots. Rugged, yet pious. Undisciplined, yet tenacious." He raised his glass to his mouth. "I find myself intrigued and somehow equally perplexed, and concerned."

Another laugh from Higley's harem pranced toward her and she bristled. Allowing herself a perusing glance, the sight of his easy smile and relaxed stance as he stood close to the brunette injected a vicious kind of bravery through Caroline's veins, giving strength to say things she might not have.

She swiveled back to Anderson. "Concerned that we might be victorious, are you?" Quirking a brow, she baited him.

The man was impossible to read. Not that she had any skill in discernment, but what looked like civility seemed to mask the shape of something else entirely. What, she couldn't tell, except that its edges were pointed.

Anderson's chest raised and lowered as he sighed. "You will find, Miss Whitney, that it takes far more than country boys and old men to be victorious over the strongest army in the world."

She conceded with a slow nod. "To say nothing of your navy."

His eyebrows hinted up. "To say nothing of our navy, indeed."

Smoothing her thumb against the delicately etched goblet, she peered at the dark liquid, the start of a smile tugging at her lips.

How alive she felt. Speaking her mind, expressing her views and opinions without Timothy to beg her to quiet and to "act the lady." Never had she been more a lady than she was in that moment. For she was herself, and it was like breathing—truly breathing—for the first time.

"Major," she said, "we may not have the vast numbers of troops, we may not have ships. We may not have ammunition or muskets or a central government to lead us." At this, she lifted her eyes, pouring into her gaze as much as her words, the conviction she'd felt but never had occasion to testify. Her body buzzed, her pulse crashing in her veins. "But what are armies and navies of men, when the army of God is on your side?"

"God?" He laughed, wicked amusement in his eyes. "You believe God cares? You believe he would be on the side of the rebels?" He shook his head, his face crumpling as if her words disgusted him. "Do you know how many have died? Do you know how many even now are in prison? Your own countrymen, Miss Whitney. Do you not feel yourself responsible for their suffering?"

The walls closed in and a sudden heat singed her back. Rolling her posture straight did little to ease the rising emotion that clutched long fingers around her throat. She pretended an unaffected exterior.

"How many prisoners have you, Major?" Smiling, she inclined her head toward her drink. "Not including myself."

"We have prisoners up and down the colonies." As if such

would impress her. "Here in Boston, under my lock and key are seven and twenty of the original one hundred and three."

Caroline's blood drained from her head, a slow drip that made every thought, every movement an agony.

Her knees locked and she reached for the chair beside to stable her. "You do not keep them here." She looked around the room, laughing playfully. "Where in heavens name would you keep such a group?"

Anderson's eyes slid down her face and stalled at her lips. Leaning forward, he whispered at her ear, his breath scented with sour wine and bitter cheese. "I might be willing to give you a hint. For a favor or two."

Caroline's skin crawled, and she leaned back to widen their distance. Playing the innocent once more, she laughed pretending she hadn't understood the horrendous conditions he'd inferred.

The room became a cage, a trap. She smiled casually and turned to see if James had yet to look her way. Still engaged and enjoying every attention the ladies shoveled on him, he appeared as if he'd never known her.

*Focus, Carrie. This is for Enoch.*

"Really, Major Anderson," she said, unsheathing the weapons she needed to keep herself safe in this sea of monsters. "If you are unafraid of a smattering of country boys and old men, why keep them in prison at all? King George is so frightened, is he?"

Anderson straightened, unspeaking, but the twitch on his forehead revealed the truth he failed to hide. The British were afraid of them. They were afraid of losing.

She poked the already angry lion. "After your losses at Bunker Hill, I would have imagined you might have given up."

He stared her down, the unaffected expression a lie. *Dangerous, Carrie. You go too far.*

But the sounds from the corner were heightened again and this time she didn't need to look to have the imagined sight fuel her ire.

Swerving to face Anderson completely, Caroline stepped further onto the battlefield. "What will you do when you discover our humble country folk have overcome your trained and tailored soldiers?"

His mouth pursed and his brow crunched. Slowly his mouth opened but snapped shut when someone called from behind.

"Major Anderson?"

The man heard his name called, surely, but he didn't move. His entire countenance was a barrage of cannon-fire. But the incoming rain of iron created only dents where holes should have been. Her offensive had thwarted his bombardment and she reveled in the way her strategy made his jaw harden and nostrils widen.

"Major Anderson?"

He inhaled and shook his head, shedding the momentary trance. "Aye?"

A nameless soldier neared and leaned forward. "There's a man here to see you."

"Now?"

"He claims 'tis urgent."

Anderson grumbled something under his breath about never fully having the pleasure of leaving duty behind him, and after bowing curtly, strode out.

No sooner had he gone then two more soldiers neared, and Caroline steeled herself. These were shark infested waters, and she had better take care, or be torn apart.

"What can I do for you, Captain Greene? As you can see I am in the middle of a friendly gathering, to which, I might add, you were not invited."

"Forgive the intrusion, sir." Greene bowed, restraining himself from mentioning the fact that, had he not been otherwise engaged, he most certainly would have been among those to receive an invitation. "You may be assured, Major, that I would not have interrupted were not this a grave matter." The man's face was taut with lines of anger in his forehead, so Greene finished the rest. "I understand Major Pitman is here, sir, and 'tis imperative that I see him."

"About what?"

At least the man was interested enough to refrain from throwing him out. "I have recently escaped capture from a Patriot camp and must inform him of the man I believe to be the informant."

His eyes narrowed. "Informant?"

That moment, Pitman parted the crowd and entered the hall, every bit the storm cloud to which Greene had grown accustomed.

"What are you doing here?" Pitman pulled back, his eyes at the bandage on Greene's neck. "What happened?"

At last. Greene bowed, motioning down the hall. "I would be most happy to tell—"

It couldn't be.

Frozen, Greene stared at the woman in blue, skirted by a good handful of soldiers. He couldn't move. There she stood, the very she-devil herself. How had she gotten here?

"Well," Anderson said, a definite groan in his voice. "This way."

The major motioned for the others to follow and somehow Greene made his immobile limbs bend and obey, carrying him away from the sight that stabbed him through the stomach.

They passed the parlor and dining room, finally ending their journey at a large office at the end of the hall.

Anderson closed the door and turned, arms crossed, waiting.

Greene swallowed and grappled for a calm tone as he addressed Pitman. "I came in search of you, sir. But it seems I found more than I came for."

Pitman eyed Anderson, his austere presence out-bellowing Anderson's. Only his eyebrows lifted in a demand for the rest.

His pulse pounded, the gash in his neck once again starting to seep. "I see you have a young woman in your home, sir."

Anderson nodded. "I have more than several young women in my home, Captain."

"I mean one in particular, sir." Greene stomped forward. "I know not how she came here, but I must tell you she is not a woman to be trusted."

Anderson leaned back and tilted his head. "Is that so?"

Why the mocking tone? Swallowing the urge to retort, he nodded. "Aye, sir. She is a Patriot spy."

"My, my. Do you hear that Pitman? A female spy in our midst?"

Idiot. Greene hated the man and he'd only known him for a handful of minutes. "I regret to inform you, sir, but you are all at risk. She is—"

The laugh that bubbled from Anderson's chest flew through the air like hurled blades. "Forgive me, Captain Greene."

Greene stalled, swiping his gaze between the majors as confusion and embarrassment heated his chest. "I'm sorry?"

Anderson looked to Pitman, then to Greene. "You are referring to Miss Caroline Whitney, are you not?"

His coat started to shrink. "I am, sir."

Pitman remained taciturn, expressionless.

Anderson motioned to the wall beyond which was the party. "Captain Higley brought her to me. An envoy of sorts. Said Stockton wished to welcome me, and what better way to prove our work here is needed than with a Patriot spy he'd apprehended. A woman at that."

Greene's skin pricked with hot animosity. "Did you say, James Higley brought her?"

"He did, and I daresay, he's made quite an impression."

"He's made quite an impression has he? Brought the woman in himself?" Greene shook his head, a bitter laugh streaming out of his chest. "Did he say anything else?"

"Your tone is unwelcome, sir." Anderson's reprimand did nothing but spur him on.

"Did he say anything about his fellow soldiers being captured by rebel forces fifteen miles south?"

Finally the man looked interested. "Can this be verified?"

Greene pointed a rigid finger at his neck. "She attempted to kill me."

Eyes narrowing, Anderson ground his teeth, his absent response a verification he had not known.

Greene pivoted toward Pitman who stood motionless, his face crunching as his mind worked. "Sir, I have said this before, I believe him to be the infamous informant we have searched for for so long, and after his last exploits, I am more than confident. You must give me leave to arrest him."

Pitman's thin brows flicked up. "You have evidence I presume."

Greene closed his eyes. Why did everyone care about evidence? Would that everyone could be as clear minded as he and see what was so obvious.

Anderson pressed out a deep breath and finally released his arms. "I thank you for your troubles, Captain, but as there is nothing pressing, I will return to my guests." He rounded the table, irritation on his wine-laden breath. "Get yourself a doctor, Captain. Your injury leaks."

With a curt bow Anderson marched out leaving Pitman at Greene's side, the wake of their combined irritation leaving rough terrain for Greene to traverse.

"You failed, Greene." Pitman's bass voice rumbled through the room. "And now I must suffer the humiliation of having chosen you for the mission in the first place."

Greene shook his head. "Nay, sir, please. I know I am close."

"The same excuses will get you the same results."

The finality in his tone made the blood in Greene's head drain to his feet. "Sir, if you will give me one more chance to prove—"

"I am finished giving chances."

He made for the door, but Greene called after him.

"Wait!"

Brilliance flashed through him like a bolt from storm-blackened skies.

Pitman slowed, turning half way.

Greene pulled from his pocket the letter he'd taken days ago from the woman's pack. "You should look at this, sir."

Brow a deep V, Pitman took the paper with a muted growl and opened it. His eyes scanned back and forth and Greene held his breath.

At the end of the second page his gaze shot up. "Where is the last page?"

"There is none."

His glare narrowed further. "When did you get this and from whom?"

At last the man would listen.

"When first I attempted to apprehend them, Higley…" *Just admit it.* "Higley beat me down, sir. And refused to bring her in. After he'd taken her I found this in her pack."

Once again studying the letter, Pitman's vision tugged sideways, his mind cranking over some unspoken realization.

"You say Higley beat you, took the woman, and fled?"

Finally! "He wished to set her free, as he did the others. You must see it, sir. Higley is the man we've been searching for."

"But he didn't set her free." Pitman's chin dipped. "He brought her to Anderson—the man who is, in fact, in charge of all the rebel prisoners."

Outwardly, Greene nodded, inwardly, he raked his hands at the heavens. "I know, sir, but he did it only as a ruse, he did it to gain Anderson to his side."

"Enough." Pitman stared, motionless, his long face twisted

with rage. "I believe you. But I doubt you will get Anderson to do so."

"I will, sir." Greene's body buzzed. "I will."

# CHAPTER 29

"It seems someone is riled."

James snapped up, curious of whom Edmond spoke, when an alarm sounded through him, rattling his bones.

Anderson marched through the doors, his complexion flushed and mouth chiseled with rage.

"Something has happened." James hadn't meant to speak the thought aloud, but he had, and looked to Edmond as he finished the rest. "He's had some news. But what?"

Edmond shook his head. "I don't care to find out."

Choosing to keep his own frustrations behind iron bars, James nodded, pretending concurrence. *You don't, but I do.*

As if the major could hear his secret thoughts, he pivoted and skewered James with a look that had the strength to kill.

Whatever he had learned, the man looked ready to tear him limb from limb.

"Edmond, I need your help."

Brow crunched, Edmond pulled back. "What is it?"

James handed Edmond the empty glass and started for the exit. "Go to Caroline, stay with her until I get back."

"Where are you going?"

There wasn't time to talk. He waved back as he moved. "Stay with her."

As James reached him, Anderson spun, red in his eyes. "I've just had my evening most egregiously interrupted."

"Sir?"

Anderson released a sigh through clenched teeth. "A Captain Greene has just arrived, making wild claims about you, in fact."

What? His mind stalled, struggling to find reason in what Anderson had said. It wasn't possible. Greene had been taken. Henry and Nathaniel had him in bonds. There was no way for him to be here.

Unless...

His stomach turned to stone. He'd escaped. But how? If Greene had killed his friends...

James stared down the major and composed himself, continuing the outer charade despite the barrage of shock and questions that exploded within him.

'Twas easy to act the honor-defiled gentleman. "Claims?" James stood erect, pure dread taking the reins of his pulse. "What kind of claims?"

"He has the audacity to name you as the informant that has plagued this army for so long."

Jaw tight, James pointed toward the hall. "How dare he defame my honor in such a way. I will see him at once—"

"I will not have you confronting him, 'tis not the time for a duel." Anderson turned away, fuming.

"Let me speak with him at least. Do I not have the right to confront a person willing to make such abominable accusations?"

As if his assertion was well founded, Anderson spun on his heel and motioned for James to follow him. "Come."

James's stomach spread shocks of cold then hot through his middle. It could be a trap. If it were, how would he get Caroline to safety?

Castigating his foolishness, James prayed for a strong dose of grace.

Anderson strode forward at a brisk pace, briefly stopping at the door where Greene and Pitman conversed. "Leave us, Pitman. I should like the three of us to chat."

Pitman's skin went ten shades of red, but he complied nonetheless, bowing and marching away in fuming silence.

Anderson strode into the office, Greene behind him. "This is not the way I wished to spend my evening."

Entering with a shallow bow, James took the temperature of the room. 'Twas hot as hell.

Anderson walked to his desk, and turning, leaned against it.

"Greene informs me that you knew of his injury and capture, and yet you never mentioned any of that to me."

*I'm certain he told you more than that.*

"An oversight, sir. Forgive me." In truth, he'd prayed the man would never be heard from again, though he knew such a dream was hardly realistic. "I was so occupied with getting our prisoner to you, I—"

"I know what is really going on."

James pulled back. He did?

"'Tis quite clear." Anderson grinned briefly before growing earnest. "I have seen this before but never to such a degree." He paused. "You are both in love with her."

"*What?*" Greene's outburst cracked the plaster on the walls.

Anderson ignored him, shaking his head. "She spurned you, choosing James instead. Now you wish to see him take a fall."

"I can tell you in all veracity, sir, that I do not *love* that woman." Greene's face was crimson. "I wish to see her immediately tried and hanged as a traitor."

"Do you?" Anderson looked to Higley. "And what about you?"

Drips of sweat trailed down James's back. "I do not love her, sir. But I believe hanging a woman might subject you to harsh criticism despite her traitorous actions."

Anderson chuckled. "You wish to hide the truth, do you? Can't say I blame you." He raised his brows, giving Greene a plaintive look. "I must say I am in agreement with Captain Higley."

"Agreement?" Greene balked. "This man wishes to detain her longer so he can think of a way to set her free." His volume rose higher. "He has, just days ago, set free two Patriots who were under his watch. I know he will do this for her as well. You must believe me, sir."

A thorny silence loomed. James ground his teeth and focused on keeping his fists from forming. *Do not believe him.*

Anderson, arms still folded, bounced his gaze between them. "Your anger is no friend to you, Greene."

"You must listen to me!" Greene's neck bulged. "Think of the implications, Major, and do not wait, or the ramifications might be—"

"Do not lecture me, boy." Eyes like pools of fire, Anderson's glare hardened. "I will do what I see fit, when I see fit."

Greene pointed a rigid arm toward James. "Pitman has given me the assignment of uncovering the informant—a man who has time and again thwarted our efforts, given away our positions and weakened the placement of our troops. And I tell you, this is the man!"

"Silence!"

Anderson stood, moving more like machine than man. His voice rattled, leaving scars on the air. "I care not for what happened to you, or for anything that has happened in the past. And I most certainly do not care about your so-called assignment to catch a man who is of so little consequence. All I care about is the future and winning this bloody war."

Greene straightened, his lips pursed tight and jaw thrust forward.

Anderson looked from one man to the other. "My goal, gentlemen, is to see that these headstrong colonists get their just reward. I do not wish to spend my time breaking up squabbles between grown men." He turned to Greene. "Any informant you seek will not be in these ranks, Greene. I guarantee you of that. And as for the woman, she is *my* prisoner now, and I will do with her as I see fit. Do I make myself clear?"

Skin red and steaming from rage, Greene nodded. "You do, sir." His face lifted. "But before you go, you may wish to have a look at this."

Anderson snatched it from his hand and stood in front of him, nose to nose. "Good evening, *Captain*."

Greene gave a brisk nod and turned on his heel, but not before branding James with a look that promised war.

Anderson let out an audible breath. "I do not like that man."

Shaking his head, James fought the urge to race down the hall and tackle the belligerent enemy to the ground.

"But what is this about you deceiving me?" Anderson said. "Why not tell me the whole truth?"

The jaws of a trap sprung up around him. "I didn't intend to deceive you, sir. My intent—my mission was to be an envoy to you from Stockton, and when I encountered the woman I knew 'twas my duty to bring her to you. En route, we were captured by a Patriot encampment which was then attacked by Greene." The explanation sounded even better than he'd hoped. "Greene wished to take the woman for himself, so I was forced to escape with her, and leave the others behind."

Nodding slow, Anderson bit the inside of his cheek and looked at the door. Then, with a flick of his wrist, he unfolded the paper. The quiet mumble of voices from the adjoining room whispered through the walls.

Anderson's face crumpled in thought before he lowered the note and stared away. He handed the note to James. "Have you seen this?"

James took it, examining the two pages briefly. "Nay."

Anderson paced toward his desk, then took the leaning position he had before. "An interesting development."

Anxiety whipped through James as he devoured the words. His heart trembled, but he hid it behind a scowl. This was Caroline's note. From her brother.

The implications were clear, deadly.

James shook his head and evened his voice, refolding the paper. "It seems her brother is a prisoner of war."

"Indeed." Anderson's expression lost every hint of softness. "And she plans to set him free, as well as the others."

His lungs refused air. "Sir, I do not see how this letter is any indication of covert activities. You are already aware that the prisoners are attempting escape. This is not any new information."

"You didn't hear her speaking to me earlier."

*Caroline, what did you say?*

"Did she mention her plans to you?"

"Not in so many words, but her intention was simple to extract."

Why anyone figured the woman for a spy was beyond comprehension. She couldn't even keep the smallest of secrets. The thought, though fringed with frustration, endeared her to him all the more. Such perseverance in the face of adversity was enough to cause any man to go beyond his strength.

"If this woman is the nose of the fox, we must wait for the tail." Anderson's eyes glowed as he leaned over his desk. "With what information she hands to her compatriots, she will be the means of leading even more of the bloody Patriot's right into our hands."

Remaining cool, James nodded. "And what will you do with her then? When we've accomplished our goal?"

Pointing to the wall, Anderson grinned with sickly pleasure. "You have seen what a spectacle she is. I will use her as long as I can." He turned to his papers again. "The rest of the Patriots will be hanged Saturday. I've had enough of their drain on our resources. 'Tis time to be done with them."

Dearest Lord in heaven. He would kill them all.

Perdition opened up beneath him and swallowed. They had only one more day.

Before James could smooth his thoughts, he spoke. "If I may be so bold, Major." He cleared his throat. "All due respect, I do not believe she will be of any additional use to you."

At this Anderson looked up, one eyebrow swooping.

James continued. "She knows nothing and if you will consider the—"

"I have already warned you, James. Take care." Fatherly admonition fenced his words. "I know you feel an infatuation for her, but the enemy is the enemy and can never be trusted. No matter how good they are in bed."

The chuckle at the end of Anderson's words made James's stomach roil.

"You will have to forget her," Anderson said, "or suffer the pains of a broken heart when her fate is sealed."

Her fate is sealed? Every minute that ticked past slapped James in the face. He should never have brought her.

Rounding the table, Anderson clapped him on the shoulder. "Come, we've been too long away as it is." He marched to the door. "After that encounter with Greene we'll certainly be needing a good drink with the ladies, hmm?" He winked and exited, making his way through the hall.

James followed behind, grinding his teeth.

He must make the most of the last hours they had left. He had to speak with Caroline before the evening was over. He had to warn her. She had to know she must keep quiet. He must teach her that things spoken, even in innocence, could mean the death of them.

He must teach her how to truly become a spy.

∽

Greene marched to the front door, hands shaking with rage. Did

Anderson really think to take the word of a man so clearly driven by fiendish motives?

At least Anderson had taken the note. Was it even likely he would read it? He might think it proof of Higley's valiance in taking the woman rather than what it really proved—that she was indeed nefarious and should be dealt with as such.

The wound on his neck ached and he pressed a hand to it as he reached the large front door.

"Greene." Major Pitman neared, his long face still harboring tints of red. "Do you still have the letter?"

A curse rolled over his tongue. "Nay, sir. I gave it to Major Anderson." Perhaps he should explain. "I believed that if he read it perhaps—"

"It matters not what he thinks of it, or even if he thinks of it at all. Only what we do."

We?

"Aye." Confusion rose through him, but he pretended he saw the meaning of the forthcoming conversation. "'Tis proof she intends to free them. We must act."

"With Higley and the girl here, 'twill be difficult, but not impossible." Pitman looked behind him to the room that still bustled, not even attempting to hide the sneer. He shook his head. "I find myself in a precarious place. You are the only one who cares to find the informant as much as I and yet I wonder if I can really place my trust in you."

Was there yet a chance? He dare not ask should the answer be otherwise.

"You can, sir. I will not give up." He neared, speaking through his teeth. "I need only—"

"You must catch him in the act." Pitman's command resonated through the quiet entry.

"So you believe me. You too believe Higley is the informant."

Pitman's eyes narrowed to black slits. "I have long despised him. But Anderson's attachment to him is aggravating beyond what I can endure—the man is blinded by Higley's faux amiability, his status and relations. I for one can see that his actions are suspicious and I believe he has something to hide."

This proved there was a God in heaven. "And the woman?" *Say you believe the same of her.* "She is culpable as well, you must believe me."

"I heard her drivel long enough this evening to make me believe her capable of anything. Culpable or not."

Any pain, any discomfort or malady he'd endure the past days drained away. He was believed. That was all that mattered.

"What would you have me do, sir?"

Though he knew well enough what he wanted to do, even what he could, keeping himself in the good graces of that man who'd placed so much trust in him would secure the advancement he craved. Humility could be demeaning, but it had its place.

Looking out, Pitman stared as if he were already imagining what he wished. "Snare them. Bring them to me."

He would have him set a trap? Glee, like a mountain spring welled up in him. How had he not thought of it before? There was nothing so easy. Higley was a man of honor, a man of duty. Should there be any distress, a person in need, a Patriot in trouble, James would come to their aid. Greene need only manufacture the deceit and the valiant man would be bound to oblige.

'Twas simple and glorious in its purity.

"You can depend upon me, sir."

Pitman's small eyes thinned all the more. "I would not, if I did not feel there was no other choice."

Greene prepared to speak when Pitman pointed, finishing the rest. "Were it not for my hatred of the man of this house, or my new-found disdain for this mysterious Patriot woman, you would already now be among the soldiers on the common."

That shrinking sensation he knew so well clouded over him, and though he straightened his shoulders and back, still he felt he was growing smaller. Here was the castigation he'd expected.

"I will choose to see your failure to this point as an unfortunate volley of circumstance, but believe me, I will be watching you. I will be waiting for you to bring me my prize."

Greene swallowed, feeling a different kind of weight upon him now. A broader one. A heavier one. "I understand, sir."

"You were the reason for the success of the raid. Do it again. And make me glad I didn't have you thrown out." Whipping past Greene, he stormed to the door. "You will take a detachment of men, and the moment you have the plan in place, send for me. I want to be there for the whole of it."

A blast of cold air hit Greene in the back and he turned, watching as the man marched down the steps, barking orders to a soldier to get his horse.

While the cold bled around him, something warmer bled through him—the taste of impending victory.

# CHAPTER 30

*C*aroline hadn't moved from her spot since the moment the party began. Her legs were wooden, refusing to take her anywhere else. One man after the other came around her, questioning, flirting, demeaning. The women refused to even look her direction, except to point and snicker. How many times was she to be informed that her "cause was already dead", or to "use your beauty for better things than spying?"

Thank the good Lord that Edmond had come beside her, without his soothing presence she might have given in to the fears that berated her. Where had James gone to? Was he coming back?

"So," Edmond said, "what think you of your new-found celebrity?"

Caroline peered at Edmond whose smile and bright eyes made her all the more curious of him. He seemed too genuine, too kind to be a man of the army. Just like James...

She shook the thought of him away. "That was the intent of this evening, was it not? A jolly gathering where officers might get a chance to speak with a *real* Patriot spy." The more she spoke it, the more it raked over her, but she smiled anyway.

"They find you intriguing, true." Edmond's lips pulled up. "But they do not know you, miss. If they did they would find much more to admire than your looks, I am certain."

Struck, Caroline found herself almost mute with gratitude. "Lieutenant, that is the kindest thing anyone has said to me in a long while."

His cheeks bloomed seconds before his attention was drawn to the doorway.

"He's returned."

Caroline followed his gaze, her pulse instantly rising when her own vision struck the man she'd pretended to care nothing about. Striding with long, purposeful steps, James entered, his attention on Edmond.

He came forward, not once shifting his eyes even an inch to land on her.

"There you are." He stood beside her, but spoke to Edmond. "How are things here?"

As if Edmond could sense something unspoken, his tone widened. "As you would expect." He nodded his head toward Caroline. "Your girl is quite the popular one."

*Your girl.*

Edmond said the words so directly. Did James think of her as such?

James responded with a deep nod, then cleared his throat. "Will you excuse us for a moment?"

"Indeed." Edmond bowed. "I have been feeling somewhat parched. I shall find my way to the refreshment table."

Caroline stared after him, a villainous dichotomy warring in her chest. She didn't want Edmond to leave. She liked him. He was easy to talk to. Kind. *He's safe.* She slapped at the chiding truth. Perhaps he was safe. James was...he was...complicated. That is, her feelings were. At the same moment she craved his nearness, a bitter heat rose in her lungs, driving the thought of him into the caverns of her heart. Where was his gaggle of women? Why didn't he find them and fall into their tempting smiles? He hadn't spoken to her all evening, so why did he wish to now?

She kept her gaze outward. "You are having a good time this evening, it appears."

He didn't speak right away. "'Tis a grand party, indeed."

Did she detect a strain of sarcasm?

Despite the fact that she still didn't care for her drink she'd clutched all evening, she sipped it. "It seems you found a good many women to entertain."

He shifted and tugged on his jacket. A wash of satisfaction smoothed over her. Good. That must mean he was uncomfortable. As well he should be. Taking the opportunity to look, she regretted it instantly. His shaven jaw ticked, while his dark hair pulled into a queue begged her to touch. The masculine scent of soap and spice wafting toward her made her mouth dry. Her lungs stilled and every forbidden thought caressed her heart until it pulsed with longing.

She looked away again, angry with herself for allowing such weakness. Why would her spirit give way to him so easily? The answer sprung out, but she ignored it, though it stared her full in the face.

*You care for him.*

She didn't. Not really. Perhaps she held affection for him, but that was all she would admit.

"Did you enjoy the books I sent to you?"

The question startled, but she kept her gaze forward. Of course he would broach such a subject. Books were her home, her respite. How could she not at least answer civilly?

"I did, sir." She gazed down into the dark liquid, then toward the party. "Thank you."

*How did you know I love Cato? Where did you find a copy in so short a time?*

"Good." His posture relaxed, and she could feel his eyes on her before he too stared out. "You seem the kind to prefer intellectual books over most fiction." There was a smile in his voice. "I am pleased you liked them."

The edges of her frustration threatened to transform to warm streams of affection. She should find a curt reply, say something of how he shouldn't suppose to know her. That he shouldn't be two people at once—the man who was warm, kind and kissed her, and the man who ignored her all evening in the company of other women.

*How selfish you are, Carrie. Really.*

Her pride was wounded, and her heart nearly so. In truth, only she was to blame.

"That dress becomes you."

Caroline flicked her head toward him, not trying to hide her surprise.

His tender admission made her posture drop and she nearly thanked him, but she glued her tongue to her teeth. Any politeness between them only doused her raging barrier of protective distance. He'd kissed her. Or hadn't he remembered? If he wished to go about giving kisses to women and then refusing to speak to them, he was welcome to—but not with her.

She clutched the glass tighter. "'Tis passable."

"Passable?" Was that a hint of amusement in his voice? "You are harsh this evening, madam."

"Harsh?" She turned to him, reminding herself this was not the place to make a scene. Keeping her voice low, she allowed her anger to burn in her eyes. "Thus far this evening I have endured enough criticism to last a lifetime, *Captain*." A flood of emotions raced up from her ankles, and she spoke to ease it back. "And you, who I thought my friend, have only just now come to speak to me."

His expression went hard, the muscles of his face flexing. "I am not your friend."

Like a knife, the words stabbed, and she winced.

Releasing a quick breath, he closed his eyes and shook his head. "I didn't mean…that's not what I meant."

"Nay, you are right." Her voice came out more pinched than she wanted. She tried again. "You and I are in opposition."

"Caroline." A small heave of air pressed out. "Come with me."

"What?"

"I must speak with you."

For all her ridiculous pining, she didn't care to be alone with him. Not right now. He might see through her, catch a glimpse of the embarrassing truth she tried so desperately to hide.

She shook her head. "I am needed here, James."

Taking her by the arm, he nudged her to the exit. The urge to refuse pinched her tongue but she resisted it utterance. She'd learned in the time they'd been together, to follow his lead no matter how aggravating it might be.

"I am sorry you are feeling unwell." He eyed her, and she took the message, following his lead despite the biting questions.

She touched her forehead. "Thank you, sir." Once in the hall, she whispered. "Where are you taking me?"

"You need a bit of cool air." He didn't tamper his volume. "A few moments outside will set you to rights."

They passed a soldier, who seemed to have heard James's profession. He motioned to the left. "The veranda is this way, sir."

James nodded his thanks and Caroline continued her act, one hand to her head the other to her stomach.

When she was sure the soldier was fully out of earshot, she whispered again. "Why are you doing this?"

Holding to her arm, he opened the large door, completely ignoring her question. "There. 'Tis not terribly cold."

He lied. The chill was suffocating.

Once the door had closed completely, she crossed her arms. "We will catch our death." She kept her ire fresh, her mountain of protection against the feelings that pressed like a seedling, ready any moment to burst free.

Lanterns flickered in the moonlight, sending mists of gold light around them.

James neared, his stern voice more than a mere warning as his breath billowed in the frigid air. "We have very little time."

Her chest pumped harder and she rubbed her hands over her arms. "What do you mean?"

"Here. You are freezing." He shrugged off his jacket and draped it around her. The warmth was heaven and she prepared to thank him when he continued. "I have just learned the prisoners are scheduled to be executed Saturday morning."

*Nay.*

Her mind trailed into the unknown, taking her strength with it. "Are you certain?"

He nodded. "I've just heard it from Anderson himself."

Caroline pressed a hand to her chest. "This cannot be."

"There is still time."

There was conviction in his words, a steadfastness that granted strength to her weakening hope. "I am ready."

"I have yet to learn where the prisoners are being housed."

"He said they were at a chapel—"

"They have been moved. With so many attempts at escape, Anderson has changed their holding place and is keeping the location a secret from all but a select few. Sadly, what little investigation I have done has produced nothing. And I fear appearing too curious lest our innocence be questioned."

What could they do?

*Dear Lord, grant us wisdom.*

He pulled his bottom lip through his teeth, his gaze drifting away. "There were papers on his desk, and I am certain some of them will contain information helpful to finding your brother."

"Then we must get the papers."

"'Tis not that simple."

"Is it not?"

James rubbed his fingers over his eyes. "Nay, and even if it were simple..." He went on. Explaining how she hadn't been taught the art of secrecy and trickery. There were ways to act, and ways not to. He wished to instruct her, but there wasn't time. She didn't know the proper tactics and if she weren't careful she would put herself at greater risk. He would have to extract the information himself, but how he didn't yet know.

Caroline listened, and though he spoke one thing, her mind saw another—a scenario that filled with such real action, 'twas as if she'd already lived it.

"Wait." She reached out to him and shook her head, memorizing the vision as it played a second time. "There is another way."

James shook his head. "There is no other way, Caroline. I must—"

"I will do it."

James's mouth hinged open before he snapped it shut and pulled back. "Absolutely not."

"'Twill work, I am certain of it." She spoke the vision as she'd seen it. "When the party is over, bring Anderson into the parlor, offer him some wine, talk with him, be friendly. Keep him occupied in conversation. While you are thus engaged, I will go to his office and discover what information we need."

"Absolutely not." His eyes were soft and hard simultaneously. "I would not begin to imagine placing you in such a position."

"How hard can it truly be?" She grinned, unable to ignore the opportunity for a simple jest. "Besides, who is the spy here? Me or you?"

A flicker of something lit behind his eyes as they trailed over her. Admiration? It grew stronger and her heart fluttered.

"You have charmed many a soldier into thinking you are exactly that." His look grew richer. "Though I know what you really are."

*Don't ask him.* But the urge was too much and she nibbled at the bait. "And what am I, Captain Higley?"

His rich, smooth voice warmed over her like a summer breeze as he took a step closer. "You are a fearless, determined woman. A woman who will, without inhibition, speak her mind."

Her defenses raised their fists, but the way his words rolled from his tongue held none of the familiar angst as when Timothy had said them. Gone was the jealousy, the anger she'd felt some hours ago. Gone were the self-serving thoughts that barred her nearness to him.

She held tight to the jacket. "I suppose I was a bit over zealous."

"Nay." His quiet protest tugged her vision up. "Do not change." Again his gaze smoothed over her like a silken robe. "Do not still your words. Women's voices are what our country needs. Silence is as great an enemy as any."

What did he mean *our* country?

"You baffle me, James Higley." She stared up at him, trying in vain to slay the yearning that breathed through her soul. "I wonder if I will ever uncover the mystery of you."

He said nothing, but his eyes flickered as if he tucked her words away somewhere deep inside of him. After a glance to the door, he spoke. "We should go back in."

"Not until you accept."

"Accept what?" His brows folded.

"The plan." Did he not remember? "I will go into his office—"

"Nay. We've already discussed this."

"I can do it."

"I've explained to you, Caroline. 'Twould be dangerous."

"Am I not already in danger? What more could I risk by doing this?"

That look returned, his gaze smoothing over her like a lover's hands. "I cannot let you."

She bent toward him, as much seriousness in her tone as levity. "Then you will have to stop me."

His eyes stilled, and he sighed. "I can see you are unmoved."

"I am." Would he give?

He closed his mouth and breathed out long through his nose. "I cannot say I approve."

Caroline grinned, hoping the draw of her lips would pull him closer. "I would do so without it."

"Ah, there you are."

Caroline jumped and James spun in front of her.

Edmond was at the door, half of him in, half of him out, his expression alight with amusement. "Anderson sent me in search of you." He smirked. "I might have known you would seek some place to be alone."

James took Caroline at the arm and led her inside. "Will you inform the major that Miss Whitney is unwell and must return to her room. I fear this cool air has done little to improve her."

Caroline held her hand at her middle and offered a meager grin to her new friend. "Forgive me, Lieutenant."

"No apology necessary, miss."

Caroline halted and slipped the jacket from her shoulders, returning it to her gallant knight. "Give my regrets to the major and the others."

She made for the stairs, feeling the eyes of the other two upon her. She might not be returning to the party, but for her, the evening had only just begun.

～

James watched as she ascended the stairs, praying his scheme would play out in reality as it did in his mind. With Caroline gone, the party would disperse more quickly, he hoped, then he and Anderson could have time to speak alone.

"Overwhelmed, is she?" Edmond looked up until she'd disappeared into her room. "I suppose this means my time at the party is over as well."

"Sorry, old friend. It appears all the attention was too much for her."

"Too bad. Though I cannot say that I blame her." Edmond made a face. "I wonder what Anderson will say when he learns his prize is not returning?"

"I doubt he will find reason to accuse her." He reached for his pocket watch. "Already half past midnight. The party has been going for some time."

Nodding, Edmond started for the stairs. "Must be at my post."

"Wait."

His friend halted, and James's stomach turned stone-like. He must ask him. There was no other way. "Tonight...I mean when everyone is gone...I need you to do something for me."

"Anything."

James swallowed, letting out the words before they refused him. "I need you to let Caroline out of her room."

Edmond lowered his chin and raised his eyebrows. "You are asking me to neglect my duty?" He grinned suspiciously. "I did that once before, and I still haven't recovered from the guilt. I don't wish to take such a risk again."

He'd suspected he would say as much. "I beg you, don't ask me to explain." James prayed the goodness of the man would win over his dutiful side. "I need only to—"

"Oh." Edmond's face brightened. "Ohhh. I understand."

He did? Not until Edmond's grin grew into a playful one did James fully comprehend what his friend implied.

A strain of panic inked through him. If he allowed this kind of reputation for Caroline...He groaned in silence. And yet, was there any other way? Best that it be known she was his.

James peered toward her room. "I don't intend anything." Perhaps he could soften things. "I just wish a little time—"

"No need to explain, friend." Edmond started up the stairs and winked. "I shall expect her back before dawn at least."

*Good man, Edmond.*

A thread of guilt needled through him. If Edmond were caught, the damage to his military career would be catastrophic.

What a friend he was, to be willing to turn his back for James with hardly an explanation.

Yet if they could not get what they needed...

James stared after his friend. Let him think what he would. The Cause, and Enoch, depended on them.

# CHAPTER 31

$\mathcal{O}$nly a handful of minutes had passed since the last partygoer bowed their thanks and drifted into the night. James watched from his hiding spot in the sitting room, listening and waiting for the moment to strike.

Edmond, good man that he was, had given a note to Caroline from him, saying what time she was to come to him. If Edmond had given in to curiosity, he would have read nothing suspicious.

Having watched from the darkness of the room, he knew all had left or gone to their beds. All except Anderson. A providential event, surely.

Stepping out of his hiding spot, he moved into the silent hall. A dim light draped over the carpet from the wide-open doorway of the room Anderson still employed.

James flexed his fists and inhaled like a gladiator preparing for the arena. This was no amphitheater and he no warrior, but this room, small as it was, was the battlefield.

Striding into the parlor, he stopped hard. "Oh, forgive me, Major, I didn't know you were still up."

Anderson turned from his place at the table, pouring himself a drink. "James. Can't sleep, can you?" He raised his glass, a sly expression over his mouth as he lifted his glass. "Any reason?"

He implied Caroline, and James chose to take the easy route. "You see through me, sir."

"A man can't help but enjoy beauty when he sees it." He ambled toward him. "So long as it does not impede your soldiering, I cannot see how Stockton or anyone, for that matter, would disapprove."

James shrugged and strode to the table. "Greene disapproves."

Anderson grumbled. "I suspect that man would disapprove of a sow eating slop." He chuckled. "Miss Whitney might be the enemy, but that shouldn't stop a hot-blooded man from enjoying himself."

Entering further, James worked his theatric skill and changed the disturbing subject. "I cannot forgive myself for not having spoken of Greene's capture. I should have—"

"Oh, don't harass yourself." Anderson released a gruff sigh when he sat. "I spent two minutes with the man, and I can tell you, I would have forgotten about him just the same."

James allowed a polite laugh to ease from his chest before moving to the table to pour himself a drink. "Your party was a success."

Anderson leaned back in his chair, a satisfied grin across his lips. "I do think so myself."

Full glass in hand, James took the seat opposite. Warmth from the fire rippled through the air toward him. "So, what know you of Howe and his plans for the Patriots?" He sipped, oozing confident nonchalance. "We do nothing but wait. He must have some sort of plan?"

"I suppose he must, but he's breathed nothing of it to me." Anderson stretched out. "If the king is willing to put the entirety of the nation in their hands, I have a hard time opposing it."

"What of Dorchester? What are the plans there? Should we not take it?"

"The Patriots are surrounded, there is little they can do. With this weather as bitter as it is, they cannot move this way or that."

"Do you suppose they plan to attack us then?"

"Nay, but if they do 'twill be a futile attempt." His expression turned somber. "I will tell you this, if we don't move quickly our forces will be diminished to a ragged army unfit for warfare. They are defeated as it is. This town is rotten as hell."

James said nothing. Staring into his glass, he nodded to indicate he heard and let the words roll over him.

*Speak more.*

As if Anderson heard him, he did. "We are expecting more troops from Quebec, and another fleet of ships in the next weeks."

"More troops?"

At last. Information he could use. James soothed the rise of his pulse, the thrill of learning something Washington would wish to know.

Pressing the glass to his lips, he swallowed the tangy liquid, praying that Caroline would have as much success as he. That she would be swift and silent. That she would be safe.

And by heaven's grace, that she wouldn't get caught.

Caroline stared at the clock, her pulse matching the rhythm of its quiet tick. She licked her lips, watching the minute-hand twitch until at last it reached the twelve.

Edmond's delivery of James's note was fortuitous. They'd not had time to discuss the hour of their action, but now there was no question.

*Lord, protect me. Give me strength.*

Going to the door, 'twas as if she could hear James's words from the note.

*Swift and silent. Two o'clock.*

Though he'd promised she would get past Edmond without his

questioning, she hadn't any idea how James would arrange it. If she couldn't get past—nay. She raised her chin, sloughing away the doubt.

She must, and she would.

Prying the door open a mite, she peeked out to her guard and he turned her way, shoulders down and eyes wide.

He rose from his chair and stood tall. "Good evening." His whisper was polite, curious. Not cautious. She smiled inwardly. What had James told him?

Edmond peered down the hall before facing her. "Where are you headed this time?"

Her mind went white, every excuse obliterated with fear.

"I...I'm..."

"Be careful." Edmond smiled sideways. "Wouldn't want you getting caught."

Did he know?

She tried to swallow. What should she say? He didn't seem at all upset if indeed he knew what she planned to do.

A jovial expression eased over his face. "A soldier and a Patriot. An interesting match indeed."

Caroline didn't move as the meaning of his statement fell in soft pieces around her.

He thought she and James were...

Her cheeks flamed and she stepped back, forcing a grin to cover the heat of embarrassment.

Edmond nudged forward with his chin. "Go. So long as you are back before sunrise, I will pretend I know nothing."

Never had her limbs felt so stiff. How was she ever to turn and get down the stairs without tripping and rolling head over heels?

Nodding her thanks, she started the perilous journey. Though 'twas only down the stairway, around the corner and down the hall, it might as well have been fifty miles. She held her breath, allowing only the tips of her shoes to touch the floor as she went.

*If you are caught, Carrie, he will not hesitate in killing you. Are you certain you wish to take that risk?*

Her heart pounded against her ribs like a prisoner begging for freedom. Her mind continued the barrage of questions. *Are you sure you are strong enough? What if you fail?* She stopped at the end of the stairs and looked both directions before continuing down the hall, her thoughts rolling to a stop at the foot of the truth. This was for Enoch—for him and the rest of the men trapped and begging for rescue. *You can do this, Carrie. You can do all things through Christ.*

She swallowed, calling again on the name of The One who would carry her on silent feet.

*Please, Lord. Help me.*

Careful not to make a sound, she started for the office. Every brush of shoe against floor, every creek of wood, every swish of her skirt made her hairs stand ever more on edge.

Though she couldn't see the doorway where James and Anderson spoke, their voices pranced merrily toward her. Knowing James as she did, he would keep every possible attention away from the hall, but—

Her toe caught on the carpet and she stumbled forward, her hands flying out to the wall. She didn't move, her pulse exploding with every pump. Motionless, she listened to the sounds from the parlor, her stomach in her throat.

After a few seconds, she breathed again. They were unchanged. Thank heaven.

Straightening, she lifted her skirts and tip-toed faster and with more care. There was painfully little time.

She halted at the open doorway before she bound and gagged the fear that promised to smother her.

There was no turning back now.

~

"Did you hear something?" Anderson swiveled in his seat, scowling toward the doorway.

James's heart was in his neck, pulsing with wild panic. *Aye.* He frowned, shaking his head. "Nay, sir."

Blinking, Anderson hummed and switched his attention too slowly back to his glass. James willed him to forget, to ignore, to speak of something else. Anything.

Satisfied with the simple answer, Anderson readjusted his position in the large chair, neckcloth slightly askew. Ominous curiosity needled his voice. "Do you really think Miss Whitney so innocent?"

The question smacked James across the face. Worry bled up his neck, but he pretended otherwise.

"I have told you time and again, sir, I do not believe her culpable in any crime. I believe her to be nothing more than a puppet."

"Aye, but puppets are inclined to act as their masters say, no matter the consequences." He bit his lip, studying the dark liquid in his glass. "She is not imbecilic—she has a mind. A strong one. And I dare say I would be a fool to underestimate her."

"I would say that is wise, sir."

James prepared for another sip, but pulled the glass away from his mouth. The thought of anything more in his belly was nauseating.

He rested the cup beside him. Looking at the wall, he prayed more fervently than he had in his lifetime.

*Get in, Caroline. Then get out.*

Caroline entered the office, keeping her motions slow, deliberate. Dark as ink and riddled with unseen furniture, the room offered little light. What glow there was, came from the sconces on the veranda outside the large paned window. At least it was something.

Holding large handfuls of gown, she moved her way around the desk and studied the shadowed papers. She tightened her jaw. This wouldn't work. She had to see.

Scanning the desk, she spied a candle, and without counseling wisdom, lit it.

She swallowed and looked up. She should have closed the door.

Pulse thick and steady, Caroline studied the papers. There were so many. Moving them around, she prayed God would guide her. She slid a map of New York aside, revealing a few letters. None were of consequence.

Her muscles began to spasm, panic smacking her on the shoulder. *Hurry.* There had to be something.

Bending, she slipped open a drawer and gasped. A stack of folded letters winked at her in the dusty light. She set the candle on the table and lifted them out, hastily reading the first one. Nothing.

The voices from the adjacent room crescendoed and she froze. Were they coming? Nay! The sound dimmed again and she took it as hope that she yet had time. She flipped open two more. Again, nothing.

The next, the same. Her fingers quivered. She had to know where Enoch was held. It had to be here somewhere.

The hum from the parlor grew louder. There was no time left. She had to go.

*One more.*

Like a celestial admonition, the prompting urged her with such force, her arms seemed to work without her permission.

Opening the crisp parchment, she read—and instantly stilled.

*...Patriot prisoners held beneath Rockford's Tavern on Newberry Street...*

Rockford's Tavern. Newberry Street.

There it was.

A flood of relief washed through her limbs.

*Thank you, Lord.*

A mumble of voices struck her ears, followed by the rhythmic *ta-tum* of boots against the floor. Vice-like panic gripped her lungs, shaking her entire frame.

She gasped for breath. *They're coming this way.*

Stuffing the letters back in the drawer, Caroline blew out the candle and dashed for the doorway when two figures appeared and made their way down the hall.

Numb, she lunged for the door and hid behind it seconds before their voices became clear.

"It will take only a moment to discover it."

James's robust tone was smooth. "Really, sir, I needn't—"

"Nonsense." Anderson lingered in the doorway. "Light that candle beside you, will you?"

*Nay!*

If any candle were lit, he would see the one she'd just blown out...*Lord, help.*

James walked in, stopping beside him. "Sir, I—"

"Major Anderson?"

There was a scrape of shoe against floor, and Caroline could only suspect Anderson had turned to see who addressed him.

"Private Welsh." Anderson's growl gouged the air. "What is it? Why must I always be interrupted?"

"A courier, sir," the man answered. "Returning with the information you requested."

"Well." All ire had gone out of his tone. "About time. Tell him I shall be there in a moment."

Anderson marched toward the door, still shrouded in black.

At the doorway he stopped and she held her breath, spying him from the space between the hinges of the doorjamb. "I'll see to this business with Private Welsh then I'm to bed. 'Tis too late already with dawn only a few hours away."

"Good night, sir," James said.

The stomp of Anderson's boots echoed through the hall, then fell silent.

James didn't move. Not right away. Almost as if he knew Caroline was hidden just inches from him and wished to guard her.

Caroline's lungs refused to take air, and she pleaded with heaven. Never had the confines of her prison-room been so coveted.

In the space of two strained breaths, James strode away, leaving Caroline in the dark, monitoring the sounds of the hall, and calculating the steps it would take before she was once again safe behind her door.

# CHAPTER 32

*I*n his room, James stared at the door, his racing pulse beating hard through his veins.

Had he waited long enough?

He took the watch from his pocket and squinted to see the time in the almost absent light.

Half past three.

Plenty long enough. He bit his cheeks. Perhaps a few more minutes just to be sure. Though he would be shocked if Anderson wasn't already sleeping. The man pretended to hold his liquor but no doubt he was in a heavy stupor.

The darkness cooed around him, luring his memory to places he had, until now, found the strength to resist. He brushed his fingers over the letter in his pocket, recalling the words Caroline's brother had so lovingly penned. No wonder she cared for him so. Courage and caring ran in their blood it would seem.

He'd addressed her as Carrie. The name was an endearment, and its mellifluous sound nested in James's mind.

The need to free Enoch became more than a political one, as Caroline's needs became his own.

The need to get her away from here was paramount.

James closed his eyes to hone the recollection of her. How he longed to hold her again. To kiss her and relive all those pleasures he'd felt the first time their lips had touched in the cabin.

He shook his head. *Come man, you are better than this.* There was no way to give to the cause he loved, and to love a woman.

*Liar.*

Growling, he turned and rested his back against the door, cutting down his foolish inner-man. Nay. In the far future perhaps, when all was over and life was peaceful. Not now.

He checked his watch again, but didn't really look. It had to be enough time by now. He needed to see her, to see what she'd gotten—if anything. That was all. Nothing more.

*Liar.*

He ground his teeth, and without allowing himself the counsel of a second thought, he hurdled past the pleading parts of him and hurried from his room and up the stairs.

Edmond rose even before James reached the top, his brow creased. "What did you do to her?" he whispered.

James halted, mimicking his friend's hushed tone. "What do you mean?"

Edmond pointed at the door. "She raced up here like she was fleeing the gates of hell." He scowled harder. "I am almost certain she was trembling. I beg you to tell me you weren't the cause of her distress."

She'd been trembling? Something must have happened.

"Edmond, I—"

"When she left there was a sprite-ness in her step. When she returned, it had vanished."

Realization flickered and James shook his head, recalling the implied nature of his earlier request, and how Edmond had grinned over it. "Oh. You think that I...that she and I—" He shook his head and hoped to white-wash his friend's concern with a layer of thick sincerity. "I give you my word, I didn't do anything—"

"I don't know her well, James," Edmond interrupted, timbre rough but sincere. "And despite the fact she is a Patriot, she deserves to be treated well. Especially by you."

Was Edmond scolding him? The thought brought a smile to his lips, but he resisted its freedom. Staring, he puzzled over the best way to answer. There were several paths he could traverse to reach the safest resolution. He chose the quickest.

James practiced a remorseful expression. "You must know, I never intended to hurt her."

"I know, James. You're a good man." Edmond dipped his chin. "She looked so lovely tonight. And I know she was jealous—all those ladies vying for your attention."

"Jealous?"

"How did you not notice?" Edmond's expression sloped to disappointment. "You should have gone to her sooner—"

"Do not accuse me of being oblivious." A burst of James's own hidden jealousy popped to the surface. "It seems to me she had plenty of gentlemen interested in her."

"Aye," Edmond said, almost on top of him, "and not in ways I would imagine you'd approve."

A billow of indignation smoked through James's lungs. He'd known she would be the recipient of some untoward gentleman, but the way Edmond said it, sounded like 'twas blatant. He ground his teeth, feeling the muscles in his jaw tick as he chewed over the grisly truth. As much as he'd wished to be at her side, he couldn't risk the appearance of attraction. Already Anderson knew it, and that alone was dangerous. At least the man seemed to find it amusing. For now...

He shook his head, looking at the door. "If I had known I would have—"

"'Tis not about knowing, James. Rather about noticing."

That was the problem. If he noticed her as often as he wished to, thought of her often as his heart desired, it would be the blow that shot him through, sinking not only his ship, but the entire flotilla.

Where once he'd feigned the part of a guilty lover, now he felt it. He'd asked Caroline to do and be something she never intended. She'd risked her life. For him. For The Cause. In truth, what she'd done tonight was nothing short of heroic.

Never had he known such a woman.

Of a sudden, the need to see her clawed at him like never before.

"Women are tender creatures, James." Edmond rested a hand on his shoulder. "They must be treated with care."

If his friend wasn't so sincere, James might have found his admonition aggravating. Edmond meant well, but Caroline's tenderness was not in the sense of weakness, timidity. Nay, she was fearless. Brave. 'Twas her heart that was tender—she cared, she loved, she hoped.

Staring down, the weight of all he'd carried—all he'd forced her to carry—rested on his back, hanging there, refusing to let go.

The core of his thoughts breathed free. "I need to talk to her." Lifting his head, he studied the kind expression of the man who thought to lecture him.

'Twas a moment before Edmond responded with a nod. He twisted the handle. "If you aren't careful, James, you might lose her."

James laughed through a whisper. "That would imply that I have her."

Edmond chuckled and released his hold. "Don't pretend with me."

"Pretend?" James bristled.

"This charade? I cannot be the only one who sees through it."

Sees through *what*? "What do you mean?"

"'Tis only a matter of time before the truth comes out."

Whatever his friend implied he couldn't be sure, but he didn't like the way this conversation tended. "Open the door, Edmond."

"Falling in love with your prisoner—with the enemy? 'Tis a dangerous game."

Love? How could Edmond even suggest such a thing? Anderson had done so, but he'd dismissed it, thinking it to be only a silly notion. Now that Edmond did the same it made his back tighten. James might feel affection, even deeply, but love was something else entirely.

Irritation pooled in his limbs, and he jerked his hand toward the door, a wide-eyed stare on his face. "Will you not let me in?"

Edmond shrugged, once more reaching for the handle. "I've warned you."

He gave his friend a glare and hurried in, grateful when the door shut immediately behind him.

"Caroline."

"James." She spun from her position by the fireplace and hurried forward, stopping inches from him.

He took her at the elbows, holding her, resisting the need to pull her to him. "Are you alright?" Beneath his grip he could feel her shaking. "Were you seen?"

"Nay. I don't believe so." She shook her head. "But I was hidden behind the door when Anderson entered—I feared I would be discovered but...I believe I was not."

James nodded, recalling the doorway, the office. He hadn't detected her. And he detected everything. He inched closer. "A true spy then."

She grinned at the implication. "They are being held at Rockford's Tavern on Newberry Street."

Inwardly calculating, James diverted his gaze. "'Tis not far. Two streets down and one over."

"Our work is nearly done then." Her voice wobbled, and her visible quaking refused to subside. "We will save him after all...if he still lives."

The fragile edge on which he stood gave way. Distance be hanged. He tugged her near and wrapped his arms around her.

Stroking her silken hair, he relished her sweet scent and the way her head fit perfectly under his chin. He gently hushed her, hoping his embrace could calm her anxiety. "You are safe now."

She sighed against him. "I feel safe—in your arms."

James closed his eyes, letting the tender confession wink around him like a starry night.

His pulse raced and no amount of defiance would cut its pace.

Everything wailed within him, jumping and shouting for him to retreat, but he couldn't. Some desires were born of something too grand to disclaim.

Nudging her forward, he cupped her face. "I shouldn't have done this to you."

Her eyes, usually clear and blue in the sunlight, were deep and dark, inviting. Irresistible.

"You didn't force me, James." Husky, her voice lulled him closer. "We help each other to reach our goals."

"I'm sorry I neglected you so long tonight." When she didn't reply, he finished the rest. "I saw you walk in, and in truth, I kept my distance because I didn't wish to make a scene—to show how I wished to be near you."

Her dainty brows lifted. "Really?"

He nodded, memorizing the way her hair fell around her ears.

"Why didn't you say as much?"

"How could I?" Dusting his finger along her feather-soft hairline sent a jolt through his skin. "I wish to close the distance between us. But I fear what might happen if we try."

Caroline lowered her head, robbing him of the joy of her face. "There are oceans between us, James." At this she looked up, a gleam of hurt in the shadows of her face. "A distance we will never traverse. So long as you and I are enemies."

"Are we?" He stroked her cheek. "Are we enemies?"

Her face crumpled, and she pulled away. The ribbon her closeness had tied around his heart tugged until his chest ached.

"I don't know what we are."

All that couldn't be spoken, but that lived in his heart, played its mournful melody.

She crossed her arms and focused her attention somewhere in the corner. "When will we free him?"

"Soon, Carrie. I promise." The name he'd read in her brother's note gripped his heart and came out in his words.

The stones of the wall he'd erected fell away with every tick of the clock behind her. He took another step, and another.

"Your brother is indebted to you." *As am I.*

Her throat bobbed as her vision moved from his face to his chest and back up. "I would do anything for him."

He took another step, aching to touch her. "As you have done for your country."

She swallowed. When she spoke, her whisper was thin, fragile. "James, what are you doing?"

"I am thanking you."

There was a pull, that need that drew her near him, the likes of which he had no control. It was a thirst sated only by the sweet nectar that poured from her soul to his.

Perhaps it was the dark, the heightened sense of danger. Perhaps it was his admiration of her courage and strength.

Nay. It was more. And it begged to be tested, tried and purchased.

But at what cost?

A shadow passed over the thought, and he continued into the tempting waters.

He reached out and untangled her folded arms, allowing his body to move even closer to her.

Her breath raced, luring thoughts to his mind he knew could be deadly. But he didn't care.

Were she to move, to resist, to plead him away, he would obey.

Slowly, he moved his fingers against her cheek before cupping her face. "I could not do what I do, without you."

Her body tensed. "I don't...I don't know what you mean."

He moved his thumb along her velvety skin, feeling the wild pulse in her neck, the delicate shape of her collarbone.

Her throat bobbed, her voice quivering. "You are a man of secrets."

"Ask me." He felt his lids growing heavy, his head nodding toward hers. "Ask me what you wish to know."

At long last the trembling melted away, and she peered at him through dreamy eyes. The tips of her fingers dusted over his scar, her gaze a delicate kiss.

"Tell me...of this."

# CHAPTER 33

*R*everent, the silent dark took its place around them. His arms at her back, her hands at his face, Caroline's spirit melded with his. Though it shouldn't.

For now, she didn't care.

"You wish to know how I came by this do you?" His voice was rich, warm. "I fear you may not like the telling."

She touched it again, its red and uneven edges smooth to the touch. "I feel I should know at least something of you."

His gaze drifted off, as if he were tugged into some place that required him before he could speak.

Taking her hands, he brought them down and held them in his own. "Once, in a prison cell much like the one Enoch suffers in, I visited a prisoner." Strains of pain weaved through his words. He cleared his throat. "While I was speaking to him, a man attacked with a broken bottle and I swerved in time, but not soon enough to save my ear."

Imagining the horror of such a thing, she touched it with her vision now, not her hands.

"That must have been horrible for you." Then the real question lunged from her chest. "The prisoner you went to see...who...who was it?"

He stepped away, and instantly she regretted the question, wishing she could take a hold of time and wrench it back.

Still looking away, James sat on the bench at the edge of the bed, speaking to the fire as if it had been the questioning party.

"I was the friend of a well-known Tory some five years ago." He opened his mouth as if he were to speak more, then closed it and waited several breaths before he finished. "Anyone who knew him considered him one of the wisest, most honorable men in Boston. I never knew anyone so generous and kind." He paused, visibly aching. "But he was taken in the forgery of official documents and found guilty of treasonous actions against the king."

Caroline didn't move, hardly even wished to breathe. He was there, in the past. She could see it undulating over his face. She sat next to him, careful not to touch him though she wished to, afraid the action would be not only too familiar, but would drag him away from the place he seemed to want to be.

"He begged me to listen to him. To believe him." His voice grew deeper. "Claiming that he hadn't done it, but I didn't believe him. Not at first. I told him there were rules, that there was evidence against him and that I could not in good faith go against what so clearly was true."

He pressed out a quick, curt breath. "I was disillusioned and full of pious beliefs of duty and honor. I told him that there was nothing I could do for him. His family was afraid, hurt, shocked. They too turned to me, but what condolence could I offer?"

Caroline studied her fingers. Regret choked through his words. Whatever had happened beyond what he offered was wrenching, that was certain.

"He was held for three months," he said. "Every time I went to him he begged me to speak on his behalf, to say that I knew he was a good man and devoted to the crown, but I was too shocked and hurt to believe him. He'd been like a father to me, and the pain I felt was beyond compare." His voice wavered and he cleared his throat. "Then, hours before he was to be hanged, I learned of a rumor that in fact he had not done what he was accused of. I went to him and inquired, and truly, the holes were filled in his story and I saw what I had been too blind or too foolish to see. He was innocent. And I had done nothing in his defense."

"Was he killed?"

Caroline snapped her mouth shut, ashamed she'd spoken the question out loud.

"I hastened to the prison yard and found him there, almost too sick with grief to speak my regret. I told him how sorry I was, that I should have believed him. I told him I would do my best to get him out, but I knew it was too late. That was when I was attacked. My assailant hated that I would think to defend a Tory convicted of crimes against the king, and wished to 'end' me, as he put it."

James touched the top of his ear, then looked at his fingers. "I carry with me daily the reminder of the vow I made that day."

Vow?

This time Caroline was able to keep the question behind her teeth. Thankfully, he answered the very thing she didn't say.

"I told myself I would do whatever it took to avenge him. To live a life worthy of the man who'd been slain. To help the innocent, to defend the weak."

James pushed from the bed and went to the fireplace. Slowly, James reached for his pocket and revealed the lovely timepiece she'd seen before. "He gave me this, on his way to the gallows."

'Twas too dark to see it in detail from her place on the bed, but she knew it as well as if she saw it in daylight. The delicate inscription beamed across the room and into her heart.

*To have all, you need only have hope.*

"I was beside myself." At this he looked up. "Edmond knew him too, knew everything as I did. We were heartsick. But no one felt the depth of responsibility that I did. I loved him as a son loves a father, and I am as guilty as if I had sentenced him."

As if burying his friend all over again, James tucked the piece carefully in his pocket.

Benumbed with shock and working through the intimate revelation, Caroline sat motionless, her knitted fingers in her lap.

"I am sorry I made you speak of it."

He shook his head, still looking at the fire. "Nay. 'Tis good to do so. I have not ever spoken of it. Not since it happened." At this he turned his head. "Something about you makes it easy to bare the unpleasant parts of myself."

"There is nothing you have done for which you must be ashamed."

"Is there not?" He looked away.

"You did what you thought was your duty. What else could you have—"

"I could have believed him." He spoke words heavy and sharp. "I knew him so well, I should have taken his word over the evidence of strangers."

"We all have regrets."

She stood and walked to the fire, keeping her stare away from his. "We all live with things we wish we hadn't done, or had done differently. Sometimes we wish we ourselves were different."

Though she still looked forward, she could feel his gaze on her. "Different?"

That tender familiarity that had grown since their first meeting now plumed into a large, soft cushion. She called it home, settling into its welcoming center. Where with Timothy she'd hidden, with James she was free.

"I have long since been told my outspoken ways, my political leanings and such were unbecoming." Just saying the words made her fingers clench. She looked down and rubbed her thumb over her fingers, lest the pity she knew she would see in his downcast eyes would drag down her already limp spirit.

Thinking of the truth always weighed upon her, anchoring her, impeding the progress of a life she wished to have, and likely never would.

"I..." Caroline pulled her bottom lip through her teeth. What was it about him that made her feel so comfortable? Dare she say what she nearly did? Why not? What did it matter? In a few short days, hours even, she would never see him again. At least now, in this moment, she enjoyed that comfortable compatibility she always hoped for herself, but never knew was possible.

She licked her lips and tried again. "I was engaged once. Three years ago." Braving a look, she spied him and found none of the pity she expected, but compassion, sincerity. A tremor started behind her breast, and she took a breath of courage before she continued. "I thought myself in love. I thought, 'now I shall have the life I wished.'" Pausing, Caroline inhaled. "But I was not the real Caroline. I dressed and spoke and acted in the way I thought I should—the way Timothy wished me to. And when he asked for my hand, I believed myself validated in that facade, proving to myself that indeed my real identity was not fitting, not appealing or attractive. Until the charade became too heavy to wear, and I began to shed the layers."

"You didn't marry him?"

The smooth embrace of his voice lured her to him, but she forced her frame to keep still.

"Nay." She fought a silent laugh. "The longer our engagement progressed, the more I allowed my true self to come alive, and when I did—when I spoke of politics or went riding or fired a musket with Enoch—Timothy would scold me, saying he was marrying a lady not an overmountain man. I did my best to appease him—so he would tell me that he loved me once again." She shrugged. "I would habitually don the approved pretense over and over, but 'twas not long before Timothy said he'd witnessed enough of the real Caroline, and that he could not love me the way I was. And he left."

Warm fingers took her at the elbow, and she looked up, enclosed in the evergreen eyes of the man she had grown to trust.

"The man was a fool."

"Nay, I was." She swiveled to face him. "I was a fool to be heartbroken over such a man, foolish to attempt to be anything but who I am." She paused. "We all do things we regret and must carry those things with us."

His mouth hardened. "But you didn't kill anyone."

"Neither did you."

He turned away, as if her words cut. The pain he felt reached from his heart and into hers. Aching for him, she held his arms, craning her head so he could see her. "You cannot live with that, James. You must learn to let it go."

"How can I?" He pulled away and stepped back to the fire. "You speak of paltry things when I live daily with the reminder that the man I cared for was killed because of my negligence."

His gaze fell away, and she reached up to his face, relishing the roughness of his unshaven jaw. "I do not intend to compare my suffering to yours. Any regret a person feels—great or small—can be overcome. But only through God. No vengeance or vow or attempt to forget will ever take the place of grace."

His throat worked. "This need to right my wrong—it gives me purpose."

"It is not all that gives you purpose." She forced him to look at her by sheer strength of her gaze. "There is something deep within you, James, something even more powerful that gives you strength to do what you do." He didn't look away, so she finished. "I have not known you more than a few days, but I see it—I feel it."

That sacred silence returned, and his eyes flickered as if by God's goodness her words filtered over him. Would that he might do more than toss them away. Would that he kept them there and made them part of him.

She moved forward, taking his hands in hers. "You are more

than your mistakes, James. Let your deeper need impel you, and I know you will gain more than you believed you could."

His eyes shimmered for a moment before the emotion that lived in his gaze settled on one more tender, one that resembled longing.

Studying her face, he brushed a hand along her ear, tucking a stray hair behind it. "I cannot endure the thought of a *different* Caroline." He continued to trail his fingers along her skin, down her neck. "Your mind is as beautiful as your heart." His already hooded eyes drooped in dreaminess even more. "Do not keep it hidden from the world. Especially not from me."

Her pulse quickened. The agonizing reality she'd ignored barreled forward. "We are strangers, James."

His voice was a warm, welcome bed. "Are we?" Without stopping his fingers along her skin, he moved them up behind her neck and into her hair. "I feel as if I have known you far longer than mere days."

'Twas true. Her spirit spoke to his, and his to hers. But how could such a thing be? He a soldier and she...she the enemy? His were the men who caused such grief to her family. Could she love such a man?

Love.

Dear Lord. She loved him.

She hadn't long to study the realization before he reached for his pocket and removed a folded paper. Gently, he nudged it toward her. "Here."

Taking it, Caroline unfolded the letter and her lungs hitched. She shot her head toward him, eyes burning. "Where did you get this?"

"From Anderson, who got it from Greene."

"Greene? How did he..."

James's expression hardened, worry chipping into the angles of his cheekbones and jaw.

Her pulse went shallow. "What is it?"

Slow, deliberate, he smoothed his hands over her cheeks, stroking his thumbs against her skin.

"When we find your brother..." He stopped, his timbre thick as if the words were too unpleasant to let out. "When he is free, you must go with him."

Caroline shivered as the cold truth poured down her back. The same thought had lived in the far shadows of her mind, but she'd ignored them. She couldn't reply, though his anguished expression begged for it.

"You must. For your safety, and his." James brushed his thumb against her cheek, his voice a whisper. "'Tis best, I believe, that we never see each other again."

# CHAPTER 34

*J*ames's legs went rigid, his chest to stone. The thing he'd loathed to speak was now free, floating in the air and releasing its poison.

Slowly, Caroline backed away, tearing the tender cord that drew them together.

"I suppose you are right." Sighing, she studied her hands. "We are enemies after all."

He reached for her arm and tugged her toward him. "We are not enemies." *We are anything but enemies.*

"You are a good man." Her voice trembled. "You have proven my previous assumptions about every soldier to be wrong. And for that I am indebted to you."

"Is that all you have seen from me?"

There was more she wished to say, he could see it in the bob of her throat, the sheen in her eyes.

"I have seen bravery and chivalry." She stepped back, her posture adjusting as if she wished to remove the bit of familiarity that had grown between them. "I have seen that a soldier, when he is a good one, can be trusted."

The throbbing in his chest consumed him and he took her

hands in his, drawing them around his back. "Is there nothing else? What do you see of the man who holds you?"

Her blue eyes, like clear spring pools, washed over him. "Honor. Devotion. Duty."

*Aye, but more. You should see that I love you.*

As the words flowed through his mind and down to his heart, he held them there, examining them as one would a precious gem. He did love her. It seemed he had almost from the moment he'd seen her. How such a thing could be, he didn't know but didn't dare deny. Yet despite the beautiful truth, ghostly eyes threatened mutiny behind the door of his conscious. He could not do this. Could not betray the promise he'd made.

But was love a betrayal? Was giving way to this yearning that was larger than heaven a betrayal or a deliverance?

Perhaps God had given him this woman to bind the wounds he carried, keep him strong. Keep him alive in the valleys that filled with phantoms, both real and imagined.

*Tell her.*

The admonition whispered through him, a golden thread twining around his inner wounds. Should he? *Could* he? Would she even believe him?

Before he'd known her, his life had been driven by guilt, by need and the quest to give back by helping others, by striving for liberty. Now, with the world wrapped in his embrace, he could see as he had never seen before. He could be driven by something else. Something infinitely more powerful.

*Tell her.*

She stroked him with that gaze he'd grown to love, and he could not hold back.

"Carrie..."

Her lips slipped upward at the ends, revealing what he'd hoped she would feel at his calling her thus.

"Aye?"

His throat thickened, and for a moment, his tongue refused to function. What he wanted more than anything was also the greatest risk. Revealing his devotion to and work for The Glorious Cause, his love of liberty and freedom—revealing his position would put not only him, but her in ever greater danger.

"There's something I need you to know."

With her soft, cool fingers on his jaw, she carried him in a gaze that softened the worries that pricked him. "Tell me." Slowly, she rose to her toes, caressing his jaw before pressing the cushion of her lips perfectly against his. "Tell me..."

Bolts of passion chased through him, releasing in him all the forbidden pleasures he'd bound in the treasure chest of his soul.

Unlocked and unfettered, he let free his desires. Holding her against him, he nudged her lips open, savoring the way her soft breath hitched when he held her face, how she melted against him when he deepened the kiss. How could he let her go? This was living. This was joy and hope and love all in a single soul. Nay, in two souls together. In theirs.

The tiny sounds from her throat were a drogue and he found himself losing strength, losing the will to hold back. Slowly, he allowed one more kiss, relishing the smooth warmth of her mouth before he pulled away.

If he waited to speak, to reveal the truth, he might lose the strength. "Carrie, I must tell you something that—"

The knock on the door was swift and firm, but quiet.

"James. James!"

Edmond's voice carried through the cracks in the door and the earnest waves destroyed their precious moment.

Flinging her an apologetic look, James rushed to the door and swung it open.

"What is it?"

The tight expression over his friend's typically placid face jarred him. "You're needed immediately," Edmond said, "below stairs."

"By whom?"

Edmond looked to Caroline before clutching James with a look so hard it strained his throat. "The prisoners have attempted another escape."

"Tonight?" *Please no.* "Tell me you are not serious."

"Aye, only hours past."

Caroline remained motionless, while the pain in her downcast shoulders, her knitted hands, spoke her worry in a thousand tongues.

James turned back to Edmond, lowering his voice. "How many this time?"

"Five."

Blast. "Is Anderson already there?"

"Nay." Edmond moved closer, speaking against his ear. "The guard of the prison came, asking for you."

He jerked back, not hiding the scowl. "Me?"

"He's frightened, James," Edmond said, "says he wants you to come down first, or he fears Anderson will hang him along with the others should his blunder be discovered."

Suspicion cramped over his shoulders. "What does he expect me to do?"

"I cannot say."

Muscles ticking, James chewed his lip. "You know what you are asking?" He shook his head. "I will not do such behind Anderson's back. Should he find out I acted without his direction we all could be—"

"James you are good." Edmond's petition knit through the thick panel of resistance. "Your goodness precedes you above all else. Please help him. He's young and he's scared. See if you can resolve this and perhaps Anderson might never know of it."

"James…"

From behind, Caroline's voice fell over him, draping him like a wounded soul waiting for relief.

His heart twisted in his chest. The faith in her stare, the way her mouth held tight and her entire frame inclined toward him—there was no way to deny her.

He looked to Edmond. "Where is he?"

Relief flooded his friend's tense posture. "At the back door."

Nodding, James raised a finger. "I'll be there in a moment."

Edmond shot a look to Caroline before bobbing his head and slipping into the hall.

Rushing to her, James pulled her against him, asking her forgiveness in the strength of his embrace. "I shall return shortly."

Her arms around his back, she rested her head against his chest. "I want to go with you."

"I know."

She perked her head up, pouring into him a confidence so deep he could have climbed the stars to the farthest edge of heaven. "Bring him back to me."

Gripped by a need, a power so rich and pure, the sweet words he longed to say almost slipped from his lips. *I love you.*

Instead, he spoke what he should. "I will do everything I can."

Her dainty brows flexed in the middle, her blue eyes shimmering with tears. "I know." Rising to her toes, she pressed her lips against his, holding his face in her hands. "I shall pray for you."

Of a sudden his throat grew thick, as every thought, wish and want for his future converged in the woman he held.

"James." He turned to see Edmond waving to him from the doorway. "Come."

Stepping away, he held her fingers as long as he could before hurrying from the room and down the stairs, his soul cracking.

*Pray on, Carrie.*

For though he liked to believe what was ahead of him would bring no harm, premonition hovered like a cloud. And somehow he feared the worst was yet to come.

Never had she known such a moment, such a feeling—the kind that drilled through her bones with the power of a grim foreboding.

James rounded the corner to the stairs, not looking back, and dread wound its dark ropes around her chest. As if God's very angel came down to whisper to her, there lived in her mind a vibrant scene—another act she must pursue.

*Follow.*

Her pulse flicked to rallying speed and she raced to the window, but the dark denied her vision of what she might have seen—James racing into the night, the frightened soldier leading him toward the very place her brother might even now be.

*Follow.*

The admonition was so strong, she didn't think to deny it. She had to follow them. When God directs, the wise obey.

Spinning around, she snatched her cloak and hurried for the door, halting in shock when her door was neither closed nor guarded. Where was Edmond?

Her palms went sweaty, and she tapped her toes in her shoes. Craning her neck, she looked down the shadowed hall but saw no one, heard only silence.

The need to stay close behind was paramount, for surely they would be on horseback and her on foot. Without consulting her inner cautions, she tip-toed down the stairs and out the back door as she'd done the night before. Allowing her eyes to adjust to the dark, she placed her trust in that Omniscient Being who held all life in His hands, clutched her skirts and ran.

# CHAPTER 35

$\mathcal{T}$he tavern was unlit and perilously devoid of sound, human or otherwise.

James dismounted and scanned the empty street. Thankfully, the ride had been short and uneventful. No doubt Anderson had decided on the place because of its proximity to Beacon House— and its immense size. Even in the dark, it was obvious this was no typical tavern.

"Here," the soldier said, motioning him forward. "I'll show you what I've found."

Checking behind him, James followed, unable to shake the apprehension that clawed at his back. Something was not right.

Hunching at the back door, he looked down into the basement of the tavern, the stench of sickly bodies and rot stinging his nose. Two torches burned on either side of the door. Their pitiful light tripped down the stairs and spilled over the mess of bedraggled men below.

And to think these were his fellow Patriots suffering in this horrid state. *Lord, help me to save them.*

James turned to the frightened guard. "Did you apprehend the five? Or have they disappeared for good?"

"They've gone, sir. I need your help in finding them." His voice was tight as a bow string. "If I cannot bring them back, Anderson will hold me responsible."

Rubbing his hand across his jaw, James nodded, giving the frantic boy the idea he considered what might be done, when in truth he had no intention of racing through the night to find the fortunate ones who'd managed to make their way to freedom. His attention was on the remaining men, and how, God willing, he would make a way to free them as well.

He lowered his hand. "I must question them."

The soldier jerked back. "Who?"

"The men below. They might know something, and if we tread with caution, the few left behind might be willing to impart some information that can help us find who we seek."

"Of course."

The boy started down, but James stopped him. "Nay. I'll go. You stay here and guard from above."

"Aye, sir."

James stalled on the steps, and his chest flexed. That hadn't been a smile had it—a small one—on the young soldier's face? His blood quickened to his limbs, thickening his muscles. The thought that this could be a trap had occurred to him more than once. But what choice did he have? He'd given his soul to The Cause and his heart to Caroline. Finding Enoch and setting these men free— these were not options, they were imperatives.

He took a moment to yet again listen for any rustle or whisper or breath, and upon hearing nothing, resolved to do what he planned and made his way down the short, steep steps. Within seconds, his eyes adjusted to the black, thanks to the pitiful light from the torches, and every vein and sinew that before then had been stretched with panic, was now near to tearing.

His soul cried out at the sight, his nose and eyes burning from the stench. Skirting the walls were men, but not recognizable as such. Wearing threadbare clothes, their unshaven faces were skeletal, their eyes gaunt. Some huddled in corners. Some lay on their sides, their knees curled up to their chests. Others were stretched out, their hands over their bellies as if they thought only of the food that might fill them, though in truth, death might be only hours away.

This was what war brought. This was the cost of freedom, the drive for the thing that mattered most. These men had given everything.

A flash of memory consumed him as Loden's words coated the sudden pain. *To have all, you need only have hope.* Was that what allowed these men to give so much? Their hope for liberty? Their belief in something greater?

Faith was the carrier, it seemed. Hope, the treasure. Love, the fountain of strength.

"Where is Enoch Whitney?" The words escaped him before he had time to consider their weight. At least his voice had been sure, heavy.

*Dear God, help him to still be living.*

Silence alone returned his question.

He tried again, willing the men to see past his coat to the truth —that he was one of them. That he too had given everything. That he now, had come to save them.

"I shall ask again. Where is Enoch Whitney?"

None spoke, but a shifting in the far corner turned him further, and his stomach lifted to his throat. A man stood, tall and imposing. Bearded, his clothes hung on a broad but malnourished frame. He pulled back his shoulders, bound hands in front of him. "Who asks?"

James showered heaven with prayers he felt more than thought. Nearing him, he studied the man's face, hoping by some fate he could detect a resemblance, assuring him indeed the man was Caroline's brother.

The more he looked, the more his confidence rallied. 'Twas not so much the physical appearance of him, rather the confidence, the determination and courage the man wore, the unyielding strength in his eyes. That, and the indisputable blond of his hair.

"Enoch Whitney?"

The man's head twitched sideways. "Here to hang me at last, are you?"

Flicking his hand toward the door, James forced a menacing scowl. "Follow me."

Enoch moved only after a threatening look, ducking low to exit from the shallow stairway.

Outside, the light from the torches revealed the true nature of the horror. Covered in filth and clothes in tatters, Enoch stood rigid.

*Dear God, help me help them. All of them.*

"Who is this?"

The young soldier neared them, musket in hand.

"I intend to get what I need from him." James motioned around the corner. "Set up a watch out front to be sure no Patriots await to attack from that side. Be quick!"

With a single nod, he raced out of sight and James snatched his dagger from his belt.

Before the wearied man could jump in fear, James swiped the blade through the rope that circled his wrists.

In a single swift motion, James gripped the man at the shoulder. "How many are left?"

Enoch jerked away. "What are you talking about?"

"Do not ask questions, only answer." James looked over his shoulder and replaced the blade. "How many are left? How many can walk and are any able to fight?"

"Fight?" Enoch's face crumpled in confusion. "Who are you?"

James's back cramped at the man's question, and he peered around to be sure they were still alone. There was no time for questions.

He filled his lungs with a patience he no longer possessed. "All that matters is getting you to safety."

Enoch rubbed his wrists, bitterness hissing through his tone. "I see what this is. You wish to use me as an example—tell me to run only to shoot me in the back. Punish me like the others. I will never—"

"Caroline is here."

James spit the words into the angst-ridden air, praying his revelation would subdue the brother who had learned to live in fear and distrust.

Enoch's expression went slack. "What do you mean?" In the next breath, rage filled his posture and he rose as if some unseen power owned him. "What have you done with her?"

"She is well, I give you my word." James patted the air, berating himself for his clumsiness. "'Tis she who brought me to you—to all of you." *Lord, help him see.* "To help you escape."

After a handful of quiet thoughts, Enoch's composure regained and his jaw shifted. "Escape?" By degrees the resistance gave way to belief and he stared out as if he could sense her nearness and the thought of it renewed his strength. "Where is she?"

"I will tell you all once you are secured. We must find a way to get you and the others—"

He stalled, cold dread shooting up his legs as an orange glow brightened the snow around him, the familiar stomp of boots growing louder.

Then, from the shadows in front of him, a nightmare appeared.

"Good evening, Captain Higley."

## CHAPTER 36

The look of shock on James's face would be the fuel for his life for years to come, Greene was certain of it.

With Pitman at his side, Greene felt his posture rising. "You see, Major, just as I told you. The man will always come to the aid of a Patriot in need. We need only supply the situation and the benevolent James Higley is duty bound to appear."

Pitman looked at him briefly before examining their captives. "You are right indeed, Captain Greene."

"We have found the traitor at last." How sweet the words. "What more evidence need we? I am certain we have enough proof to secure a hasty execution."

"I am impressed."

Always laconic, Pitman's simple admission made Greene's pride burst across the Atlantic, to shine in the face of his father's disdain. He had done the impossible thing. And he had done it himself.

"What of the woman?" Greene kept his eyes on his victim, knowing full well he had better keep James fully under his watch, for the risk of his flight was not to be taken lightly.

James answered nothing, but kept his glare steady, his mouth firm and fists round.

Greene scanned the yard, his instincts scouting around him like a small band of warriors. "You did not tell her you were coming then?" He spied the other man at James's side. A pitiful creature soon to be put out of his misery.

Securing his attention to James, he tried again, amused at his tenacity for silence. "Do not think me ignorant of her ways—or yours. She has tried before to kill a man of the king and I would not dismiss her intention to do such again. Which is why I feel it my duty to have her brought here as well."

"Leave her alone." James's voice rumbled along the cobblestone. "Your quarrel is with me as it has always been."

"This is certainly true, but I will not forget one who intended to take my life as she did. The law requires she pay the price."

"What is he talking about?" The prisoner looked to James then to Greene and instantly Greene realized who it was who stared at him as if he were a serpent from the underworld.

"So." Greene gestured to Pitman, then to the prisoner. "It would seem that this is the man who started it all."

The prisoner stepped backward, eyes narrow slits. "If you mean that I was one of the prisoners instigating the escapes, then indeed I am and I refuse to deny it. But I don't see how any of this relates to this woman you speak of."

He wouldn't admit the woman was his sister then? Perhaps she wasn't. Their relationship mattered little, only their predilection to do evil.

"This woman I speak of, when I found her days ago, had a letter. Claiming you and others were attempting to escape prison. It seems she was on her way to give you aid, *brother*."

His thin face went slack and he looked to James, who revealed an expression of hate chiseled from rock.

"Excellent work, Greene." Pitman stepped forward. "I should like to be the one to inform Anderson of the horrifying reality we have discovered here tonight. As I see you have everything in hand, I will bring the news of this man's betrayal and return Anderson here to witness it for himself."

Bowing, Greene gripped the hilt of his sword. "As you wish, sir."

With a flick of his fingers, two men followed Pitman, and as he walked out of sight, Greene wasted no time.

"Tell me." He kept his jaw firm and spoke through clenched teeth. "I shall give you one last chance. Where is the woman?"

Still, James remained silent, hurling spears through glaring eyes. Did the man think to frighten him?

"Where is she, Higley?" Greene stalked forward. "Did you leave her unprotected? Is she there all alone and whimpering that her protector has left her unattended?"

James leaned into the enmity that spilled from his mouth. "She is not afraid of you."

The sneer Greene released over his mouth and nose did nothing to express the depth of his contempt. James thought he was so valiant—thought the woman so noble. He thought his relation to a man in the highest rank of the army might spare him the punishment that awaited? It would do none of that.

"You will not tell me where she is? Then you leave me no choice but to go in search of her."

"You claim only the guilty run. Yet, I am here. And she is there. What proof have you that she is as evil as you claim?"

"What proof have you that she is innocent? You saw that moment she attempted to shoot me in the head—"

"She acted only in the defense of her own life—"

"You are daft!" Greene looked to the brother, then back to James. "You've allowed yourself to be so blinded by her charms, her looks, and whatever else she'd opened to you—"

James's fist plunged into his jaw, a shock of pain bursting over his face and into his head.

Greene bent forward, struggling to retain his posture. He tried his voice and found it still held strength. "Bind them and hold them below!"

Three men rushed forward and did as commanded when Greene called for four more, his head screaming in pain. He leveled his shoulders when the other soldiers stopped at attention in front of him, unwilling to give his enemy the satisfaction of knowing his blow had pained.

The streets were too quiet, and his instincts were never wrong. The woman was here. He could feel it.

"Search every darkened door and alley." He looked down the road. "I have a feeling a woman is lost and in need of assistance." He turned back to James, smiling with all the rancor his soul had to offer as he finished giving his command. "Find her and bring her back to me."

The door to the basement slammed shut as James stared at the beams of light squeezing through the slates on the door. Utter shock filled his bones like a plaster, binding his joints and rendering him motionless. How could this have happened? How had he not seen? He could only pray Caroline would find some way to escape—that God would grant her His all-seeing wisdom and show her a way to safety. This fate should not be hers.

"Tell me everything. Now."

Whipping around, James stepped into the chasm of Enoch's angry stare. "I am not who I seem. You must believe me."

"Then who are you?" Enoch tipped his head sideways. "And take care, these men can smell a lie under twenty feet of—"

"I am James Higley." He lowered his voice and narrowed the darkness between them. He dare not expose everything, but he must reveal something or risk losing all he'd worked for. "I am a captain in the British Army and..." He let the rest spill from his heart. "I am in love with your sister."

"In love?" Enoch sounded as if he choked on the expression. "You cannot be in earnest. How do you know her? How can I be sure you aren't using her—"

"I have only my word to give you, but as God is my witness, I love her." Would the man believe him? He pressed devotion into the peaks and valleys of his words. "I would do anything for her—which is why I am here." Could he, he would share with them his work for Washington, his love of liberty, but he'd sworn secrecy and must hope his other revelations would prove sufficient. "She asked that I use my position in the army to see you secretly out of prison, and I vowed I would do exactly as she requested."

"Don't listen to his drivel." A stranger from a darkened corner approached, a glistening something in his hand. "He is like the rest of them."

A memory of a similar night lurched and James cursed the binds that held him. Should the man lunge, he would have no way of protecting himself from the incoming blow.

Enoch hushed the man with a glare before turning to James. "This man—Greene—he says she is—"

"I rescued her from him." He had best spill the truth before Enoch decided to make assumptions that would close his mind to James completely. "He would have her taken and tried for spying, when she in truth was only searching for a way to help you." When Enoch didn't reply, James went on. "She has spoken of nothing but you and her affection for The Cause. I vow before you and before God, I would give my life for her."

Another man grumbled in protest but Enoch hushed him into submission before facing James, his voice solemn. "Does she return your affections?"

James stared out as the memory of her touch, her gaze, her kiss, the way his spirit twined with hers, took hold of him and clutched his reply. "She does."

Enoch's mouth narrowed, his gaze averted. "I should never have sent that letter. I am to blame for this."

Such was hardly true, but convincing the man was impossible, 'twas clear from the way his shoulders pressed down. James inhaled and released his breath slowly. "All is not lost."

"Is it not?" Enoch's outburst splintered the air. "You speak as one who has not been imprisoned these many months. You, with a full belly and clothes to warm you. If you speak the truth, and you are interested in our rescue, then it appears your attempt has failed and we will all die, only sooner."

The burn of unseen eyes singed through James's coat and it seemed the very walls crept toward him. Would they jump him? Beat him? He'd heard tales of it, and he knew they were not fables. These men were not to be taken lightly.

"I speak..." James weighed his words on the scale of truth, determining how much was too much. "I speak as one that cares for all humanity, no matter their political connection."

"You care, do you?" Enoch scoffed. "We are casualties of war, forgotten men who must wallow in this hell until our last breath, simply for the want of something far too few are willing to stand for."

The shadows continued to inch toward him, the shapes of men drawing nearer. "You are not forgotten," James said. "And your cause it not lost."

"Perhaps not. And neither is my will." Enoch's chest rose as he spoke. "But our bodies are withering away, and a man can only suffer neglect so long before he gives up the ghost."

The door to the cellar burst open and a single soldier descended, torch in hand. "James?"

"Edmond?" James's muscles flexed. "What are you doing here?" His heart pitched and the horror he instantly realized came out in his words. "Where is Caroline?"

His friend of years past marched part way through the room then stopped, peering about him with the look of a child too afraid to venture into the dark.

Hurrying forward, James cursed his tied hands. He needed to shake the shock out of the man's face. "Edmond! Where is she?"

"I don't know where she is, and I didn't know that you..." Edmond's voice was fragile, ready to snap. Gripping James with wilted eyes, he refused to stop his words. "I didn't know they would do this to you, you must believe me. When you left, another soldier came, begging for me to come along. He was so persuasive that I—"

"You left your post."

How this man ever got in the army James would never know. His heart was too good and his intentions too innocent, too naive. There was no way Edmond could ever fathom the harm his neglect had done.

"She is clever, is she not?" Edmond swallowed, and looked around him again, voice shaking. "I am sure she is well."

"And I am sure she is no longer there." James would be a fool to think Caroline would have stayed behind, especially when there was no guard at her door. "We can only hope she will stay away from here and out of sight."

A glimmer of suspicion that she might make her escape for good was quickly snuffed out by the knowledge that her heart was here—with Enoch.

He peered to Enoch whose face refused to produce anything but a contemplative glare.

Edmond's skin paled in the wan light of the flickering torch. "You do not think she would follow you?"

"I should have supposed by now, Edmond, you would have expected as much."

His urge was to find fault with him, be angry and blame the gentle ignoramus, but Edmond's penitence was as plaintive as his own. James huffed away his frustrations. "'Tis not your fault."

Edmond shook his head, his voice a taut whisper. "I should have known. I—"

Again the door burst open and Greene stomped down, two

soldiers flanking him. "Anderson has just arrived. But to my surprise, he refuses to see you." He neared, stopping within inches and excusing Edmond with a stabbing look that would have killed him had Edmond not retreated in haste.

Turning back, Edmond tossed James a look with so much remorse it dissolved any lingering resentment. They both had been used, both had been taken in Greene's plan. Edmond was no more to blame than he.

Greene continued across the darkened space. "It seems Anderson cannot control his rage and is most interested in arranging your speedy demise." He pretended a look of sorrowful shock. "'Tis only too bad Stockton could not be here to learn of your capture."

"Anderson knows only what you've told him." James's wrists ached as his instinct to pull free of them consumed his mind. "Let me speak with him."

"Never." Greene stopped hard, his shoes scraping over the dirt floor. "You have been taken in the very act of subterfuge. I am certain when Stockton arrives he will be no less shocked. He has long suspected you."

Stockton might in fact be the only ally he had remaining. The man was a tender cub in his center, softened by tales of love, and if James were to appeal to that side of him, knowing how he too had fallen for such a woman, perhaps he might have a chance.

"I have done nothing but my duty, Greene." He growled between words, wishing Greene had come alone, so they could have taken him down. "But what do you know of duty? You know only of self."

"Duty, hmm?" Greene moved only his head, bypassing the accusation James had hoped he would spar over. "What duty do you speak of? Duty to the crown or your own pitiful conscience?"

James's mind stormed, picking up the pieces he'd been unable to place and thrashing them to bits. No soldiers had escaped that night. Greene had constructed the story to lure him here, knowing he would come. Another more ominous thought followed. He'd insisted Edmond follow as well. Leaving a way for Caroline to be more easily taken.

"This is all your doing." His voice grated up his throat as he spoke the wretched truth. "You put me to this—you *made* this happen."

Greene meandered carelessly backward. "Say what you will. If you claim this is my doing then I suppose it is only fitting."

Secreted in his words was something akin to poison, and in a puff of memory, Loden's face appeared before him. The accusation, the trial, the hanging.

He could hardly take breath. "What do you mean, 'fitting?'" The pump of James's chest increased by increments and the muscles of his back clenched.

Greene continued his movement toward the stairs, his ugly casualness cinching a rope of revelation around James's throat. "Your old friend never saw it coming. And neither did you."

James's heart stuttered.

It was he. Greene had done it. All this time, and James had never known it.

Red sheathed his vision, and he was consumed by something not himself. Roaring he ran forward, kicking Greene in the back. Greene sprawled forward onto the stairs. Ready to kick again, James growled while the two soldiers grabbed him and held him back.

Slowly, Greene rose, brushing his hands on his thighs as he straightened. His eyes were black as he neared, taunting him as a trapper to a caged animal. "I had to do it." He stepped nearer. "He refused to see things my way. I had to make the point that if you cross me, you will pay." Nearing, Greene stopped, his nose almost touching James's. "He did. You will."

Waves of hate crashed over James's back and into his chest. Breathing from his nose, he clenched his teeth to keep from yelling. Loden's life was ended by this man? All for the sake of pride.

Would to God he could break the bands that held him and ease his rage around Greene's neck, feel the last beat of his pulse as he went speedily down to hell.

"You will not go unpunished for what you've done. Someday, you will pay."

"I will?" Greene pivoted, the ripple of a laugh in his reply as he made for the stairs. "When? After you are dead? I do not believe in ghosts."

Rage rendered him mute. He could hardly think for the emotions that tightened around him like iron bars.

"For one so keen," Greene said, opening the door, "I'm surprised you didn't learn it earlier." He shook his head. "'Tis a shame, I suppose, for him as well as for you. For myself, 'tis a pleasure to rid the world of its barnacles."

He motioned for one of the men to release James, and they did, shoving him. "Your execution is slated for sunrise." He grinned. "I look forward to it."

The steps creaked as he exited, before he slammed the door shut behind him.

James couldn't move. Couldn't find a way to take breath.

Rage cramped his shaking body as the realization weaved past his skin and into his bones.

The sounds from the street increased as Greene barked orders. Soldiers shuffled this way and that, while the men in the room around him mumbled indistinguishable things.

Enoch stayed beside him, as if he sensed James's need for some modicum of comfort. "We are grateful for your efforts."

James ground a refusal between his teeth. What efforts? He had failed.

Loden's lined smile filled his memory, his kindness and resolve. His love. His acceptance in the face of death.

The past lulled him backward.

*"Here."*

James's eyes burned at the memory, and he shut them to flee the remembrance, but it only heightened his senses.

*Loden turned to him, his shoulders even, no hint of fear in the creases around his eyes as the afternoon sun blazed hot, the soldiers shuffling and scoffing around them as the gallows was prepared.*

*Holding out his pocket watch, the man took James's hand in his. "I want you to have this."*

*James shook his head. "I cannot." How could the man look upon him with so much love?*

*"Do not hold yourself in contempt." Loden pressed the object into James's palm and forced his fingers around it. "Hold to hope."*

*Hope? Loden had been sentenced to death for a thing he had not done and he spoke of hope?*

*"How do you not hate me?"*

*"I never could do such a thing, James. You are like a son to me."*

*"But I—"*

*"You did not arrest me, you did not throw me in prison, you did not accuse me. You followed duty, and there is no shame in that." His face softened. "I am blessed at least to know you have seen the truth—that I am not the man you feared. I am at peace, knowing that I go to my death innocent before you, and in the eyes of God."*

Innocent. James fell upon that word like a man falling on his sword. His worst fears were to be realized. Not only had he failed, he would now be forced to accept that his life, and the lives of all these men, and Enoch—and Caroline—would die because of him.

*Dearest Carrie, forgive me.*

Falling to his knees, James gave way to the monsters of regret that opened their jaws to consume him.

He slammed his eyes shut as the teeth of that monster pressed into him. Of all his failures, 'twas the one to Caroline that made his heart bleed within him.

His lungs convulsed and his neck thickened until he was certain his veins would burst.

If only he had the strength of some mythical creature. He would fly from this dank prison, find her and free her.

For now, he had only a sorry past to reflect upon and regrets to fill his grave.

A heart full of love and no way to reveal it. A life of regrets and no way to right them.

*Forgive me, Carrie. I love you.*

# CHAPTER 37

*C*aroline hurried along the road, grateful that the few lights on the street still glowed. A tender mercy, no doubt.

*'Tis not far,* James had said. *Two streets down and one over.*

Putting speed in her feet, she hurried down the quiet road, following this path then that. Every step made her blood pump faster, carrying heat through her limbs and down to her cold-bitten toes.

At the corner of one brick building, she halted and gazed down the street. Her lungs stilled and she strained her eyes against the dark. Was that...? She leaned forward. Aye. Those were figures, no denying it.

Two buildings down, in the same street as she, were the silhouettes of two men. One disappeared into the building while the other stayed out. If not for the lights that glimmered from the building, she would not have seem them at all.

Their shape and color of their coats bore witness who they were but 'twas only when one of them walked and entered a doorway did she know the man to be James.

Her hands slicked with moisture and her pulse rammed

through her veins. There was too much in her heart to pray, too many thoughts to form the proper words, so she prayed her feelings—her hope and her fear. Was Enoch still there? If so, how would James get him away without either being detected?

A mumble of whispers cut her ears. Or was it just the breeze against the shingle above her? Caroline held her breath and strained her hearing. Nay. 'Twas nothing.

Alone and shivering, she pondered what to do. Stay hidden? Offer help? The thought almost made her laugh. What help did James need from her? Aye, she'd done what little she could, but he was so capable, so strong and courageous...Nay. Should she reveal herself, James would surely castigate her for risking herself in such a way.

Mayhap she—

The crunch of boots in the snow echoed between the buildings and down to where she stood, and she held her breath, praying to remain undetected. Hugging the side of the building she peered to where James had reemerged—with another man beside him.

Her heart leapt from her chest to the heavens. Could it be? The thin, bearded man, the rags of clothes he wore, the rope that bound him—even from a distance, those squalid trappings could not mask the brother she knew so well. Tears burst to her eyes and she covered her mouth to keep her joy from crying up her throat. He was alive. Praise God, he lived!

James motioned something to the other soldier and the man jogged away and out of sight.

That whispering she'd heard before crawled menacingly through the snowy street and she turned, but saw no one. It had to be a trick of the night, that the voices she heard were James's and Enoch's echoing off the brick that surrounded them.

Moving her attention to James and her brother, the cold dark alley began to glow, followed by the distinct rhythmic stomp of an approaching crowd.

*Dearest Lord, no!* From her position she saw the soldiers

approaching before James did, but was helpless to stop them. Swinging out of sight, she pressed her back against the brick, panic squeezing her neck.

It couldn't be what she thought. Nay. She rounded her eyes to keep the fears from clouding her vision. 'Twas expected. The soldiers knew James, and his presence there would be no great surprise. Would it?

Caroline breathed deep. There was no need to become frantic. James was trusted by all. Wasn't that what Edmond had said?

Flipping around, she peeked again to assure herself that indeed naught was awry, when instantly she froze.

Nay. It couldn't be.

*Dearest Lord, no.* 'Twas Greene.

She craned her neck forward. Greene was alive. But how could he be here? He'd had been captured. Henry Donaldson and Nathaniel Smith had taken him and the others. Impossible. There was no way she saw whom she did. Drips of horrid disbelief trailed down her back as she accepted what she wished were only a dream. Like a Roman victor, Greene stood tall, his legions on either side of him.

Caroline stared in stunned disbelief as three words echoed through the ice-covered street in Greene's own tongue. *Traitor. Evidence. Execution.*

Sucking in a shock of cold air, Caroline swung around, slamming her back against the brick wall. She put a hand at her chest, her lungs pumping. James had been caught. Why? How? Had Greene known he'd be coming?

Tremors of panic raced up and down her spine. If the Lord had not led her here she would not have known. But what could she do?

More sounds filtered down the street and her proximity to the melee shot through her conscious and she shuffled deeper into the alley and the safety of the shadows. She looked left and bit her lip. The outlet was open, but the rump of a horse blocked half the exit. Most likely the animal belonged to a soldier and she dare not think of escaping from that route as surely there would be men there eager to take her. She'd have to go out the way she came in.

A steady parade of nightmares marched through her mind, scenes of horror she could hardly endure. James and Enoch would be killed. Nothing was more certain.

She slapped a hand to her mouth, admonishing her fright to ease. Panic would not help him, or her. Breathing hard through her cold fingers, she schooled herself in calm. Clarity, planning—work. Prayer. Those were the ways to victory. Long, labored breaths allowed her to think. She could not do this alone. There must be—

*Go for help.*

The piercing whisper spoke through the cacophony.

Aye, she must get help. But whose? How? Where was there anyone that would—

*Patriots.*

She pulled away from the wall, her legs already prepared to do whatever amount of running or riding it took to get her message to anyone that would aid her.

Cambridge was not that far, was it? There were soldiers there, were there not? On a swift mount, the journey 'twould take no time at all. But where was a horse?

The sound of voices marched toward her, followed by the stomp of boots, and she froze, pressing flush with the brick, praying the shadows concealed her. Holding her breath, she looked to the entrance as three soldiers passed, disinterested in examining her hiding place, thank the Lord.

When their silhouettes and sounds of movement passed, a wave of energy rolled over her then drained out her legs. That was too close. She needed to get away. Now. *Lord, help me.*

Then, as if an angel held her head and turned it, her vision landed on the thing she had previously dismissed. Motionless but for the tail that moved ever so slight, the horse that waited patiently at the end of the alley came into view.

Her pulse thundered. Should she?

Holding her breath she tiptoed along the ice and slush, praying God would keep her steady and silent. If she were heard, seen— detection at all would be their doom. She was James's and Enoch's last hope.

Moving her hand along the wall, she steadied herself, stopping in silence at the end of the alley.

The horse was within inches of her, the saddle so close she could reach out and touch it.

Caroline swallowed before taking an inhale that filled her lungs, as well as her strength. She'd tried before to make an escape on Ginny with undesired results. Should this horse prove as stubborn, she would be in the cellar along with James and her brother.

Another volley of questions collided with her resolve, but she toppled them with a determination strengthened by love. Love for James, for Enoch. Love for The Cause and all that it meant for their future. Inching forward, she peered around the corner and her breath caught, this time, with gratitude. There was no one. The soldiers were two buildings down, their backs were to her. With their torches giving only small circles of light, she was invisible to them in the dark that encompassed her.

Caroline looked back to the animal, studying her salvation. An impossible thing, yet here it was. Untied and without a rider, it seemed as if her ever-loving, ever-providing Father had placed it just for her.

Resting her future in the hands of God, she moved forward, slow, deliberate, careful. The horse's ears perked back as she neared and his muscles flicked and twitched when she touched his soft coat.

"Shh."

Placing her foot in the stirrup, she lauded her former self for all the times she'd ridden stride against Timothy's prodding, for all the times she'd raced Enoch across the fields. She could do this. She needed only God's hand to shield her from the enemy's view.

Clutching the reins with one hand and holding the pommel, she gripped the back of the saddle with the other. With a jump and a swing of her leg, she mounted, breathing a prayer of thanks when the animal obeyed her prodding to turn.

A kick of her heels against his flank, and the animal lurched into a full run.

# CHAPTER 38

The sound of a horse's hoof-beat against the cobblestone echoed through the empty streets and Greene jerked around, his eyes instantly spotting the rider—and the fact it was a woman.

Neither the darkness of the night, nor the distance she'd already put between them, could diminish her frame or the blonde of her hair.

He'd known all along she had been there.

"Lieutenant Blakely!"

Greene stomped forward, a mix of rage and pleasure kneading his back as he stared after her, not wanting to lose her direction. "Lieutenant Blakely!"

The man approached from the side. "Aye, sir?"

"You were responsible for watching the female spy were you not?"

His face paled. "I was, sir, but I was called away—"

"Well she has fled and you are responsible for her!" Greene growled, pointing over the man's shoulder. "Follow her and bring her back to me if you wish to avoid an immediate court martial!"

The worthless man jumped on the nearest horse and raced from the torch-lit yard into the night.

Greene stared, his nostrils ticking, as the rider sped farther into the midnight shadows. Imbecile. How could Anderson see the man as worthy of such a position? Greene had intended for him to leave his post, but not for her to make it all the way here. What had happened to the soldier who was supposed to take her from her room? How could things have gone so wrong? His plan had been flawless. It was the faulty men he was forced to work with that made his job impossible. At least she wouldn't be hard to catch. Even a sot like Blakely could force her back, and within seconds no doubt.

"What is it? What's happened?" Anderson marched toward him, Pitman as the man's perpetual shadow. "What are you yelling about?"

Greene motioned to the road. "The girl was here."

"Here?" Pitman rounded him, then looked where she had ridden. "How did she get away?" He turned to Anderson. "Did you not set a guard at her door?"

The muscles in Anderson's face twitched at the accusation. "The man I put there is as capable as any."

"He was here now, sir. And I've sent him after her."

"What?" Anderson spit when he spoke. "He would not have left—"

"'Tis not his fault, sir. I am certain she tried to escape and he followed her here." Greene placed his palm against the handle of his sword, realizing he stood on faulty ground. If he revealed 'twas his doing that forced the man to leave his post, Anderson would forget in an instant the growing trust he placed in Greene. "She won't get far."

"She will not indeed." Pitman twisted and yelled toward the group. "Miller! *Miller!*"

Greene pulled back, shocked at the man's sudden action.

In seconds, the man he'd called for approached, all six feet, two hundred pounds of him. "Aye, sir?"

Pitman moved with more animation than Greene had ever seen from him. "Anderson's prisoner has escaped and you must bring her back. Immediately. Follow that rider."

"Aye, sir."

Without a second glance, the man found a horse, mounted, and like an unearthly creature, raced into the wintery blackness, out of sight.

Anderson shook his head. "I cannot believe this of Higley."

Could he not?

"I tried to warn you, sir." Now was not a time to prove his previous point, but he couldn't help the way the need to speak it cut over his tongue. With a kinder smile, he offered a rebuttal to his statement. "But Higley has been apprehended, and soon the woman will be. Any further damage will be averted. I am grateful at least he did not take more advantage of your situation."

"But the Patriot." Anderson stared in the direction the riders had gone. "Have you ever known a woman so remarkably fearless?"

Greene pulled back, fighting the sickness that clutched him at such a statement. He found something redeemable in such a person? She was a Patriot, a spy, a fugitive. What in any of that merited admiration?

"She is foolhardy and feckless," Pitman said, perfectly reflecting Greene's unspoken sentiment. "I doubt she will find anyone to heed her foolish cries for freedom when her time for judgment comes."

Anderson shifted his weight, looking out. "I aim to send her to England."

"England?"

Both Greene and Pitman spoke the word, and Anderson nodded. "Think of how perfect it would be—a real Patriot spy to parade down the streets? 'Twould be an utter spectacle and would no doubt bring an unfathomable amount of fame upon anyone associated with her, would it not?" Anderson grinned as he bowed. "I have matters to attend. Gentlemen."

Greene watched him go, a sudden urge swelling his chest as a single word flashed before him. Fame. The need to ride behind both men, to be sure neither of them failed in returning her, nearly drove him to leap for a horse.

But he stalled the sensation, knowing such an act would prove his leadership unworthy.

Still, the tempting thoughts, like a hearty ale, swam through his blood.

To see his name atop the London paper, to know that his father—the man who had derided him, belittled him and spoke nothing but derisive auguries to him since his youth—would see what he had become, that he had been part of something great. Something historic.

'Twould be worth a thousand cuts to know he'd proved him wrong.

No Greene would ever amount to anything?

Nay. Not until now.

# CHAPTER 39

$\mathcal{N}$ever had she ridden so hard. Though, 'twas the animal's legs that thumped rhythmically along the solid ground, Caroline's heart pumped as if she herself were running all those miles.

Again she glanced behind, but saw no one.

By God's grace alone she'd made it over the neck without so much as a question. Saying she was a midwife on the way to deliver a child in Roxbury had been enough to let her through. But Cambridge was still miles away, and having not crossed the river, she was forced to go the long way and it would be hours before she reached the men.

*Lord, help me. Guide me.*

Looking across the road, she saw a figure, and something about him bid her to slow.

His cocked hat and the musket at his shoulder attested to her he was no British soldier, nor was he a regular townsman.

"Sir!"

Expression hidden by his hat, he looked up, resting his musket beside him. "What are you doing about this time of—"

"What direction is Cambridge? I must make it there on urgent business."

"Cambridge?" His posture jolted, and he twisted to point behind him. "You will find the militia camped here, Miss. If you seek Washington then—"

"I seek anyone that will help."

With a long sweep of his arm, the old man motioned up a slight hill.

"You'll find plenty of help up thatta way."

Nodding her thanks she barreled forward, the few trees lining the road soon giving way to a clearing. Row upon row of tents and huts of all shapes and sizes consumed her view.

"Halt!"

Pulling her horse to a stop, Caroline raised a hand to show submission when she reached the sentry. "Please, sir. I need help."

The man stepped forward. "Miss Whitney?"

He knew her?

In a swift motion, he swung off his hat, his black hair and keen expression unmistakable.

"Mr. Watson?"

'Twas Eliza's husband. She'd been acquainted several times before, but they had never formally spoken in any place other than a social gathering. How had he recognized her?

"What are you doing here?"

Swinging down from her mount, she forgot all counts of propriety and grabbed his arm, driven by the angst that pooled in her blood. "My brother is in danger—all the prisoners are. I need help to free them or they will be executed."

"Your brother?"

"Aye. Please, I beg of you."

Without another word he yelled to the next nearest sentry. "Get Donaldson and Smith. Now!"

Caroline's heart leapt. "They are here?"

"Arrived just this evening." He shook his head. "Thank the Lord 'twas my time to keep watch."

Another mercy of Providence, indeed. Henry Donaldson and Nathaniel Smith knew of her plight. They'd seen James take her. Perhaps they knew enough of him to believe her when she told them he was not as terrible as they might think him to be, and that he too deserved to be rescued.

In seconds, a pair ran toward them, and Caroline rushed forward, knowing who approached even before she saw their faces.

"Praise the Lord, I have found you."

"Miss Whitney?" Henry's face contorted as concern lifted from him like fog. "What are you doing here?"

Both men looked to Thomas for explanation and he complied. "Her brother and other Patriot prisoners are to be executed. She wishes our help to save them."

When the three men forced their attention on her, the words began to fly. "I have been held at the headquarters of a Major Anderson. James Higley brought me there under cover of a spy, even though he knew I was not one. He told me he would help me rescue my brother and the others, and we had nearly done it —*he* had nearly done it—when the man who attacked your camp discovered him, and now they are both being held and will be executed if we do not get to them in time."

She'd made it through without a single crack in her words. A feat of strength if ever there was one. Her hands shook and throbbed with cold as she studied the men's shocked expressions.

Nathaniel rushed to her, taking her arm. "You are shivering. Come, you must get warm." He glanced behind. "Henry, go for Mrs. Lindy."

Henry raced away without a word.

As Nathaniel led her to the nearest tent, Thomas came at her other side, opening the door. "Rest here."

Too benumbed with cold and shock to speak her thanks, she nodded it.

Seconds later, Henry arrived, a dark-haired woman at his side. "Mrs. Lindy, this is Miss Whitney."

Not wasting a moment, the woman hurried in, motherly concern on her lightly-lined face. "Sit, my dear." She snatched a blanket and swung it around her. "You best get warm. I'll fetch some soup for you."

As she ushered Caroline to a seat, the men smiled their farewells. Caroline's mind was a gale. Would they know where to go? What to do?

"Stay here." Mrs. Lindy patted Caroline's shoulder before heading to the door. "Keep that blanket about you while I go in search for something warm for your belly."

With that she was gone.

Caroline's muscles continued to quiver, her knees bouncing as she sat. How could she remain here when James and Enoch were in so much peril? There must be something she could do. The urge to burst out the door and name her myriad reasons for going with them stalled in her throat, as if a higher purpose required her to stay. She shook her head. Nay. There must be a way to—

"Did she say how long ago he was taken?" Henry's whisper filtered through the thin canvas.

"It can't have been long." Thomas's tone raked the chilled air. "We received word from him just yesterday."

"Aye," Nathaniel said. "The information he shared was vital, and Washington was immensely pleased to have it."

Washington? Confusion blinded Caroline's already darkened vision. James had sent information to the leader of the Continental army? Why?

"He has long been my friend, and I cannot stand idle when he has done so much for us." Command billowed through Henry's hushed words. "We must get him out. Now."

Caroline pulled away from the canvas. Shaking her head, she

whirled around, her fingers at her temple, fighting the fog of confusion. They were friends? What did Henry mean James had done so much for them? Why would James be—

Her back went straight and her mouth nearly dropped open. A spray of tingles trailed from her head to her feet as the truth of James's work broke through the clouds like a beam of light. Her heart pounded, the thing she'd not considered before growing in her mind like a mountain out of the sea.

*He is a spy.*

She spoke under her breath. "He's a Patriot."

Bursting through the tent door, she halted, each man staring at her with troubled eyes.

Caroline rushed the few feet that separated them. "He's a spy."

No one spoke, but their gazes jumped back and forth, mouths tight.

Would they not speak?

"Do not pretend it isn't true. I know I am right."

As if to avoid the spreading of some dangerous contaminant, the men stepped back, resting their gazes at her and answering more with their silence than they knew.

The more the veracity of what she'd discovered settled over her, the more her body needed to move. She hugged her arms then dropped them to her sides, shifting her weight over her feet. Oh, dearest Lord in heaven, how had she not known it before? All those times he spoke of "our" cause, the times he'd seemed to want to share something but didn't. The secrets in his eyes...

"I didn't know." She sent her gaze around the circle of men. "I didn't know..."

Nathaniel neared, resting his hand on her shoulder. "You must not speak it. Must not tell a soul. The Cause depends on him."

She nodded. "Of course." *Dearest James.* If only she had known.

"What do we do now?" Henry's question formed in the air like an apparition. "We cannot leave him helpless."

Caroline stared, touched by the taut expressions of such stoic men. One man looked away and another down, one had his hand on the back of his neck—as if the thought of losing this intimate friend crushed the very center of their hearts.

"I should like to be of some service."

Gasping, Caroline spun about, nearly shrieking at the sight of a British soldier that stalked from the shadows.

The metallic sounds of sabers drawing fast, the glimmer of steel in the dim light of camp made her skin shrink and she stumbled back.

"Speak your name." Henry stood in front of her, his sword extended, the other two men at his sides, one with a sword, the other a pistol.

"Edmond." He raised his hands. "Edmond Blakely."

"Edmond?" Caroline pried through the men's tight guard and clasped him at the arms. "What are you doing here? Where is James? Have you seen him?"

"You know this man?" Thomas's eyes were narrow when he looked to her, his mouth twitching with unrestrained contempt as he turned to their willing prisoner. "If you cannot vouch for him, his remaining moments of life are few."

With one hand at Edmond's arm, she faced the others. "He was my guard at Beacon House." She spied Edmond again, speaking what she had somehow always known. "He can be trusted."

Edmond's downtrodden expression was enough to make her already weeping soul weep harder. "I didn't know they would take him." His throat bobbed as he looked to Caroline. "I was asked to follow you and bring you back."

"Bring me back?" Pressing a hand to her chest, she forced herself to take in and let out the air that seemed clogged in her lungs. "Do not, Edmond, I beg of you. I cannot—"

"'Tis why I am here." Edmond's jaw shifted as his gaze moved across each man. "Greene wishes ill upon James, but for what wrongs I cannot comprehend." He shifted to where the three still eyed him with contempt. "James is a friend to me—he is a friend to many. We suffered much together and I cannot bear the idea of him being accused of a wrong on my account." He paused, nodding with such conviction it plumed from his shoulders like an impending storm. "I must help. I will not be persuaded otherwise."

"You wish to help him, do you?" Henry's blade inched closer. "Then you will leave here. Without the woman, and let us do our work."

"You'll never get past the neck. 'Tis stocked with soldiers."

The small bit of land that connected Boston to the mainland was heavily guarded. 'Twas one thing for a woman to pass over, but a group of Patriots? Impossible.

"You will need me," Edmond said. "There would be no way for you to make it to him in time on your own." He moved his feet and relaxed his stance, apparently buoyed by their collective quiet. "We fight on opposite sides, but in this, our differences work to our benefit."

"He is right." Henry stepped away, replacing his weapon. The others did the same. "If we wish a speedy extraction we can only do so by covert means."

"I am pleased you agree." Edmond looked behind him before taking a step forward, lowering his voice. "I have a plan."

Caroline realigned her legs, her cold hands at her chest. "God be thanked. We shall work together for him."

Henry shook his head, lips between his teeth. "There will be no *we*, Miss Whitney."

She pulled backward. "What do you mean?"

Eyes gentle as always, Henry neared, taking her at the elbow. "James would wish you to stay here."

"Stay?" Shaking her head, she offered a polite smile to the man who seemed more than determined. "Forgive me, Henry, but the man I love and my brother are in grave danger and I could not imagine—"

"Love?" Nathaniel blurt out the word then looked around. "You are in love with him?"

Had she spoken it aloud? Her cheeks blazed, but there was no taking it back. She did love him, and the need to see him again—to tell him of her feelings became almost unbearable. "I am. I love him, which is why I must see him again. I must do my part to help—"

"I know you wish to assist, and your determination and bravery are commendable," Henry said. "But if I know James, and I am certain I do, then he would not wish you anywhere near the fight."

She shot a frantic look to each man, their even shoulders and unwavering stares as formidable as any army. "Please." Her voice wavered and she didn't wish to stop it. "There must be something I can—"

"You cannot put yourself at such risk, Miss Whitney," Thomas said. He too, came near. "I can say with certainty that were any of our wives in a precarious circumstance we would not wish them anywhere near danger." He looked about him, collecting hums of approval before he finished. "And we would make sure they did not place themselves in such a situation either."

She looked to Henry. Did they think she would be satisfied with staying behind? Surely Anna would not have complied were she told to stay behind.

When no one spoke again, Caroline took the moment for herself.

"I will go with you, but will stay in the shadows. You must let me come. You must let—"

"Worry not," Thomas said, all kindness in the way he smiled. "We shall not return without him."

All four men turned toward the road, Edmond at their front, already speaking.

"Wait." Caroline hurried in front of them, hands out. "I have been in agony of finding my brother. And knowing now that

James too has been taken, I cannot bear the thought of giving no aid."

"Miss Whitney, please." Henry took her at the shoulders, his kind insistence a credit to his character. "What danger we must face we know not, and I am sure James would have our hides should we let you come along."

Mouth sealed from penitence, Caroline swung her gaze to Edmond who nailed her with a harsh stare meant to plead her into submission. Thomas and Nathaniel too, nodded. Were they all so blind? Could they not see, not comprehend her need?

"The greatest thing you may do for us now—for James—is to pray," Henry said. "Stay in the tent. Mrs. Lindy will have something warm for you and will keep you well until we return."

With a tap on her arm, and a look so tender it threatened to melt the ice of her resistance, he released her and the men continued on. Only Edmond looked back, his eyes round with emotion.

She stared after them, and 'twas not long before the shadows enclosed them from her view.

Her legs urged her to follow, to race after them and demand to be one of them. Shivering, she clutched the blanket harder, knowing she should return to the tent, but her legs refused to move. *Dearest Lord, lead them safely there. Bring Enoch and James back to me.*

"There you are, Viper."

Caroline spun at the hissed sound, her back instantly seizing. She gasped, preparing to cry out but the stranger jerked her back, tying a cloth over her mouth.

He chuckled, and the shadows of the night went pitch as he snapped a sack over her head. "You're coming with me."

# CHAPTER 40

*A*rms and shoulders aching, James rested with his back against the wall of the prison cell, Enoch beside him.

The road outside the window of the cellar was a thoroughfare, soldiers tromping this way and that, talking and laughing in hushed voices.

Though death was hours, perhaps minutes away, his mind refused to stop its feverish pace. He must get them out. The Benevolent Hand that carried all the earth would hear their cries, would He not? Provide them escape?

Sweeping his gaze around the dimly lit room, any flicker of hope that remained grew dimmer. He had no way of escape, no way of seeking help. No way of letting Caroline know of their fate. He lowered his head, squinting his eyes. His fate was nothing to hers, and the mere thought of it threatened to cut through his flesh.

"Tell me of her."

Twisting his neck toward Enoch, James quirked his brow to the man who stared at him. The sudden and quiet petition rested solemnly between them. "Of Caroline?"

Enoch nodded, smiling as his gaze drifted downward, no

doubt pulled by the heaviness of happier times. "I have thought of little else than family since our imprisonment." He looked out first, then to James. "I would so liked to have seen her again. But now I suppose any hope of that is far gone."

James fought the raw aching that grew in his throat. How he wished he could have done more. If only he had—

"You say you love her, and that is good," Enoch said. "She deserves love. From a good man." He paused, his stare as clear and sharp as broken glass. "Are you a good man?"

The pointed question, smeared with the rarest of poisons, pressed deep into his heart. How could he answer? Was he good? He'd brought her to capture, brought her to a life of prison and solitude—perhaps even death, if in fact she were taken to trial and found guilty. A good man would never have done such a thing.

"She is deserving indeed." It seemed strange to him, and yet wholly real and irrefutable, that his love for her had taken root in him in so little time. He stared down, the weight of his past pressing heavy, wishing for her comforting touch to soothe the hurt he carried. "Am I worthy? What man is worthy of such a woman?" At this he looked to Enoch. "I can only pray my love for her is strong enough to cleanse me from past wrongs, making me worthy of such a future with her."

"You see a future with her?" Enoch's question was quiet, hooked in reverent shock.

James stilled, surprised at the sudden intimacy of their speech. The men around them were as withdrawn as they had ever been, too consumed with their own suffering to be concerned with him.

"I saw one, aye. Believed perhaps it might have been." When faced with death, 'twas easy so speak of things he might not have. To share with a stranger the lush dreams in the garden of his heart. "I would have liked such a life, if she would have agreed." He looked to Enoch. "Now I suppose I shall never have a chance to see how near she might have been to accepting me."

Unmoving, Enoch studied him, the hidden wisdom in his

shadowed eyes beaming past the darkness. "I thank you, Captain Higley. For the attempt you made." He looked out, toward the door that had not opened since last Greene had locked them in. "I am certain not many men would have taken such a risk—not many would see past our politics. And it shows of a character rarely witnessed in mankind."

Though James had known him merely hours, Enoch's words melted against his spirit, coating him in a brotherly bond he had never known. "I wish you to know, had not Caroline driven me to act, I would have done so nonetheless." *I am one of you.* "If there were any way to—"

The door to the cellar burst open and a solitary figure hurried in.

"James."

James jutted forward, blood shooting through his aching arms. "Edmond?"

Hurrying through the dark, Edmond knelt before him. "Thank God you are still here."

"What is it?" From the angle of his stride, James could sense something was wrong.

"There is little time. But I believe..." Edmond looked back then inched closer, his volume under a whisper. "I believe there may be a way to get you out."

Dearest God. An answer to prayer. "How?" James looked to Enoch who mirrored his posture.

"I've just been sent on the lookout for—"

The door to the cellar slammed open. "Lieutenant Blakely!"

'Twas Greene.

Edmond shot to his feet and whirled around, standing stiff at attention. "Aye, sir."

"Pitman told me you returned, but you neglected to report to me?"

"I report to Major Anderson, sir."

He stopped hard and skewered James with a glare. "And yet

345

you are here with the prisoner? Perhaps I should bind you as well."

"I was only—"

"But you have returned to me empty handed?" His timbre crawled across the dirt at their feet. "Why?"

"Forgive me, sir." Edmond remained still, his reply revealing more than James believed he meant it. "I did my best to find her, but it seemed she…she slipped away."

"Slipped away? Is that so?" He stepped closer and Edmond was forced to raise his chin to look him in the eye. "Then I suppose 'tis good Pitman sent another man—a *real* soldier—to do the job you could not."

"What do you mean?" The words strayed from James's mouth before he could tie them back.

Greene stepped around Edmond, all shades of disdain apparent in the shadows of his face. "Did you know, dear Romeo, that your fair Juliette has fled?"

*Carrie, you didn't.*

"But not to worry." Greene smiled with hate. "We shall be returning her to you in short time."

James schooled his features to show none of the emotions that rose like a flood in his chest. *Why, Carrie?* Didn't she know the danger?

"You will not find her," James said. 'Twas a mere hope, but he spoke it nonetheless.

"'Tis noble of you to wish the best for her." Greene chuckled. "Not to worry. I am certain she will be found soon, for 'tis not as if she has been so difficult to discover in the past."

"You best pray I am dead before you find her, or I shall tear your limbs from their sockets." Enoch's eyes glowed red as he spoke.

James reserved a grin, though within him it grew as wide as the sea. He had thought he liked the man before, now he was certain of it.

"Your threats are vain," Greene said, turning for the door. "For Anderson has your last moments well laid out." He pivoted at the door. "It isn't long now. Come, Lieutenant. I should like to hear the sorry excuse for your ineptness as you explain it to Anderson."

Without looking back Edmond hurried forward, his head straight and arms firm at his sides.

When the door was closed again, Enoch twisted toward him. "What will they do to her?"

James stared in bitter silence as the future was laid out like a map before him, and his gut cramped so hard he strained not to buckle. "There is naught we can do for her, but pray. For her fate, I fear, is a nightmare."

# CHAPTER 41

"I've found her, sir."

Iron fingers gripped her at the waist and yanked Caroline from the saddle. The sack around her head might have shielded her vision, but it did nothing to deaden the sounds of the soldiers or the scents of the burning torches. 'Twas clear. She was back at the tavern.

Her captor shoved her forward, and she fell to her knees.

"Who have we here?"

Greene's eerily melodic tone penetrated her fragile constitution, and she prepared to cry out when the sack flicked off and her surroundings came into perfect vision.

He stopped some inches before her. "Lieutenant Blakely!"

Edmond? Caroline craned her neck to look behind, shock consuming her frame. He was here?

Face contorted, Greene kept his eyes on her new friend until he stopped in front of her.

Greene pointed down. "Here is our prisoner."

Edmond swallowed and tossed her a fleeting glance. "I see that, sir."

All disdain and contempt, Greene kept his mouth hard. "I am

sorry to see you were not the one to find her." He peered at the man who still guarded her from behind. "Excellent work, Lieutenant Miller."

"Forgive me, sir," Edmond said.

"Forgive you?" He shook his head wildly. "You have failed, Lieutenant. Failed. And you will suffer the consequences."

He looked to the group, squinting in thought. "Where are the men for the execution?"

Though it seemed his question was meant solely for effect, Edmond responded. "They are waiting in the back, sir. I called for them as Major Anderson instructed."

"As Anderson instructed? When did he instruct such a thing?" Spinning on his heel, Greene looked ready to explode from frustration. "Where is he?"

Edmond peered down at her, a kind of gentleness in his eyes she'd not seen before. 'Twas almost as if...as if he wished to tell her something.

When he couldn't find the man he sought, Greene turned back to them, speaking almost under his breath. "Why the man would leave anything to you after all you have done, I cannot comprehend." He faced Edmond with ticking jaw. "Get out of my sight."

Bowing, Edmond stepped backward, but not before granting her one last appeal through eyes of friendship. She savored the bit of kindness before he turned and marched from sight, leaving her in the muck of her enemy's rage.

Greene crouched in front of her, resting one arm over his knee. She'd never seen him so close. The high cut of his cheekbones, the narrow set of his eyes, the rough look of his skin. 'Twas the face of evil.

"You are lucky, my dear."

"Am I?" How her voice found strength, she didn't know.

Still at her level, he nodded, his thin lips pulling tight. "It seems Anderson doesn't wish you dead, as I do."

He didn't?

She threw her gaze to the tavern only yards away. Was James still there?

Pushing against his knees, Greene stood, staring down at her. "Nay, he wishes something more grand for you, it would seem." He sighed. "And though I am inclined to protest, I must say, his proposal is far grander than the end I would have for you."

Every vile thought she could produce went wild through her head, and she stilled from their madness. Would she be used? Tossed from man to man? Would she be made a slave?

His answer slashed through her questions. "Your fate awaits you in London."

"London?" She couldn't have heard him right.

Anderson appeared from around the corner, gestured to the few he spoke with, then started toward them, granting her only a cursory look before he spoke to Greene as if he had never seen her. "We are ready."

Greene's wicked grin stretched over his lips and he gestured to the men by the door. "Bring them up."

"What do you mean London?" Caroline's stomach lurched to her throat, the wet ground seeping through her petticoat while dread seeped through her chest. "What will you do with James?"

Just then he appeared—followed by the person she'd prayed for since the moment she'd known there might be hope.

"Enoch!"

Her brother turned to her. His blond hair was matted and dirty, his bearded face gaunt, but his eyes were alive.

"Carrie!" He lunged to her but two soldiers held him back. "Get away if you can. Don't let them take you!"

Her vision flung to James, as tears burned her eyes. She wanted to speak his name, to launch to her feet and run to him. His hands were tied and two men gripped his arms as if he were a criminal, but his gaze leapt across the distance, beyond the sea of red coats and thundering voices. He tried to comfort her, to say he wished it were different. She could almost hear his voice. Her throat ached and all the words she'd wished to say, every part of her that yearned to run to him, was rendered inert.

*Forgive me.*

She opened her mouth to call to him when the man behind her yanked beneath her shoulders and tugged her to her feet.

"Wait!" Greene reached out, his brow creasing. "Nay. She remains here."

"What do you mean? I thought I was meant for London?" Caroline's heart beat so quick she feared her knees would lose their strength. "Am I to be killed with them after all? I doubt you would be so merciful."

"Indeed, you are correct. I am not in the least bit merciful." Greene sneered. "You, my lady, will not die. You will have, however, the honor of watching them breathe their last."

Held on both sides, James looked to Caroline whose washed complexion and sorrowed eyes gave him strength enough to throw off the men that bound him and fly to her. But doing so would be futile, and more dangerous. 'Twould bring about a skirmish that would end in more lives lost than merely his own. And he could never risk Caroline's life with such an action.

"We are ready, sir."

Speaking to Anderson, who approached from the crowd, Edmond neared and stopped just in front of James, not once looking at him despite the fact moments ago he'd spoken so cryptically, there was surely more he wished to say. James dare not believe his good friend would go against the demands of his superiors to hint at a rescue, yet the thought plagued him like a disease. Edmond was a good man, but would he attempt such a thing for him?

Anderson peered casually around, hurt mixing with resentment in the lines of his mouth. "Excellent."

Edmond nodded and motioned to a line of soldiers, their muskets in hand. "At your command."

"Nay, I believe this honor should be saved for someone else."

Edmond's face twitched. "Someone else?"

"Captain Greene." Anderson called to him from his conversation with Pitman and he bowed himself away before marching over.

"Aye, Major." He stood erect, pride thick in his voice. "Everything is prepared. The common is not far, we shall do it there." Casting a brief look to James, his pleasure shone like a light behind his eyes.

Anderson motioned to a soldier who brought his horse through the gathering crowd. "'Tis perhaps not customary, but I have been impressed with your work, your dedication in the face of so many obstacles, and I think indeed you should finish what you started."

A stone formed in James's stomach. How ironic it would be, the man who had forced Loden's demise would now take his own life as well. Perhaps 'twas fitting, as Greene had said.

And yet…

He looked again to Caroline who remained motionless, tears falling over her cheekbones. His heart pitched. This could not be the end. Not for her.

"Will you stay, sir?" Greene's polite question plucked every taut string in James's chest.

Anderson adjusted his gloves, shaking his head. "I shall not. What I have been subjected to is intolerable, and I have no interest in witnessing this depressing spectacle. So long as it is accomplished, I am satisfied."

"What of the other prisoners, sir? Shall I bring them as well?" Greene's pretended calm could not cover his tone that screamed with enthusiasm.

Raising his dour look toward the tavern, Anderson shook his head. "Let them wait. I have a sufficient gallows prepared for the rest. These men—though deserving of a noose—will get a more immediate end. This gloom deserves its own audience."

A sheen of disappointment veiled Greene's acquiescent bow. "Of course."

Anderson sighed, looking to Caroline, then to Pitman. "Major Pitman will be present to oversee the execution. Report back to me immediately when it is complete. Harris," Anderson said, turning to the soldier nearest him. "Bring the woman. We shall return to Beacon House."

"Nay, sir." Greene reached out and Anderson halted with a scowl. "I would wish her...if you are agreeable, I would wish her to stay."

Already narrow, the man's eyes thinned more as questions formed over his brow. "To what purpose? You know I intend her for England, you cannot go against my—"

"I would not think of it, sir. I wish only to have her see what truly comes of those who wish to work against the sovereign."

Anderson's jaw hardened, his gaze swinging to Caroline. "Have her on the Verity by sunrise."

England? James bypassed one horrid revelation to focus on another. "How dare you!" James clenched his teeth and wriggled his wrists against the rough rope that tied them. "You would make her witness our deaths to torture her with grief."

"How right you are." Greene's unaffected expression twisted a knife through James's gut. "As I cannot have my wish to see her suffer for trying to take my life—"

"Enough!" Anderson shook his head. "This contempt between you drives me to madness."

"Sir, I beg you." James stepped as far as his guards would allow. "Do not allow him to do this—"

"You are in distress, are you?" Anderson looked to James, no hint of compassion in his tight mouth. Hate turned his dark eyes a heavy black. "You should have heeded my wisdom. Now look where your ill-begotten love has brought you." Voice sharp as a blade, Anderson held nothing back. "Take them away—and finish them."

He marched off, two men beside him, leaving James exposed to the barbs of Greene's vile rancor.

Greene motioned toward Caroline and the men who held her. "Bring her."

The march to the common seemed a lifetime to complete. James tried and failed to keep Caroline in his sights, but as the light of morning had barely shown, the trees still cast too many shadows.

He strained his back another time to look behind, but saw only Enoch marching in silence behind him. 'Twas clear from the heaviness of his step that he too had thoughts of Caroline on his mind, and his heart. Their death would be quick, almost painless. Hers would be anything but.

As the sun rose, the slightest hint of lavender and pink brushed across the wintery sky. The common was lined with men, soldiers come to witness the excitement and drama about to unfold. One of their own, a traitor. No doubt the rumors had licked through the ranks like fire in a field.

"Line up!"

Greene marched forward, heralding instructions to the men who would do their duty and take the lives of their fellow soldier.

James spun, straining against the hold of his captors. His heart burst within him. There she was, some yards away, restrained as he was, with a soldier on either side, forcing her to watch from a near enough distance to see in gruesome detail the way their lives would end.

"Do you think they will spare her?" Enoch's voice was taut, strained with emotion.

James shook his head. "I don't know."

"Your time has come." Greene marched to stand in front of them. "Prepare to meet your maker."

∼

Greene's chest pounded, pleasure twining with rage and streaming liquid fire through his chest. *At last.*

He turned away from the men and marched to the one who held the lighter portion of his hate. "All this time you wished to subvert the ways of the king, to be part of this rebel movement. But in the end, you bring only death upon yourself, and upon those around you."

"Do not do this!" Her voice cracked. Face red, she struggled against the men who held her, as if she might by some way get free again. "Please, I beg you not to do this! If you must take someone, take me!"

"Nay!"

The shout of two voices came at once as both her brother and James called out.

Greene twisted at the waist. "You think to be honorable do you?" He finished his about face and stalked toward James. The smile that lifted his face could not be helped, and he allowed it. He'd done the impossible. None believed in him and yet here he was, basking in a glory even his own father thought him incapable of receiving.

"I have caught you—you, James Higley, the uncatchable informant." He looked to Caroline's brother, his gaunt face a pitiful incarnation of the rebel's unifying force. "You have thought to best the most powerful army in the world, have you? And here you are, in bonds and your life moments from ending."

None moved. James's jaw ticked as his eyes carried a will almost laughable. Did he think to intimidate him? "Come now, James." Let him boil in the putrid scraps of his dismembered ideals a moment longer. "'Twas foolish to think you would never be caught. I distinctly remember you telling me the person would never be found, but here you are. In my hands." He chuckled, savoring the memory of the shock on Pitman's and Anderson's faces when indeed his tale had proven true. He could live on that memory through the end of time.

"I may be in your hands, Greene, but my death will not end this fight."

"Perhaps not." Greene's fingers itched and he relieved their stress by gripping one hand to his sword, the other to James's face. "But I will have ended you and that is enough for me." He released his hold with a shove and pointed to the man at the head of the line. "Ready your men."

"NAY!"

Spinning, Greene lunged for the woman. "I have had enough of you."

"Stop!" Neck lined with veins and skin crimson, the woman appeared as if her spirit would fling from her own body to strangle him. "If you kill them you must kill me as well."

"Oh no, my dear." He stalked to her, the sensation of power almost too perfect. "I would not think of it."

All the fight drained from her, that darkness in her cheeks fading through shades of pink to near white. Her eyes moved from him to James.

Her voice quivered. "Let me speak with them. One last time."

Ready to deny any such mercy, he opened his mouth, but snapped it shut as he caught sight of the few men he had beside him. One might have thought him a monster from the way their brows all pinched together.

He rolled a shoulder. Well, there was a reason he would rise in the ranks and they would not. Leadership took work, determination and required impossible things. Compassion was a crack that once allowed, grew, until it shattered the very vessel that held the army together.

She blinked and tears streamed down her face, the fall of it doing something to the boy in him. He wasn't a monster, and though he wished his men to fear him, he didn't wish them to despise him.

"Fine." He flicked a wrist at the soldiers guarding her. "Release her, but don't let her out of your sight."

# CHAPTER 42

*L*ike a captive animal set free, Caroline bolted the moment her bands were loosed, racing the small distance that separated them.

Her heart was cut in two, bleeding out in her core. She went to Enoch first, flinging her arms around his neck and bathing his skin with her tears.

Feeling his body against hers, the boney remnants of the man she'd known pulled more grief from her eyes. She hugged harder. "Enoch, I tried. Forgive me."

"Carrie." His rich voice, and the love that heaved it, forced her back and she gripped his arms, looking at him when he spoke. "There is nothing to forgive."

Despite the grime upon him, despite the rags he wore, there was light in him. All he'd endured had not dimmed the conviction within his soul, and there it was, smiling back at her—a glimmer of heaven in the center of despair.

"Do not fret so." He winked. "You always did worry overmuch."

Her throat ached as it swelled. Did he think to tease her at such a time? Her head grew heavy from grief and she dropped her gaze, but his voice tugged her eyes back to his.

"Carrie." Enoch's bearded face flicked up with a smile. "Where is your faith?"

She might have asked the same thing of herself. "Gone, I suppose."

"Why ever would it flee when there is so much to be hoped for?"

"You will die, Enoch—"

"But not in vain. Not for nothing and not without my honor."

Caroline fell against him, holding him as she had dreamed she would a thousand times. "I will strive to live worthy of you. To make you proud."

"Come now, Carrie. I go to a better place, to sit among the angels and sing praises to our God." His tone changed to polite firmness, as his gaze slowly detached from hers. "You have another who wishes to see you."

Enoch's vision swung to James, and the unspoken message in her brother's small nod made all that still had strength in her, crumble.

Turning to the man to whom she'd given her heart, she willed her knees to keep her erect.

James's shoulders were even, his posture upright, but red rimmed his eyes. That pain in her throat moved down through her chest, squeezing the two parts of her severed soul until tears poured down her cheeks.

A world lived in her heart, but how to speak it? How to reveal all the hurts and passions with only seconds to share them?

"I didn't know." The words squeaked out and she swallowed, praying for strength. But no use, her voice was a bumpy road her sorrow was forced to traverse on the way to her lips. "I didn't, and yet...I did. All this time I—"

Her throat grew too thick to speak, the ache in its center consuming every part of her, down to her soul.

Hands still at his back, his eyes did the caressing. He too swallowed, his neck working as if he strained to keep his own voice from cracking. "There is something you must know."

Her chin wobbled and her vision misted, hot tears threatening to fall.

"Your cousin is well." There were tears in his own eyes, but somehow he kept them from falling. He needn't say the rest for her to know it. He'd let them free. 'Twas the next confession that left her shock-ridden. "Your uncle, Ensign. He is alive and under the care of Kitty Smith."

A gasp of joy squeaked through her and she flung a hand to her mouth. "Alive? How do you know this?"

His face told her before his words did. "I took him there."

"You saved him."

"I knew he would not otherwise survive. But I had to protect the belief of his death. For his safety, as well as mine."

What a man James Higley was. He had saved her uncle—released her cousin. If only she had known this from the beginning. Horror rifled through her joy. He had done so much for her, and here he would die in innocence—*because* of her.

Smiling with more joy than she might have ever seen, James reached out with his gaze. "I could not die without you knowing I had done everything in my power to help your family. And though, until a few days past, we were unknown to one another, I see now that I did it all for you. I am certain, Carrie, God meant for us to be together."

Hand still pressed to her mouth, Caroline tried in vain to quell her falling tears and quivering face. "I cannot bear the thought—"

"Be strong." His voice was a fortress, his presence a pillar of strength she needed, and yet would be taken from her. "Be strong. You must be. The Cause will need you."

Was there a way to be strong without him? Before James Higley she'd seen a future of moderate love if she were lucky, perhaps solitude. Now—now that she knew James, there was no other choice. There was life with him or no life at all.

She shook her head. "I cannot."

"You can." The tears were gone from his eyes as if he knew she could only survive on his strength, and would gift it to her. "You can and you will."

His admonition sealed her lips. If he wished her brave, she would be so, though only by God's grace would she keep her knees beneath her.

His eyes tugged her close and she shuffled toward him, fearing that should she feel him one last time she might not have the strength to let go. Driven by a power nearly void in her muscles, she wrapped her arms around him and wept, willing his bands to break and his comforting embrace to circle her in a hundred sacred promises.

She savored the feel of her cheek against his chest. "I love you."

His lips rested against her head and he nodded, not speaking, but sniffing. He cried. The mere thought forced her grip to harden.

"Carrie..." He coughed to clear his throat and lifted his head. "Carrie."

She pulled back, still holding him at the waist.

"My pocket." He motioned with his head toward his side and she reached in, instantly knowing what he asked.

Lifting free the timepiece, Caroline's frame went numb. All the memories, all the tenderness behind such a thing shuddered through her bones, and she sucked in a quaking breath. "James, I—"

"Who better to have it than the woman I love." James's timbre was thick, all the dreams she'd wished for them cradled in his words. "What a pity it is that I can die but once—for you."

She shot her head up, unable to quell the sudden shaking. Would he quote Cato now? It tore her heart even more. "I cannot live without you."

He smiled, gifting her strength through the courage that lifted from him like streams of light. "You can. You will."

He lowered his head and pressed his lips to hers. Holding his head in her hands, she pressed against him, willing every measure of her love to fill the void that would soon leave her lifeless. Savoring his masculine scent, the feel of his whiskered face on her skin, the warmth of his mouth—she imprinted it on her soul.

Pulling away, she rested her head against his chest before looking up, cradling him in her gaze. "I love you, James."

His jaw went tight, and his lips pressed. Tears welled. "I love—"

"Enough." Greene marched forward.

"You are a devil." Caroline whirled, the soldier's who'd held her before once more gripping her arms and tugging her back. "They are innocent—"

The strike to her face burned as the salty palate of blood coated her tongue.

"Hold her back." Greene pointed casually to the small clearing. "Show them their places."

All life went still, all sound silent but the heavy in and out of her breath, the thundering of her pulse. Led by Edmond himself, Enoch went first, followed by James until they reached the middle of the clearing.

Tying each man's eyes with a blindfold, Edmond spoke to them, quiet and with such a solemn expression she could only pray to God his words brought comfort.

There, bound and blinded in the middle of the field with an audience of hundreds, was her life, her heart. Her future. Had she not been restrained she would have run and forced herself between them, showing her devotion to the cause she loved and the men she had no way of living without.

His job complete, Edmond stepped away as the men readied their weapons. A cry leapt from her throat. Never again would she be found in the green fields of his eyes, never again would she feel his strong arms at her back. Any hope of love and life would die in front of her. Perhaps 'twas better that he not witness her weakness. For that's what she was. Weak. Pitiful.

Shameless, she wept, the men still holding her arms. What hope was there? Where was the balm God promised? The heavy watch in her hand begged a different thought, but she pushed it away. What hope would she have when all she wished for, all she wanted would be taken from her?

Greene pointed and shouted commands, but she couldn't hear him. A line of soldiers stood ready at the other side of the field, machine-like, muskets at their shoulders. Again he yelled a command, and their weapons rose.

Then time went still. No movement, no sound, no cold. Only she and James. Only Enoch.

Only the end.

Greene's red face trembled as he yelled one last time, and her entire frame seized.

An explosion and plume of smoke moved slow through the air, a scream scraping hard up her throat.

Their bodies crumpled, face forward on the ground.

Wild and raving, she pulled against her captors until her legs refused to hold and she fell, sobbing, unable to look away from the two who lay motionless.

She continued to scream as they dragged her away, her body convulsing with the need to get free, to run to them. To prove to herself they were dead.

Everything blurred, became masses of color and muffled sounds. Hard hands gripped her arms and pulled her back, before picking her up and forcing her onto a mount.

She couldn't look away.

Edmond neared their bodies, his gait heavy, as if he were weighed down almost as much as she.

A soldier mounted the horse behind her and her hand slipped, nearly dropping the watch from her fingers.

She gripped tighter to the treasure, frantic that she would lose the only thing left of him.

The horse lurched forward and she wrenched herself to look

behind.

The inscription burned into her fingers, while the truth burned into her heart. She had no hope. She had nothing.

∼

James fell face first into the dirt and rolled enough to allow air through his mouth.

He didn't move, sure to keep his muscles limp and still, while every part of him swelled with agony, aching to fly to his feet and soothe Caroline's wrenching cries.

"Take her away." Greene's voice waded toward him, growing quiet as his enemy distanced himself from the clearing. "She leaves at sunrise and we haven't much time."

Nay, they hadn't much time. And if Edmond's hasty plan hadn't worked they would be too late going after her.

'Twas a miracle he lived, and the seconds he spent with his face in the mud plastered his soul in gratitude. He didn't know how his friend had accomplished it—an entire Patriot band over-taking the intended executioners and donning their uniforms. Shooting with empty barrels.

He could have groaned with shock. It had taken him nearly all his strength to remain brave for Caroline. She'd looked so defeated, so lost and afraid. Had he known he would not die, he might have offered some kind of cryptic hope, a message of some kind to let her know all would be well. For now, he could only hope the rest of Edmond's plan could be executed as simply as this had been.

The murmurs and grumbles from the crowd dissipated as the men returned to their duties, and in seconds, his arms were yanked back and the tie around them sliced through.

"Take them away."

"Nay! Nay, I beg you, let me see them!" Caroline's sobs and guttural cries refused to abate as they carried her away, until finally, they were gone. His heart crawled after her, reaching for her in the dusty light of morning. The effort needed to remain motionless—to give the appearance of death—was all but impossible. And certainly he would not have done it if Edmond had not made his plan clear in the seconds before the shots were fired.

Still acting the part, he let his head fall back when two men grabbed him at the arms and legs and carried him to a wagon, resting him in the cold hard bed. Another thud beside him let him know Enoch had been brought as promised, and in seconds, the wagon lurched forward.

They rode for what seemed a lifetime, until at long last the wagon stopped. Only when the driver jumped down and came to him, did he dare sit up.

Henry extended his hand and helped James up the rest of the way, while Nathaniel did the same to Enoch.

James smirked, rubbing his red, raw wrists. "Back in uniform I see."

Chuckling, Henry clapped him on the shoulder. "I would not do it for anyone less worthy."

James swelled with gratitude for such a man as Henry. "I am grateful indeed."

"'Twas your friend's brilliance that allowed for it."

Henry motioned to the horses behind the wagon where Edmond and another man he didn't recognize dismounted and came forward.

Palpable penitence in his round eyes, Edmond stopped before him. "James."

He smiled. "Edmond."

The other man neared and Henry gestured between them. "James, this is Thomas Watson. A good friend of ours and staunch Patriot."

Thomas bowed politely before turning his attention to Enoch. "If Caroline had not found us, 'tis certain we would not now be here."

"Caroline?" James looked between them. "What do you mean?"

'Twas Nathaniel who answered. "She came for help and found friends."

She'd gone for help? Then how had she been captured?

"I can see the questions on your face." Henry shook his head. "We tried to detain her, to keep her safe at the camp, but it seemed she would not be restrained."

He would have supposed as much. *Dear, Carrie.*

James's heart leapt and he turned to Enoch, wanting to speak of her, but the man's sorrowful look stabbed his gut. "Are you hurt?"

Still on the edge of the wagon bed, he shook his head. "I am grateful for what you have done. But what of the other prisoners? What will happen to them?"

Edmond gestured behind him. "These three were not the only ones to act the part of Redcoats." He looked to James. "Henry's men subdued all twelve who were brought to bring death upon you. The other nine are there now, preparing a way to arm them, and get them free."

Enoch's face softened as relief visibly smoothed over him. "We are in your debt, sir."

"There is no debt," Henry said. "We are brothers in this cause."

Nathaniel motioned for Enoch to sit. "I am a doctor and should like to examine you, if you are agreeable."

"I thank you." Wearied, Enoch shuffled back to the wagon and once again sat.

Peering at the others, Nathaniel motioned to his patient. "He needs my care. If you can do without me, I should like to stay with him."

James gave an insistent nod. "Of course."

"We haven't much time." Edmond spied the lightening horizon. "The ship that will carry her to England leaves at sunrise."

"Where are they now?" James spun about, locating the direction of the sea. "Do you think they already boarded?"

Sighing, Edmond shook his head. "I cannot say. They will shove off from an inlet not far from here. Anderson claimed he wished not to create a scene and preferred it to having them leave from town."

"Fortunate for us." James looked to the other men. Their expressions carried his same sentiment.

Edmond continued. "I did my best to detain them with paperwork and formalities, but I cannot trust Greene will go by protocol."

The thought of Caroline's suffering, of her grief and of Greene anywhere near her made rage blaze up his back. He fought the pounding need for revenge—revenge for Loden, for Caroline, for him. For all who had suffered needlessly under Greene's hateful pride.

He knew 'twas not his place, that his peace was found in grace, in forgiving. But for now, he could not endure the thought of it.

"Greene says he does not believe in ghosts." James hurried to a saddled horse Thomas had brought with his own. Mounting, he tugged on the reins. "Let us change his mind."

## CHAPTER 43

*T*here was no way to say no to morning. No way to deny the sun's rising, to refuse the light it gave. No way to forget.

Benumbed with grief, Caroline rested against the tree they'd tied her to, every part of her body detached from another by grief. There was too much of it to be held together. Too much shock and pain.

Her dry eyes wished for tears, but they had all fallen. One gentlemanly soldier had insisted she wrap in his blanket, but she could only shake her head in refusal. There was no warmth or cold. Only the rift in her soul.

The image in her mind refused to fade. James and Enoch face down in the mud. When the deed was finished, they had dragged her away, refusing even to let her watch them being carried from the clearing.

Her throat swelled and she ground her teeth to keep from weeping. Greene had said Anderson wished her on the boat *Verity*, a vessel scheduled to leave port that morning. And morning was here. So here they waited, at a small inlet, by the rowboat that would take her to the *Verity*, where it in turn would take her away from America, away from the only home she had ever known, to stand trial for something she hadn't done, in a body devoid of will. Devoid of joy.

The soldiers around her mumbled to one another, speaking of her, of the death of the hated informant. Of the bone-thin Patriot and how the others were next to find relief from their sufferings in death. How long she'd waited there she didn't know, nor did she care.

Greene marched forward, command in his step and his sound. "Get her up."

Once Caroline was on her feet, Greene stopped before her, examining her wrists to make sure she was still bound. "You are most fortunate, my lady."

The source of his jovial nature made her very bones brittle. An army of blade-like words readied on her tongue, but she saved them. Despite their barbs, he was immune to them, and speaking likely would injure her more than him.

He tugged on a glove, his brows lifting in genuine surprise. "For once you will not speak, hmm? Well, never mind. I have a feeling where you go you will not have the luxury of silence."

Despicable.

He gave a sweeping gesture to the rowboat. "Your vessel awaits."

In the sea, some distance from shore, awaited the majestic looking ship, its masts tall and sails being prepared.

The urge to resist, to tug away, to cry out consumed her mind, but her muscles had given up, her voice had gone mute. She had no strength left to fight.

The soldiers pressed her forward and her shoes brushed the edge of the frigid water when a voice shot like cannon fire from the wood.

"Greene!"

Caroline whirled around, utter disbelief shocking through her body.

It couldn't be.

James stalked forward from the wood, begrimed but bloodless. Her mind could not work out what she saw. He'd been shot. And yet...he was here. Alive.

Greene's face was white, his mouth round and eyes bulging. "It cannot be."

The other soldiers were equally still, their grips on her arms slacking.

He offered her a brief glance and she savored it before he turned his gaze on Greene. "Surprised?"

Greene retreated a step, shaking his head. "You were shot. I saw you die."

"Perhaps I am dead." James stalked forward. "Perhaps I am come to haunt you."

Just then three more stepped from the shadowed wood and instantly she knew them. Thomas, Henry and Edmond—all in red uniforms—surrounded Greene's small band of six men with a combined strength powerful enough to spark the chilled air.

Greene transformed. His countenance reddened and his voice pitched an octave higher as he yelled like a mad man. "Get them!"

Greene's small group of Redcoats flew to action, but their work was too slow. Two pistols fired and two of Greene's men fell mid-stride, the remaining four still lunging with heads down.

James grabbed for a dagger and rushed for Greene as Thomas and Henry lunged for two more heaving soldiers.

Caroline's pulse throbbed through her veins, and she raced forward, thirsty for freedom. Greene yelled just as James reached him. "Take her to the boat!"

The remaining soldier beside her hooked his arm around her waist and dragged her into the water. Kicking and flailing, her instincts overcame her until every muscle was engaged in the need for escape.

The man's grip tightened, and so did her fight. A cry scraped up her throat before she called out. "James!"

James whirled to look when Greene's fist struck the side of his head, forcing him back, and the realization hit like a blow. What if he could not get to her? He would try, surely, but Greene would stop at nothing to see them suffer.

With one arm, the soldier lifted her into the rowboat and sheer panic sucked away every thought but escape. Standing in the rocking boat, she called again, and though she was certain he could hear, he could not turn his back or the blade Greene now held in his hand would find its mark in his back.

*Think. Think, Carrie!*

The soldier prepared to shove off when her vision landed on an ore in the center of the boat. She went for it. Hands still bound, she swung it around and cracked its thin side against the soldier's head like an axe.

Slumping, he buckled at the knees and fell into the water, blood gushing from his skull. Grimacing, he shoved the boat with a roar before falling face-first into the water.

*Nay!*

Caroline looked to shore. The fight between the men grew more violent. Thomas struck at one man while another came from behind. Edmond and Henry fought hand to hand with teeth-baring Redcoats while James and Greene continued to battle on the sand.

The farther she drifted the more panic tried to murder reason. She should jump. She should—

From the water, the injured soldier rose, shaking his head as blood streamed down his wet face.

Without thinking she jumped. Stumbling, her knees hit first, keeping the top of her from submerging. The ice-cold water gripped her like the fingers of some invisible creature.

She struggled to get to her feet as the soldier splashed toward her, but the length and weight of her petticoat held her down.

Within feet of her, he reached out then froze, went limp, and fell forward.

Jumping aside with a scream, she looked up and relief took the place of fear. "Henry!"

Her rescuer replaced his blade and stepped over the man's body. "Come. Quickly."

She raised her wrists to his outstretched hand then stopped, all energy converging in her voice. "Behind you!"

Henry whirled and slammed the blade into the gut of the incoming soldier, tossing him aside and pulling her beside him almost in the same breath.

"Get to safety." He hurried her to shore. "Find a way to stay warm."

Out of the water, he raced to Thomas who still fought one man. Edmond was on the ground, motionless. Was he dead?

Her body convulsed, then froze as her vision landed on James and Greene, both crouched and blade-baring.

The end was near. *Dear God, help him. Make us free at last.*

# CHAPTER 44

*C*rouched, a dagger in his hand, James readied for the attack Greene would spring on him.

"This is over, Greene."

Greene tilted his head, mouth contorting as he shrugged off his jacket and threw it aside, his own blade aimed and shimmering. "This will never be over. Not until you are dead."

A sound from the shore urged him to look, but he dare not move his gaze from his enemy. From the edge of his vision he could see Henry at the lip of the water, Caroline at his side.

She was safe.

The sight of her, however brief, granted him another measure of strength. He motioned to his friends with a wide sweep of his arm. "Keep her away from here."

Henry rushed forward. "James, let us—"

"This is my fight, Henry." He kept his stare upon Greene. "And I will end it."

"Noble to the last," Greene mocked with a forced smile.

James too removed the coat that encumbered him. Rolling his shoulders back, he adjusted his grip on his blade. "You cannot know the pains you would suffer if she had not survived."

"Who says she will live?" Greene stared, motionless, fists at the ready.

"You would risk Anderson's rage by going against him? Foolish."

"I do what must be done." Greene swiped with his blade.

James lunged back. "You tried to kill me once before, and you failed."

The place above Greene's eye where James's blade had earlier nicked the skin, dripped red. He sneered, baring teeth. "I will not fail a second time."

He charged and James swerved right, grabbing Greene's outstretched arm and throwing him to the ground. The kick to the back of James's legs was swift, knocking the dagger from his fingers. Falling backward on the sand, he rolled to dodge the impact of Greene's incoming elbow.

Both surged to their feet. James wasted no time, plowing his fist into Greene's jaw. The hit sent him reeling, and the grip on his own blade weakened.

James knocked the weapon from Greene's fingers then shuffled back. His chest pumped, muscles throbbing. "Are you finished?"

Greene stumbled, a hand at his bleeding mouth. "Never."

He swung again and James ducked, plunging his fist into Greene's soft middle. Greene buckled then sprang forward, slamming his shoulder into James's stomach.

The hard ground met his back and all air left his lungs.

Instantly, Greene's hands were at his throat. "This is over." His grip tightened. "You've lost."

"James!"

Caroline's cry put steel in James's hands and he squeezed, pressing against Greene's iron-like hold. The man's rage made him invincible.

Gasping, James choked for air and the action seemed only to harden his enemy.

Greene bent down, pressing his thumbs harder into James's throat. "This is not such a terrible way to go." He leaned closer, taunting through closed teeth. "And don't worry, your death will be swifter than hers will be."

With a roar that surged from the depths of him, James shoved him aside and lunged for the nearest blade.

Strength borne of an unseen power, he dodged Greene's incoming attack and held him at the shoulders, rolling until James was atop him, his knees on his arms.

Yanking Greene's hair at the root, he held the tip of the blade at Greene's throat, ready to let free all the years of grief and pain as he plunged the dagger into his flesh.

He stared into his enemy's eyes. "You are done."

*Nay, James.*

The quiet voice filtered through the suffocating rage and rested in the center of him.

*Do not become him.*

'Twas Loden's voice. Did he watch from heaven? Or was it only James's inner soul that spoke with the sound of his beloved friend's caring wisdom?

James's grip did not weaken, but somehow, within him, something changed. He'd not become a Patriot to kill his enemies, he'd not made a vow to murder those who opposed him.

He'd made a vow to live higher. To give, not take.

The inner struggle shook his arms. If he did not kill him, how was he to know the man would give up the fight? How would he know his life and Caroline's would ever truly be free?

Pressing down harder, he let the point of the blade brush against Greene's skin and for the first time, he saw it—the fear in Greene's eyes. The regret, pain and loneliness that he'd never known lived in the heart of such a man.

*Let him go.*

Nay. He couldn't.

*You must. Leave it to God.*

Releasing a guttural yell James plunged the blade into the sand beside Greene's neck.

Dumb with shock, Greene stared up at him as James pushed to his feet. He stepped away, refusing to remove his vision from Greene as the man hurried to his feet.

Greene's brow creased with confusion and disgust, as he spewed hate through his teeth. "You should have killed me."

James shook his head, his chest pumping. "I am not like you."

Greene looked around him, chuckling. "Nay, you are not."

There was no use in speaking to him. The man had gone mad. James turned, making his way to where his companions and Caroline beckoned him. All the anger he'd felt moments ago dimmed, the fire of rage receding the more he allowed himself a vision of his future. One of devotion, dedication and love.

"You are not like me!" Greene yelled from behind. "Because you refuse to do what must be done!"

In that moment, everything slowed.

Caroline's face lengthened as she screamed his name, pointing. Henry and Thomas lunged, and he turned to see Greene's frame streaking toward him, a knife in his hand.

Inches from impact the report of a pistol ripped through the trees and Greene's body went slack. Limp, he crumpled to the ground at James's feet and rolled onto his back, a stream of dark blood seeping across the sand.

James hurled his vision to the other side of the inlet. His back seized at the sight. Should he run? Grab Caroline and make for the trees?

But the look on Stockton's face as he sat upon his horse, a smoking pistol in his grip, gave no indication of malice. Rather, relief. Contentment. Resolve.

James hadn't yet the strength to force his legs to move. How had he...

There were too many questions to form into proper thought.

Dismounting, Stockton marched across the sand, his eyes

darting from one man to another as he secured his used weapon inside his jacket. "Higley." He stopped, his eyebrows rising. "Captain Donaldson. I have been looking for you."

James whirled to see his friend's reaction, and the stunned look in Henry's face was every bit the war of confusion he expected.

Spinning back to his superior, James did his best to smooth his tone. "Major..."

Stockton stopped his approach, staring down at Greene's body between them. "I arrived not an hour past and had the tale from Anderson."

From Anderson? What exactly had the man said?

James looked behind. If Henry and Thomas left now, they could take Caroline to safety before Stockton went in search of them.

"He tells me you are the informant." Stockton slowed his words, looking to sea as he spoke. "That you were caught in the act."

Feuding replies cut each other down on their way to his mouth, rendering him mute. What could he say? There was no going back to the army now. His reputation as a man of honor in the British Army was forever destroyed. Anderson would have him killed most certainly if Stockton did not.

James opened his mouth to rebuttal, but Stockton spoke before him.

"But I had heard...I heard you were killed." He paused, dotting his stern gaze from man to man. "Imagine my surprise when I came in search of the mysterious female spy, and upon finding her, I found you—and Donaldson, as well." Again, Stockton peered down at Greene. "I could not let this man have his way with another Patriot woman and I'd determined to see for myself that he had not taken Hannah after all." His expression went wistful for a moment, before settling on solemn. "Had you killed him, my opinion of you might have lessened, Captain." He raised his eyes to James. "Somehow, I knew you would not do it. And standing idle while he took your life instead, would not have sat well with me."

James's entire frame twitched as surges of shock, confusion and gratitude took turns in his muscles. "I am...I am indebted to you, sir."

Stockton turned his attention to Henry, but his words were for all of them. "I am tired of this war. I am tired of the fight that will only bring more bloodshed and tears." He aimed his thin gaze at James. "If you wish a different path, I suggest you take it while you can, before you end up too deep and only death alone can separate you."

He turned, slowly, making his way to his horse. He mounted, and pulled his horse around.

Silent, he nodded to James, grazing his eyes across the others before he kicked his horse and disappeared.

Caroline ran to him, while Thomas and Henry went to each soldier on the ground determining their state of injury—or death.

"Thank God you are safe."

James held her to him, growing more alive the more he inhaled her scent and memorized the feel of her body against him. He pressed his lips to her hair, fighting the truth that pressed against his tongue. They could not stay here. She needed safety, and that, she could only find far away from here—and from him.

Looking toward heaven, he prayed for strength to say what he must. He tugged her to the edge of the wood, away from the dead and dying, away from the horror they both had somehow survived.

"I know what you will say to me." Her face slackened and her eyes filled with tears as she looked at him. "Enoch is dead."

"Nay." He stroked her cheek, hoping his smile would wipe away the inner wounds she suffered. "Nay, he is well."

"Praise the Lord!" Her eyes filled with tears. "I must see him."

"You will." Her joy filled his own heart. "He was too weak to come aid you, or certainly he would be here now."

"I understand." Her chin quivered and she looked behind her. "Edmond!"

Racing forward, she neared and James followed as Henry helped their friend to sit. A wound wept along his side and a dark bruise started at his eye.

James put a hand at his back to steady him. "How bad is it?"

Edmond shook his head. "Not bad." He eyed James, a slyness in his words. "I fear Anderson might wish my head in a bag if I were to return to his service." He looked to Henry. "I suppose I am one of you now."

Grinning, James held him at one side while Henry held him at the other. "I suppose you have always been."

Henry assisted Edmond to a horse while Thomas neared where James and Caroline stood. "We have to go." He cast his gaze around the wood, then the water. "I hate to leave the dead here, but I fear staying any longer might mean our fates will mirror theirs."

"You're right." James held Caroline at the arm and led her to a horse. "You will see her to camp won't you, Thomas? Then prepare a way for her to return home. I must make my escape to Washington."

"Nay. What do you mean? What are you saying?" Caroline spun about and pressed a hand to her chest. "Nay, I will not let you."

"Caroline, this is no time for argument. Your safety is above all—"

"I don't wish to argue, James. I wish to tell you…" She stalled and Thomas bowed himself apart from the conversation as if he knew they would wish a moment alone. When he was with Henry, she continued, her eyes brimming. "I love you. I *have* loved you. I cannot endure the thought of being apart, I beg of you, take me with you."

She loved him. Those words he'd longed to hear bade him honor her wish, to answer that his feelings were the same. That not only would he give his life for her, he would *live* for her.

He raised a hand to her cheek and she rested it against his palm. "'Tis dangerous, Carrie. I do not know how—"

"There is more danger when we are apart than together." She took his hand from her face and held it to her chest. "Let me live this life with you. Let me be part of this conflict as you are. There are plenty of women who follow their husbands to camp and—"

"Husband?"

"James! We must go!" Henry called.

James pivoted to see both Henry and Thomas already mounted, and he waved to them. "Coming."

He turned back to Caroline to find her cheeks flushed, her lip in her teeth. Her worried expression toyed with a smile that began deep within him. She saw herself as his bride?

All the needs and wishes he'd held so tightly in the bonds of his former life, he at last let free. "Caroline, I—"

She shook her head. "Forgive me, I shouldn't have said anything. I shouldn't have assumed—"

"Will you marry me?"

Her eyes shot to his. "What?"

He nodded sideways. "I know this is hardly the proper place to ask but as we haven't much time—"

"James! Now!" Thomas's voice was cannon fire.

James rushed her to the nearest horse and readied to help her mount, but need stalled his movement. Holding her arms, he poured every part of his soul through his words. "I love you, Carrie. You are the beat in my chest and the breath in my lungs. You are my smile, my voice, my wishes and wants together. If you will have me, if you will have this life, I give you my word, I will devote my soul to you."

A sound from the wood snaked up the part of him still attentive to the danger. Taking her at the waist, he didn't wait for an answer. He needed to get her to camp not only for safety, but to get her warm.

Taking his place on the saddle, he wrapped his arm around her as he had done those days not long ago.

As the horse began to move, Caroline's answer met his ears. "I will." She turned, craning her neck, gifting him through a smile every joy and spark of love he never dared believe would be his. Facing forward again, she hugged his arm against her. "How could I not? You are my life, James. My hope. To have all, I need only have you."

# EPILOGUE

*ay 1, 1776*
Cambridge, Massachusetts

Warm spring air, scented with rose, drifted down the small path behind the house. Bees hummed and birds trilled their happiness as Caroline filled her basket with stalks of pink and yellow blooms.

She could hardly believe only months ago this place was covered in snow, the river edged with ice. If ever she'd imagined Cambridge would become her home, she would have chuckled in disbelief. If someone had told her she would meet and marry the second part of her soul in a matter of days, she would have laughed them to scorn.

But thanks to God in his goodness, both had happened. And she couldn't think of a life she would wish to have more.

Plucking another pink flower, she tucked it into the basket on her arm. Washington had gone with his army to New York, having some time ago vanquished the British army from the city, but she and James were to stay, per Washington's command.

James was to keep guard over the city with a select number of men, to be sure the British didn't attempt a return.

Her cheeks blushed at the thought of James in his blue and buff uniform. Two months of marriage they'd enjoyed already, and somehow, it felt like a lifetime, and yet no time at all.

She peeked at the road the third time in as many minutes. With his business for Washington so often taking him into town, she was used to his tardiness. It was never his intention to be late. It was duty that required him, and she did her duty in supporting him.

"I've made sure the hedges are properly trimmed, as you commanded." Enoch teased as he rounded the corner of the house, brushing his hands. "What other jobs would you wish for me, Mistress of the House?"

"Thank you. I could not have prepared for this day without your help." She smiled at his approach, motioning him to her. Without his permission, she stepped forward and brushed a smudge of dust from his jacket. "Did you see James on the road? I worry he shall be late."

"I didn't see him." Enoch's shaven face had filled out, the previous handsomeness she'd remembered before his time in captivity, having returned. "But don't worry, I have no doubt he will—"

"Carrie?"

Caroline's heart burst at the sound of James's voice. "Thank heaven." Though she couldn't yet see him, she knew he'd arrived.

Enoch nodded toward the front of the house. "What did I tell you?"

Touching his arm, she offered a humble smile, acknowledging her penchant for worry. "I am so pleased you stayed. I could not think of having you leave again."

Enoch looked up as James rounded the corner. "When your husband asked for my assistance, how could I refuse knowing I should be near you?"

"And of course Mama and Papa will be elated at seeing you again."

His eyes beamed. "You say they shall be here by week's end?"

"Aye. Sooner, if travel permits." Caroline reached up and corrected the position of his neckcloth, her joy brimming. "I had word from them two days past, saying they were journeying as quickly as they could, eager to embrace you."

Satisfied with the lay of his collar, she stepped back. Seeing him like this, healthy and happy and strong, it started a yearning in her that she could almost not contain. Enoch must find love as she had. He deserved a good woman who would love and care for him.

He shuffled backward, as if he could see into her thoughts and wished to escape some impending lecture. "I should like to check something in the barn."

She opened her mouth to answer when James hugged her from the side. "There you are."

Resting her basket on the ground, she swung her arms around his neck, his blue uniform accentuating the depth of his green eyes. "I almost feared you wouldn't be here in time."

He kissed her gently on the mouth before hooking one arm around her waist as he walked to the back of the house where she'd waited for him. "You know I would not miss this day for the world."

"Everything is prepared." She pointed to the spread she'd worked on all morning, and into the afternoon. Two long tables, bedecked with cloths and glasses, china and silver. The food she'd prepared was still inside. Hurrying to the flowers she'd picked, Caroline worked to place them in the pewter pitchers, one in the center of each table.

"This should be perfect, should it not?" She stepped back, admiring her work before eyeing James for endorsement. "Do you like it?"

"I do. The ladies will be much impressed, I can assure you." He neared, a contemplative slope to his brow. "Are these lemon tarts?"

He reached for one and she batted his hand away, fighting a quiet laugh. "You must wait."

"Alright, I shall behave. However..." Tugging her to him, he dusted his lips over her ear. "There are certain things I cannot wait for."

"James..." Her heart quivered when his mouth found the soft place behind her ear, and she forced herself to push him away, fully laughing to cover the embarrassment. "They will be here any moment."

Just then, the sound of an approaching horse and carriage met her ears.

Gasping, Caroline jumped back, catching a glimpse of James's conquering smile. He leaned down. "Do not worry, we were not seen. And even if we were, 'tis nothing to be ashamed of. They know what it is to be in love."

"You are right." She took his hand and squeezed, grinning coyly, assuring through her touch she would give him more than kisses when once the evening lights were out.

His eyes hooded with love before he released his hold and hurried to greet their guests as they piled from the coaches that parked at the front of the house.

Caroline followed close behind, unable to bind the gleeful joy at seeing her friends after so long. "Anna, Henry—what a joy to have you!"

"Greetings to you both." Henry helped his wife from the door and she rushed to Caroline, wrapping her arms around her as if they were sisters more than friends.

"Oh, my dearest Caroline, how good it is to see you both so well."

Caroline held her friend at the shoulders. "I have missed you more than I can say."

The two spied the men who were exchanging warm hand-shakes and chuckling about the length of the journey.

"Here," Caroline said, "let me help you with your things."

Caroline prepared to take a trunk from the back of the carriage when Anna stopped her, a hand on her swelling middle. "Let the men take them. I am famished and dying for a glass of refreshment."

"Of course. Why don't you—oh look! There are the others!"

Two more carriages rolled up the path to the house. In moments, Thomas and Eliza rushed out, baby Mary on Eliza's hip, followed by Nathaniel and Kitty, whose own belly was rounder than Caroline had seen it.

"You have arrived!" She rushed over to them sharing embraces and smiles she hoped would never end. "I must admit we have been waiting none too patiently."

Caroline motioned the ladies to the yard at the back of the house, as the men were already engaged in conversation and starting that direction as well. No doubt James would take them straight to the tarts. She couldn't help the smile on her lips at the thought.

"We couldn't be more pleased." Eliza adjusted the babe in her arms. "When Thomas learned that Washington had chosen James to stay behind in Boston and head the remaining portion of the army here, he was thrilled."

Kitty nodded, peering to the ladies as they walked. "Even more thrilled to know James had been given authority to choose his own men to help him, and that our husbands will now work together…" She sighed, the weight of worry and relief cradled in her words. "It gives me more joy than I have words to express."

Caroline hummed in agreement. "I am grieved only at the thought that Hannah and Joseph could not join us as well. But they have their own journey, and God will lead them back in time, I am certain."

She'd had word from Hannah, relating her cousin's story, and the relief Caroline enjoyed at knowing her beloved cousin was safe and happy with Joseph was enough to fill any void that was left.

"To know we shall be quartered here, with you," Anna said, "I am certain I cannot think of any ladies I would rather share a home with."

"Nor I," Eliza said. "I can only hope this little one will not be a bother."

"Nonsense." Caroline motioned to the table, laughing quietly when she spied the men, each with a tart in their hand. "Besides, 'tis only temporary. You shall have your own quarters once a home is found for you. The positions our husbands employ will not be permanent. Before long we shall be able to return to Sandwich and resume our lives as we wish."

"Has the party started without me?"

Enoch jogged from the barn toward the men, shaking hands as James and the others exchanged fond greetings and jeers as men were wont to do.

"My goodness, Carrie, is that your brother?" Eliza whispered.

Kitty's eyes rounded when she spied him, and she turned immediately to Caroline. "Good heavens, he is quite a handsome specimen, isn't he."

"And you say he isn't married?" Anna, too, appeared shocked and shook her head with the look of one scheming. "I daresay, we shall have to find a girl to help remedy that, shall we not?"

"You echo my thoughts completely." Caroline leaned in, grinning with glee and hoping her brother's ears didn't edge their direction. "I was just thinking this morning that—"

"Ladies."

All straightened at the sound of James's voice.

He spied Caroline, motioning her toward him. Once beside him, he hugged her against him before reaching for a glass.

"Friends, I should like to offer a toast."

Each man and woman reached for a glass and mirrored his

action. Thomas hugged Eliza and the baby close, while Kitty rested her head on Nathaniel's shoulder.

James smiled, eyeing each person in the group and a burst of pride warmed Caroline's chest. Henry came behind Anna, wrapping his arms around her middle. A smile beamed through her eyes as her gaze landed on Caroline, as if to say she'd known all along how well it would end.

"Here we begin a new chapter, a new time in our lives," James said, lifting his glass. A hum made its way through the group. "Our individual paths, though different, have knitted our lives indelibly together, in our united struggle for The Glorious Cause."

Thomas raised his arm. "Hear, hear!"

The others echoed him and Caroline's throat began to ache, her eyes stinging. A reverence settled over them, the birdsong and hum of bees a heavenly hymn to herald their treasured moment. The men cleared their throats and women sniffed.

"I, for one, cannot forget what we have come through, what we have endured. No doubt you feel the same." James looked down, studying the glass in his hand before once more peering out. "God has carried us through trial and sorrow, and brought us here. We are family to one another, lifting and helping in our times of need, sharing the joys and tribulations that is the lot of every child of God. But He is good, He is faithful. He is our Protector and our Stay. Whether in this fight for freedom we are victorious it matters not. For in Him is our salvation and our joy."

As one, the group nodded and hummed in unified agreement, still gripped silent with emotion.

James lifted his own glass higher as joy spilled over Caroline's cheeks.

"A toast," he said.

"A toast," all echoed.

"To freedom." James pulled Caroline tighter to him. "To faith and family. To all that awaits in this life and the next. We shall forever be joyful, no matter the outcome. For how can we not, when with God, we look to the future with so bright a hope."

Dear Reader,

How bittersweet it is to know this series has come to an end. I have grown to love these characters as real friends, and I find myself growing teary at the thought of no longer spending time with them.

For that reason, I have chosen to write a spin-off series titled The Glorious Cause. The first book in that series (yet to be titled) will feature Caroline's handsome and courageous brother, Enoch, as the hero.

Thank you for coming along on this journey with me. My readers bring me so much joy!

As always, please feel free to review this book, and/or contact me with your thoughts and comments. I love to hear from readers.

From my heart,
    Amber
    www.amberlynnperry.com

Made in the USA
Columbia, SC
28 May 2020